ALSO BY SCOTT MARIANI

The Mozart Conspiracy

THE
HOPE
VENDETTA

SCOTT MARIANI

A TOUCHSTONE BOOK
Published by Simon & Schuster
New York   London   Toronto   Sydney   New Delhi

Touchstone
A Division of Simon & Schuster, Inc.
1230 Avenue of the Americas
New York, NY 10020

Originally published in Great Britain in 2009 by HarperCollins Publishers, Ltd.

Published by arrangement with HarperCollins Publishers, Ltd.

First Touchstone hardcover edition March 2012

TOUCHSTONE and colophon are registered trademarks of Simon & Schuster, Inc.

For information about special discounts for bulk purchases, please contact Simon & Schuster Special Sales at 1-866-506-1949 or business@simonandschuster.com.

The Simon & Schuster Speakers Bureau can bring authors to your live event. For more information or to book an event contact the Simon & Schuster Speakers Bureau at 866-248-3049 or visit our website at www.simonspeakers.com.

Designed by Renata Di Biase

Manufactured in the United States of America

10   9   8   7   6   5   4   3   2   1

Library of Congress Cataloging-in-Publication Data
Mariani, Scott.
    The hope vendetta : a novel / Scott Mariani.
       p.   cm.
    "A Touchstone book."
    1. Prophecies—Fiction. 2. Conspiracies—Fiction. I. Title.
PR6113.A745 H67 2012
823'.—dc92
                                    2011041333

ISBN 978-1-4391-9347-1
ISBN 978-1-4391-9350-1 (ebook)

Blessed is he that readeth, and they that hear the words of this prophecy, and keep those things which are written therein: *for the time IS at hand.*

—BOOK OF REVELATION 1:3

THE
HOPE
VENDETTA

1.

t was night when they took her.

They'd found her living on the lush island and watched for three days in the sun before they figured out their move. She was staying in a rented villa, isolated and shaded by olive trees, high on a cliff above the crystal-clear sea.

She was living alone, and it should have been easy to snatch her. But the house was always filled with party guests, and the dancing and drinking was virtually round the clock. They watched, but they couldn't get close.

So the team planned. Right down to the last detail. Entry, acquisition, extraction. It had to be subtle and discreet. There were four of them, three men, one woman. They knew this was her last day on the island. She'd booked the flight from Corfu Airport next morning and was flying back home—where she'd be far, far harder to take.

So it was tonight or never. Strategically, it was the perfect time for her to disappear. Nobody would be looking for her in the morning.

They waited until evening, when they knew the farewell party would be well under way. Their car was a rental sedan, bland and inconspicuous, paid for in cash from a local hire firm. They drove in silence and parked off the road, unseen in the shade of the olive grove a hundred yards from the villa.

And watched quietly. As expected, the villa was lit up and the sound of music and laughter drifted through the trees and across the cove. The white stone house was fine and imposing, with three separate balconies where they could see couples dancing and people standing around drinking, leaning out over the railings, taking in the beauty of the evening.

Down below, the sea glittered in the moonlight. It was warm and the air was sweet with the scent of flowers, just the gentlest breeze coming in from the shore. Now and again a car would pull up outside the house as more guests arrived.

As 11 p.m. approached, the team put their plan into action. The two men in the front seats stayed where they were, making themselves comfortable for what might turn out to be a long wait. They were used to that. The man and woman in the back exchanged a look and a brief nod. She ran her fingers over her glossy black hair, pulled it loosely back, and fastened it with an elastic tie. Checked her makeup in the rearview mirror.

They opened their doors and stepped out of the car. They didn't look back. The man was carrying a bottle of wine—something local, expensive. They walked out of the shadows and up to the villa, through the gate, and up the steps towards the terrace and the front doors. The two in the car watched them as they went.

The couple walked into the villa, adjusting to the light and the noise. They said nothing to each other and moved casually but expertly through the crowd. They knew how to blend in. Many of the guests were already too out of it to notice them anyway, which suited them perfectly. There were a lot of empty bottles lying around and a lot of the smoke wasn't tobacco.

The couple wandered through the cool white rooms, gazed around them at the expensive décor. They located their target quickly and kept her carefully in sight the whole time.

She suspected nothing.

She was very much the center of attention, and she looked as though she loved it. They knew that she'd been spending the money freely, carelessly, the way a person does when they're expecting a whole lot more of it. There was plenty of champagne on offer. People milled around the self-service bar in the corner of the main room, helping themselves to as much as they could drink.

The couple watched her the way a scientist observes a rat in a tank, knowing exactly what will happen to it. She was young and attractive—just as in her photographs. Her blond hair was a little longer now, and her deep tan made her eyes stand out a bright and startling blue. She was wearing white cotton trousers and a yellow silk top that had many of the men glancing appreciatively at her figure.

The woman's name was Zoë Bradbury. They knew a lot about her. She was twenty-six and had carved out a remarkable career for her age as an author, a scholar, a historian, and a biblical archaeologist with a solid reputation among her peers. She was single, though she had a crowd of men around her and liked their company. The couple could see that much for themselves from the way she was flirting and dancing with all the good-looking guys at the party. She was English, born and raised in the city of Oxford. They knew the names of her parents. A whole raft of information about her. They'd dug deep, and they were good investigators. It was what they were getting paid for.

The plan was simple. The woman would drift away after a few minutes, and the man would get closer to the target. Offer her a drink, maybe flirt a little. He was in his early thirties, toned and handsome, and he was pretty sure he could get close enough to slip the dope into her drink.

It was a slow-acting chemical whose effects looked exactly like those of too much wine, except that it made the victim sleep for hours. The way she was knocking back her drinks, nobody would make a big deal of it when she had to retreat to her bedroom to sleep it off. The party would wind down, people would leave, then they'd move her out to the waiting car. The motor launch was already waiting at the rendezvous point.

As they'd anticipated, it wasn't hard to get close to her. The guy introduced himself as Rick. Chatted and smiled and flirted. Then he offered her a martini. She wasn't about to say no. He walked to the bar, mixed her drink, and quickly added the contents of the vial. All very professional. He was smiling as he brought it back to her and placed it in her hand.

"Cheers," she giggled, raising the glass in a mock toast, the gold bracelet on her wrist slipping down her tanned forearm.

And that was when the plan started going wrong.

They hadn't noticed the man standing in the corner of the room until he suddenly strode across, moved in fast, and took Zoë's arm, asking her if she wanted to dance. They knew his face. They'd seen him a few times while watching the villa. He was about forty-five, slim and well dressed, a little graying at the temples. A good bit older than her other boyfriends. They'd paid him little heed—until now.

She nodded and put the glass down on the table untouched. Then the man did something strange for someone who looked so sober. He nudged the table with his knee, a clumsy sort of movement, but almost as if he'd done it deliberately. The glass toppled and the drink spilled to the floor.

And they had only one vial of the stuff. They watched as the older guy led her onto the terrace, out into the starry evening where the people were dancing to the slow jazz beat.

So the couple did what they were trained to do: they improvised. Their communication was all in the eyes and the minute gestures undetectable to anyone who didn't know why they were there. In seconds they had a new plan. To hang around, merge into the background. Slip through a door and stay hidden in the house until the guests left and she was alone. Easy. They were in no hurry. They moved quietly out onto the crowded terrace, leaned against the wall, and sipped their drinks.

They observed some kind of tension between the target and the older man. The two of them danced for a while, and he seemed to be attempting to persuade her of something. He was whispering in her ear, looking anxious but trying to keep it discreet.

Nobody noticed except the couple. Whatever he was saying, she refused. For a second, it looked like an argument was brewing. Then he backed off. He ran his hand down her arm in some kind of concil-iatory gesture, pecked her on the cheek, and then left the party. The couple watched him walk to his Mercedes and drive off.

It was 11:32.

By quarter to midnight, they saw her glancing at her watch. Then, unexpectedly, she began making moves to usher the remaining guests out of the villa. She turned the music off, and the quiet was abrupt. She made her apologies to them all. She had an early flight in the morning. Thank you all for coming. Have a great night. See you sometime.

Everyone was a little surprised, but nobody was too upset. There would be plenty of other parties going on across the island on a warm summer night.

The couple had no choice but to leave with the others. There was no chance to slip away and hide. But they hid their frustration well. It was only a minor glitch, nothing to worry about. They walked quietly back to where the car was hidden under the shade of the olive trees and got in.

"What now?" said the driver.

"We wait," the woman replied from the backseat.

The fair-haired man scowled. "Enough of this bullshit. Give me the gun. I'll go and get the bitch. Right now." He reached over and snapped his fingers. The driver shrugged and unholstered the 9mm pistol under his jacket. The fair-haired guy grabbed it from him and started getting out of the car.

The woman stopped him. "Low profile, remember? We keep this clean."

"To hell with that. I say—"

"We wait," she repeated, and flashed him a warning look that si-lenced him.

That was when they heard the motorcycle.

It was exactly midnight.

2.

Ben Hope had been standing there a long time in the darkening room, long enough for the ice in his whisky to melt away to nothing as he stared out of the window. The sun was dipping behind the Atlantic horizon, the sky streaked with crimson and gold, clouds rolling in from the west as night fell.

He stared at the waves as they crashed against the black rocks, lashing spray. His face was still, but his mind was racing and filled with a pain that the whisky couldn't ease. Visions and memories that he couldn't shut out of his mind, and didn't truly want to. He thought about his life. The things he was sorry he'd done in the past. The things he was sorrier he'd never be able to do again. The emptiness of the only future he could imagine lay ahead. The way the lonely days kept turning into lonely nights.

Perhaps it didn't have to be that way.

The bottle stood behind him on a low table. The whisky was a fine malt Scotch, ten years old. It had been a full bottle that afternoon. There were just a couple of fingers left in the bottom now.

Beside the bottle lay a Bible. It was old, leather-bound, worn with use. It was a book he knew well.

Next to that lay a pistol. A Browning Hi Power 9mm, well used, clean and oiled, thirteen shiny rounds in the magazine and one in the breech. It had been lying there for hours, cocked and locked, the sleek copper nose of that first round lined up with the barrel and its tail exposed to the striker, ready and waiting for him to make his decision.

That one bullet was all it would take.

From somewhere in the shadowy room, the phone rang. Ben didn't move. He let it ring until whoever was calling him gave up.

Time passed. The sun slipped down into the sea. The waves darkened as night crept across the sky and he could see only his reflection standing there in the window staring back at him.

The phone rang again.

Still, he didn't move. After half a minute the ringing stopped, and the only sound in the room was the distant roar of the Atlantic.

He turned from the window and walked across to the low table. He put down his empty glass and reached out for the pistol. He picked it up and weighed the heavy steel in his hand. Stared at the weapon a long moment as the moonlight glimmered down its length. He clicked off the safety.

Very slowly, he turned the pistol towards himself until he was looking down the barrel, holding it backwards in his hands, thumb on the trigger. He brought it closer. Felt the cold kiss of the muzzle touch against his brow. He closed his eyes. In his mind he could see her face, the way he liked to remember her, smiling, full of life and beauty and happiness, full of love.

I miss you so much.

Then he sighed.

Not today, he thought. *Today's not the day.*

He lowered the pistol to his side and stood there for a while, letting the weapon dangle loosely in his hand. Then he clicked the safety catch back on. He laid the pistol down on the table and walked out of the room.

3.

Zoë Bradbury felt the cool wind in her hair as the big Suzuki Burgman scooter carried her up the winding country lane.

As she rode, she noticed the strong headlamps of a car behind her, lighting up the road ahead. The lights flashed at her. She wondered who it might be. Maybe the last straggler leaving her party?

Strange, though. She hadn't noticed any cars left outside as she closed the shutters and locked the place up to leave.

She rode on, twisting the throttle a little harder. Trees flashed by on either side as she gained speed. The wind tore at her hair and clothes, and the lights shrank away in her mirror.

She smiled to herself. She was glad that Nikos had taken all her gear away to his place. It was too much to carry on the Suzuki, and this way she could enjoy her last ride before going home to Oxford in the morning. The 400cc scooter was fast enough to scare her—and thrills and risk were things she loved. She opened up the throttle and her grin widened.

But then the lights reappeared in her mirror. The car had crept up even closer this time, its headlights on full beam, dazzling her. She slowed a little and moved aside to let it pass.

It didn't. It just hung back, matching her speed. Irritably, she waved it on. It still hung there behind her. She could hear its engine over the whir of the Suzuki.

OK, then, it was some arsehole who wanted to race. That was fine with her. She cracked open the throttle and accelerated hard through the bends, leaning the bike this way and that. The car followed. She pushed harder, widening the gap between them. But not for long. The car came right up behind, and for a terrifying instant she thought it was going to ram her.

Zoë's heart was beating fast now, and suddenly the idea of racing along the dark empty road, with trees rushing by on either side, didn't seem so much fun.

A farm lane flashed up on the right a little way ahead. She remembered where it led. She'd been walking down that way a couple of times. At the bottom of the lane was a gate that was always padlocked, barring the way—but between the gatepost and the crumbled stone wall there was a gap just big enough to get a bike through.

The Suzuki hammered down the farm lane, barely in control. The ground was little more than soft earth, loose under her wheels. She skidded and regained control. In the mirror, the lights were coming closer again.

What did they want?

The gate was coming up fast. Thirty yards. Twenty. She squeezed the brakes, wobbled, but hit the gap. The Suzuki scraped through with a grinding of plastic. The car skidded to a halt behind her, and suddenly she was leaving the lights behind again.

She whooped. She'd made it.

But then she looked back in the mirror and saw the figures in the lights of the stationary car. Figures running. Figures with guns.

There was a loud crack from behind her. She felt the machine shake violently. The rear tire was blown.

She lost control of the bike, and suddenly it had slipped out from under her. She felt herself falling. The ground rushed up to meet her.

That was all Zoë Bradbury remembered for a long time.

4.

The high gilded gates were open, and Ben Hope drove on through the archway. The private road carved its way through a long woodland tunnel, cool and verdant in the heat of the afternoon. Round a bend, the trees parted and he saw the late-Georgian country house in the distance, across sculpted lawns that looked like velvet. Gravel crunched under the tires of the rented Audi Quattro as he pulled up in the car park alongside the Bentleys and Rollses and Jaguars.

Stepping out of the car, Ben straightened his tie and slipped on the jacket of the expensive suit he'd bought for the occasion and was pretty sure he'd never wear again. He could hear the sound of the big band drifting on the breeze. He followed the sound, cutting across the lawns towards the back of the house. The sweeping acres of the estate opened up in front of him.

Guests were clustered around a striped tent on the lawn. Laughter and chatter. Long tables with canapés, waiters carrying trays of drinks. Women in summer dresses and big flowery hats. The wedding reception was a lot more opulent than Ben had expected.

Charlie had done well for himself, he thought. Not bad for the practical, down-to-earth Londoner who'd started out driving supply trucks with the Royal Engineers. He'd been in the service since leaving school. In 22 SAS he'd never gone higher than trooper. Never wanted to. His only ambition was to be the best. It was strange to imagine him marrying into wealth. Ben wondered if he'd be happy surrounded by all this.

Charlie and his new bride were among the dancing couples on the lawn. Ben smiled as he recognized him. He didn't seem to have changed a lot, apart from the tuxedo. The band had struck up an old jazz number Ben vaguely remembered, Glenn Miller or Benny Goodman. Their trombones and saxes glittered in the sunshine.

Ben kept his distance, stood listening to the music and watching the people, taking in the scene. Thoughts came back to him of the day he'd got married, just a few months before. His hand instinctively went to the gold wedding ring that he wore on a thin leather thong around his neck. He fingered it through the cotton shirt, trying to stop the other memories that bubbled up, the bad ones, the ones of the day it had all ended.

For an instant he was there again, seeing it unfold. He blinked the images away, battled them back into the shadows. He knew they'd return.

The dance ended. There was applause and more laughter. Charlie spotted Ben and waved. He kissed his bride, and she went off with a chattering bunch of friends towards the tent as the band started up another number. Charlie trotted over to Ben, visibly buzzing with excitement, unable to repress the broad grin on his face.

"You look a little different in that outfit," Ben said.

"I didn't think you'd come, sir. Glad you could make it. I've been calling you for days."

"I got your message," Ben said. "And it's Ben, not sir."

"It's good to see you, Ben."

"Good to see you too." Ben clapped Charlie affectionately on the shoulder.

"So how've you been?" Charlie asked. "How are things?"

"It's been a while," Ben replied, evading the question.

"Five years, give or take."

"Congratulations on your marriage. I'm pleased for you."

"Thanks. We're very happy."

"Nice place you've got here."

"This?" Charlie swept his arm across the horizon, at the house and the neatly tended acres. "You must be kidding. This belongs to Rhonda's folks. They're the ones paying for this do. You know how it is—only daughter and all. A bit over the top, between us. All about flaunting their money. If it was up to Rhonda and me, it would have been the local registry office and then off to the nearest pub." He smiled warmly. "So what about you, Ben? Did you ever take the plunge?"

"Plunge?"

"You know—normal life, marriage, kids, all that kind of stuff."

"Oh." Ben hesitated. *What the hell.* There was no point pretending. "I did get married," he said quietly.

Charlie's eyes lit up. "Great, man. Fantastic. When did that happen?"

Ben paused again. "January."

Charlie looked around. "Have you brought her with you?"

"She's not here," Ben said.

"That's a real shame," Charlie said, disappointed. "I'd love to meet her."

"She's gone," Ben said.

Charlie frowned, confused. "You mean she was here, but she left?"

"No. I mean she's dead." It came out more abruptly than Ben had meant. Still hard to say it.

Charlie blanched. He looked down at his feet and was quiet for a few seconds. "When?" he breathed.

"Five months ago. Not long after we married."

"Jesus. I don't know what to say."

"You don't have to say anything."

"How are you?" Charlie said awkwardly. "I mean, how are you handling it?"

Ben shrugged. "I have good days and bad days." The cold touch of the Browning's muzzle against his brow was still a fresh memory.

"What happened?" Charlie asked after another long silence.

"I don't really want to talk about it."

Charlie looked pained. "Let me get you a drink. Shit, this is terrible. I was going to ask you something, but now I don't—"

"It's fine. Ask. What is it?"

"Let's talk in private. See if we can find somewhere quiet."

Ben followed him across the lawn to the tent, through the crowds of people talking and sipping champagne. "A lot of guests," he commented.

"Mostly Rhonda's side," Charlie said. "I hardly know anybody, outside of the regiment. And Rhonda didn't want army people here." He rolled his eyes.

"That's your brother over there, isn't it?"

Charlie stared at him in amazement. "It must be seven years since you last saw Vince. And he doesn't even look anything like me. How the hell did you recognize him?"

"I never forget a face," Ben said with a smile.

"You certainly don't."

By the tent, a waiter was offering drinks from a silver tray on a table. He handed Ben and Charlie a glass of champagne each.

Ben shook his head and pointed. "The bottle."

The waiter stared for a second, then set down the glasses, took a fresh bottle from the ice, and passed it over. Ben grabbed it with one hand and scooped up a couple of crystal champagne flutes with the other. He and Charlie walked away from the throng and the chatter. He sensed that Charlie didn't want anyone listening to what he had to say.

They sat on the steps of a gazebo, a little way from the reception. Ben popped open the bottle and poured them each a glass.

"You're sure you're OK with this?" Charlie said nervously. "I mean, under the circumstances—"

Ben handed him a glass and took a long drink from his own. "I'm listening," he said. "Go ahead."

Charlie nodded. He took a deep breath and then came straight out with it. "I've got some problems, Ben."

"What kind of problems?"

"Nothing like that," Charlie said, catching his look. "Like I said,

Rhonda and I are happy together, everything's cool in that department."

"So is it money?"

In the distance, the band started up a version of "String of Pearls."

Charlie made a resigned gesture. "What else? I'm out of work."

"You left the regiment?"

"Just over a year ago. Fourteen months. Rhonda wanted me out. She was scared I'd get myself killed in Afghanistan or somewhere."

"That's fairly understandable."

"Well, it nearly did happen. More than once. So, what the hell, it's civvy street for me now. Problem is, I'm no damn use in it. I can't hold down a job. I've had four since I left."

"It's a common problem," Ben said. "Hard to adapt, after the things we've seen and done."

Charlie took a long drink of champagne. Ben reached for the bottle and topped up his glass. "We bought a house a while ago," Charlie went on. "Just a small place, but you know what property prices are, and this is hardly the cheapest part of the country. Even a bloody cottage is worth half a mil these days. Rhonda's folks put up a deposit for us as an engagement gift, but we still can hardly keep up with the mortgage payments. It's killing me. I'm just drowning. I don't know what I'm going to do."

"What about Rhonda? Does she work?"

"For an aid charity. It doesn't pay much."

"Plenty of desk jobs in the army. Why don't you apply?"

Charlie shook his head. "They'd go crazy if I went anywhere near that again. Scared I'd be tempted back into active service. God knows I probably would be too. Rhonda's dad made his money selling cell phone ringtones. Wants me to go and work for him. He's putting a lot of pressure on me. The whole family is. I mean, fucking *ringtones*. Can you imagine?"

Ben smiled. "Maybe you should go for it. Sounds cushy—and lucrative. And safer than getting shot at."

"I wouldn't last long," Charlie said. "It would put a strain on the marriage." He took another long gulp of champagne.

"I didn't bring you a wedding present," Ben said. "If it'll help, I can give you some money instead. I could write you a check today."

"No way. That's not what I want."

"Then you could consider it a loan. Until you get on your feet."

"No. I wanted to ask you something else."

Ben nodded. "I think I know what. You want to ask me about working together."

Charlie let out a long sigh. "OK, I'll be frank with you. How is the kidnap and ransom business doing these days?"

"Better than ever," Ben said. "Snatching people and holding them for ransom is a growth industry."

"I was talking about your end of the business."

"There's always call for people like me," Ben said. "Involving the police is nearly always a bad move. K and R insurance agents and most of the official negotiators are just nerds in suits. People in trouble need an extra option."

"And you're it."

"And you want to be part of it."

"You know I'd be good," Charlie said. "But I can't just set up on my own. I don't know anything about it. I'd need some training. You're the best teacher I ever had. If I was going into something like that, I'd want to work for you."

"From what you tell me, I don't think your new family would approve."

"I'd tell them I was a security consultant. It can't be as dangerous as what we've seen in the regiment, can it?"

Ben said nothing. Both their glasses were empty, and the sun was beating down. He poured out the last of the champagne and set the bottle down with a heavy clunk of glass on concrete. "Problem is, I can't help you," he said. "If I could, I would. But I'm out. Retired. I'm sorry."

"Retired? Really?"

Ben nodded. It had been his promise to her, the day she'd said she would marry him. "Since the end of last year. It's all over for me."

Charlie sank back against the steps of the gazebo, deflating. "You have any contacts?"

Ben shook his head. "I never did. I always worked alone. Everything was strictly word of mouth." He finished his drink. "Like I said. If it's money I can help."

"I can't take money from you," Charlie said. "Rhonda can ask her folks to bail us out anytime, and they probably would. But we see this as our responsibility. Our problem. We need to deal with it ourselves. I was just hoping—"

"I'm sorry. There's really no way."

Charlie grimaced with disappointment. "But if you hear of anything going, you'll let me know?"

"I would, but it won't happen. I told you, I'm out of it."

Charlie sighed again. "I'm sorry I brought this up." He paused a long time, watching the people dancing and having fun in the distance. "So what are you going to do next?"

"I'm going back to Oxford. I'm heading there right after this. I've already rented a flat there."

"What's in Oxford?"

"The university," Ben said. "I'm going there to study."

"You, a student? To do what?"

"To finish what I started before I went crazy and joined the army almost twenty years ago. Theology."

Charlie's eyes opened wide. "Theology? You want to be a priest?"

Ben smiled. "Reverend. Once upon a time, that's all I wanted to be. Seemed like the perfect life."

"So you went off to war instead. Makes sense."

"Sometimes things don't work out the way you think," Ben said. "It just happened that way. Now I've come full circle. The time is right for me. They let me back in to finish my course. One year to go, then I can start thinking about entering the Church, just like I'd planned years ago." He slapped his hands on his knees. "So that's it."

Charlie was staring at him in disbelief. "You're kidding me. You're winding me up."

"I'm serious."

"This just doesn't seem like you. I still have this image of you—that time with the tank, in the desert? We were pinned under fire, you only had three rounds left. I've never seen anything like it. Guys in the regiment, guys who never met you, still talk about it—"

"Well, I don't want to talk about it," Ben said, cutting him off. "Whatever I did in the past, whatever I was or wanted to be, that's finished. I'm tired, Charlie. I'm thirty-eight years old and all I've ever known is violence and killing. I want a life of peace."

"A dog collar and a little cottage, with a Bible in your hand."

Ben nodded. "That's it. About as far away from the past as I can get."

"I can't see it."

"Maybe I'll surprise you."

"I should have waited awhile," Charlie said. He laughed. "You could have married us."

They hadn't noticed Rhonda striding across the lawn towards them. They stood up as she approached. She was tall and slender, with reddish hair that looked as though she'd colored it with henna. She had a stud in her nose. A bohemian kind of look that contrasted with the high heels and the expensive dress she was wearing. She was pretty, but Ben thought he could see a hardened look behind the eyes. There was suspicion in them as Charlie introduced her to him.

"Heard all about you," she said, looking him up and down. "Major Benedict Hope. The wild one. I know all the stories. Really impressed."

"I'm not Major Hope. I'm just Ben. Forget the stories."

"Well, Ben, I suppose you're here to talk my husband into joining you on some—"

"I invited him here," Charlie said. "Remember?"

She looked up hotly at Ben. "I don't want him getting mixed up in anything dangerous."

"I'm the last person who would get him into any kind of danger," Ben said. "You can trust me on that."

She snorted. "Yeah, right. Now, can I have my husband back, please? And someone over there wants to meet you."

Ben followed the direction of her pointing finger, and his gaze landed on a stunningly attractive woman standing over by the tent. She was waving coyly, smiling in their direction.

"That's Mandy Latham," Rhonda said. "Her parents own half of Shropshire. Deliciously nouveau riche—even worse than my lot. Winters at Verbier, drives a Lambo. She's been asking me who the gorgeous, tall, blond, blue-eyed guy with Charlie is."

"He's going to be a priest," Charlie said.

"Why don't you go and ask her to dance?" Rhonda snapped at Ben.

"Rhonda—" Charlie started.

"I don't dance," Ben said. He smiled at Charlie. "Nice party. See you around." He walked away.

"You'll phone me, then?" Charlie called after him.

Ben didn't answer him. He made his way back across the lawn, placed his empty glass on the table at the tent. He looked at his watch. Mandy Latham approached him, slinky in a shimmering blue silk dress that matched her shining eyes. "Hi," she said tentatively. "I'm Mandy. Were you really Charlie's commanding officer in the SAS?"

"You shouldn't believe everything you hear," Ben said. "Great to meet you, Mandy. I have to go now."

He left her staring after him as he walked away.

5.

Professor Tom Bradbury shut the front door behind him, put down his old briefcase, and laid his car keys on the oak stand in the hall, next to the vase of flowers.

The house was quiet. He hadn't expected it to be. Zoë should be home today, and her presence was always made noticeable by the hard-rock sound track that she insisted on blaring at full volume from the living-room hi-fi.

Bradbury wandered through to the airy kitchen. The patio windows were open, and the scents of the garden were wafting through the room. Remembering the half-finished bottle of Pinot Grigio from the night before, he opened the fridge. Inside was a freshly prepared dish of chocolate mousse, Zoë's favorite pudding, which her mother always prepared for her visits home.

He tutted and poured himself a glass of the chilled wine. Sipping it, he stepped out into the garden and saw his wife, Jane, kneeling at the flower beds, a tray of brightly colored annuals beside her.

"You're back early," she said, looking up and smiling.

"Where is she?"

"Not here yet."

"I thought it was quiet. Expected she'd have got in by now."

Jane Bradbury stabbed her trowel in the ground, stood up with a grunt, and dusted the earth off her hands. "That looks good," she said, noticing his glass. He passed it to her, and she took a sip and smacked her lips. "I wouldn't worry about it," she said. "You know what she's like. She probably stopped off to stay with some friend in London."

"Why couldn't she just come straight here? She's always with some friend or other. We hardly ever see her."

"She's not a child anymore, Tom. She's twenty-six years old."

"Then why does she act like one?"

"She'll call. Probably turn up tomorrow like the bad penny."

"You indulge her too much," he said irritably. "You've even prepared her favorite pudding."

His wife smiled. "You indulge her as much as I do."

Bradbury turned towards the house. "The least she could do is bloody well let us know where she is."

6.

Zoë Bradbury woke up with a gasp. The first thing she was aware of was the strong sunlight in her face, making her blink. She tried to focus, but her vision was hazy. Where was she?

After a minute the cloudiness melted away and things were clearer. She was in a bedroom. Was it hers? She couldn't remember, and that was the strangest realization.

She was lying on a bare mattress, a rumpled sheet draped over her. She sat up in the bed and suddenly felt a sharp pain cutting through her side. She winced and clutched at her ribs. It felt as though one was cracked. Her head was on fire and her mouth was dry. She looked down at her palms. They were scuffed and tender, as though she'd landed heavily and put her hands out to protect herself.

Flashes. Bright lights. Sounds. Places and people. It was all there in her mind, but jumbled and obscure, all shadows and echoes. She vaguely remembered the sensation of falling. Then the impact to the head. She rubbed it and felt the bruise. Struggled to clear her mind. Nothing would come. She blinked and shook her head. Still nothing.

Panic began to grip her. She couldn't remember anything. Didn't know anything about what she was doing there or, she realized with horror, even who she was. Something had happened to her. A bad fall. Some kind of damage inside her head. She prayed it was only temporary.

All she knew was that she was in danger. It was the instinctive knowledge of a trapped animal in the presence of a predator.

That instinct helped her focus. *Get out of here first. Worry about the rest later.*

There was nobody in the room with her. But as the breeze ruffled the drapes she saw the man in the chair on the balcony outside.

The first thing she noticed about him was the gun. It was clasped loosely in his hand, a big boxy thing, pointing right at her. He was sitting facing her, leaning right back in a deck chair in the sunshine, and at first she thought he was staring at her through his wraparound shades. But his chest was heaving slowly, and from the way he didn't respond to her waking up she guessed he was asleep. At his feet were a bottle of ouzo and an empty glass. His fair hair blew lightly in the sea breeze.

Zoë struggled out of the bed, clenching her teeth against the tearing pain in her side. She planted one foot on the tiled floor, then the other. The tiles were cool against her soles.

The man didn't move.

She slowly stood up and stepped away from the bed. Her head was spinning wildly and she reached out to steady herself. She saw that she was fully dressed, in white trousers and a yellow top. The clothes felt grubby on her skin, as though she'd been sleeping in them for a couple of days. The right knee of the trousers was ripped, and there was a smear of dirt up her right side where the pain was. From the fall, she guessed.

Wobbly on her feet, she reached for the pair of heeled sandals by the bed. They matched the yellow top. Were they hers? She didn't know. She carried them by their straps as she crept towards the door, praying the man in the chair wouldn't wake up.

When she grasped the door handle and felt its initial resistance, she was sure the door would be locked. But then it turned and her heart surged with excitement. The door opened without a sound. There was a hallway outside, and a flight of stairs leading down.

She tiptoed across the hall and peered down over the metal rail into the stairwell. Voices, far away somewhere in the house. She heard a woman talking, and a man laugh.

Her heart was hammering now. She started down the stairs, wincing at every step, her bare feet padding silently on the ceramic tiling. The fear sharpened her mind. She had no idea where she was, but she knew she had to get away from this place.

She made it downstairs without anyone hearing. Nobody had come running from the bedroom. She was safe—so far.

At the bottom of the stairs was another door. It was open, and bright light was shining in from outside. She hobbled out, clutching the shoes and her ribs, and found herself standing on a little terrace with potted plants and flowers. Down three steps was the white pebbled beach. The stones were sharp against her feet, and burning hot. She pulled on the shoes. They fitted her perfectly, even though they seemed like a stranger's.

She crept down the beach and looked back at the house. It was a pitted white stone block with shuttered windows and a red tile roof. Through the railings of the first-floor balcony she could see the back of the man's deck chair. Behind the house, a wooded incline rose up steeply to the cliff above. There was no way she could climb it. She looked around her in desperation. The beach was empty. There was a long ramshackle wooden jetty with a small motorboat moored up to it, bobbing gently on the swell.

She headed for it, her steps quickening. She stumbled in the slim three-inch heels. Kept glancing back at the house. Nobody. She was getting away.

She made it to the jetty. The boards were solid, and she could run better than on the loose stones and sand. She hurried on, the pain in her side forgotten now.

That was when she heard the yell. It came from the house. A man's voice, loud and full of rage. She gasped and spun round. Her heart jumped. It was him—the fair-haired man from the balcony. The gun was in his hand. He bounded down the steps to the beach and sprinted towards her, screaming.

Then more of them came from the house. A woman and two more men. The woman pointed at her. They all started running. More yells.

She was halfway across the jetty. She could make it to the boat. Could she get the outboard motor started? Would they shoot her? What did these people want from her? Her legs were shaking as she stumbled along.

Then she fell. She sprawled across the rough wood and felt her ankle twist. Her heel was caught in a gap in the planking. She jerked and struggled. It was jammed tight. She reached down and tried to tear the shoe off.

They were coming. Footsteps thundered on the jetty, and then there was a gun pressing hard into the back of her neck, heavy breathing in her ear. She looked up to see the man's face contorted in anger, teeth bared.

The others caught up.

"What the hell happened?" one voice said.

"The bitch came round," the man with the gun snapped back over his shoulder.

"And what the fuck were you doing?" the woman's voice demanded. "Sleeping?"

He ignored her and yanked Zoë to her feet. The four of them marched her roughly back along the jetty. She was kicking and screaming hysterically. They said nothing to her. Dragged her, limping, back to the house, back up to her room, and shoved her down on the bed. Her ankles and knees were roughly bound together with duct tape. The fair-haired man thrust the pistol into the back of his belt and grabbed her right wrist. His grip was crushing. He jerked her arm up and there was a rattle of metal as he cuffed it to the bed frame. Then the left arm.

She fought them wildly. "What do you want with me? Let go of me! *What do you want with me?*"

Then they pressed a length of the tape across her mouth, stifling her screams. Tears poured uncontrollably down her face.

The man took the gun out of his belt and pressed the muzzle to the side of her head. She tried to shrink away from the cold steel, screwing her eyes shut.

Then he smiled and took the gun away. They all stood back and watched her. She was too exhausted to fight any more. Her breath came in gasps and she felt she was going to faint.

The woman had her hands on her hips, head cocked to one side, a thin smile on her lips. "Leave her awhile," she said. "I have to make a call. Then we can go to work on her."

"*What do you want?*" Zoë tried to scream again through the gag.

Nobody answered as they filtered out one by one.

The fair-haired man was the last to leave the room. "I can hardly wait to get started," he said, grinning down at her.

7.

Ben surfaced slowly from a murky sleep filled with threatening dreams, and his mind drifted back into focus. He remembered now. He was in his new flat. Oxford was hardly a strange city to him, but it felt weird actually to be living here again after so many years. He wouldn't be home in Ireland until December.

Fighting away the numbing torpor that made him want to crawl back deep under the covers, he kicked his legs out of the bed. He shrugged on a tracksuit top, walked through to the living room, stepped over the mess of half-unpacked luggage that was in there, and headed for the kitchen. The flat was tucked into a secluded block of apartments in the quiet northern end of the city. It felt modern and compact, so different from the rambling old seaside house in Ireland, with its stone floors and drafty fireplaces.

He listened to the twitter of birds and the distant traffic rumble as he made some coffee. No milk, no sugar, nothing to eat. He left the radio off. He wasn't interested in whatever might be happening in the world. He sat for a while at the small table in his kitchen, the coffee cup hot between his hands, emptying his mind, trying not to think about things. Most of all, trying not to think about the two bottles of ten-year-old Laphroaig in his suitcase—and how easy it would be to walk over there and open one of them. Too easy. He knew he'd get there in a moment of weakness, when the demons came. But this wasn't it.

At three minutes to eight he stood up, walked back to the living room, and found the fabric shopping bag he'd left on one of the armchairs the night before. He picked up the heavy bag, carried it across the room, and dumped the contents out across his desk. Books spilled everywhere.

There were over twenty theology textbooks in the heap, and he'd set himself the task of reading them all in the next few days. Acres of Hebrew and Latin to pore over. Thousands of pages of abstruse philosophy. Aristotle. Spinoza. Wittgenstein. Stacks of essays and interpretations of Bible scripture. It was a mountain of work, and he relished the prospect. It would keep his mind occupied and get him in training for when term began in October. Nineteen years was a long time to catch up on.

He worked for six straight hours, stretched and stood up, and then headed for the tiny bathroom. After a quick shower he pulled on a pair of jeans and a white cotton shirt, and ate a stale tuna sandwich that he'd bought at a filling station on the M40 the day before. Sometime after two he left the flat and did the half-hour walk into the heart of the city in twenty minutes. He headed straight towards the Bodleian, the university's grandest and oldest library, just off the city center.

The sun was beating down strongly. As he walked, he took off his jacket and slung it over his shoulder.

That was the moment, strolling through the old city under the clear blue sky, when it hit him.

What is this feeling?

He stopped. It was the strangest thing.

I'm just a normal person. I'm a student about to start college, walking to the library. That's all I am.

Suddenly, and for just one wonderful instant, it all seemed possible. That he could live the simple life he'd dreamed about, far away from the violence and ugliness he'd been immersed in for what seemed like an eternity. That he could be happy again one day, that the pain would come to an end.

It was just a taste of that happiness, a simple taste of normality and freedom and the promise of some kind of life again. He knew there would be more bad days ahead—days when he didn't even want to go on living. But here, now, for the first time in months, he could feel the sun on his face and he was thankful to be alive. Maybe the worst of the grief was over. Maybe he was coming through. Maybe he was going to be OK.

It was what she would have wanted, he thought. He saw her face in his mind and felt the loss and guilt stab deep inside him. He wanted to reach out and touch her. Then she smiled, and it made him want to cry but smile too.

Oh, Leigh. I'm so sorry for what happened.

I know, her distant voice replied in his mind.

He was still smiling sadly to himself as he walked through the stone archways of the Bodleian. The main reading rooms smelled of old leather and burnished wood. He approached the desk and showed his card to the librarian.

Twenty years before, the women behind the desk had been notorious battle-axes with intimidating stares that had frightened most of the students. He'd been idly wondering whether he was going to find them still here, grayer, fatter, and even more formidable.

The librarian flashed a smile at him. She was about twenty-eight or twenty-nine, with sandy curls tied up loosely in a ponytail, little wisps hanging down and framing her face. It was a pretty face, open and natural. She glanced twice at his name on the card and smiled again. He requested the book he was after, and she told him in a low voice that it would have to be fetched up from the bowels of the library.

He thanked her, and spent the next half-hour flipping through periodicals in a booth in the reading room across from the main desk. Every so often, he was aware that the librarian was glancing over at him. Then another member of the staff brought him the book he'd come to read, and he didn't see her again.

It was late afternoon by the time he left the library. The heat and sweat of the bustling city center were a strong contrast to the cool silence of the Bodleian reading rooms. He filled his lungs with the smell of the old city.

"Well, I'm back," he said quietly to himself.

8.

s this line secure? I have to talk to you."

"It's secure. Why haven't you reported sooner, Kaplan?"

"We've had a problem here."

A pause. "The girl?"

"I'm afraid so."

"You killed her, didn't you? You had strict orders to take her alive."

"She's alive."

"Then what?"

"She's alive but she's no use to us."

"You're trying to tell me you screwed up."

"We had her, OK? She was right in our hands. But she was hard to catch. She was on a motorcycle. We chased her for about three miles, from the villa up into the hills. Those roads are twisty, and there's a lot of forest. We tried to head her off, but she panicked. She went off the road, where we couldn't follow. I left Ross and Parker in the vehicle and took Hudson with me. We went in after her on foot."

"And she got away."

"No. We got her. She didn't get far before she came off the bike."

"What's the damage?"

"No serious external damage. A few cuts and grazes. But she suffered a head trauma, and that's the problem. She was unconscious a long time, nearly thirty hours. Came round yesterday. But she has some kind of traumatic amnesia. She can't answer our questioning, because her memory has blanked out."

"You're sure you got the right person?"

"One hundred percent sure."

"How bad is she?"

"We can't really say. The amnesia might be short-term."

"You'd better hope so. Have you any idea how serious this is?"

"It's under control."

"Doesn't sound much like that from this end, Kaplan. If she doesn't regain her memory soon, you'll have to get her back here, where there are proper facilities."

"There's another small problem."

"You mean this gets worse?"

"All her things have disappeared from the villa. We went there to collect everything. It's not there anymore. Luggage, papers. All gone. She wasn't meant to be leaving until morning. It means we have to replan. It can't look like an accident anymore."

"Nice work, Kaplan."

"One more thing. There was someone at the party, some boyfriend, we think. He'd been hanging around. We didn't think anything of it. But then at the party he spilled her drink just after Hudson spiked it. Looked deliberate."

"So he knows something. Who is he?"

"Just a local guy, as far as we know. One of her many boyfriends. Probably married, so he was real discreet. The villa has a linked garage, and he always parked his Mercedes there where we couldn't see it. Now we think he took her things away, in the car, earlier on. And we're pretty sure she was RVing with him when we took her."

"So he could know everything."

"Basically. But there was no way we could have known that."

"You have any information at all on this person?"

"We're working on it."

"You're going to have to rescue this situation quickly. We're on the clock here. People will start to miss her."

"We'll find him."

"You'd better. And when you do, you contain the situation. There might still be a chance of saving this mess. This goes up in smoke, you're dead. Understand?"

9.

After two solid days of study, Ben felt ready to breathe some air again. The sun was shining through his window, and he felt the tug of the outdoors. Back in Ireland, he made a point of running ten miles every day.

He put on jogging pants and a T-shirt and walked briskly into town, where he picked his way through the shoppers in Cornmarket and walked down towards his old college, Christ Church. Entering through the main gates, he found himself looking across the vast main quadrangle. He took a deep breath.

He walked across the quad, gazing around him at the regal old sandstone buildings as they caught the gold of the sun. Distant memories flooded back. In the center of the quad, surrounded by neat lawns and perched above an ornate stone fountain, stood the familiar statue of Mercury, the winged messenger. Ben walked past it, trotted up some steps to the far side of the quad, and headed for an arched entrance. Tucked away behind it was the cathedral, one of the smallest in England, which doubled as the college chapel. Ben hadn't planned on going in, but now he felt himself drawn to the place. He slipped in through the door.

At the far end of the cathedral, a morning service was in progress. Ben didn't recognize the priest in the pulpit, but he was sure he'd be meeting him sooner or later in the course of his studies. The man's voice was solemn and gentle as he read from the Gospel of St. Matthew. His words echoed off the twelfth-century columns and walls and drifted up to the magnificently ornate ceiling. The small congregation was clustered near the front, listening attentively.

Ben stepped quietly across the polished mosaic floor, took a seat near the entrance and watched and listened from a distance. He tried to imagine himself standing there in the pulpit, wearing the dog collar and that earnest expression, conducting the service. That was his planned future up there: the role he was supposed to be preparing for, something that had been part of his life, on and off, for as long as he could remember.

Sitting here now, it seemed hard to imagine. He'd wanted this thing so much, dreamed of it so often—but was it really within his grasp to make it happen?

He stayed a few minutes longer in the cathedral, bathing in the soft light from the stained-glass windows, head bowed, letting the serene atmosphere penetrate deep inside him. Then he very quietly got up and slipped back outside into the sunlit quadrangle.

He turned left and made his way towards the sprawling meadow behind Christ Church. He jogged for half an hour, making himself feel the burn in his calf muscles as he ran along the towpath by the river. Then, satisfied that he wasn't letting himself become too unfit, he jogged back towards the college.

He was so deep in thought as he walked through the main quad that he didn't see anyone approach.

"I was hoping I might bump into you," a voice said.

Ben turned and saw the tall, gray-haired, tweedy figure of Professor Tom Bradbury approaching. He hadn't seen Bradbury since his interview six weeks before with the faculty admissions board.

"Professor. How are you?"

Bradbury smiled. "Call me Tom. I think we've known each other long enough for that."

Tom Bradbury and Ben's father, Alistair Hope, had been at Cambridge together. The friendship between a devout theology scholar and a law student might have seemed unlikely, but it had lasted many years and ended only when Ben's father had died. That had been the year Ben broke off his studies and joined the army. He had few fond memories of that time, but he'd always remembered Tom Bradbury, even though he'd lost contact with him all those years ago. As a teenage student he'd come to think of him as an uncle. His presence had always been warm and reassuring, with the aromatic smell of pipe tobacco ingrained in his clothes. His tutorials had been the liveliest of all the classes Ben could remember. His speciality was the Old Testament—scripture that was so ancient and dense and obscure that it was hard to bring to life. But Professor Bradbury could do that, and the students had loved him.

"I wanted to talk to you," Bradbury said. "Are you free tomorrow lunchtime?"

"I had a date with Descartes," Ben smiled. "But lunch with you sounds a lot more appealing."

"Wise choice," Bradbury said. "Not my favorite philosopher, I have to say. I was thinking you could come over to our place."

"Still up in Summertown?"

Bradbury nodded. They agreed on a time, and the professor smiled weakly and headed off towards his rooms in Canterbury Quad. Ben watched him walk away. Bradbury was a sprightly, upright sixty-three. He was normally jovial and full of life, with a mischievous twinkle in his eye. But today he was different. There was something missing. He looked old and weary, subdued. Was he ill? If that was the case, why invite someone for lunch the next day? Something was wrong.

10.

GREECE

THE SAME DAY

t was a Buck clasp knife, and the fair-haired man loved to sharpen it. When he was sitting out on the balcony with nothing much else to do except soak up the sun, drink ouzo, and watch over the bitch, he would spend hours carefully whetting the blade with an oiled sharpening stone. He had the edge so perfectly honed that he could lay the knife on its back, edge-up, and leave a banknote lying across it overnight, and when he came back in the morning the banknote would have cut itself in half with just its own weight.

He took the knife out of his pocket and clicked the blade open with one hand as he walked slowly up to the bed. Her eyes rolled across to look at him, and she let out a stifled cry of terror behind the gag. Her arms were strapped down to the bare mattress. Her fingers were clawing and straining as she struggled.

He rested on the edge of the bed, leaned across her, and let her see the blade up close. He could smell the fear coming from her. "Looks sharp, doesn't it?" He ran his thumb gently down the cutting edge, splitting the first layer of skin. "You have no idea how sharp it is. But maybe you'll be finding out pretty soon."

He pressed the flat of the blade against her cheekbone, and she drew in a gasp. Her throat fluttered.

"Now, I'm going to take this gag off, and you're not going to start

THE HOPE VENDETTA | 37

screaming again. You're going to talk to me. You're going to tell me everything. Because if you don't, I'm going to put your eye out. Pop it, just like that."

The dark-haired woman was standing and watching from the other side of the bedroom. Her arms were folded and her face was tight. She wanted to intervene, but she checked herself.

The man ripped away the gag. Zoë's breath was coming in rapid gasps. She swallowed hard, and gave a whimper of terror as he ran the cold blade lightly down her temple and traced a line around her eye.

"I don't remember," she gasped.

"Yes, you do. Don't lie to us."

"I swear to you, I don't remember."

"One little push of the blade," he said. "That's all it takes, and I'm going to watch that pretty little blue eye come spilling out. You ever seen a burst eyeball? Looks like raw egg." He smiled, let the touch of the knife linger on her skin, then drew it away.

She was shuddering with horror. "I don't know what to say to you," she sobbed. "I don't know."

"Cleaver," he said. "You remember Mr. Cleaver, don't you? You re-member what you did to him?"

She shook her head violently.

"Where is it?" he said.

"Where is what?"

"*Where is it?*" he screamed in her face.

"*I don't fucking know,*" she screamed back. "I don't fucking know what you want from me!" Her eyes were desperate, her hair sticking to the tears on her cheeks. "You've got to believe me! I don't know anything! You've got the wrong person!" She began to cry harder. "Let me go," she pleaded. "Let me go. I won't tell anyone. I promise."

The woman stepped forward and laid a hand on the man's shoul-der. "We need to talk."

He tensed, still staring at the girl on the bed. Then he sighed, turned away, and followed the woman out of the room.

They stepped into the hallway outside the bedroom. The woman shut the door so that Zoë Bradbury wouldn't hear. "This isn't working."

"She's faking it, Kaplan," he whispered furiously.

"I don't think you can know that."

"Give me half an hour alone with the bitch. I'll get it out of her."

"How? By putting her eyes out?"

"Just let me."

"We haven't exactly been easy on her. What makes you think you can get it out of her?"

"I will. Give me more time."

The woman bit her lip, shook her head. "She can't stay here. We don't have the facilities. I'm getting her out."

"Give me ten minutes with her first."

"Negative."

"Five minutes. I'll make her talk, believe me."

"You're enjoying this too much, Hudson."

"I'm doing my job."

"What if you kill her? Then we're all dead."

"I won't kill her. I know what I'm doing, Kaplan."

She snorted. "Do you? Listen to me. I want you to put that knife away. If I see it again I'll put a bullet in your head. Is that completely clear to you?"

The man went quiet, staring at her sullenly.

"They'll get it out of her," she said. "They have other ways."

11.

Ben leaned back in the hard seat and watched as the audience trickled into the room. The acoustic amplified every sound, and people kept their voices down. He was in the back row and the place was filling up slowly, but he didn't think the concert was going to draw a big crowd.

He'd spotted the flyer a couple of days before, and he was glad he was here. He wasn't much of a concertgoer, but the idea of an hour of Bartók string quartets appealed to him. It was the kind of edgy music that made a lot of people restless and uncomfortable, but which he liked. It was moody and dark, introspective, a little dissonant, filled with a tension that somehow relaxed him.

The Holywell Music Room was tucked away down a winding side street not far from the Bodleian Library. It wasn't a big or opulent venue, just a plain, simple white room with a low stage at one end and capacity for about a hundred people. The lighting was stark and the stepped banks of seats seemed designed to be as uncomfortable as possible. The program said it was the oldest concert hall in Europe, and that Handel had played there in his time. There was a short blurb about the composer and the music, and a little paragraph on each member of the string quartet. They were all postgraduate music students, teaching and gigging their way through college.

The low stage had four plastic chairs, four music stands. The musicians were due out any second. Maybe they'd hold out a few more minutes, hoping more people would come in. But it didn't look promising.

Ben felt, rather than saw, her walk into the room. He turned, and the first thing he noticed was her smile as she recognized him. The librarian from the Bodleian. Her sandy hair was down over her shoulders, and she was wearing a light jacket that hugged her figure. He laid the program down on his knee as she came over to him.

"Are you on your own?" she said softly. "Mind if I sit here?"

His jacket was folded over the back of the seat next to his. He grabbed it and stuffed it down at his feet. "No problem," he said.

She sat, still smiling. She had a little bag, which she set down beside her. "I didn't expect to see you here," she whispered. "I'm Lucy, by the way."

"Ben."

"It says Benedict on your library card."

"Just Ben."

She took off the jacket, and he noticed she was wearing the same crisp white blouse she'd been wearing when he'd first met her. "Been working late?" he said.

She rolled her eyes. "You guessed it."

He was about to reply when the musicians walked out onto the stage, carrying their instruments. There was a smatter of applause from the small audience as the two violinists, the viola player, and the cellist settled themselves into their seats. They took up their bows, nodding to one another. Then the playing began.

As the edgy music filled the room, Ben became aware of Lucy's perfume. From time to time she shifted in her seat and he felt her knee brush his lightly. He idly wondered why she'd wanted to sit next to him when the place was half empty. She seemed pleasant enough. He didn't mind the company.

Sunset was falling as they left the Holywell and walked up the narrow street.

"I enjoyed that," Lucy said.

"Relaxing," he answered.

"You think? It's pretty intense."

"That's what I find relaxing."

"Fancy a drink?" she said.

"Why not?"

The Turf was just nearby, a pub he remembered from years ago. They crossed the road and headed towards the sound of music and laughter. The interior was traditional—low ceilings, exposed beams, with a pitted wooden bar that looked at least two centuries old. The place was heaving with people. A contingent of Italian tourists was taking up several tables, making too much noise. Ben bought a double Scotch and a glass of white wine, and he and Lucy took their drinks out to a tranquil corner of the beer garden surrounded by old stone walls and climbing plants. The air was thick with the scent of honeysuckle.

Ben took out his cigarettes. "You mind?"

"I'll join you," she said. He gave her a light, and they clinked glasses. It seemed a little strange to him to be sitting there with her, yet at the same time she was easy to be with.

"Great concert," she said. "Shame about the audience."

"I guess Bartók's an acquired taste."

"If it had been Chopin's greatest hits, or some frilly baroque thing, the place would have been packed out." She smiled. "So, Ben, are you a postgrad or what?"

"Undergrad. Waiting to start my final year at Christ Church."

She seemed surprised.

"I know," he said, catching her look. "I'm old."

"You're not old."

I feel old, he thought. *And tired*. "I took some time out," he explained. "Did two years of my theology degree, long ago. Too long ago. Now they've let me back in to finish it."

"Career change?"

"Definitely."

"What did you do before?"

He thought for a moment. Even thought about telling her the truth—then decided against it. "I was self-employed. Kind of a freelance consultant. Troubleshooter. Specialist stuff. I traveled around a lot."

It was meaningless, the vaguest answer he could think of, but she seemed satisfied with it. "Career change would suit me too," she said.

"You don't like working at the library?"

"It's OK. But I want to paint. I'm an artist. The Bodleian job's only a few hours a week, to help with bills. I'd go full-time with the art if I could make a living out of it. But things are tight."

"Tough business," he said. "I hope you succeed. What kind of art do you do?"

She chuckled. "Oh, you wouldn't be interested."

"No, I am interested."

She reached into her bag and brought out a business card. On one side was printed LUCY WILDE, FINE ART PAINTER and a phone number and website address. Ben flipped it over. The back of the card was printed with an abstract design, clean and geometric, a style that reminded him of Kandinsky. "This is one of yours?"

She nodded.

"I like it. You're pretty good. I hope you do well with this stuff." He made to hand her back the card.

"Keep it," she said. He smiled and slipped the card into his pocket.

There was silence between them for a few moments. He twirled the glass on the tabletop, then glanced at his watch. "Maybe I should be going." He drained the last of his drink.

"Where do you live?" she asked.

"North Oxford. Woodstock Road. What about you?"

"Up in Jericho."

"I'd offer you a lift," he said. "But I'm on foot."

"Same here. But you're going my way, as far as St. Giles'. Walk with me?"

He nodded. She smiled, and they left together. They didn't talk much as they walked back along the narrow street. Their footsteps echoed up the pitted old walls of college buildings as they made their way back towards the center of town. A crowd had spilled out of the New Theatre and the kebab vans were busy, filling the warm night air with the smell of grilled meat. Past St. John's College, up the broad St. Giles'. The streets were quieter there, and the streetlights cast off a dim amber glow.

Lucy stopped. "I go this way," she said, pointing to a side street. "So I'll see you sometime? The library?"

"I suppose so." He was about to turn to walk away.

"Ben?"

"What?"

Her voice was hesitant. "I was thinking—would you like to go to see a film with me tomorrow night?"

He said nothing.

"It's a movie about Goya," she said nervously. "The artist."

"I know who Goya was." He hated the abrupt way it came out.

"I don't know if it'll be any good. But I thought you might like—" Her voice trailed off. She shuffled a little, looked down at her feet, fiddled with her bag.

He hesitated. "Sorry, Lucy. I don't think I can make that. I'm busy."

"What about some other night? Maybe a drink?"

"I don't think so," he said.

She looked flustered. "OK, I understand. See you round, then." She turned to go, and he watched her walk away. She didn't look back. He carried on up the street.

After about a hundred yards he slowed his step. Stopped. Stood under the amber lights and shook his head. *What an asshole*, the voice in his head told him. He'd handled that all wrong. Stupid and clumsy and callous. She obviously wasn't the kind of woman who asked men out on dates every day. It had been an effort for her to come out with it, but he'd stepped on her like an insect. She deserved better than that. He needed to go back and explain the situation. That he liked her, but just couldn't see much of her. How he could never possibly be attracted to anyone, not for a long time and maybe never again. That it wasn't personal—it was just him and his problems. That he was sorry.

He turned and strode back to the cobbled side street where he'd watched Lucy walk away from him. It was poorly lit and narrow, and the high buildings either side threw long black shadows across the cobbles. Little more than a long alleyway. There was nobody around.

Just Lucy and the three guys.

They were thirty yards away. They had her pressed up against the wall. One in front with his hand on her throat. One each side, blocking her escape. She was struggling and kicking. One of them had her bag, and she was holding on to the strap, trying to snatch it back away from him. Then she let go, and Ben heard a laugh over her faint cries.

He moved stealthily against the dark shadows. They were too preoccupied with Lucy to notice his approach, but not even a professional soldier would have heard him. Two of them were white, and the third one who'd ripped her bag out of her hands was Asian. The one holding her throat looked the most useful. Shaved head, nose ring, confident attitude. Definitely the leader. The other white one was short, chunky, mostly fat. They were little more than kids, probably between seventeen and twenty, all in the same kind of designer sports gear.

Just kids, but dangerous kids. Something glinted in the dull amber light. The leader had reached inside his jacket and drawn out a blade. A kitchen knife, black plastic handle, maybe eight inches of serrated steel. He waved it in Lucy's face. She let out a stifled scream, and he growled at her to stay still and shut the fuck up.

Ben's fists tightened at the sight of the knife. He moved closer, completely quiet. They still hadn't seen him.

The Asian kid was rifling through her bag, looking for her wallet, whilst his fat friend grabbed her arm, trying to pull off her watch. Her eyes were locked open in terror.

Ben stepped out of the shadows. They froze. Stared at him. Lucy gasped his name.

His mind was full of the ways he could take them out. Three seconds, and they could all be down and broken on the ground. As for the knife, it was big and scary to the average victim, but the leader kid had no idea how to use it. Not against someone trained to take it off him and drive it into his brainpan before he could even draw a breath.

They were dangerous kids. But still kids.

"Open the wallet," he said to the Asian one. The kid glanced down at it, then back at Ben. He blinked.

"Go on, open it," Ben said, keeping his eyes on the leader. His voice was steady and soft.

The knife kid was frowning, and Ben could see the confusion in his face. He knew what he was thinking. Three against one, but something was horribly wrong with the balance of power. His confidence was ebbing away fast, and the defiance in his eyes was fading into fear as he fought for words. The knife was wavering a little in his fist. He slackened his hold on Lucy, and she wriggled away from him.

The Asian kid did what he was told. The wallet was tan leather, well worn. He unsnapped the catch and opened it.

"How much cash is in there?" Ben asked.

The kid dipped his fingers inside the wallet and came out with a twenty.

"Not much of a haul, boys," Ben said. "Less than seven pounds each. Then you'd find that the debit card's no good because the account is already in the red. And the credit card is maxed out. Let's face it, she doesn't have the money. So you go home with seven pounds. Real hard guys. A great night's work, something you can go and boast about to your friends."

The kid with the knife finally found his voice again. "Fuck you," he said. But he couldn't hide the quaver in his throat.

Ben ignored him. "OK, let's make a deal here." He reached into the back pocket of his jeans. Took out his wallet and flipped it open. Inside it was a sheaf of fifties, crisp from the cash machine. He counted through them slowly, taking his time, feeling their eyes on him. He picked out six notes and tucked the wallet back in his jeans. "Three hundred. A hundred each. Better than seven. And much more than you're worth." He held it out to them. "It's yours."

The knife guy stepped forward to take it.

Ben pulled the money back. "This is a trade. That means I want something from you in return. Four things. One, let her go free. Two, give her back her bag. Three, put the knife on the ground. Then I'll give you the money. Nice and easy. Four, then you leave, and I don't ever want to see you again."

They hesitated.

"If you don't want to trade, that's OK too," Ben said. "The only thing is, you'll all be dead within the next half-minute because I can't think of any other options. It's up to you."

The Asian kid was beginning to tremble violently. The knife kid's eyes were bulging wide. Nervous glances passed among them all.

"I'm offering you a way out here," Ben said. "I'm buying your lives back from you, so that I don't have to kill you."

The leader stooped and laid down the knife. The blade clinked against the cobbles. The Asian kid handed the bag back to Lucy, and then they all moved quickly away from her. She was shaking, pale. She scurried over to Ben's side, and he laid a hand on her shoulder.

He kicked the knife away across the alley. "Good choice. A defining moment. You've no idea how lucky you were tonight." He held the money out. The leader kid's fingers were trembling as he went to take it. Then all three of them turned tail and ran like hell.

"Are you all right?" Ben asked Lucy.

She looked up at him. Her eyes were wet in the darkness. "I can't believe what you just did. How did you do that?"

"Let me walk you home," he said.

12.

SUMMERTOWN, OXFORD
THE SEVENTH DAY

The Bradburys lived in a large Victorian semidetached house on the edge of the leafy suburb of Summertown. Ben arrived at twelve-thirty with a bottle of wine and some flowers for Jane Bradbury. He hadn't seen her in a very long time. Physically, she'd changed little, other than some gray streaks in her dark hair—and he thought he could see a certain fragility in her thin frame that hadn't been there before. He remembered her as a quiet woman, slightly in the shadow of her ebullient husband. But today she was even quieter than he recalled.

Lunch was served on the patio at the rear of the house. The garden hadn't changed much in almost two decades. Tom Bradbury's rose bushes were even bigger and more colorful than Ben remembered, and the high stone walls around the edge of the garden were now covered in ivy.

After lunch they sat and sipped wine and made small talk for a while as the Bradburys' Westie, a sturdy little white terrier, all muscle and hair, ran to and fro across the lawn, sniffing through the grass on the trail of something. "That dog looks exactly like the one you had last time I was here," Ben said. "Surely it can't be the same one?"

"That was Sherry you remember," Jane Bradbury said. "This is Whisky. Sherry's son."

Hearing his name mentioned, the dog stopped what he was doing and came running. He trotted up to Ben, sat back on his haunches, and offered his paw.

"Our daughter, Zoë, taught him that," Bradbury said. "He's really more her dog. But we look after him most of the time, since she's not here very often."

"How is Zoë?" Ben asked.

It was just a casual question, but it seemed to have a strange effect. Bradbury shifted uncomfortably in his seat and looked down at his hands. His wife paled noticeably. Her face tightened and her movements stiffened. She caught her husband's eye, her look full of meaning, as if she was urging him to say something.

"Is anything wrong?" Ben asked.

Bradbury patted his wife's hand. She sat back in her chair. The professor turned to Ben. He seemed about to speak, then instead reached across the table for the bottle and topped up all three glasses. He set the bottle down, picked up his glass, and gulped half of it back.

"I'm getting the impression this isn't just a social occasion," Ben said. "You want to talk to me about something."

Bradbury dabbed the corners of his mouth with a napkin. His wife stood up nervously. "I'll fetch more wine."

Bradbury reached into the hip pocket of his tweed jacket, brought out the old briar pipe, and started packing the bowl with tobacco from a plastic pouch.

Ben waited patiently for him to speak.

Bradbury was frowning as he lit the pipe. "We're happy to see you again," he said through a cloud of aromatic smoke. "Jane and I would have invited you here to have lunch with us, even in normal circumstances."

"So you've asked me here for a particular reason," Ben said. "Something's wrong."

Jane Bradbury came back out of the house carrying another wine bottle, which she placed on the table. It looked from their faces as though they had a lot to tell Ben, and it was going to be a long afternoon.

The professor and his wife exchanged glances. "I know it's been a long time since we were in touch," Bradbury said. "But your father and I were good friends. Close friends. And we think of you as a friend too."

"I appreciate that," Ben said.

"So we feel we can trust you," Bradbury went on. "And confide in you."

"Of course." Ben leaned forward in his chair.

"We need your help." Bradbury hesitated, then continued. "It's like this. When you left Oxford, all those years ago, we heard rumors. That you had drifted for a while, and then joined the army. Apparently done very well there. Just rumors, nothing specific. Then, six weeks ago, when we interviewed you as a returning mature student, you told me and my colleagues a little about the career you had pursued in the meantime. I know you didn't want to go into too much detail. But you said enough to give me a clear impression. I understand you're a man with a very specific set of skills and a great deal of experience. You look for lost people."

"I was a crisis response consultant," Ben said. "I worked freelance to help locate kidnap victims. Especially children. But not anymore. As I told you at interview, I'm retired."

"Especially children," Bradbury echoed sadly.

"This has something to do with Zoë," Ben said.

Jane Bradbury got back up from her seat. She walked through the french windows into the house and came back a few moments later holding a framed photo. She set the silver frame down on the table and nudged it towards Ben. "Do you remember her? She was just a child, the last time we saw you."

Ben cast his mind back to those days. It all seemed so distant. So much had happened since. He remembered a sparkling little thing running across the lawn, with the dog trotting happily after her, sunlight in her hair and a world of joy in her gap-toothed little smile.

"She was about five, six years old then?"

"Almost seven," Bradbury said.

"So she's twenty-five, twenty-six now." Ben reached out for the photo. The silver frame was cool to the touch. He turned it towards him. The young woman in the picture was strikingly pretty, long blond hair and a full smile. It was an honest, happy picture of her hugging her little dog.

Bradbury nodded. "She turned twenty-six in March."

Ben put the picture down. "What's wrong? Zoë's in some kind of trouble? Where is she?"

"That's the problem. She was supposed to be here. And she's not."

"I've had too much wine already," Jane Bradbury said suddenly. "I'll go and make us some coffee."

Ben watched her go. There was a lot of stiffness in her movements, like someone under enormous pressure. He frowned. "What's the problem?"

Bradbury toyed uncomfortably with his pipe. He glanced over his shoulder. Whatever he was about to say, he obviously preferred to say it without his wife there. "We've always loved her deeply, you know."

"I'm sure you have," Ben said, not sure where this was going.

"This is a little hard for me to talk about. Personal things."

"We're friends," Ben said, meeting his eyes.

Bradbury smiled weakly. "When Jane and I got married, it took us a long time before we could have a child. It was nobody's fault." He made a face. "It was my fault. Embarrassing. The details are—"

"Never mind the details. Go on."

"After five years of trying, Jane became pregnant. It was a boy."

Ben frowned. The Bradburys had no son.

"You can guess what happened," Bradbury continued. "His name was Tristan. He didn't see his first birthday. Crib death. One of those things, we were told. It was devastating."

"I'm sorry," Ben said, and meant it. "That must have been tough."

"A long time ago now," Bradbury said. "But it's still very raw. So we tried to have another, but again it was hard for us. We were on the point of giving up, and talking about adoption, when Jane conceived. It seemed like a miracle to us. Nine months later we had the perfect little girl."

"I remember her well," Ben said. "She was lovely. And bright."

"She still is," Bradbury replied. "But for so many years we were terrified of losing her. Irrational, of course. Her health's always been excellent. But these things leave a mark on you. I admit we spoiled her. And I'm afraid we perhaps didn't bring her up quite the way we should have."

"What is she doing now?"

"She went on to become a brilliant academic. She's never really had to try. She sailed through her studies. Archaeology. First class from Magdalen. She was all set for a glittering career. Biblical archaeology is a major field of study. It's a relatively new science, and Zoë has been one of its pioneers. She was part of the team that found those ostraca in Tunisia last year."

Ben nodded. *Ostrakon*, from the Greek, meaning shell. In its plural form, it was the name archaeologists gave to fragments of earthenware that once served as cheap writing materials. Ostraca had been widely used in ancient times for recording contracts, accounts, and sales registers, as well as manuscripts and religious scripture.

"I read about that find," he said. "I had no idea I knew one of the people responsible for it."

"That was such a wonderful moment for her," Bradbury replied. "In fact, what her team discovered was the biggest haul of intact ostraca found since the 1910 excavation in Israel. They were buried deep under the ruins of an ancient temple. An amazing find."

"She's clever," Ben said.

"She's exceptional. But that's not all she's done. She's written papers and coauthored a book on the life of the Greek sage Papias. She's even been on television a few times, interviewed on an archaeology channel."

"You sound very proud of her."

The professor smiled. Then the shadow fell back over his face. His chin sank down to his chest. He fingered the pipe. It had gone out. "Professionally, academically, she's wonderful. But her private life, and our personal relationship with her, is a disaster." Bradbury raised his hands and let them flop down on his thighs. A gesture of helplessness. "What can I say? She's wild. Has been since the age of fifteen. We just couldn't control her. She was in trouble with the law a few times for petty crimes. Shoplifting, picking pockets. We used to find stolen items in her room. It was all a joke to her. We hoped she would grow out of her wildness in time, but she didn't. Drinking. Parties. All kinds of reckless behavior. It's been fighting and difficulty all the way. She's argumentative, aggressive, terribly headstrong, always has to have it her way. It takes very little to provoke her into a quarrel." He looked up at Ben with red-rimmed eyes. "And I know it's our fault. We spoiled her completely, because we felt so lucky to have been given a second chance at having a child."

Ben had been sipping his wine steadily as Bradbury talked. He filled his glass again. "Let's talk straight, Tom. You told me you were concerned that she wasn't here. Has she gone missing?"

Bradbury nodded. "Nearly a week now."

"And you think she's in some kind of trouble?"

"We don't know what to think."

"A week isn't a long time, under the circumstances. You said yourself, she's wild. She'll turn up."

"I wish I could believe that."

"You're telling me all this because of what I used to do."

"Yes."

"So you'll listen to my professional opinion."

Bradbury shrugged. "Yes."

"People do go AWOL from time to time," Ben said. "Now, if someone does go missing and there's clear evidence that something has happened to them, there are things we can do to get them back. But you need to distinguish between a legitimate missing persons case and someone who's just a little wayward, argues with her parents, likes to have fun, and has gone off the radar for a short while."

"She's done it before—gone off the radar, as you say," Bradbury said. "We're realistic. We can accept a lot of things. We accept that she's free and likes to enjoy herself. Sexually, I mean." He flushed with embarrassment. "But this time it's different. This time it's really strange, and we have the most terrible feeling about it."

"So what makes this time different?"

"The money. I mean, where did all that money come from?"

"What money?"

"I'm sorry. Let me backtrack. Zoë was working on an excavation project in Turkey. It was meant to last until the end of August. But then the next thing we knew, she left it early and was on Corfu. We have some friends there. She was staying with them for a while." Bradbury paused. "Then, suddenly, she seemed to have all this money. She's a doctoral student. She doesn't *have* money, at least no more than she needs. According to our friends she was suddenly loaded with it. Thousands. And the way she was spending it, it was as though it would never run out. Started partying all the time, coming home drunk with a different man every night."

"I know that shocks you, but—"

Bradbury shook his head. "That's not really the point. She had a row with our friends, and then she moved out. She booked into the most expensive hotel on the island. Until she was kicked out of there for causing disruption. Then she rented a villa on the coast. Big place, luxurious, expensive. Partying all day and all night, from what our friends heard."

"Go on."

"And then she just vanished. We had a drunken message on our phone late one night, a week ago. Saying she was flying back to Britain and would be here the next morning. That was it. We're still waiting. Nobody seems to know where she went. We've tried all the numbers we could think of. She's no longer at the villa. Nor in any hotel. The Corfu airport people said she didn't get on the plane. She just seemed to vanish." He looked earnestly at Ben. "So, what do you make of it?"

Ben thought for a moment. "Let's go through it. You say the money issue is perplexing you. Fine. But you also told me she has plenty of boyfriends. How do you know she hasn't hooked up with a rich one? The evidence is simply that she hasn't left Corfu. She's a fine-looking girl. There are lots of wealthy young guys out there enjoying the good life. She could be sitting on the deck of a yacht somewhere right now, as far away from harm as anyone could ever be."

"That's true," Bradbury agreed.

"Then there are credit cards. You spend a couple of hundred on your Barclaycard, the next thing you get a letter offering you a loan, and they up your credit limit another couple of grand to boot. That could easily explain where she got a pile of cash from."

"That makes sense too," Bradbury admitted.

"So what makes you think anything's wrong?"

"It's hard to explain," Bradbury said. "It's just a feeling. It's not just our protectiveness. This time is different." He leaned forwards in his chair and looked Ben in the eye. "We would be so grateful to you, Ben. All we ask is that you travel there and find her. Make sure she's all right. That she's not involved in drugs, or some awful thing like pornography . . ." There was a tortured edge in his voice.

"Come on," Ben said. "Why would she be?"

Bradbury stared at him. His hand was gripping the table edge. "Will you help us? We trust you."

Ben was silent.

"We're desperate, Ben. It's not that we want you to persuade her to come back here, or anything like that. Just find her, make sure she's safe and well. And ask her to please, please get in touch with us. Tell her we're sorry for all the quarrels and anything we might have said. And that we love her."

Ben didn't reply.

"We've thought of flying out there ourselves and looking for her," Bradbury said. "But even if we did find her, she'd never want to talk to us. She'd only go into one of her moods—start accusing us of parental interference or something, and run a mile. I know what she's like, and it would only make things worse." Bradbury grimaced. "We need an outsider, someone who's a friend of the family but more objective. Someone who can approach her, who would know how to handle this."

Ben drained his glass and put it down on the table. "I'm sorry for what's happened to your family, Tom. Truly, I am."

Bradbury bit his lip.

"But I can't help you," Ben said.

"Naturally, you'd be paid," Bradbury said, looking agitated. "I should have mentioned that. We have savings. I can pay ten thousand. That should cover all the expenses with plenty left over. I can do an Internet bank transfer. The funds would be in your account instantly. I'm just sorry I can't pay more."

Ben smiled. "It's not the money. I'd do it for nothing. But I'm retired. That's why I'm here. I'm finished with all that. Trying hard to put that life behind me."

"But this would be different," Bradbury said. "This is nothing compared to the things you've been involved in. Please. I'm begging you."

"I'm sorry, I can't." Ben paused. "But let me tell you what I *will* do. If you want someone you can trust to go out there and find Zoë, there is a guy I would recommend . . ."

When he left the Bradburys' place Ben walked straight back to his flat. He picked up the phone and punched a number into the keypad. Charlie answered.

"That thing you were asking me about," Ben said. "Would you still be interested, if I told you an opportunity had come up?"

Charlie didn't need time to decide. "I'd be interested."

"Good. Now listen." Ben told him in careful detail what Bradbury was offering.

"That would take care of the mortgage for a year," Charlie said. "But I already know what Rhonda will say."

"All you have to do is find Zoë. You don't have to try to bring her back. She shouldn't be too hard to track down, by the sound of it. Just follow the party music and the trail of empty bottles. All her parents want to know is that she's safe. The most you'd need to do is persuade her to make contact with them."

"It sounds easy."

"That's because it is easy," Ben said. "It's low season there at the moment, so you won't even make much of a hole in the ten grand. You can tell Rhonda that all you're doing is delivering a message—surely that won't be a problem for her? This is the Greek Islands, not Afghanistan. And you'll be there and back inside five days, maximum."

"I'm interested," Charlie said again.

"I need to call the Bradburys right now and tell them yes or no. It's your decision."

"Count me in," Charlie said.

13.

At that moment, one and a half thousand miles away on the tiny Greek island of Paxos, Zoë Bradbury was being roughly shoved and prodded down the beach, back towards the jetty where she'd tried to escape four days before.

It was the first daylight she'd seen since then. For four days she'd been tied down to the bed, only allowed free when she screamed to be allowed to use the toilet. For four days, they'd been questioning her around the clock.

The whole time, she was racking her brains to remember. *Who was she?* Sometimes there was just nothing there, nothing but a big empty blank. But then, every so often, it felt like something was stirring in her mind, as though the drifting fragments of memory wanted to gel together and fall into focus. Faces, voices, places. They hovered tantalizingly in her head. But just when they seemed so close and she tried to reach out to them, they would suddenly dissolve back into the mist.

She stared for hours at the tiny scar on her finger. A childhood injury, maybe. But how had she got it? She had no idea. A thousand other questions crowded and jostled in her mind. Where was she from? Who were her family and friends? What was her life like?

And then there was the most horrifying question of all. *What did these people want with her?*

As her initial acute terror faded into a new kind of steady, chilling horror, she watched and listened to her captors. Two of the men never spoke to her and she saw little of them. It was the woman and the fair-haired guy she had the most contact with. The woman had a hard look about her, but there were times when it seemed to melt a little, and she spoke more kindly.

The fair-haired guy was a psychopath. Zoë hated him profoundly, and the only thing that had kept her going throughout those endless hours had been her fantasy of somehow getting free, getting that gun or the knife from him, and using it on him.

But however they tried to get the information out of her, whether the threats were implicit or they were obscenely violent and screamed in her face, none of it was working. She could see they were getting increasingly desperate.

Then a new thought had come into her mind. What if her memory *did* come back to her? What would they do to her, once they had whatever it was they wanted?

She had a good idea what the fair-haired man wanted to do, if the woman let him. Maybe her amnesia was the only thing keeping her alive.

And now they were taking her somewhere. But where? Had they finally given up on her? Her heart raced at the thought. Maybe they were letting her go, taking her home.

Or maybe the time had come when they'd decided it was pointless, and they were going to finish it. End her life. Here, now, today. Her hands began to shake.

The fair-haired guy's pistol was pressing hard against her spine as he shoved her across the beach. "Move it," he muttered. She tried to walk faster, but the soft sand was heavy going in her bare feet, and her legs felt like jelly. She stumbled. A rough hand grabbed her arm and jerked her up to her feet. The gun stabbed painfully into her.

She risked a glance over her shoulder. The man was glowering at her. Behind him, the woman was following with a pensive look on her face, checking her watch and gazing up at the sky. The other two men tagged along quietly with blank expressions. One of them was holding a gun loosely against his side.

Zoë trembled violently. They were going to kill her. She knew it.

"I know what you're thinking," the low voice said behind her. "You want to run." He chuckled. "So run. I want you to run, so I can shoot you down."

"Keep your mouth shut," the woman snapped at him.

They reached the edge of the sand. Zoë was shoved towards the wooden jetty. She stepped up onto it, feeling the hard salt-encrusted planks against the bare soles of her feet. They followed. Were they going to drown her?

Then she heard it. The distant buzz of an aircraft approaching. She shielded her eyes and looked up to see a white dot against the sky. She kept watching it as she walked slowly along the jetty.

The white dot grew bigger until she could make out its shape. It was a small seaplane.

They reached the end of the jetty. The clattery rumble of the seaplane's twin engines filled her ears as it sank lower and lower in the air. Its underside skimmed the waves, bounced, and then touched down, sending up a fan of spray. It settled in the water and came round in a wide arc, leaving a churning white wake. It drew up level with the jetty and sat bobbing in the water. The spinning props settled down to an idle. The sound of the engines was deafening, and Zoë cupped her hands over her ears. The gun was still pressed hard to her back.

A hatch opened in the slim fuselage, and a man peered out. He stared coldly at her, then nodded to the others. He and another man moored the plane up to the jetty and slid out an extending gangway, like a narrow bridge over the water. Zoë felt herself being pushed towards it. She staggered across the wobbling gangway into the plane. It was hot and cramped inside. A strange man thrust her down into a seat.

"Where are you taking me?" she gasped in terror.

The fair-haired guy appeared in the hatch, and for a moment she froze at the thought that he was coming with her. Then the woman put a hand on his shoulder and shook her head at him. He seemed to protest, then relented. He stepped aside and it was the two other men, the quiet ones, who climbed into the plane and sat down beside Zoë. They ignored her completely. Then the hatch was shut, and she felt the vibrations mount as the twin aircraft engines revved up for takeoff.

Hudson and Kaplan stood and watched the plane skim across the waves. It climbed into the blue sky and became a fading white dot. Then it was gone.

"Out of our hands," Kaplan said.

Hudson cast a sullen look at her. He'd been counting on getting on the plane and being there when they went to work on the girl. After days and days on this rock, now he'd been cheated. "Then we can get out of here," he muttered.

"Not yet," she said. "We have other work to do."

14.

t had been a blur of time for Ben as he sat endlessly hunched over the desk in his flat, deep in study, completely immersed in textbooks and dictionaries and piles of notes, stopping only to eat and sleep. No phone calls, no visitors. It was a time of total focus, and his mind thrived on the concentration. It helped him forget.

By afternoon on the third day of it, his eyes were burning. The spread-out papers on his desk were turning into a mountain. The coffee at his elbow had gone cold hours ago, neglected while he'd been trying to decipher page after page of knotty Hebrew. It was driving him crazy, but as the lessons of twenty years ago slowly filtered back into his brain, things were coming into focus for him.

For the first time in days, his phone rang. He felt its pulsing buzz in his pocket, dug it out, and answered. It felt strange to hear his own voice again.

It was Charlie. He sounded far away, anxious and agitated.

"Ben, I need your help."

Ben leaned his weight back in the reclining swivel chair and rubbed his eyes, light-headed from concentration. He forced himself back into the present. "Where are you?"

"I'm still here on Corfu," Charlie said quickly. "Things are turning out more complicated than you said they would. I'm running into problems."

"What do you need from me?"

Charlie said something Ben didn't catch.

"You're breaking up."

"I said, I need you to come out here as soon as possible."

"I can't do that. Can't you just tell me what's going on?"

"I know it sounds odd, but I have to explain it to you face-to-face. I can't talk about this on the phone. There's a situation developing here."

"It's a simple job, Charlie."

"That's what you told me. But believe me, things didn't turn out that way."

Ben sighed and was quiet for a few seconds.

"Ben, please. This is serious."

"How serious?"

"Serious."

Ben closed his eyes. *Shit.* "And you're absolutely certain you can't handle this on your own?"

"I'm sorry. I need backup. You know this kind of stuff better than me."

Ben sighed again. Shook his head. Punched out his left fist and looked at his watch. He did a quick calculation. He could catch the Oxford Tube into London and be at Heathrow in a few hours. Catch a flight to Athens and from there to Corfu. "OK, copy that. Give me an RV point and I'll be with you by midday tomorrow."

He was there by breakfast.

It was an island Ben had never been to before. He'd expected an arid landscape, but from the air Corfu was strikingly green, a paradise of woods and wildflower meadows, mountains and blue ocean. In the distance he could make out rambling ruins and sleepy villages nestling in the pine forests as the plane circled and dropped down towards the airport at Kérkyra, Corfu Town.

But he didn't have much time for the beauty of the place. He was tired, and fighting to contain his annoyance. He couldn't understand why he had to be here, why Charlie couldn't deal with this on his own. Had he misjudged him? The man had been a good soldier. Tough, determined, resourceful. But maybe he'd lost his edge. Ben had seen that happen before.

He stepped off the plane into the warmth of the sun. In the small airport he rented a locker and stuffed into it his passport, his return tickets, and the thick hardcover philosophy book he'd brought to read on the plane. He wasn't planning on staying long, and he wanted to travel light. The only items he kept with him were his wallet, his phone, and his whisky flask.

He wondered about the Bible. He'd been carrying it around a lot lately, and had got used to having it on hand to dip into. It was compact and not too heavy. He decided to bring it along. He slung the lightweight duffel bag over his shoulder, secured the locker, and put the key and his wallet into his jeans pocket.

Outside the airport, he hailed a taxi. He leaned back in the noisy Fiat and took in the scenery. The driver talked incessantly in such rapid broken English that Ben couldn't understand a word. He ignored him, and pretty soon the guy shut up. It was only two miles into Kérkyra, but traffic was already building, and by the time they entered the city the roads were badly snarled up. Ben paid the driver in crisp euros, hauled his duffel bag out of the back, and decided to walk it.

He walked fast, impatient to hear what Charlie was going to tell him. The rendezvous was at the guesthouse where Charlie was staying. Ben had the address and used a cheap map he'd bought at the airport to find his way through the old town.

He walked up narrow streets where washing hung like banners on lines strung between the houses. The place was crammed with life and bustle—shopping arcades, tavernas, hot food bars, and cafés. He walked through a thronging marketplace, rich with the salty tang of lobster and squid. Stand after stand of fresh olives glistened in the sunshine. In the hectic buzz of San Rocco Square people were sitting outside cafés, taking their morning coffee. Traffic rumbled through the old, twisty streets.

Just before nine he reached Charlie's guesthouse, a faded stone building on the edge of a busy road right in the heart of the old town. It had a café terrace outside, tables lining the pavement and shaded by wide parasols and dozens of trees planted in big stone urns.

Charlie was sitting at one of the tables, a newspaper and a pot of coffee in front of him. He saw Ben across the street and waved. He looked relieved more than happy, and he wasn't smiling.

Ben threaded his way across the brisk traffic and between the tables to where Charlie was sitting. The place was already busy with families eating breakfast, the season's first tourists with their cameras and guidebooks, people grabbing a bite on their way to work. A small man in a light cotton jacket was sitting alone near the edge of the terrace, working on a notebook computer.

Ben hung his jacket over the back of the empty wicker chair at Charlie's table, dumped the duffel bag on the ground, and sat down. He leaned back in the chair, kicked his legs out in front of him, and crossed his arms.

"Thanks for coming," Charlie said.

"This had better be good. I'm tired and I shouldn't have to be here."

"You want coffee?"

"Just talk," Ben said.

Charlie was frowning. He looked even more agitated than he'd sounded on the phone. He folded up his paper and laid it on the table beside him, took a sip of coffee, and looked hard at Ben.

"I have a bad feeling," he said. "About Zoë Bradbury."

15.

came here as a messenger and ended up like a detective," Charlie said. "You told me she wouldn't be at the villa, but I checked anyway. No trace. The owners didn't know anything about where she'd gone afterwards. She didn't make her flight either. Then I went to see the friends of the family that she'd been staying with initially. Couple of expats. A bit stuffy, middle-class prigs. I could see why she didn't get on with them. They told me the same story they'd told her parents—that she'd argued with them, left, got booted out of the hotel, rented the villa. Nothing new. So I started scouring the island. I've been to every bar and café, showing her picture and asking if anyone has seen her, saying I was a friend of the family trying to get in touch about a pressing legal matter at home. I've spoken to everyone. Police, the ferries, the airport, taxi drivers, hotels, hospital. You name it. I gave out cards with my number on, in case anyone knew anything. Must have given out fifty or sixty of them. And nothing. She just isn't here."

"So what makes you think something happened to her?" Ben said. "Plenty of ways off an island without leaving a paper trail. She could have caught a ride on someone's yacht. She could be sitting a mile offshore as we speak, lounging on deck sipping on a cool drink."

Charlie listened. He shook his head.

"There's always a trace you can follow," Ben said. He let the irritation show in his voice. "You didn't have to press the panic button so soon."

"There's a lot more. When you hear it, you'll understand why I called you." Charlie was talking fast, looking jumpy.

"I'm listening."

"Then I got a call from this guy. Said his name was Nikos Kara-piperis and that someone had told him I was looking for Zoë. He sounded concerned. Said he knew her and had something to tell me. But he didn't want to say much on the phone. Preferred to meet up somewhere."

"So he's married," Ben said. "Respectable local guy. His wife is away and he's been dallying with our girl."

"You got it. About forty-five years old, businessman. Something big at the golf club. Pillar of the community. Posh house here in Corfu Town, and also this little hilltop hideaway out in the country-side, a good place to chill out and bring girls. He didn't want to talk to me at his main residence, because his wife and kids had just got back from holiday. He invited me up to his hideaway. I went there to meet him. He seemed really nervous. Told me a lot of things."

They were distracted by a child running by the terrace tables. He was seven or eight, a typical little Greek boy, black hair, dark eyes, deeply tanned. He wore a striped T-shirt and red shorts. He was playing with a soccer ball, bouncing it skillfully like a basketball player, with a rhythmic slap of rubber against pavement. He ran round the edge of the tables, chortling to himself, bouncing the ball as he went. A couple of women at a nearby table smiled as he ran by them.

As Charlie reached for the coffeepot to top himself up, Ben twisted in his seat, admiring the kid's skill with the ball. The kid was too in-tent on keeping the rhythm going to notice anyone watching him. But then he missed a bounce and the ball went sideways and hit the leg of the table where the small man with the computer was sitting. The man swore at the boy in some language that Ben didn't recognize over the traffic noise. His face was lean and angular, and his eyes blazed for a second. The kid picked up his ball and backed off.

"I wish that damn brat would go and play somewhere else," Charlie said.

Ben turned back to face him. "Just tell me what Nikos Karapiperis told you."

Charlie continued. "They'd been seeing each other, discreetly, for a while. It started as a one-night stand. Apparently she had quite a few of those. Then it got more serious, and they saw each other again and again. He was pretty frank with me. He'd had flings with girls before, but this was different. He was beginning to really care for her. Liked buying her things, he said. But then, suddenly, she didn't need his money anymore. She had plenty of her own."

"Did you find out where she was getting it?"

Charlie nodded. "It came from the States. Someone sent her an international money order for twenty thousand dollars. She wouldn't tell Nikos who sent it, but she did tell him that there'd be more of it coming her way very soon."

"More?"

"A lot more. The kind of money that would free her up for the rest of her life, she said. Apparently she was talking about coming back and buying a big house here, settling. She said she'd never have to work again. So if it's true, we must be talking millions." Charlie paused. "But here's the really strange bit."

Ben blinked. "What?"

"She never told him who sent the money, but she said it was all because of some prophecy."

"What prophecy?"

"That was all Nikos knew. She was vague about it. The prophecy had something to do with the money. I have no idea what that means. Someone predicted that she'd win the lottery?"

"When was the last time he saw her?" Ben asked.

"At the party she threw on her last night here, the night before she was due to catch the flight back to England. He didn't really want to be seen at her parties, but he drove down there and hung around for a while, trying to keep a low profile as best he could. He was there until around eleven-thirty. They had an arrangement that afterwards, she'd ride her scooter up to his hideaway. They were going to spend a last night there. He was supposed to wait for her at his place." Charlie reached back across for the coffeepot and refilled his cup.

"But she never got there," Ben said.

Charlie shook his head. "That's the moment where we lose track of her. Sometime between Nikos leaving the party, around eleven-thirty, and the time she should have turned up at his place, she disappeared."

"Did you say she was using a scooter?"

"One of those big fancy super-scoots. It was a rental. She never returned it. It's disappeared too."

"So maybe we're looking at a road accident. A little drunk, after the party. She could be lying in a ditch somewhere."

"Maybe," Charlie said. "But there's more to it. Nikos said he thought something weird happened at the party. He knew she liked men, and there were a lot of much younger and fitter guys than him there. So he was keeping an eye on her. Jealous type."

"Go on," Ben said.

"Apparently there was this guy hanging around her. Nikos described him as young, early thirties or thereabouts, good-looking, fair hair. He came in with a woman, but soon afterwards he started flirting a lot with Zoë. Said his name was Rick. Nikos thought he sounded American."

"What about the woman?"

"Could have been Greek, according to Nikos. But he didn't hear her talk at all, and he didn't take a lot of notice of her. He was more worried about this Rick character, because it looked like Zoë was responding to him. Then Nikos said Rick went to the bar and fixed her a drink. He couldn't be sure, but he said there was something furtive about the way he did it. He was standing with his back to the room. Nikos thought maybe he was slipping something into the glass."

Shit, Ben thought. He'd been here before. At best it was a guy loading the dice by slipping a woman an aphrodisiac. A little worse than that, it could be a date-rape setup. The worst possibility was abduction. And that was the option that seemed to fit the picture. "This isn't good," he said.

"Nikos wasn't totally sure of what he saw," Charlie said. "But he went over and butted in right away. Asked her for a dance. While he was at it, he spilled the drink, kind of accidentally-on-purpose, just in case there was something in it. They danced, and he warned her about Rick. Told her to stop the party and come away as soon as she could. She argued with him, and he was scared she was going to cause a scene and draw attention to him. He warned her again to stay away from this Rick guy and not to touch any drinks anyone gave her. Then he left, went back up to his hideaway, and waited for her."

"How do we know she even intended to go to his place? She could have been stringing him along."

"I don't think so," Charlie said. "Because then she wouldn't have let him put her baggage in his Mercedes earlier that day, and drive it up to the hideaway. A rucksack with all her clothes and things. And a travel pouch with her passport, money, plane tickets, the works. She was serious about going up there to meet him."

"So it looks as though perhaps this Rick person didn't give up so easily," Ben said. "What happened next?"

"When Zoë didn't turn up that night, Nikos tried to call the landline at the villa. No reply. Then he went down there. It was all closed up, empty. The scooter was gone. She'd vanished. That's when he began to worry."

"And he couldn't call the police about the disappearance," Ben said. "He'd have to let out about their relationship, and he'd have been scared that if she just turned up after a couple of days, he would have compromised himself for nothing."

Charlie nodded. "He was in a fix. When he heard that I was asking questions and I told him I was employed by her family, he was very happy to give me her stuff."

"Where is it now?"

Charlie pointed upwards to a window. "The rucksack is in my room upstairs. The pouch is right here." He reached over and grabbed a plastic shopping bag off the seat next to him.

Ben took out the travel pouch and sifted through it. The contents were all the usual items a traveler would carry. Passport. Cell phone. A fabric wallet, stuffed with euro banknotes, all five hundreds. He counted quickly through the cash and stopped at six thousand.

"There's more cash in the rucksack, under her clothes," Charlie said. "She made a good dent in the twenty grand, but she still had quite a bit left."

"I think you're right," Ben said. "She must have been serious about joining Nikos. Nobody walks away from that much money."

He rummaged deeper in the bag. Her air tickets were folded in a glossy travel agent's paper wallet. He opened it. The destination was Heathrow via Athens, dated the day she'd disappeared. Under the tickets was a little book, good quality leather jacket. An address book. From its crisp edges he could see it had been bought recently. He picked it up and flipped through it, looking for a Rick. Rick was what worried him the most.

But it was a long shot. As he'd expected, there was nothing. He flipped through the pages and took note of the names she'd written in it. There were few entries. A handful of numbers with the 01865 Oxford code. One of those numbers was her parents'. Then there were some overseas numbers. Someone called Augusta Vale. Someone else called Cleaver. That seemed to be either a nickname or a surname. Or else maybe a company name. There were no addresses, just phone numbers. The Vale and Cleaver numbers had the international prefix for the U.S.A.

"Who or what is Cleaver?" Ben asked. Charlie just shook his head. Ben flipped a few more pages, and a business card dropped out onto the table. He picked it up. The card read: *Steve McClusky, Attorney.* The address printed under the name was in Savannah, Georgia, U.S.A. He slipped it into his pocket. "Apart from the money and the clothes, is there anything else in her rucksack?"

"Nothing else," Charlie said. "I went through it all."

"Then this is all we have to go on." Ben thought about the money from America. And Rick, the American at the party. "A lot of U.S. connections. Did Nikos mention anything about that?"

"Apart from the fact the money came from there, no."

"Then I think I'd like to meet him and talk about this, in case he knows something. Can you arrange it?"

"It's not going to be possible, Ben."

"I understand it's delicate for him. Tell him it'll be very discreet. All we want is to ask him a few more questions."

"That's not what I meant," Charlie said. "You can't talk to him."

"Why not?"

"You think I'd have called you all the way here for nothing?" Charlie picked up the folded newspaper, opened it out, and handed it to Ben. "Front-page news, yesterday. You don't have to read Greek to get the idea."

Ben ran his eye down the page and it settled on a grainy black-and-white photo. The picture showed a couple of police cars and a bunch of uniformed officers standing outside what looked like a small villa surrounded by trees. Next to that picture was another, of a man's face. The man looked to be in his mid-forties. Olive skin, strong features, mustache, graying at the temples. There was a little caption under the picture.

"Don't tell me," Ben said.

Charlie nodded. "I said this was serious, didn't I? As soon as I heard he was dead, that's when I called you. The house in the picture is the hilltop place. That's where they found him. It's the talk of the island."

"Who found him?"

"Somebody tipped off the cops. He was dead long before they got there. Massive heroin OD, and they found drugs all over the house. It looks like he was involved in it big-time. Either OD'ed by accident, or it was suicide or murder. Nobody knows. The police are all over the place. It's already turning into the biggest scandal they've seen here for years. Nothing like this ever happens on Corfu."

Ben was thinking hard. None of this was making sense. The drugs and the sudden appearance of the money went well together. Heroin, cash, and death. A classic combination. But if Nikos and Zoë were mixed up in some kind of drugs business, the story he'd told Charlie was bizarre. He wouldn't even have approached Charlie. Wouldn't have drawn attention to himself like that. Unless there was something else they were missing.

And what about the prophecy? He couldn't even begin to understand what that could be about.

"And there's another thing," Charlie said. "Someone's been tailing me."

"Since when?"

"Since pretty soon after I got here. After I started asking questions about Zoë Bradbury."

"You're sure about that?"

Charlie nodded. "I'm certain. They're good, but not so good that I didn't spot them. They're working as a team."

"How many?"

"Three for sure, maybe a fourth. A woman."

Ben frowned. If a former SAS soldier said he was being followed, that was how it was. "What about now?"

Charlie shook his head. "Pretty sure I lost them. So what do we do? Do we tell the cops what we know? Just hand it over to them?"

"I don't like dealing with the police," Ben said, "unless I absolutely have to."

"Then I don't see any way ahead," Charlie said. "At least, not for me. This was meant to be a straightforward job. That's what I told Rhonda."

The kid with the ball was making another pass through the tables, bouncing it as he went. He ran past the table where the man with the laptop had been. It was empty. The guy had left. The boy suddenly stumbled, and the ball bounced away from him. He ran after it, towards the edge of the pavement. The ball rolled into the road.

Out of the corner of his eye, Ben was suddenly aware of what was happening. There was a van coming down the street. It was green, battered, some kind of delivery vehicle, moving fast, in a hurry to get somewhere. And the boy was chasing his ball right out into its path.

Charlie was talking, but Ben didn't hear. He turned and looked at the oncoming van. The driver was talking to his passenger, eyes off the road. He hadn't seen the child.

The ball stopped rolling. The kid crouched to pick it up. Saw the van and froze, wide-eyed. It wasn't slowing down, and Ben realized with a chill of fear that it couldn't stop in time to avoid him.

When the mind is working at extreme speed, things seem to happen in ultra–slow motion. Ben burst out of his chair and launched himself into the road. Cleared the six yards between him and the kid.

He bent low as he sprinted, wrapped an arm around the boy's waist and scooped him off the ground. He heard a grunt of air escape from the kid's lungs with the impact.

The van was almost on them. Ben dived across its path and hit the ground sliding, using his body as a shield to protect the child from the road surface. The kid was screaming.

The van brakes screeched and the wheels locked up, leaving snakes of rubber on the road. It slewed around and came to a halt at a crazy angle between Ben and the café terrace, rocking on its suspension.

Time restarted. Ben could hear cries and shouts from the tables as people realized what had happened. He could feel where his shoulder had scraped the tarmac, pain beginning to register. Over the hood of the van he could see Charlie up on his feet on the café terrace, staring wildly, one hand gripping the back of his chair.

Then the world exploded.

16.

One instant, a café terrace, families and friends sitting having breakfast. The next, a blast of fire engulfed everything, blew everything apart. The shock wave rolled across the pavement and out into the road, tearing down everything in its path. Pieces of tables and chairs and parasols were hurled into the air, tumbled and spun, burning, in all directions. Flying glass exploded across the street like a giant shotgun blast. The shock lifted the van off its wheels and threw it sideways, its windows bursting outwards.

Ben had been clambering to his feet, still holding on to the child, when the stunning force of the explosion blew him down. He instinctively rolled his body across the boy's to protect him. Wreckage rained down.

Just as suddenly, and for one eerie moment, everything was completely still. Then the screams began.

Ben's ears were ringing badly and his head was swimming. His first thought was for the boy. He slowly raised himself up, kneeling in the broken glass. The boy's eyes met his, wide and terrified. Ben checked for injury. There was no blood. The kid hadn't been touched. He was just rigid with shock.

Then Ben thought of Charlie. He staggered to his feet, suddenly aware of terrible pain in his neck and shoulder. His shirt was ripped and wet with blood. He raised his hand up to his neck and his fingers felt something there that they shouldn't. But he ignored it. He stepped out from behind the burning van and saw the full devastation of the explosion.

It was carnage. Blood-spattered corpses and smoldering body parts were strewn across what used to be the café terrace. People were screaming in horror, others moaning, calling for help, others dying. Some of the wounded were already up on their feet, staggering dazed through the wreckage. Black smoke and the acrid smell of burning filled the air. The street was littered with little fires.

Ben shouted for Charlie. Then he saw him.

Charlie's hand was still gripping the back of his chair. The hand ended at the wrist. The rest of him was spread across the pavement. Ben looked away and closed his eyes.

It wasn't long before the screech of sirens drowned out the screams of the survivors and the urgent shouts and chatter of the people flocking to help them. Then all was frantic activity. Paramedics waded in, hard and fast like soldiers through the wreckage. In minutes the street was flooded with emergency vehicles and equipment. Police streamed everywhere, yelling into radios, working fast to cordon off the scene, holding off the hundreds of onlookers crowding in from neighboring streets. People were crying and hugging one another, faces contorted in anguish.

Meanwhile the ambulances and coroner's teams carried out their grim work. The dead were covered with sheets where they lay, waiting to be bagged and loaded. The medics did what they could to patch up the wounded before the ambulances took them away. One by one, vehicles screeched away up the street, fresh ones arriving in a steady flow.

Ben watched the whole thing from across the road. Beside him on the edge of the pavement, the boy sat quietly with his ball between his feet, staring at the scene in front of them. He looked up at Ben with questioning eyes. There was a cut oozing blood above his left eyebrow. Ben patted his shoulder.

Then the boy seemed to see something. He straightened up and then jumped to his feet and ran off before Ben could stop him. He disappeared into the crowd and then was lost in the milling chaos.

After another minute, a paramedic pointed Ben out to his team-mate. They jogged over to him, and he remembered that his shirt was soaked in blood down one side. He hardly felt the pain anymore. He was numb all over, and he couldn't hear properly. He tried to protest as they wrapped a blanket over his shoulders and attended to his wound. He didn't understand what they were telling him, but they seemed to think the injury was serious. He didn't have the strength to resist them as they walked him to an ambulance.

He looked over to the terrace. What was left of Charlie was lying under a bloody sheet. The hand had been removed from the back of the chair. In his daze, Ben wondered where they'd put the hand, and whether they'd found all of him. Then the paramedics got Ben inside the ambulance and made him lie on a bunk. Doors slammed, an engine revved, and the siren started up.

He felt the ambulance accelerate hard up the street. He looked around him. Saw medical equipment, tubes dangling and rattling with the motion of the vehicle. A drip swinging on a stand above him.

He wasn't alone. Hands were moving over his body, faces peering down at him, the sound of voices somewhere behind the constant ringing in his ears. The distant impressions began to blur. After that, he was drifting, spinning weightlessly into a black space. He dreamed of fire and explosions, saw Charlie's face smiling at him. Then Charlie's face was the child's face, giving him a last look before he ran away into the crowd. Then it became nothing at all.

17.

Ben woke with a start and sat bolt upright. He blinked and looked around him, disorientated for a second. He was alone in a room. Everything white and clinical. The smell hit him—a sickly combination of disinfectant and hospital food. A trolley clattered past the open door, pushed by an orderly in a blue smock.

As he shifted on the hard bed, Ben winced at the tearing pain in his neck and shoulder. He reached his hand up and felt the big dressing. He remembered now. The moment of the blast. The shards of glass sticking in his neck. The paramedics taking him away.

Then he remembered something else.

Charlie was dead.

His diver's watch and the wedding ring on its leather thong were on the bedside table. He reached for them gingerly, feeling the pull of the stitches. He stared at the date and time. Nearly twenty-two hours since the explosion. He'd been asleep all day and all night.

He climbed slowly out of bed and walked around his hospital room, slipping on the watch and hanging the ring around his neck. He found a small private bathroom and wandered in to inspect his dressing in the mirror. He peeled back the edge of it and looked at the wound.

He'd had worse. He couldn't afford to let a couple of slivers of glass stop him. He pulled the hospital gown off over his head, washed quickly in the sink, and then walked back into the room to dress. What was left of his clothes had been folded and left on a chair near the bedside. The ripped, bloody shirt was gone. He stepped into his jeans and shoes.

A nurse came into the room, stared at him, and started talking in rapid Greek.

"I'm sorry," he said. "I don't understand."

She gestured towards the bed, trying to shoo him back into it.

He shook his head. "I'm getting out of here. But I need a shirt."

"You no leave," she said, and pointed to his neck. "You hurt."

"I'm OK," he said. "I want to leave now."

"I call the doctor." She turned and went off, shaking her head and muttering to herself. She slammed the door behind her.

He sat down heavily on the edge of the bed, ruffled his hair, and waited. After a couple of minutes there was a loud knock at the door. For a second Ben thought it was the doctor come to scold him for wanting to check out too early and to give him the whole bit about complications and infections.

But it wasn't the doctor. The door swung open and a huge bear of a man walked in. He was several inches taller than Ben, and he had to stoop as he came through the doorway. He stared at Ben with glittering eyes and a wide grin as he strode across the room and grasped his hand in a strong fist. A small dark-skinned woman followed in his wake, beaming at Ben.

The big man shook Ben's hand vigorously, clinging on as if he never wanted to let go. Tears welled in his eyes. "You are a hero," he rumbled in heavily accented English.

For a second Ben was bemused. But then he saw the child appear in the doorway. He had a plaster over his left eyebrow and a couple of scratches on his cheek. Ben knew him immediately. The boy with the ball.

"You are a hero," the big man said again, still clutching Ben's hand. "You saved our son."

"I didn't do much," Ben replied. "He saved me as much as I saved him. If he hadn't run out into the road, I'd have been blown to pieces."

"But if you had not acted, Aris would have been killed." A tear ran down the man's cheek and he sniffed and wiped it away. "I am Spiro

Thanatos. This is my wife, Christina. We own the guesthouse where the bomb exploded." His gaze landed on Ben's neck and bare shoulder. "You are hurt."

"It's nothing," Ben said. "Just a few bits of glass. I'm leaving soon. Just need something to wear."

Spiro smiled. He immediately started unbuttoning his shirt, revealing a Hotel Thanatos T-shirt underneath. "Take mine. No, please. I insist."

Ben thanked him and slipped it on, wincing a little at the pull on his stitches. The shirt was light-blue cotton, a little baggy on him, but it felt cool and crisp.

Spiro talked and talked. He and Christina had been in the kitchen when they'd heard the explosion. They'd thought their boy was surely lost. It was terrible. People dead, maimed, buildings ruined. Drug-dealing murderers on their peaceful island. The world was going to shit. Their business was devastated, but they didn't care as long as Aris was unharmed. They would do anything, anything to repay their debt to him. Anything he wanted, anything they could do. They'd never forget . . .

Ben listened and protested, "Anyone would have done the same."

"What hotel are you in?" Spiro wanted to know.

"None," Ben said. "I only just arrived. I wasn't planning on staying."

"But you must stay for a while, and you must be our guest."

"I haven't made my plans yet."

"Please," Spiro went on. "If you stay, you must not book into a hotel." He dug in his pocket and dangled a key from his fingers. "We have a place on the beach, just outside the town. It is simple, but it is yours until you leave Corfu."

"I wouldn't dream of it," Ben said.

Spiro grasped his wrist in a strong, dry hand and dropped the key in his palm. Attached to it was a small plastic tag with an address. "I insist. It is the least we can do for you."

Spiro and Christina left reluctantly, with more smiles and gratitude. Ben was tucking the borrowed shirt into his jeans when the door swung open again.

He turned, expecting the angry doctor this time. But it was another visitor.

Rhonda Palmer's face was pale, puffy, and streaked with tears as she walked into the room. An older man and a woman came in behind her, watching him grimly. He knew them from the wedding. Her parents.

"I wanted to see you," Rhonda said.

Ben didn't reply. Didn't know what to say to her.

"I wanted to see the man who killed my husband, and tell him how I feel about that." There was a quaver in her voice. She reached up and wiped a tear away.

Ben felt suddenly weak at the knees. He wanted to tell her he hadn't killed Charlie. That he would never have involved him in anything like this if he'd known.

But it seemed so lame, so pointless, to tell her those things. He stayed silent.

Rhonda's face was twisted in fury and pain. "I knew, when you turned up at my wedding, that you would bring trouble into our lives somehow. Major Hope, luring my husband to his death."

"I'm not Major Hope anymore," Ben said quietly.

"I don't care what you call yourself," she fired back at him. "You've ruined my life and my family. You took my child's father away."

Ben stared at her.

"I only found out two days ago," she sobbed. "I was going to tell Charlie when he came back. But now he's dead. My child will never know its father. Thanks to you."

Then she broke down, weeping loudly, swaying on her feet. Her father held her, supporting her. She broke free of him. She looked at Ben with hate and disgust in her eyes. *"You're a fucking murderer!"* she screamed at him. She spat in his face. Slapped him hard across the cheek.

He turned away from her. His cheek was stinging. He looked down at his feet. He could feel all their eyes on him. Two nurses had come running when they heard the raised voices. They stood staring, frozen in alarm.

Rhonda was bent double, racked with sobbing, shoulders heaving. Her mother put her arms around her. "Come on, darling. Let's go." They turned to leave. Rhonda's father shot Ben a last look of venom as he pushed past the nurses.

Her mother hovered in the doorway, clutching her daughter tight in her arms. She turned and looked Ben in the eye. "God damn you," she said, "if you can live with this on your conscience."

18.

Just over thirty miles away, on the island of Paxos, the fair-haired man called Hudson was sitting at a table in the empty house by the beach. The woman, Kaplan, was standing behind him, looking over his shoulder as they both stared intently at the laptop screen in front of them.

The digital video image was as crisp as it had looked through the lens when they'd filmed the scene from the apartment window the previous day. The camera was zoomed in on the two men sitting at the table near the edge of the terrace. For now, they were calling them Number One and Number Two. Number One was the man they'd been monitoring after he'd started asking questions about Zoë Bradbury. Number Two was the man who'd unexpectedly come to join him. They knew less about him, and that bothered them.

What bothered them more, in the aftermath of the bombing, was that he was still alive. It was what was keeping them here, when they should be packing up this job and heading for home.

On-screen, the conversation was intense. Then the child with the ball appeared. After a moment one of the two men jumped up from his chair and ran out into the road. Seconds later, the café terrace was engulfed with flames.

"Pause it," Kaplan said.

Hudson tapped a key. On-screen, the unfolding fireball and flying debris stood still, sudden terror frozen on the faces of the victims caught in the blast.

"Scroll it to the left," she said.

He held down another key and the image panned across. The green delivery van was slewed at an angle in the road. On the other side of it, the man who had leaped from the café terrace was sprawled on the ground, shielding the child.

She watched him thoughtfully, pressing a finger to her lips in concentration. "Did he know something?" she said. "Did he see it coming?"

"Doesn't look like it to me," Hudson said. "He ran out to save the kid. A second later, he'd have been caught up in it too."

"What if he saw Herzog? What if he remembers him? He's a witness."

"No way. It was just chance. He had no idea what was coming."

She frowned. "Maybe. Go back. OK, stop. Replay."

"We've been through this a hundred times," Hudson said.

"I want to know who this guy is. I get a bad feeling about him."

They watched and listened again. The audio was scratchy and filled with background sound—jumbled conversation from other tables and passersby, traffic, general white noise.

"The sound is shit," Kaplan muttered.

"Yeah, well, we didn't exactly get much time to prepare," Hudson said. "If I hadn't thought to bring the stuff just in case, we wouldn't even be listening to this conversation at all."

"Just shut up and let the damn thing play."

He went quiet. Kaplan was in charge, and he already knew she could be pretty mean if he pushed it too far.

"Pause," she said. "Did you hear that? He mentioned her name again. Go back."

He rewound the image a few frames. "It's hard to be sure."

"I'm sure. Turn up the volume," she said. "Can you clean it up any more?"

"I've cleaned it up all I can," Hudson replied irritably. He'd been up most of the night working on it, painstakingly whittling away as many unwanted frequencies as he could isolate. "I'll need a few more hours to get the best out of it."

"If you could get that fucking kid out of it," she said, "I'll be happy." The percussive *tap—tap—tap* of the child's bouncing ball each time he came into the range of the mike was cutting out a lot of the precious conversation and driving her crazy.

Hudson restarted the playback and they listened carefully.

"There it is," she said. "Bradbury. Comes out clearly now."

"Yup. Definitely Bradbury."

"Shit. OK, let it play on." The video played on a few more seconds. She focused hard on the sound, closing her eyes. Then she opened them, and her jaw tightened. "Stop. Cleaver. He said '*Cleaver.*'"

Hudson was annoyed he hadn't picked up on it before. "Copy. What did he say about him?"

"Run it back. Slow it down."

They listened to the hissy, muffled recording again. "I think he's saying '*Where is Cleaver?*'" she said. "That's what it sounds like to me."

"But how could he know about Cleaver?"

"Means he's been talking to Bradbury. Means he's in on it."

"Or he just saw it in the address book."

"Either way," she said. "That isn't something we want him to know."

They watched more. On-screen, Number One unfolded the newspaper and leaned across the café table to show it to Number Two.

Kaplan reached for the copy of the same paper on the desk. Followed Number Two's gaze down the front page. She nodded. He was definitely looking at the report on Nikos Karapiperis's death.

Then the child came into the frame, his ball went out into the road, and they watched again as Number Two leaped out to save him. Then the explosion burst across the terrace all over again.

"You can shut it down now. I've seen enough," Kaplan said.

"Fucking baby-saving hero," Hudson muttered.

Kaplan started pacing up and down. "Put it all together. They knew everything. Bradbury, the money, Cleaver, Nikos Karapiperis. And Number One knew we were tailing him."

Hudson swiveled round in his chair to face her. "How did he know that?" The screen went black as the laptop shut down.

Kaplan shook her head. "He wasn't just some friend of the family. This is a professional at work. No way anyone could have spotted us otherwise."

"So who are these people? Who are they working for?"

"I don't know."

"You think they know where Bradbury put it?"

"I'm going to have to call this in," she said. "I don't like either of them. And I don't like that Number Two is still around."

She walked to another room, where she could speak in private, and dialed the number. It was a long-distance call. The same man's voice answered.

"We might have another problem," she told him. She explained the situation quickly.

"How much does he know?" the man asked.

"Enough. About the money, and about Cleaver. And about us. And maybe more."

There was a long silence. "This is already getting messy."

"We'll deal with it."

"You'd better. Get me names. Find out everything he knows. Then take care of him. Do it properly and quietly. Don't make me have to call Herzog in on this again. He's too damn expensive."

When the call was over, Kaplan went back to the other room. "Let's go," she said.

19.

Ben checked out of the hospital still feeling drained and numb. He shambled out of the glass doors and into the hot morning sun, hardly feeling the warmth on his face. His mind was blank as he stood there on the pavement, not knowing what to do next.

Approaching footsteps made him turn: two men. One had a camera, the other a notebook. Reporters. They were looking right at him.

"You are the man who saved the little boy," the one with the notebook said. "Can we ask you some questions?"

"Not now," Ben replied quietly.

"Later? Here is my card." The reporter pressed it into Ben's hand. Ben just nodded. He felt too weary to say more. The photographer raised his camera and fired off a few snaps. Ben didn't try to stop him.

As the reporters were turning to go, a Corfu police four-wheel drive pulled up with a screech of tires at the edge of the pavement. The doors opened and two men climbed out, one in uniform and one in plain clothes. The plainclothes officer was short and dumpy, bald-headed with a trim beard.

They walked up to him. "Mr. Hope?" the plainclothes officer said in English. He reached into his jacket and took out an ID card. "I am Captain Stephanides, Corfu police. I would like you to come with me, please."

Ben said nothing. He let them usher him into the back of the four-wheel drive. Stephanides climbed in after him and said something in Greek to the driver, and the car sped off. Then he turned to Ben.

"You are leaving hospital early? I was expecting to find you still in bed."

"I'm fine," Ben said.

"Last time I saw you, you were lying on a stretcher, covered in blood."

"Just a couple of cuts. Others got it a lot worse."

Stephanides nodded gravely.

In less than ten minutes they had passed through a police security point and were pulling up at the back of a large headquarters building. Stephanides bundled out of the car and asked Ben to follow him. They walked inside the air-conditioned building, into a comfortable office.

"Please take a seat," Stephanides said.

"What is it I can help you with, Captain?"

"Just a few questions." Stephanides rested his weight on the edge of the desk, one chubby leg swinging. He smiled. "People are calling you a hero."

"It was nothing," Ben said.

"Before you acted to save young Aris Thanatos, you were with one of the victims on the terrace of the establishment."

Ben nodded.

"I must ask you whether you noticed anything strange or suspicious."

"Nothing at all," Ben said.

Stephanides nodded and picked up a notepad from the desk beside him. "The victim in question. Charles Palmer. Was this man a friend of yours?"

"We were in the army together," Ben said. "I'm retired now."

"And what was the nature and purpose of your visit to Corfu?"

Ben had known men like Stephanides for a long time. He was smiling and working hard to come across as kindly and unthreatening, but he was deadly serious. The questioning was dangerous, and Ben had to focus hard to avoid saying the wrong thing. "I was here for Charlie. He needed my advice about something. But I never got to find out what it was. The bomb happened first."

Stephanides nodded again and made a note in his pad. "And this advice, you have no idea why it could not have been given by phone or e-mail?"

"I prefer to talk face-to-face," Ben said.

The cop grunted. "So you came all this way just to have a conversation, not even knowing what it was going to be about?"

"That's right."

"That strikes me as being rather extravagant."

"I enjoy traveling," Ben said.

"What is your line of business, Mr. Hope?"

"I'm a student. Of theology. Christ Church, Oxford. You can check that."

Stephanides raised his eyebrows and made another note on his pad. "I suppose that would explain why you were carrying a Bible with you." He glanced up. "There are things about your friend that concern me. He was here asking questions about an Englishwoman."

"I don't know anything about that," Ben said.

Stephanides raised his eyebrows. The look that flashed through his eyes said *gotcha*. "This is not what his wife, Mrs. Palmer, told me last night. She told me Mr. Palmer was working for you to find this Miss Bradbury."

Ben closed his eyes and rubbed his temples. He'd walked right into that one.

"I have seven bodies in the morgue," Stephanides said. "And another eleven people who have suffered injury. One will never see again. Another will never walk again. Someone planted a bomb in the middle of my town, and I will find out who and why."

Ben didn't reply.

Stephanides smiled, but it was a cold smile. "You have been through a shock. Perhaps you should not have left hospital so early. It may be you need a day or two to recover and clear your mind. When you are feeling more like talking, I would like to run through these questions again. In the meantime, I want you to remain here on Corfu. I must ask for your passport, please. We will retain it until we no longer require your assistance."

"I don't have it," Ben said.

"Where is it?"

"It was in my jacket pocket when the bomb went off. So were my tickets. My jacket was over the back of the chair. Everything burned."

Stephanides stared at him long and hard. "I notice you carry your wallet in the back pocket of your trousers. Can I see it, please?"

Ben handed it over, and the captain searched briskly through it. He scrutinized Ben's driver's license, put it back, and riffled through the thick wad of banknotes. "A lot of cash to carry around," he noted. "Especially for a student."

"I don't use credit cards," Ben said. "And I don't carry my passport in there either."

"You are a very unusual man. Someone who would travel over a thousand miles rather than talk on the telephone. Who carries thousands of euros in cash, uses no credit cards. And checks himself out of hospital before his injuries have even begun to heal. It's my job to notice unusual things like this. And I have to ask myself why you were in such a hurry."

"You think I'm involved in this?"

"I think you are not telling me everything," Stephanides said. "And I think you should reflect carefully about what you would like to tell me. We will talk again. You may go now."

Ben was heading for the door when Stephanides called him back. He handed Ben a black plastic rubbish bag. "Your belongings," he said pointedly. "Those that did not burn in the fire."

Ben took it and left.

He walked out of the police station in a daze, clutching the plastic bag. He hardly took in his surroundings. He just kept walking, one foot and then the other, staring down at the ground. His thoughts were screaming. He wasn't thinking about the conversation with Stephanides, or that he'd let the cop entrap him with his questions, or that he was getting deeper in shit, or that he had no idea what was going on.

My child will never know its father.

You're a fucking murderer.

God damn you, if you can live with this on your conscience.

The words were like knives stabbing into his brain. He kept walking, trying desperately to shut them out. He wandered away from the town and found himself on a quayside, some moored fishing boats drifting lazily on the water below. He made his way down a crumbly flight of steps and walked out onto the soft sand. The deserted cove curved round in an arc, with the rocky shore sloping upwards behind and a thick pine forest edging the shoreline all the way to the horizon.

He slumped against a rock and tossed the garbage bag down between his feet. He closed his eyes. It felt as though all his strength had left him.

He gave way to despair. He could see Charlie's face in front of him. Rhonda's voice was still screaming in his head. She was right. Charlie was dead because of him. He'd led him right into it, telling him how easy it would be.

Why did you assume that? When was anything ever that easy? You, of all people, should have known. And now Charlie's dead.

He felt sweat prickling his face. He needed a drink, badly. He reached out and untied the knot in the garbage bag. In amongst the charred remains of his duffel bag he found his wrecked phone. He groped around for his flask. His fingers closed on something solid, and he pulled it out.

It wasn't the flask but his old Bible, the leather cover scorched around the edges. He stared at it for a moment, then tossed it down in the sand and reached back into the bag. Finding the battered old flask this time, he unscrewed the top and took a long swig of the warm whisky. It burned his tongue and he felt the glow immediately. It would take some of the edge off. But nothing like enough. He closed his eyes again and sighed.

When he opened them, the first thing he saw was the Bible lying there in the sand next to him. He picked it up and held it in his lap, gazing at it. He stood up, feeling the pull on his injured neck and his aching muscles. Still turning the Bible in his hands, he walked slowly towards the water's edge.

He stared again at the book and thought about the direction his life had taken. The choices and paths that lay before him now. He'd tried so hard to get away from trouble, and to find peace. It was all he wanted, to be a normal person, to get away from all this, to lead a simple and happy life. That was what the Bible meant to him.

But trouble had followed him, just as it always did, like a demon treading close behind him everywhere he went.

Would it ever stop? Was there no escape? He understood, in that moment, that there wouldn't be. It seemed to be his destiny, some-how.

The surf hissed in across the sand, caressed the tips of his shoes, and then edged away again.

And where was God? he thought.

He looked up at the clear sky. "Where *are* you?" he shouted. His voice echoed off the rocks and across the cove.

There was no answer. *Of course not.* There never would be. He was alone.

Molten rage and frustration suddenly burst through him. He drew back his arm and hurled the Bible out to sea. It arced up high against the blue. For an instant it seemed suspended, as though it would stay up there forever. Then it came tumbling down, pages flapping, and dropped into the waves twenty yards out with a dull splash.

Ben walked away and took another long swig of whisky. Wandered aimlessly up the shoreline, feeling emotion rising high in his chest. In the distance were some houses clustered at the sea's edge, with steps leading down the gentle cliffside to the beach. He heard voices on the breeze. A small group of people was ambling down the hill towards him. They were a couple of hundred yards away, but if he kept walk-ing he was going to meet them. He didn't want to be near people. He turned and walked slowly back the way he'd come, towards the invit-ing cover of the pine trees. The surf kept hissing softly in and out, as though it was breathing. The tide washed over his shoes and he felt the cold wetness on his feet. Something nudged his toe and he looked down.

It was the Bible. It had come back to him. He stared at it for a mo-ment, stooped down, and picked it up. Stood holding the dripping book in his hand. Drew his arm back again to fling it right back out to sea, farther this time so the surf wouldn't wash it back up onto the shore.

But something made him stop. His arm went limp. He stared at the book again. There was a strand of seaweed hanging from the cover. He wiped it away. Then he walked on, still clutching the soaking-wet Bible in his hand.

20.

Zoë could see that it was night through the cracks in the boarded-up windows. She leaned back on her bed and stared up at the ceiling.

Five days now since she'd been flown off the island. She had no idea where she was, but it was a lot colder here. Her captors had given her a heavy sweater to wear, and a pair of woolen trousers and thick socks. She spent most of her time just sitting there, helpless, resigned, trying desperately to remember.

It was coming back to her, slowly. As the days ground by, fragments of images kept returning to her, like a forgotten dream gradually seeping back into her conscious mind. Things that had been completely out of reach were there again now, little floating islands of memory slowly merging together into coherence. The smiling faces of a man and a woman kept coming back to her. Her parents, she thought. Trying to peer further into the mist, she saw a little white dog. He was hers. What was his name?

Bringing up these lost memories was like trying to catch a sunbeam in her hand. Sometimes a half-formed impression would dart into focus, she'd try to concentrate on it, and it would be gone. But other things were sharp and clear. The villa, for instance. She could picture it clearly. But the name of the island was lost to her. And what had she been doing there?

In random flashes, she saw herself on a motorbike. Remembered the wind in her hair. Lights in her mirror, and the feeling of fear. She tried to piece it all together. She'd been chased. Then she could vaguely recall the horrible moment of falling. She must have come off the bike and whacked her head on the ground. She rubbed the bump. There was hardly any pain now.

She tried to piece together what had happened next. She could remember the house she'd been kept in when she'd first been taken, and how she'd tried to escape. She shivered, recalling the fair-haired man. She wondered where he was now. The thought of him coming back, walking into her room, terrified her.

She thought back to the journey here—wherever here was. The seaplane had carried her over islands and across the blue sea before the bumpy landing somewhere within sight of the mainland. She'd kept asking where they were taking her, but nobody would speak to her. A speedboat had come out to meet them and taken her to shore with two of the men. They'd dragged her up the rocky beach to a deserted minor road, where a van had been waiting. The men had shoved her into the back and held her down. She remembered how hard she'd screamed and kicked, convinced she was about to be gang-raped and then murdered. But instead, they kept a grip on her arms as a third man took out a syringe from a black leather case. He'd stooped down and jabbed the needle into her. She'd cried out.

The next thing she remembered was waking up on a hard bunk in a cold room with no windows. Bare concrete walls and just a single naked bulb hanging from the ceiling. She'd been kept there for four days—four more days of slowly going insane with frustration and terror.

There'd been visitors to her cell in that time. One of them was a man who brought her food and water. She drank the water but left most of the food. A couple of times a day he'd let her out and walk with her to a stark, windowless bathroom at the end of a concrete corridor. He never spoke, never smiled.

Then there was the man in the dark suit. He'd been to see her three times now, and she dreaded his visits. He was tall and lean, about fifty, with slicked-back hair. His face was craggy, and when he smiled that cold smile his teeth were uneven and fang-like. He had the look of a wolf.

Wolfman just wanted to talk about one thing. Where was it?

All she could reply was "I don't know." It was becoming like a mantra. *I don't know. I don't know. I don't know.*

Wolfman obviously hated hearing it, even more than she hated saying it. The first time she'd seen the cold rage flash through his eyes, she'd thought he was going to start screaming and shaking her, like the fair-haired man had done. But Wolfman was more controlled. He just smiled and pressed on with the same line of questions. Where was it? What had she done with it? She had only to tell him what she knew, and everything would be OK again. They'd let her go. Take her home and make sure she got back safe.

But however hard she tried, she just couldn't remember, just couldn't give him what he wanted. After hours of it, she'd break down and start sobbing, and he'd sit there staring impassively at her for a while, then leave without a word and lock the door behind him.

The third regular visitor was the doctor in the white coat. He looked in his late forties, overweight, balding, bearded. From his first visit, he'd been kind to her, though there was something nervous about his smile. He'd checked her temperature and blood pressure, listened to her heart, examined the fading bruise on her head. He seemed sympathetic and genuinely anxious for her to get her memory back. He spent a lot of time asking her questions too, but his were gentle. Some she could answer and some she couldn't. He noted her responses on a pad.

"What's your name?"

"Zoë Bradbury."

"How old are you?"

"Twenty-six."

"What month are we in?"

"June, I think."

"Where are you from?"

"I don't know."

"Why are you here?"

"I don't know."

"What happened to you?"

"I don't know."

He never pushed harder than that, and never mentioned the things that Wolfman kept asking about. She wanted to open up to him. "I'm scared," she'd said to him again and again. "Where am I? What's going to happen to me?"

He never replied to her questions. Just smiled and told her everything would be all right. Her memory would return in time.

But she could see behind the smile, and the look in his eyes was telling her that he wasn't so sure everything would be all right.

From the doctor's second visit, two days ago now, she'd been aware of some kind of tension between him and Wolfman. There'd been angry whispers outside her door, and once there'd been an argument some way down the corridor outside that she'd strained to hear but couldn't make out.

Then, yesterday, the doctor had come to see her again. This time there'd been a woman with him. Not the woman from before. This one had auburn hair, not black. She was smiling, but when she leaned against the wall, Zoë saw the butt of the gun sticking out of the holster under her jacket.

The doctor had sat by the bed. His voice was soft. "I have some good news for you, Zoë."

"I'm going home?"

He'd smiled sadly and patted her arm. "Not just yet. But we're moving you to a nicer room, where you'll be more comfortable. I think you'll like it there."

"I just want to get out of this place!" Zoë had yelled.

He and the woman had left then. She'd waited all day for their return, and fallen asleep thinking it must have been some kind of cruel trick.

They'd finally come back this morning, along with two more men she didn't recognize. The men acted like guards and said nothing. Zoë had been thankful that Wolfman wasn't with them.

The doctor had led the way. The woman walked with her, and the guards followed quietly behind. Instead of turning left for the bathroom, they turned right and went all the way up the drab corridor to a doorway. Beyond it was another corridor, and then they'd come to an elevator. The woman had pressed the button for the top floor.

They'd stepped out into a different world. The walls were white, with sun streaming in through big skylights. At the end of another corridor they'd shown Zoë to the room she was in now. It was twice the size of the old one, with its own little bathroom. The bed was comfortable, and at the foot of it some fresh clothes had been laid out for her. In one corner was a table with some magazines and a little personal DVD player with a stack of movies for her to watch. She remembered what movies were, though she couldn't recall having ever seen one. It was a strange feeling.

"You rest awhile," the doctor had said as they left her. "Tomorrow we're going to start your therapy sessions. We'll get your memory back." Then he'd winked at her and locked the door.

Now, as she lay there waiting for tomorrow to dawn, she thought about what was in store. The doctor seemed kind, and her instinct told her she could trust him. But another voice in her head told her that the doctor wasn't in charge of things here.

Sleep was impossible. Her heartbeat wouldn't settle. She sat up in the bed, ran her hands through her hair and over her forehead. Somewhere inside here, buried deep inside her mind, was the information these people wanted.

And if it came back. What then?

21.

Ben left the cove and walked back towards Kérkyra, taking his time, deep in thought. He dumped the garbage bag with the remains of the duffel and his phone in a bin. In the center of town he stopped to buy a couple of new shirts, a new pair of jeans, and a canvas military-style shoulder bag. He stuffed the clothes in the bag, slung it round his neck, and mingled with the crowds. In the aftermath of the bombing there was a subdued feeling in the air, a tingle of apprehension, shock, and rage. The streets were noticeably emptier, and people looked tense. The carnage was on every newspaper front page. Police were everywhere.

Ben bought a prepaid cell phone from a market stall. He had a call to make. He sat on a low wall in San Rocco Square and dialed the Bradburys' number. He wasn't looking forward to talking to them, but sooner or later they were going to hear about the bombing, and Charlie's death. He couldn't afford to have them freaking out on him.

The moment Jane Bradbury picked up the phone, he knew he was too late for that. There was a muted sobbing on the line, and then a rustle as she passed the phone to her husband.

"Hello?" Tom Bradbury's voice sounded weary and strained. "Ben, where are you? I've been looking for you everywhere, all over college and in the library. I even went to your flat when you didn't answer your phone."

"I'm on Corfu," Ben said. "You've heard what happened, then."

"Is she hurt? Was she involved?" Bradbury asked urgently.

"She wasn't there," Ben said.

Bradbury sounded relieved. "Thank God. But your friend—It's terrible. I'm so sorry. What's going on?"

"I don't know."

Bradbury was silent for a second. "Forgive me for saying this. I know it sounds terrible. But before he was killed—did your friend—"

"Find Zoë? No, he didn't. I don't know where she is."

"But you'll find her?"

"Did she ever mention any connections in America?" Ben asked.

Bradbury sounded surprised. "Yes, she has a friend there."

"A lawyer called McClusky?"

"No, I've never heard that name. Her friend's an elderly lady she met while teaching a summer school course here two years ago. Her name's Miss Vale. Miss Augusta Vale. We've been out to dinner with her, and Zoë's been to visit her a couple of times."

"In Georgia?"

"Yes. Savannah, Georgia. What's this about, Ben?" Bradbury sounded more and more anxious and confused. "Has something terrible happened to our daughter?"

"What about the name Cleaver?"

"Never heard of it."

"Or someone called Rick?"

"No."

"One last question," Ben said. "Did Zoë ever talk about a prophecy?"

Bradbury was quiet for a moment. "What?"

"A prophecy that could make her rich."

"What are you talking about?" Bradbury asked, anger rising in his voice. "What I need to know is if something's happened to my daughter. I'm going to call the British Embassy in Athens. And the police. This could be a kidnapping, and all you're doing is asking me about prophecies."

"I know it sounds crazy," Ben said. "I have reasons for asking. But if this *is* a kidnapping, and you start ringing alarm bells, it just raises the stakes and will put her in more danger."

The anger in Bradbury's voice died away. He sounded distraught. "What do I do?"

"Sit tight and wait. Let me do things my way. I'll keep in contact. As soon as I know what's happening, you'll hear from me."

"What if there's a ransom demand? We've no money left. What will they do to her, if we can't pay?"

Ben already knew there'd be no ransom demand. It was much too late for that. "Let's just take this one step at a time, all right? You told me you trusted me."

"We do trust you," Bradbury said weakly.

When the call was over, Ben shut the phone and sighed. He'd needed to sound in control for Bradbury's sake. He wished he was so confident in reality.

He looked around the square and took in the scene. His mouth felt dry. He walked to a nearby café-bar and drank a couple of double Scotches on the rocks. The atmosphere in the place was somber, a mixture of gloom and rage as people watched news reports of the bombing on a TV in the corner. After half an hour or so, Ben left and hung around like a tourist for a while. He bought a kebab from a hot-food vendor. Munching as he went, he headed towards the west corner of the square and strolled down an arcaded walkway, gazing in shop windows. Then he wandered over to another bar, where he sat outside on the terrace and drank a couple of chilled beers and ate a bowl of olives.

He spent a few hours like that, just wandering aimlessly around the town center, thinking about Charlie and Zoë and all the things that were happening in his life. The sun was beginning to drop in the sky by the time he picked out a busy taxi stand and showed the driver the address on the key fob Spiro had given him.

Fifteen minutes later, he was stepping inside the Thanatos family beach house a few kilometers south of Corfu Town. It was small and simple but welcoming, with whitewashed walls and cool tiled floors.

The couple must have been expecting him. There was a vase of flowers on the table, and half a dozen bottles of local white wine chilling in the fridge along with spicy cold meats, a dish of stuffed vine leaves, a mountain of fresh green olives, and a bowl of fruit.

He grabbed one of the frosted wine bottles, pulled the cork, and walked out onto the beach. The sound of music drifted towards him on the breeze, and he looked to see where it was coming from. About three hundred yards away across the white sand there was an open-air beach taverna shaded under a long canvas awning. He set out across the sand.

By the time he reached the taverna the bottle in his hand was empty. He showed it to the bartender. "Another of these," he said, and the guy nodded. Ben pulled up a stool at the bar and slumped in it. The bartender left him the fresh bottle and a glass and went back to his chores. Ben turned on his stool, sipping the wine, and looked out to sea. The sun was dipping over the horizon, casting a red glow across the water.

At the tables around him, a few people were drinking, talking, laughing. It looked as though mostly everyone was making an effort to forget the horror of the previous day. One or two faces were showing the strain. A little five-piece band was gamely plucking guitars and bouzoukis in the corner, churning out quick-time traditional dance music. Three or four couples were up on their feet, moving to the fast rhythm.

At another table were two pretty girls. One of them kept glancing at Ben. She leaned forward and whispered something in her friend's ear, and they both smiled at him.

He ignored them and watched the spectacular sunset.

After a few minutes a woman entered the taverna. She joined him at the empty bar, and laid her handbag on the stool between them. She was in her late twenties or early thirties and wore a low-cut cream-colored linen dress. Her hair was lustrous and black, curls tumbling over her bare shoulders. She spoke English to the bartender, with a warm Spanish accent. He served her a glass of mineral water and she sat sipping it, looking preoccupied. Ben watched her for a moment and then went back to the sunset.

The woman's phone rang. She tutted and fished it out of her bag. She answered it in Spanish. Ben knew the language well enough, and he couldn't help overhearing. She was telling someone called Isabella that, no, she wasn't having a good time and that, no, she wasn't staying here any longer. She was flying back to Madrid tomorrow.

The woman shut the phone and looked apologetically at Ben.

"Happens to me all the time," he said. "People phoning when all you want to do is get away."

She smiled. "You are English?"

"Kind of."

"Tourist?"

"Not really."

She smiled again.

"You're from Spain?" he said.

She nodded. "As you heard. I'm sorry. I hate people who talk on phones in public places. It was my sister. She's concerned about me."

"You're not having a good time here?"

She frowned. "How did you know? You understand Spanish?"

"¿Qué vas a tomar?" he said.

She laughed. "You speak it well. But I already have a drink, thank you."

He pointed at her water. "That's not a drink. Have some wine with me."

She accepted, and he asked the bartender for another wineglass. She moved closer to him, lifting her handbag off the stool between them and taking its place. She laid the bag on the floor at her feet. "My name is Esmeralda," she said, offering her hand. He took it. It was soft and warm.

"I'm Ben," he said. He pointed to an empty table in the corner, overlooking the water's edge. "Shall we sit over there?"

She nodded.

"Don't forget your bag." He picked it up and handed it to her.

They carried their drinks over to the table. He bumped into a chair, spilling some wine on the floor. "Whoops. Too much to drink."

They sat facing each other and talked until the stars were out and the moon was shining on the sea.

"Why do you want to leave here?" he asked her. "It's beautiful."

"I'm freaked out by this bombing," she said. "So terrible. All those innocent people."

He nodded. Said nothing.

"And other reasons too."

"Like what?" he asked.

"You really want to know? My fiancé left me for my best friend. My sister thought it would be a good idea for me to get away for a while. But it's not working." She smiled weakly, then looked down.

"I can't imagine why he would leave you." Ben reached over and gently stroked her arm with his finger.

She flushed. "You are nice. So, Ben. What are you doing on Corfu? Vacation? Business?"

"Getting drunk." He poured the last of the wine into his glass. The band had gone into a slow, melancholy set of traditional Greek songs, joined by a female singer.

"What do you do for a living?" Esmeralda asked.

"I'm just a student."

"What happened to your neck?"

"You ask a lot of questions."

She smiled. "I would like to get to know you better, that's all."

He reached across for her hand. "Would you like to dance?"

She nodded. He led her over to the small dance floor. She glanced back at the handbag on the table. "It'll be OK there," he said.

The dance was slow and sensual. Her bare arms were warm against his hands. The strap of her dress kept sliding down her shoulder. Her skin was the color of honey, and the lights sparkled in her dark eyes. Ben drew her closer to him, felt her body crush up against him, and then the soft heat of her lips on his.

"I have a place on the beach," he said. "It's not far to walk. We could be alone there."

She looked up at him. Her face was a little flushed and her breathing had quickened. She squeezed his hand and nodded. "Let's go."

They left the taverna and made their way back across the moon-lit sand. The beach was empty, just the murmur of the surf and the music in the distance. She slipped off her high heels and walked bare-foot. He circled his arm around her slim waist, feeling the litheness of her muscles as she walked. He stumbled again, and she laughed as she helped him to his feet. "You are *ebrio*," she giggled.

"Completely rat-arsed. I've been drinking all day."

They got back to the beach house. He fumbled with his key, dropped it, and searched drunkenly around on the sandy doorstep, muttering curses. "Here it is," he slurred.

Esmeralda tried the handle. "It's open anyway," she laughed. The door swung ajar. She walked inside and he followed, holding on to her arm. He flipped on the light and let go of her as they entered. Let her move away from him until she was at arm's length.

Then he delivered a ridge-hand strike to the side of her neck and she crumpled to the floor without a sound.

It was a blow designed to stun, not to kill. He kneeled quickly over her inert body and ripped open her fallen handbag. Feeling inside, his fingers touched cool steel. He quickly pulled the pistol out. It was more or less what he'd expected it to be from its weight when he'd picked up the handbag at the taverna. A Beretta 92F semiautomatic. The hefty 9mm was cocked and locked. He flipped off the safety.

At the other end of the room, the door through to the kitchen burst open. Ben had expected that too. He fired a rapid double-tap and the Beretta bucked against his palm.

The intruder ran right into it. The bullets struck him in the chest and he crashed back against the side of the door, his gun flying out of his hand and spinning away across the floorboards. He slumped down and lay still, chin on his chest, blood on his lips.

Ben's ears were ringing from the gunfire. He checked the front door. The beach was still empty. The walls of the house would have muffled the shots enough to prevent them carrying too clearly all the way to the taverna. He strode quickly back into the room and locked the door.

The woman was beginning to stir, groaning and clutching her neck. He stepped over her and picked up the dead intruder's pistol. It was the same model of 9mm Beretta, but with a long sound suppressor screwed to the barrel. With his left hand he pulled the slide back far enough to expose the breech and reveal the shiny brass of the cartridge inside. He looked down at the intruder on the floor. The guy was fair-haired and youngish, maybe thirty, good-looking. Ben remembered what Nikos had told Charlie about the couple at Zoë Bradbury's party that night. A fair-haired guy, same age, and a woman who could have passed for a Greek.

He shoved the unsilenced gun in his belt and pointed the other at the woman's head. It was a much more useful weapon for indoor work. "Get up," he said.

She coughed and raised herself slowly onto her knees and elbows, brushed the hair away from her face, and turned to look at him. There was a very different look in those dark eyes now.

"I saw you in the town earlier," he said. "I saw you in San Rocco Square and again while I was looking in the shop windows. I saw you before you even started following me today. I made sure you could see me the whole time, so that I could watch you."

She rose up into a crouch, tensed, one hand spread out on the floor in front of her, looking up at him with tight lips. Where the thick black hair was brushed away from her forehead, he could see a vein pulsing.

"You weren't following me," he said. "You were being led. I chose a busy taxi stand so that you wouldn't lose me. You and your friend here jumped in the next cab, and I watched you all the way over here. I made it easy for you. I even pretended to be drunk. You walked right into it."

Her eyes were empty. He could see she was measuring distances, working out moves, calculating odds. She was someone trained. "You're pretty good," he said. "That was a great cover story, about your sister. But you're not good enough to get out of this. Talk to me, Esmeralda. Don't think I wouldn't shoot you."

She said nothing.

"Zoë Bradbury. Where is she?"

She didn't reply.

"Who bombed the café?" he asked. "Was it to kill Charlie?"

"I don't know what you're talking about."

He fired. She screamed and drew her hand away from the floor.

"You're fine," he said. "I aimed between your fingers. Next time I'll take one off. Let's start again. Zoë Bradbury. Where is she?"

"Gone," she whispered.

"Cooperation. That's good. Gone where?"

She hesitated.

"Pick a finger," he said. "Maybe one you don't use much. Hold out your hand. That way I won't hit anything else by mistake."

"She's not in Greece any longer."

"Then where is she?"

"You'll kill me anyway," she said. "Why should I tell you?"

"I'm not like you," he replied. "I know the kind of treatment you had in mind for me tonight if I didn't answer your questions. But I'm not a senseless killer. If you tell me where she is, what's going on, and who you are, you won't be harmed. I'll put you where nobody can find you. When I find Zoë safe and well, I'll come back and maybe I'll let you walk free. It's your choice. But understand that if you don't tell me, you're dead. Right here, right now. No more finger games." He aimed the pistol at her forehead.

"Who the hell are you?" The Spanish accent was less pronounced now. She sounded distinctly American.

"Nobody. Last chance. Where is she?"

The woman heaved a sigh. "She's been taken to the U.S. Five days ago."

"Good. We're getting somewhere. Where exactly in the U.S., why, and by whom?"

"I don't know everything," she said. "I just do what I'm told to do."

"Who tells you? Give me names."

"I don't have any names to give."

"What's yours?"

"Kaplan. Marisa Kaplan."

He watched her eyes and believed her. He pointed back at the fair-haired man on the floor. "What was his?"

"Hudson."

"Why are you here, Marisa? Who planted the bomb?"

Then the room was filled with noise. Ben felt the shock wave of a bullet pass close to his ear. A wall light shattered. He whirled round and fell back simultaneously, returning fire. The Beretta kicked in his hands. The fair-haired guy was half raised on one elbow, and the gun in his bloody fist was a small backup revolver. It fired again. The second shot went through the cuff of Ben's shirt.

Ben fired back. Saw the bullet strike. Fired again. The guy's eye disappeared and his head dropped to the floor. There was blood up the wall behind him.

Then there was silence again. Ben clambered to his feet and checked himself. He wasn't hit. But the intruder was definitely dead this time. Ben kicked the .357 Magnum snubby backup piece away across the floor.

He heard a tiny sound behind him. He turned. The woman called Kaplan was sitting up, staring at her stomach. The blood was spreading fast over her cream dress. She clutched at the wound that her partner's stray shot had punched into her gut, trying to tear the cloth to get to it. Her mouth opened and closed. Then she slumped backwards and died.

22.

Creating corpses was much quicker and easier work than disposing of them afterwards. Ben found some heavy-duty plastic garbage bags in the kitchen of the beach house. Stepping over the pools of blood on the tiles, he tore two bags off the roll, opened them out, and spread them on the floor in the passage near the front door.

He took Kaplan by the wrists and dragged her. Her head hung down, eyes still open, her hair trailing in the slick of blood on the tiles. He dumped her corpse on top of one of the garbage bags, walked back across the room to Hudson's body, and bent down and grabbed his ankles. Hudson was much heavier and much more bloody. His right eye socket and cheekbone had been smashed by the impact of the 9mm bullet from his partner's gun. Ben dragged him over the tiles and left him lying next to Kaplan.

He crouched over them and frisked them carefully. No papers, no personal items of any kind. Hudson had a phone in his back pocket. He found Kaplan's in her handbag. With a phone in each hand he redialed the last call she'd made, and Hudson's phone vibrated in his other hand. He checked through their call records. The two phones had been used only to call each other.

Ben left the corpses lying there and started cleaning up the house. The broken wall lamp had sprayed glass shards over part of the floor, and he swept them up with a dustpan and brush and shook them out into the bin. In a kitchen cupboard he found a mop and bucket and a bottle of bleach. He filled the bucket with cold water, lugged it through to the other room, and started mopping up the worst of the blood. Once that was done, he used a kitchen knife to hack at one of the doorframes, where a bullet had embedded itself deep into the wood. He dug the flattened 9mm bullet out and dropped it in his pocket. He winced at the mess he'd made of the doorframe.

As he worked, he was thinking hard. Kaplan and Hudson hadn't been the best surveillance and hit team he'd ever seen, but they hadn't been the worst either. The two Berettas were the exact same make and model. The serial numbers had been expertly removed. Those kinds of details pointed to a professional outfit. He was pretty certain that they had been sent to kill Nikos Karapiperis. If Nikos had really been involved in drugs, he wouldn't have gone to Charlie for help to find Zoë. So the killers had planted the drugs on him. That was a neat touch. Then the bombing had been orchestrated to eliminate Charlie, after they'd seen him talking to Nikos. And it wasn't a difficult step from there to figure out that they'd come after Ben for the same reason.

Those pieces slotted together neatly enough. But when Zoë Bradbury was factored into the equation, it started falling apart. There was no ransom demand. No apparent reason for snatching her. Her parents were hardly the kind of people who could be screwed for millions to get their daughter back. If Tom Bradbury had been in politics or some other kind of position to be privy to valuable information, it might have made sense. But he wasn't. He was a theology scholar in one of the world's dustiest institutions, about as remote from the real world as it was possible to get.

So whatever reason was driving someone to these extremes, it had to come from Zoë herself. But what was it? He thought about the money. She'd apparently got hold of twenty thousand dollars fairly easily, and was expecting a lot more to come soon. It certainly sounded like a blackmail deal. Whomever she was extorting the money from had to be pretty rich and powerful, and they were clearly desperate. Which meant that whatever she was threatening them with, it was real enough to be taken very seriously.

But why go to the trouble of moving her halfway across the world to the States, when it would have been so easy just to put a bullet in her head right here on Corfu? He thought about it and could come to only one conclusion. She had something they wanted, and they wanted to keep her alive until they got it.

But that led to another problem. Kaplan and Hudson weren't soft types. They were ready and willing to kill. And Zoë wasn't a soldier trained to resist interrogation. If all they wanted was to make her talk, it would have taken just a few seconds to get the information out of her. Just the sight of a knife or a gun and, like the vast majority of ordinary people, she would fold instantly.

After that, they probably would kill her. And after twelve days, there was a good chance she was dead already.

At three-thirty in the morning, the beach taverna started closing up for the night. The last of the stragglers wandered off homewards. The music stopped and the lights went off, leaving the beach in darkness.

Ben watched and waited for another half hour. The sands were deserted. He stuffed a Beretta in each of his jeans pockets, pushed open the front door and dragged Hudson's corpse out across the sand, sliding him along on the plastic bags.

It was a long drag, and a dead body on sand was a heavy weight. The pull on the stitches in Ben's neck was agonizing, and the muscles in his shoulders and forearms were pumped full of lactic acid by the time he reached his chosen spot a hundred yards away. He left the corpse in a nook between two dunes and walked back, breathing hard.

Back at the house, he took Kaplan's wrists, gritted his teeth, and hauled her out onto the beach. As her head lolled and bounced he kept imagining that her staring eyes were meeting his. He didn't like to see a woman dead like this, and he was glad that he hadn't been the one to kill her.

With the two bodies piled up next to him in the moonlight, he kneeled in the sand and dug a shallow hole in the crook of the two dunes. He rolled them in one at a time with his foot. Kaplan flopped in first, and Hudson sprawled in on top of her with a meaty sound as their heads collided.

Ben filled the hole back in with sand. They were food for crabs now.

Searching around, he found the barnacled carcass of an old rowing boat and hauled it across the sand. He laid it over the shallow grave and walked away towards the water's edge. Retracing his footsteps, he kicked over the tracks in the sand to hide them. Then he stripped the two pistols and threw the bits into the sea.

Dawn was creeping up on the horizon by the time he finished cleaning up at the house. He showered and changed, burned the bloodstained jeans and shirt on the beach, and stamped the ashes into the sand. He left five hundred euros on the table and a note to apologize for breaking a lamp and damaging a doorframe, saying he'd drunk too much of the fine wine Spiro and Christina had left for him.

Then, as the sun was breaking free of the sea, he left the house and started walking towards town. He took a taxi to the airport, careful that he wasn't being followed. The last thing he needed now was for Stephanides's men to grab him just as he was about to leave Greece. He'd be in America long before they even noticed he was gone.

At the airport he retrieved his passport from the locker and used his return ticket to board an early flight to Athens. At midday, Greek time, he was sipping whisky on the rocks in the half-empty business class section of a 747 heading for Atlanta.

He didn't know what awaited him in the U.S. But he was going to find Zoë Bradbury, dead or alive.

And then someone, somewhere, was going to pay.

23.

Georgia wasn't noticeably hotter than Corfu, but it was about twice as humid. Ben's shirt was stuck to his back within fifteen minutes of stepping off the plane at Atlanta's Hartsfield-Jackson Airport.

He adjusted his watch to U.S. time. The zone shift meant that he was arriving at pretty much the same time he'd left Greece, and the sun was high overhead. He hired a big silver Chrysler at the airport and drove the long distance to Savannah with the windows down and the wind in his hair.

It was late afternoon by the time he got there. Savannah was rich and verdant, with picture-perfect antebellum homes that looked as though they hadn't changed since Civil War times. The first thing he did was to phone the number on Steve McClusky's business card. But when he tried it, all he got was a message to say the number had been cut off. There was no landline number, and there was no S. Mc-Clusky, Attorney, listed in Yellow Pages. But he still had the address. He checked his map and turned the big Chrysler round.

He found McClusky's building on the edge of town, far away from the opulence of the old houses and the tree-lined streets. He'd been expecting some kind of proper law firm offices, either an imposing glass-fronted modern building or some elegant old place with columns and steps leading up to the front door. What he found instead was a little old barber's shop in the middle of a crumbling block. There was a small parking space outside, with yellowed weeds growing though the cracks in the concrete. He looked twice at the address on the card. It was the right place.

A bell tinkled overhead as he walked in the door. It was cool inside, air-conditioning working full blast. He glanced quickly around him. The fittings were straight out of the fifties, and the old barbers themselves looked as though they'd been there at least as long. One of them was busy cutting the hair of the single customer in the place. The other was perched up on a stool, sipping a can of light beer. He was stooped and white and looked like an iguana. A young guy of about eighteen in an apron was sweeping up bits of snipped hair from the tiles.

The old barber with the beer turned towards the newcomer. "What can we do for you, mister? Haircut or a shave?"

"Neither," Ben said. "Where can I find Steve McClusky?"

"That would be Skid you're looking for."

"The name on the card is Steve McClusky."

The old man nodded. "That's him. Skid McClusky."

"Why do they call him that?"

The barber grinned. He had no front teeth. "Well, some folks say it's the way he drives that Corvette of his. Others say Skid Row's the place he'll wind up, if he ain't there already."

"His card says his offices are at this address."

"Right there." The old barber pointed a scraggy finger at a door in the corner. "Up the stairs, turn left. Ain't much to look at, though."

"Thanks." Ben headed towards the door.

"Save yourself the trouble, mister. You won't find Skid there." The barber grinned again, flashing pale gums. "No, sir."

"So where is he? I need to talk to him."

They all laughed. "Get in line, mister," the old man said. "There's a bunch of us who'd like to talk to that sonofabitch. Skipped out of here without paying his rent. Been gone more'n two weeks."

"So you don't know where he is?"

"'Fraid I can't help you there."

He'd come a long way, and this wasn't a great start. "Thanks anyway." Ben turned and pushed back through the door. The bell tinkled again. He walked out into the hot sun and made his way towards the car, beeping the locks as he approached. He yanked open the driver's door and was about to climb in when he heard running footsteps come up behind him.

He turned. It was the young guy from the barber's shop. The apron was gone, under it a faded Jimi Hendrix T-shirt. "Mister," he said. "Wait a minute." The teenager was looking over his shoulder back at the place as though he was scared they might be watching him from inside. Must have slipped out the back way, Ben thought.

The teenager looked anxious and sincere. Whatever he was about to say, Ben believed it.

"Skid's in some kind of trouble, mister."

"What kind of trouble?"

"Don't know for sure. Something real bad. That's why he's gone." He paused. "Skid's always been good to me. Loaned me money when I needed it."

"If Skid's in trouble, I might be able to help him," Ben said. "Do you know where I can find him?"

The kid shook his head. "I know someone who might."

"Can you pass on a message to them?"

The kid threw another jittery glance back at the barber's shop. He looked back at Ben and nodded.

"Tell them a friend of Zoë Bradbury, from England, needs to talk to Skid. It's important and urgent. Got that?"

"Zoë Bradbury," the kid repeated.

"If Skid gets the message he'll understand. He needs to call this number." Ben scrawled it on a piece of paper and handed it to the kid, together with a twenty-dollar bill. The young guy nodded, turned, and ran back towards the rear of the barber's shop.

It was about an hour later, as Ben was driving back towards the middle of town, looking around for a hotel, that his phone buzzed on the dashboard. He picked it up.

"Who I am talking to?" said a man's voice, nervy, aggressive.

Ben didn't like the challenging approach, but he bit his tongue. "I'm Ben Hope. Who's this?"

"Never mind who I am," the voice said harshly. The tone of someone working hard to cover up their fear. Someone clearly under a lot of strain. He gave Ben the name of a bar near a place called Hinesville, about twenty miles southwest of Savannah, and some rough directions to find the place. "Be there tonight at seven-thirty." Then he hung up.

Anonymous rendezvous were not something Ben very much liked, but in his line of work he got a lot of weird calls from people too scared to give their identity away. Experience had proved that it was usually worth chasing them up, even it was just part of the process of elimination.

He checked his watch. A couple of hours to get there. He swung round and headed southwest, away from the neat white houses and emerald lawns and the cool shade of the tree-lined streets. He stopped at a roadside diner and drank four cups of the best coffee he'd ever tasted outside Italy. Then he checked the time again, got back in the car, and drove at a steady sixty towards his RV.

Music was thumping through the barroom walls as Ben stepped out of the Chrysler and walked up to the door. He swung it open and the noise of the country rock beat hit him, along with the heat and the smell of smoke, beer, and a hundred tightly packed bodies. He cast his eye around the place. There was a rebel flag hanging over the bar, below a couple of crossed sabers. Waitresses in high heels, tiny denim shorts, and cut-off T-shirts were weaving between the tables. On a low stage there were electric guitars, a bass, a sprawling drum kit, and a mountain of speakers and amplifiers set up and waiting for the band to come on.

Ben pushed through the crowd and headed the way the voice on the phone had told him to. A door between a pinball machine and a pay phone led him up a dark flight of creaky wooden stairs. He walked along a dingy corridor. The music was pumping up from below, vibrations pulsing under his feet. It would probably get about twice as loud when the band started to play. He came to a door and knocked.

A woman's voice called from inside. "Come in."

He opened the door and stepped inside the room. It was some kind of office, but it looked as though it had been abandoned quite a while ago. There was a desk and a plain wooden chair, an empty bookcase, and a tall withered plant in a dried-out pot in the corner.

The woman was alone in the room, standing by the desk. She was small and wiry, not much more than five-two, about thirty years old. Her hair was curly and long, dyed blond. She wore high-heeled boots, tight jeans, and a suede jacket, with a heavy-looking leather shoulder bag on a strap.

"I spoke to a man on the phone," Ben said to her.

"You spoke to Skid," she answered tersely.

"Where is he?" He took a step closer to her.

"Stay right where you are, mister. I'm the one asking the questions here." Her hand dipped quickly into her bag and came out clutching a huge revolver. She clasped it tightly, pointing at his chest from across the room. Its weight made the tendons stand out on her wrist.

"OK, you have my attention," Ben said. "What do you want to know?"

"Who do you work for?"

"What makes you think I work for anyone?"

"If you're one of Cleaver's boys, you ain't getting out of here alive." She sounded like she meant it.

"I don't know who Cleaver is."

"Sure." She frowned. "Where are you from?"

"Not around here," he said. "Look, I need to talk to Steve. Skid. Whatever the hell you want to call him. It's urgent."

She raised the gun. "Easy."

He eyed the pistol. It was a massive single-action revolver, large caliber, stainless steel. The kind of weapon hunters used to shoot grizzly bears in Alaska. He could see the noses of the fat hollowpoint bullets nestling in the mouths of the chambers. The muzzle diameter was half an inch across. Not a pistol for a woman of her build. She was having trouble keeping the long barrel level. If she let off a round, the recoil would snap her wrist like a piece of celery.

"That's not yours, is it?" he said. "My guess is, that belongs to Skid."

She grimaced. "Makes no difference whose it is. I can still blow the hell out of you. And I will. So keep your distance, and your hands where I can see them."

"He should have taught you how to use it before he sent you out here as his guard dog," Ben said. "It's not cocked. It won't fire."

She glanced down at the gun, keeping a mistrustful eye on him.

"Try pulling the trigger," Ben said. "Nothing will happen. See the hammer there? You need to wrap your thumb around that, and ease it back."

She did as he said.

"All the way back, till it clicks," he told her.

The action made a smooth metallic *clunk-clunk* in the silence of the room. The big five-shot cylinder rotated and locked.

"OK," he said. "Now you can rest easy. You can shoot me if you need to. But before you do, let me prove to you that I'm not one of Cleaver's boys. Whoever Cleaver is. Now, I'm going to move my hand to my jacket and peel it back. Don't worry, I'm not armed. I'm going to show you my passport." He slid it out and tossed it on the desk. "Freshly stamped by U.S. Immigration, just today. My name's Ben Hope. Benedict on the passport."

She reached out, picked it up, and studied it. The gun wavered, and he could easily have taken it from her. He just smiled. She glanced up at him, then back at the passport.

"Now do you believe me?"

She let the gun down to her side. Her face softened, a look of relief in her eyes. "All right," she said. "I believe you."

"Then maybe you should decock that revolver now."

"Oh. Right." She wrapped her left thumb around the hammer, squeezed the trigger, and let the hammer down slowly.

"You haven't told me your name," he said.

"Molly."

"It's good to meet you, Molly."

"So what are you doing in Georgia, Mr. Hope?"

"You can call me Ben. I came from Europe to find Zoë Bradbury."

"You don't look the kind who would hang around that little tramp."

"She's in trouble."

Molly snorted. "She *is* trouble."

"And Skid's in trouble too," Ben said. "Or I wouldn't have been looking down the barrel of that hand cannon just now."

"I'm sorry. I had to be careful."

"Where is he?"

"Hiding from Cleaver."

"Will you take me to him?" Ben said.

24.

Molly drove him through the night, southwards along the coastal highway towards Jacksonville. Gentle specks of rain on the windshield became a drumming thunder, and the road ahead was slick and glossy. They sat in silence for the first few miles, the wipers beating time.

"Boy, I could use a drink," she said suddenly. "My hands are still shaking." She glanced at him sideways and smiled for the first time. "I've never pointed a gun at anyone before."

"You did fine." He reached into his jacket and offered her his flask. "It'll calm your nerves."

She sipped. "That's good. What is it?"

"Laphroaig single-malt Scotch, ten years old."

"Nice." She took another sip, smacked her lips, and then handed the flask back to him. "See that glove compartment? Can you get me a smoke?"

He opened it. "Havanas?" he said, surprised.

"My daddy used to smoke them. I got the taste. Have one yourself."

The little Coronation Punch cigars were sealed in silver aluminum tubes. Ben opened two of them, lit them up with his Zippo, and passed one to her.

She took a long draw on hers and let out a cloud of smoke. "So, Mr. Hope. I mean Ben. Just who are you?"

"Just someone who wants to help."

"You seem to know an awful lot about guns. For an English guy. I thought they were banned over there."

"I'm not really English," he said. "I'm half Irish."

"Which half?"

"The good half."

She laughed. "That figures. Every English guy I ever met was an uptight sonofabitch."

"Tell me about Skid," he said.

"We met at law school."

"So you're a lawyer too?"

She shook her head. "Couldn't get past the bar exam. I get nervous. So I'm a paralegal. I worked with Skid for a while, but now I work uptown for a firm."

"Why did he send you to meet me?"

"Because he can't go anywhere. You'll see for yourself, soon enough."

"What happened to him?"

"Cleaver's people. They got to him. Almost killed him. Would have too, if I hadn't turned up and called the cops."

"Who is this Cleaver?"

"Skid'll tell you all about him."

"Where does Zoë Bradbury come into this?"

"Skid and I were serious for almost two years," she said. "Zoë Bradbury broke us up."

"I know she was here a couple of times," he said. "Staying with a Miss Vale."

Molly nodded and took another drag on her cigar. "It happened the last time she was here, six months ago. Skid was in a bar—he's always in a bar, somewhere—and he meets this pretty English girl, and I guess he couldn't resist. And I guess she couldn't resist him either. Skid never had a cent to his name, but he's a charmer, that's for sure." She smiled grimly. "The one time I met her was in his office. He told me that she and he had a business deal going. What he didn't tell me was, they were screwing the whole time she was here. I only found out weeks later what all those late nights at work were about." She wound down the window a crack and flicked ash out. "Skid never denied it. That's when I left him. Told him I'd never see him again. It was over. But then he kept calling and pestering me, saying he couldn't live without me. He was leaving me phone messages, crying and threatening to shoot himself."

"With that big pistol there?"

"Wouldn't be much left, I guess."

"No, there wouldn't."

"Anyway, I turned up at his office late one night to have it out with him face-to-face. As I went up the stairs I could hear all this screaming and yelling. There were three guys there with him. Beating the crap out of him. I called the cops, and there happened to be a patrol close by. They went in, but the three guys must have heard them coming. They got out the back way. Left Skid in pretty bad shape."

"When was this?"

"Just over two weeks ago," she said. "Now Skid's petrified that Cleaver will get to him again. Won't even go to the hospital, though Lord knows he needs to."

"You're looking after him."

"Guard dog, like you said. And nursemaid, all rolled into one."

"So was there a business deal between Zoë and Skid, or was that just a cover?"

"There was a deal," she said gravely. "And that's the reason Skid's in trouble."

"What was it?"

"Skid'll tell you that too. We'll be there soon." She pulled off the highway, and within a few more minutes they hit roads that were dark and narrow and twisty. Molly drove fast, her face tight with concentration. A dirt road came up on the left and she took it. The car lurched past a dilapidated motel sign. The dirt road was all churned up into mud by the rain. At the end of it, they swung into a rough earth yard. The headlights picked out clumps of overgrown grass, discarded garbage bags, broken furniture, flattened beer cans. The motel buildings were low-slung and badly in need of repair. A fly-specked neon light threw a yellowish glow over the raised porches and parking spaces out front. Molly pulled up next to a pickup truck and killed the engine.

They stepped out. The rain had stopped and the air was heavy and humid. Two Dobermans in a mesh cage barked furiously and hurled themselves against the wire, standing upright on sinewy hind legs.

"Welcome to Skid's new home," Molly said.

Only a couple of windows were lit up. The muffled sound of a TV was coming from somewhere inside. The dogs were still barking. A man's drunken voice in the distance yelled at them to shut up.

Molly led Ben to room number ten. The old door was warped and peeling. She beat on it, three loud knocks. "It's Molly," she called. She dug in her bag and took out a key, unlocked the door, and they went in.

The room was dark and smelled of must and antiseptic. Molly yanked the drapes shut and flipped on a sidelight.

Skid McClusky had been sleeping, and his head jerked up. He blinked in the light.

He was about thirty, like Molly. He might have been good-looking, but it was hard to tell under all the yellow bruises and half-healed cuts on his face. His dark hair was greasy and plastered over his brow. He was wearing a denim shirt with dark sweat patches, sitting in an upright armchair with most of the stuffing hanging out of it, his feet straight out in front of him and resting on a stool. Both legs were plastered from the knee down. There was a Mossberg pump shotgun resting across his lap, and he fingered it nervously.

He looked up. His eyes were ringed with pain and fear. They darted around the room and settled on Ben.

"He's OK, Skid," Molly said. "He isn't one of Cleaver's."

"Pull yourself up a seat," Skid said to Ben. "And tell me what you want."

"I'm going out to get some beers," Molly said. "I'll leave you boys alone to talk." She left.

Ben and the lawyer sat in silence for a minute. "I'll get right to the point," Ben said. "Zoë Bradbury is missing. She disappeared from her place in Greece twelve days ago. It's my job to find her, and I think you can help me."

"I figured they'd get to her," Skid moaned. "They made me talk."

"The men who did this?" Ben motioned to the plastered legs.

Skid nodded. "I'm a real mess, man," he said desperately. "Look at me. I'm just fucked."

"Maybe I can help you too," Ben said.

"Just how exactly do you figure on that?"

"I don't know yet. But I'm pretty sure the people who did this to you are the same people I'm after."

Skid rubbed his hands down his face. He was quiet for a minute. "OK, what do you want from me?"

"I want to know everything," Ben said. "About the deal you and Zoë had between you. And about Cleaver. I keep hearing the name. Who is he?"

Skid let out a long breath. "Pass me that, would you?" He pointed to a half-empty bottle of Jack Daniel's on the table out of his reach. Ben grabbed it and handed it to him. Skid took a deep swallow and wiped his sleeve across his mouth.

"I'll start from the start," he said. "Do you know who Augusta Vale is?"

Ben nodded.

"Then you know that Zoë was over here staying with her at her home in Savannah. That's how we met. In a bar."

"I heard that bit already," Ben said.

Skid shifted uncomfortably in his chair and winced from the pain in his legs. "She and Miss Vale were real close. At least, Miss Vale thought so. Zoë was more interested in her money. She was always dropping hints to her about this thing or that thing she wanted to do, hoping Miss Vale would pull out her checkbook. It's not every day you have a friend with a two-billion-dollar estate who calls you the child she always wanted but never had. And one thing about Zoë, she loves money."

"I don't know her that well," Ben said. "I haven't seen her since she was a child."

Skid took another swig of bourbon. "And she thought she was in with a chance to get a piece of the action. Until Clayton Cleaver came on the scene." The way Skid said the name, he seemed to think Ben would recognize it. "You never heard of Clayton Cleaver?"

Ben shrugged. "Should I have?"

"Bestselling author. Televangelist. Wannabe state governor. And now, best friend of Miss Augusta Vale, who thinks the sun shines out of his ass. Miss Vale is a good Christian lady, extremely devout, patron of a whole bunch of charities. But she's being fooled. That fucker has her convinced he's a saint. When Zoë came to stay with her six months ago, Augusta told her all about her latest plan, to give Cleaver money for his foundation. I'm talking a lot of money. A fuck of a lot."

"How much?"

"Nine figures."

"A hundred million," Ben said.

Skid nodded. "Just loose cash, as far as Miss Vale is concerned. She had some investments and bonds waiting to mature, a whole bunch of lawyers working on it and billing five hundred an hour while the money was still tied up. Clayton's due to get it sometime soon, this month or next."

"I take it Zoë wasn't very happy when she heard about this."

"Damn right she wasn't," Skid answered. "She'd met Cleaver at one of the old lady's dinners. Said he was a sleazebag and a con artist. She couldn't believe that Miss Vale was so taken with this guy who was so obviously stringing her along. She was convinced that he was turning the old lady against her."

Ben leaned back in his chair and lit a cigarette.

"You getting this?" Skid said. "So, anyway, Zoë couldn't stand it anymore. She left and went back to England. We didn't keep in touch for a while. I had my own problems this end. Molly probably told you. But then, a few weeks ago, I get this call from her. She's excited. Just came back from some dig in Turkey and has thought of a way to get a whole lot of money out of Clayton Cleaver. It was perfect, she said. Foolproof. Nothing could go wrong." Skid stared down the length of his plastered legs and grunted.

"She's been blackmailing him," Ben said. "But with what?"

Skid toyed with the whisky bottle. "Truth is, I don't know. She never told me details. Something dirty, maybe. Sex. Who knows? But whatever it was, it was working. She called him from Greece and made some kind of a proposal to him. Asked for money. She knew he didn't have the hundred million yet, so she said she'd be easy on him. For now. She wanted a down payment of twenty-five grand. Five of that was my cut. All I had to do was deliver a box to Clayton's offices."

"A box."

"A box. Just a plain old cardboard box, about this big." Skid angled his hands out to make a six-inch cube. "It felt light. Don't ask me what was in it. I have no idea. All I know is that when you shook it, it rattled."

So it wasn't photographs, Ben was thinking. So much for a sex sting.

"Cleaver took the box into a room while I waited outside," Skid went on. "I heard cardboard ripping, like he was digging in real fast. Whatever was in there, it persuaded him. He came back out with a case containing twenty-five thousand dollars in cash. Handed it right over. I took out my cut, the rest was hers."

That explained Zoë's sudden wealth, the expensive hotel, the villa, the parties.

"But she wanted more, didn't she?" Ben said.

"She told Cleaver that as soon as the big money rolled in, she wanted ten million dollars from him in exchange for whatever she had. My cut was ten percent. I didn't even have to do anything, it was just a handling fee. It looked as if Cleaver was agreeing to the deal. I couldn't believe it. A lawyer's dream. I had it all planned. I was going to get out of that rat hole office and move the practice uptown, clean up my whole act." Skid sighed. "But evidently he changed his mind."

"The night you got beaten up."

Skid nodded. "I'd been pretty sure for a couple of days that I was being followed. Never saw anyone. It was just a feeling. I was spooked enough to keep the revolver around me. Then one night I was working late at my desk. I didn't even hear these guys come in. Next thing I'm being dragged out of my chair with a gun in my face. They threw me down on the floor, started asking me where it was. 'Where is it? Where is it?' I didn't know what the hell they were talking about. Then they started asking me where Zoë was."

"And you told them."

"Not at first," Skid said. "I've taken beatings before. I'm no chicken. But then they opened up this bag and took out a couple of fucking hammers. Started going to work on my legs while the third one held the gun to my head. You'd have to be pretty damn tough to keep your mouth shut when two big guys are smashing your knees to shit. Of course I told them. You'd have done the same."

"Did Zoë ever say anything to you about some kind of prophecy?" Ben asked.

Skid looked blank. "As in reading your star signs kind of prophecy?"

"She's a biblical archaeologist," Ben said. "So, as in Bible prophecy. She told someone that the money was somehow tied up with it."

"I don't know anything about that," Skid replied. "How could a Bible prophecy make her rich? Like I said, she had some angle on Cleaver."

"Forget it," Ben said. "It's not important."

The door opened, without warning. Skid jumped and made a grab for the shotgun. The pump action was racked halfway back on its rails when he relaxed and laid it down again. He slumped back in the chair.

Molly locked the door behind her and walked into the room carrying a six-pack of beer. She dumped it on the bed. "Time for your pills, honey," she told Skid.

The lawyer nodded sadly. "And that's all I have to tell you," he said to Ben. "If it wasn't for Molly here, we wouldn't even be having this conversation."

Molly walked over to his chair and laid a hand softly on his shoulder. With the other hand she wiped away a tear. Skid stroked her arm. There was tension between them, but there was tenderness too.

"I didn't want her to go to meet you," Skid said. "It was her idea. She's a brave lady."

"What are you going to do now?" Ben asked.

"What else is there for a broke-down, penniless drunken cripple to do? I'm stuck here."

"You can't stay here forever."

"I'll stay here till Cleaver forgets about me. Or till I die, whichever happens first. I can't go home, can't go anywhere. They find me, they'll kill me. Might as well drink myself to death right here in this chair." Skid glanced up at Molly, who was smiling down at him through her tears. "What can I say?" he said. "The day I ran into Zoë Bradbury was the day I just screwed my life up into a little ball and threw it in the fire. I've lost everything. And I lost the best woman a man could wish for."

"You didn't lose me," she whispered. She leaned down and kissed his clammy forehead.

Skid turned and stared at Ben. "What about you? What happens next?"

"I think I should pay a visit to Miss Augusta Vale," Ben said.

"I have the number," Skid said.

"Good. And then I want to talk to Clayton Cleaver." Ben reached for his wallet. "But first there's one more thing you can do for me."

"What's that?"

"You can sell me that big revolver of yours. I have a feeling I might need it."

25.

It was late by the time Molly drove Ben back to Hinesville. She squeezed his hand and wished him good luck. He smiled and watched her take off into the rainy night, then climbed into the Chrysler and headed for Savannah. In his canvas bag on the seat behind him was Skid's Freedom Arms .475 Linebaugh hunting revolver and a box of hollowpoint shells.

Ben drove into Savannah and checked into a hotel. For a long time that night, he sat in his room pondering and staring out of the open window across the Savannah river. He was dead tired, but sleep was impossible with a thousand thoughts swirling in his mind.

If things had seemed unclear when he was in Greece, the picture was fuller now. And uglier. Working through the pieces, he could see that the chances of finding Zoë Bradbury alive had just slipped further away.

So now he knew the name of the rich, powerful figure who'd felt threatened enough by her to take some kind of drastic action. A hundred million dollars and aspirations to the governorship of Georgia—you couldn't get much richer and more powerful than that, without going all the way to the top.

He also knew now why the name Cleaver had been in her address book. How and why Zoë had been blackmailing him was still a mystery. But one thing was clear: she'd named too high a price. Ten million was easily enough to get him thinking about ways to avoid paying her. From his point of view, he had no way of knowing that he could trust her not to keep coming back again and again. He'd pay her the ten, then a year or two later, if what she had on him was really such a threat, she could pop up wanting another ten. And on and on, until she'd bled him dry. Once she'd tasted the money, she might never go away.

There was only one way to eliminate the threat properly and permanently. The logic was chilling, but Ben saw that it was the only answer to Cleaver's dilemma. Zoë's life was worth a lot less than ten million dollars.

That left Skid McClusky. From Cleaver's point of view, the lawyer was just another loose end needing to be tied up. The first attempt had failed, but sooner or later Cleaver would get him, and McClusky knew it. He wasn't going to stop until he'd silenced anyone who might know anything about this. First Nikos Karapiperis, then Charlie.

Now him. It all suddenly made very clear sense. If Ben didn't go after Cleaver and put an end to this, Cleaver might very well put an end to him. A hundred million buys a lot of hit men, and there would be no way to anticipate when and where one might turn up.

As he sat and worked his way through the minibar and his cigarettes, his thoughts turned to Tom and Jane Bradbury. How was he going to tell them that their daughter was almost certainly dead?

Then he shoved that thought behind him. He could worry about it later.

For now, there was just one objective. Get Clayton Cleaver.

The next day dawned in a blaze of sunshine. Ben waited until just after nine, then called the number Skid McClusky had given him for Augusta Vale. A grave, solemn man's voice answered with "The Vale residence." Ben explained that he was a close friend of the Bradbury family, just happened to be passing through Savannah, and was hoping to pay Miss Vale a visit. In an even graver voice the man told him to hold on.

When Miss Vale came on the phone, Ben liked her immediately. She sounded like a strong, confident old lady. Her tone was formal, but there was a glowing warmth to it. She told him how delighted she was to hear from a friend of the Bradburys. Why didn't he come over for coffee? She had some affairs to attend to, but she'd be free after eleven.

Ben used the spare time to explore the old town and buy some clothes. He went for smart, casual, and simple—crisp black jeans, white shirt, black jacket. Then he went back to the hotel, and drove the Chrysler to the Vale residence in the Squares.

It was more than a house. The towering white mansion stood away from the street, surrounded by verdant gardens filled with flowers and trees. He walked up to the front door and was met by the solemn, deep-voiced man he'd spoken to on the phone. The butler ushered him inside the house, into a wide entrance hall with a checkered marble floor and gilt-framed paintings on the walls.

"May I take your bag, sir?" the butler asked.

"I'll hold on to it, if that's OK," Ben said.

A grandfather clock chimed eleven as the butler led the way to the drawing room. He knocked, pushed open a set of polished walnut doors, and announced, "Mr. Hope to see you, ma'am."

Miss Augusta Vale stood up and walked across the room towards Ben, smiling. She was tall, upright, and very elegant, maybe seventy-five years old but radiantly beautiful. Her skin and teeth were perfect and her hair was more platinum than gray. She was wearing a string of pearls over a silk blouse and a black tailored skirt. She offered her hand, and a diamond glittered in the sunlight that streamed through the bay windows.

"So pleased to meet you, Mr. Hope."

"Please call me Ben."

"Ben. Is that short for Benjamin?"

"Benedict," he said. "But everyone calls me Ben."

"But Benedict is such a very fine name," she replied firmly, as though deciding that that was what she was going to call him.

She invited him to sit down and asked the butler to bring coffee and cake. She lowered herself daintily into what looked like a Louis XIV settee. Underneath it, a small Pekingese dog eyed Ben suspiciously and growled quietly.

"You have a beautiful home," Ben said.

"Thank you. It's been in the family since before the Civil War." She smiled. "So you're a friend of the Bradbury family," she said, watching him closely.

He nodded. "Tom and Jane send their regards."

"Lovely people," she said. "And Oxford is a fine city. I mean to visit there again in August, for the summer school."

"I gather you have a great passion for archaeology."

"Indeed I have," she said. "That's how I met Zoë. Such a talented young lady. Very intelligent. A little headstrong, perhaps. And rather wild too."

"That's what people say."

"Have you seen her lately?"

"The last time I saw her, she was about this big." Ben held his hand three feet off the floor.

She smiled. "So you're not one of her young bucks, then."

"No, I'm not one of her young bucks."

She didn't reply to that, but he thought he could see a look of relief and approval in her eye. "What do you do, Benedict?" she asked sweetly.

"Ben. I'm a student. In fact I'm Tom Bradbury's student at Oxford."

"My, that's wonderful. You're a theologian."

"I was planning to be."

"Then you should really be using that beautiful name of yours. You know what it means, don't you?"

He said nothing.

"It means 'blessed,'" she said.

"I think I'm more cursed than blessed."

She held his earnest gaze for a second, then laughed. "You shouldn't say things like that. Tell me, Benedict. Where are you staying?"

He told her the name of his hotel, and she shook her head and clicked her tongue. "I won't have it," she said. "You must come and be my guest here."

"I don't want to put you to any trouble."

"You won't. You can have the old carriage house. It's a special guest quarters adjoining the house. You'll be no trouble to me, and I'll be no trouble to you."

"It's very kind of you," he said.

"Not at all. I'll have one of the staff collect your luggage from the hotel."

He pointed to his canvas bag. "This is it."

Miss Vale laughed. "You certainly like to travel light, Benedict. And of course, you'll have dinner with us tonight."

"Us?"

"With myself and Clayton. He is a regular visitor to the house."

"Would that be Clayton Cleaver?"

"Why, you've heard of him?"

"Who hasn't?" he said.

"Then you must be familiar with his book," she said.

"I'm afraid I haven't had the pleasure of reading it yet."

"Then I'll give you a copy right away." She rang a little bell, and a handsome black woman came into the room. Miss Vale smiled at her. "Benedict, this is my housekeeper, Mae." She turned to Mae. "Could you have one of the girls fetch down a copy of Mr. Cleaver's book from the library?"

"Right away, Miss Vale." Mae nodded and left briskly.

Augusta Vale's eyes sparkled. "You must read it," she said to Ben. "It changed my life. You know, Clayton personally received divine illumination from the eternal spirit of Saint John the Apostle."

"It sounds like quite a book," Ben said.

After a few moments a maid entered the room with a large hardback book in her hands. She handed it solemnly to Miss Vale. The old lady dismissed her with a kindly smile. She turned the book lovingly in her hands, and then passed it to Ben.

He thanked her and laid it in his lap. The heavily embossed gold script on the cover read, *John Spoke to Me*, by Clayton R. Cleaver.

"Clayton distributes it free to all the poor and underprivileged families," Miss Vale said, glowing. "He is truly a wonderful man."

Ben opened the cover. Inside was a foreword by the author. He scanned it quickly.

Ten years ago, I completed the manuscript of this book in a moment of Divine revelation and sent copies to every publisher in the United States. Not one of them wanted to publish it. But I already knew they wouldn't, because that is what John told me. He told me to persist. That this book had to get out there. I sold my car. I sold my house. I sold everything I had. I lived in a trailer and invested every cent to set up my own publishing company and bring this book, dear reader, into your hands.

John was right in every word He said. The book was so successful that within the year I had every major U.S. publisher begging me for the rights. To date, the Word of John has gone out to more than twelve million Americans . . .

"So what do you think, Benedict?" the old lady asked.

"It certainly looks interesting," Ben said.

"Take it," she said instantly. "I have many copies."

"That's very kind, Miss Vale. I look forward to reading it very much. I'm looking forward to meeting the author too."

She beamed at him. "I believe this must have been meant to happen. I just know you and Clayton will get along."

Mae showed Ben to the carriage house. The guest quarters were situated at the back of the mansion, on the ground floor. It was a substantial apartment in its own right, with two bedrooms, a kitchen, a bathroom, a living room, and even its own dining room. The furnishings were exquisite. Ben tossed his bag onto the four-poster bed and walked back to the living room. French windows looked out over a magnificent subtropical garden filled with palm trees and Spanish moss, and roses of every color imaginable.

Looking around him at his elegant surroundings and thinking of his amiable, obviously very generous and charming hostess, he couldn't help but wonder what she was doing with a thug like Clayton Cleaver.

He wondered what kind of man Cleaver must be. He looked at his watch. In a few hours he'd find out.

26.

Far away, Zoë Bradbury was sitting up in her bed, her hands folded limply in her lap, gazing into the middle distance. At the bedside, sitting in a plastic chair, the doctor was making notes on his pad. It was just the two of them. As always, his questions were soft and gentle.

"That's a very nice bracelet you're wearing, Zoë. Is it real gold?"

She held out her right arm and stared at the shiny link bracelet as though she'd never seen it before. "I suppose so," she muttered suspiciously. She knew that every line of questioning, however indirect and subtle, was a probe searching for a way inside her head. Part of her wanted to scream and run, to fight it until she dropped, to hate this man. But there was a soft look in the doctor's eye that was genuine, and some part of her very much wanted to trust him, reach out to him. It was an inner conflict she was finding hard to resolve. She was a prisoner; she was kidnapped; yet this man seemed sincerely to want to help her.

"It looks antique," the doctor said. "Where did you get it?"

"I don't remember where it came from. I don't know how long it's been there."

"Maybe it was a gift from someone close," the doctor suggested. "Someone who loves you, like a relative. Tell me about your family."

"I see faces in my mind. I think they're my parents."

He nodded. "That's good progress. Things are starting to come back to you, just like I said they would."

"Will it all come back?"

"What you have is called post-traumatic retrograde amnesia," he said. "The memory loss is usually transient, depending on the severity of the injury. You had a nasty knock on the head. But I've seen a lot worse." He reached into his briefcase and brought out a book. "Now, I have something to show you."

"Where am I?" she asked flatly, ignoring the book. She'd lost count of the number of times she'd asked him that.

He gave his standard reply. "A place where we're going to make you better."

She sensed his discomfort as he said it. "What's going to happen to me?" she asked, looking him in the eye. A tear rolled down her cheek.

He glanced away. "You're going to get your memory back."

"But what about afterwards? If I remember, what next?"

He laid the book gently across the bed. "Let's focus on this, OK?"

She looked at it. It was a book of dog breeds, filled with color pictures. "What's this for?"

"You told me you thought you had a dog back home. Why don't we see if we can find out what kind he is?"

"Why?"

"Because it might help jog other memories. That's how the mind works, by unconscious association. One recalled detail can trigger another. So, if we can find your dog, we might remember his name. Then maybe some related incident will come back to you, like, say, a day at the beach. Before you know it, we might be able to start making all kinds of inroads into areas that are still blanked out. OK?"

"OK," she whispered.

He started patiently flipping the pages, one by one. "Let's see. Does he look like this?" He pointed to a picture of a Labrador.

She frowned. "I don't think he's that big."

"OK, let's look at some small dogs. Here's one. King Charles spaniel. Does he look like this?"

She shook her head. "No."

"What about this one?"

"I don't think so."

He flipped another page.

"Stop," she said. "There."

"This one?" He pointed. "West Highland white terrier."

She recognized the picture. It was the small white dog from her cloudy memory. "That's him. That's my dog."

"Good." He smiled. "We're making really good progress, Zoë."

"Can I go soon?"

"Soon," he said.

"How soon?"

"I can't say yet. It all depends on your recovery."

"What am I supposed to be remembering?" she asked, her voice rising fast. "This isn't therapy. I'm being held against my will. What's so important that I'm being kept prisoner in this place?"

The doctor had no answer to that. "Let's take this one step at a time, OK?"

When the session was over, he left her in her room. As the guard locked the door behind him, the doctor closed his eyes and sighed deeply.

You're a doctor. You're supposed to be helping people. This is all wrong. What the hell did you get mixed up in?

"Jones wants to see you in his office," the guard informed him.

"Later," the doctor said.

"Jones says right now."

The doctor sighed again. His shoulders drooped.

He got there three minutes later. Knocked on the door and walked in. The room was small and square. The walls were plain, the floor bare concrete. Jones's desk was clear apart from a phone and a laptop. Jones was leaning back in his chair, smirking at him.

The doctor found it harder every day to hide his hatred of this man. He would have loved to smash that smirk off his face—but he knew what Jones would do to him. "What did you want to see me about?"

"Got any good news for me?" Jones demanded.

The doctor hesitated. "Not the news you want to hear, certainly."

Jones grunted. "I didn't think so. I wouldn't say this so-called therapy of yours is getting us anywhere, would you?"

"Yes, actually I would. Besides, it's still early days."

"Maybe you don't realize what's going on here, Dr. Greenberg. We're on the clock with this."

"You can't just click your fingers and make severe retrograde amnesia disappear overnight. Her GOAT results are improving steadily."

"What the hell is a goat?" Jones snapped.

"Galveston Orientation and Amnesia Test," the doctor said, trying to preserve his calm.

"Don't bullshit me with medical jargon. She's lying."

"You saw the polygraph result."

"The lie detector isn't reliable. You know that as well as I do."

"Listen to me," the doctor hissed. "We're close. Really close. A few more days, a week. Maybe two, and it's my guess that her memory will come back completely."

Jones shook his head. "Why is it I get the feeling that you're stalling me?"

"I'm not stalling."

"Yes you are. Buying her time. You sympathize with the bitch. Let me tell you something. You're not paid to sympathize. You're paid to get results, and you ain't getting them. I've given you all the leeway I'm prepared to give. We even redecorated the whole goddamn upper floor so we could move her to a nice little room, because you said the gentle approach would help. But I've had it with gentle."

The doctor looked down at his feet and balled his fists at his sides. "So what are you suggesting we do?"

"Apply more pressure. There are ways."

"What kind of pressure?"

Jones shrugged. "Whatever works. I don't give a shit."

"You're talking about torture."

Jones shrugged again. "Like I said, whatever gets the job done."

The doctor stared. "You've got to be kidding."

Jones said nothing. His eyes were steady and cold.

"You apply any kind of severe stress to her, and all you'll do is drive the memories deeper," the doctor said. "She'll regress dramatically. And I won't have anything to do with torture. That isn't what you hired me for."

"You'll do what I tell you to do," Jones said. "And this is where we're going to start." He grabbed a sheet of paper from his desk and brusquely handed it across.

The doctor scanned it quickly. There was just one name scrawled on the sheet. It was the name of a chemical. He looked up in alarm. "You can't give that to her. You're not authorized to use it. It's experimental. And illegal."

"I can give anything I want to her," Jones said softly. "Now tell me. This shit goes a lot deeper than Sodium Pentothal, right?"

"I'm not happy with this."

"Like I give a fuck. Answer the question."

"It's designed to repress higher cortical functions and remove all inhibitions," the doctor muttered. "In theory, potentially, it's the most powerful truth serum ever developed. But—"

"That's what I heard too."

"The only people who ever used this drug are terrorists and mass murderers," the doctor said. "This is America, not Sierra Leone."

Jones just smiled, showing yellow teeth.

"You've heard about the side effects?"

Jones didn't answer.

"Ninety-five-plus percent chance of complete, irreversible psychosis. Those are the stories, and there are lab results on chimps to confirm it. That's what you want to do to this girl? Fry her brain down to the size of a peanut so she has to spend the rest of her life in a mental hospital?"

Jones nodded slowly. "If I can get what I need from her first, yes."

"Just so you can get this information from her. You're willing to make that trade?"

"Absolutely. This matters a great deal to the people I work for."

"Then you can find someone else to help you. I won't be party to this."

"Think you have a choice, Greenberg?"

"I don't answer to you." The doctor turned to go. But the metallic sound of the gun being cocked behind him stopped him in his tracks. He turned back to face Jones.

The man was aiming a pistol right at his head. In his other hand he was holding a phone. "You're going to make a call, doc. You're going to get me some of that serum. And then you're going to administer it to our little patient in there, and we'll see who's right."

The doctor hung his head. He was powerless here. They had him. "All right. I have a contact. But I can't just write out a prescription for this stuff. It might take a few days."

"Too slow," Jones said. "My employer isn't a patient man." He checked his watch. "You get it for me by tonight."

"Tonight!"

"Fail me, and you'll watch me torture the girl before I put a bullet in your eye," Jones said. "Your choice."

27.

en spent the afternoon in Augusta Vale's luxurious guest quarters, sitting on the four-poster bed and poring over Cleaver's book.

The book was two things. First, it was an account of how the humble preacher from Alabama had become the mouthpiece of John the Apostle after the saint had appeared to him years before in a miracle vision. Much of the text was devoted to persuading the reader of the truth of this, which the author did in fine style. Ben noticed that the last page of the book was a detachable slip for readers to mail their donations to the Cleaver Foundation, part of whose function was to raise funds for the author's political ambitions.

Second, the book was a scalding doomsday forecast based squarely on the book of Revelation, the apocalyptic text of the New Testament and the key biblical reference for millions of evangelical Christians, predominantly Americans, who believed in the coming End Times.

Cleaver certainly knew his Bible. His style was pounding, insistent, articulate, and utterly sincere. His book went into enormous detail about what was coming, any time now, all closely referenced from the book of Revelation: global meltdown, the destruction of social order, and the rise of the Antichrist, soon followed by the battle of Armageddon, when the returning Christ would vanquish his enemies forever and lead the faithful into eternal glory.

Ben noticed that, like most evangelical Christians, Cleaver assumed without question that all the "John" books of the Bible were the work of one man, John the Apostle—Christ's loyal follower, "the disciple Jesus loved," present at the crucifixion and the first to believe that Christ had truly risen. The traditional account, reflected in Cleaver's book, was that after the crucifixion John had traveled widely, preaching the Gospel. Then, seized by the Romans and thrown in boiling oil, he had miraculously escaped without so much as a blister. After the embarrassing miracle, the Roman authorities had banished him to the remote Greek island of Patmos, off the Turkish coast. There he had penned his strangest and darkest work, the doom-laden book of Revelation, in which he set out his vision of the future—a book so dramatic and thunderous in its terrible imagery that, millennia later, it remained more strongly imprinted on the public consciousness than ever.

The rest was Cleaver's unique twist on the tale, explaining how Saint John had personally appeared to him and confirmed in no uncertain terms that the End Times were truly coming and that the faithful must rally. Things were about to get nasty.

But Ben wondered how deeply Cleaver had looked into the theological studies surrounding Revelation. Many modern scholars didn't agree that the authors of the Gospel of Saint John and the book of Revelation were the same man. They distinguished between at least three different biblical Johns: John the Evangelist, John the Presbyter, and John of Patmos. John of Patmos, most agreed, was the author of the apocalyptic book. But was he the same John who had been numbered among Christ's twelve apostles? The blood and violence of Revelation, contrasted with the milder and more philosophic Gospel of Saint John, seemed like the work of a different writer.

Theories abounded. Some scholars were more moderate, suggesting that Saint John might have been the author of Revelation but written it under the influence of hallucinogens. Others were more hard-line, pointing out that this John of Patmos could be just about anybody; in which case Revelation might have no legitimate claim to be included in the New Testament at all and should possibly be scrapped. But the frustrating lack of proof either way prevented the issue from being settled once and for all.

Meanwhile, as Ben could see from Cleaver's book, core evangelical belief remained untouched by the raging debates within academic theology circles. As far as the Georgia preacher was concerned, his direct line to Saint John was all the proof anyone needed that this generation was living in the Last Days.

And somehow, this all had something to do with what had happened to Zoë Bradbury. Whatever hold it was she had over Clayton Cleaver, it involved Bible prophecy.

But how?

Ben thought about it for hours. He was still thinking about it as seven o'clock approached and it was time for dinner with Miss Vale and the man himself.

28.

Ben left the carriage house and wandered over to the main residence. Mae greeted him with a smile, and chatted warmly as she led him into the grand hallway. He could hear Miss Vale's voice, and a man's, coming from the drawing room. He was shown inside. Miss Vale's visitor stood up and strode over to meet him.

He was a man in his mid-fifties wearing a well-tailored light-gray suit that looked Italian. He obviously played squash or tennis and was in good shape, with only a little spare padding around the middle and under his chin. He was about Ben's height, just a little under six feet. His hair was thick and dark, swept back from his brow, maybe tinted to hide the gray. He approached Ben with a broad smile and an outstretched hand.

Miss Vale said, "Clayton, this is the young man I was telling you about." She gestured towards Cleaver with a glow in her eyes. "Benedict, it's my great pleasure to introduce you to my dear friend Clayton Cleaver. Or should I say Governor Cleaver?"

Cleaver flashed a white grin at her. "God willing, Augusta. God willing. But we're not there yet."

"With ninety percent of Georgia behind you," she said, "you soon will be."

Cleaver seized and shook Ben's hand in a dry and powerful fist, greeting him like a long-lost brother. "It is a true pleasure to meet you, Benedict," he said with absolute sincerity. "May I call you Benedict?"

"I've been looking forward to meeting you too, Mr. Cleaver."

"Please. Call me Clayton. Augusta tells me you're a believer. That's just wonderful. Just wonderful."

The maid came in with a tray of canapés and martini cocktails. They made small talk for a while, chatting about the difference between English and Georgian weather; the things Ben really had to see while he was staying in Savannah; what it was like to study theology at Oxford.

"Final year, I guess you would have branched out a little," Cleaver said. "Do you have a specialized interest, Benedict?"

"Actually, I do." Ben sipped his drink. "My special subject for my final year dissertation is Bible prophecy."

Miss Vale and Cleaver exchanged knowing, approving glances. "I just knew this was meant to happen," the old lady said. "You couldn't be in better company, Benedict. Did you get a chance—"

"To read Clayton's book?" Ben filled in. "I've been reading it this afternoon. I couldn't put it down."

"Why, thank you, son. I can sign that copy for you, if you'd like."

"That would be an honor."

The butler came solemnly into the room and announced that dinner was served. Ben followed Miss Vale and Clayton into a spectacular dining room. The table was more than fifteen feet long and glittering with silverware beneath a crystal chandelier. Miss Vale sat at the head of the table. Ben was shown to a seat on her right, as guest of honor, and Cleaver sat opposite him. The maid lifted the lid of a silver dish in the center of the table.

"The smoked salmon is from Miss Vale's own fishery," Cleaver said. "It's the best in all of the South."

They drank champagne and ate. Cleaver looked completely at home.

"So, Benedict. We were talking about Bible prophecy . . ."

"Ask him anything you like," Miss Vale urged Ben. "Nobody knows the Bible like Clayton."

"For a young Bible student, you couldn't be living at a more exciting moment of our history," Cleaver said. "The time isn't nigh. It's now."

"I noticed that in your book, you were very insistent that the great apocalyptic prophecies of the Bible are about to come true."

"You've read it, Benedict," Cleaver replied. "You know it's going to happen."

"I know about the various interpretations that scripture scholars have made," Ben said. "For instance, some theologians say that the book of Revelation isn't a legitimate part of the New Testament."

Cleaver reddened. "Interpretations my ass." He glanced at Miss Vale. "Excuse my language, Augusta, but I'm sick of hearing about these scholars. The way I see it, these fellows are walking around with their eyes shut." He clenched his fist against the table. "Look around you at the signs, Benedict. Governments, the rule of law, economies, cultures, our whole world system is just about ready to collapse. Total chaos and destruction are right around the corner. Exactly as the Good Book tells us." He wagged his finger for emphasis. "All the signs are there. Time to get ready and accept our Lord Jesus Christ into your heart, because we are standing right now on the brink of the End Times. And all these scholars can do is chase their own tails talking about interpretations? How do you interpret the literal word of God? What's wrong with just opening our ears to what He's telling us?" Cleaver paused for a sip of champagne.

The performance was beautifully polished. Cleaver was a fabulous showman, winding himself up into full-on televangelist mode, and it was all for Miss Vale. Ben could see from the rapt look on her face that she was completely captivated by this man. As far as she was concerned, he was worth every penny of her hundred million dollars. He wondered whether Cleaver had had his big payday yet. He might have, judging by his absolute confidence and composure.

"You know, Benedict," Cleaver went on, "a poll in 2002 showed that sixty percent of Americans believe the prophecies of John in the book of Revelation will come true. Twenty percent—that's fifty million Americans I'm talking about—believe it will happen during their lifetime. That's anytime now. We could walk out of here this very minute, turn on the TV, and see that the events have already started rolling right before us." Cleaver's eyes were locked hard on Ben's. He stabbed his finger on the tabletop. Then he smiled. "Notice anything strange last spring, Benedict?"

"All the plants came out too early."

"You got it. Not just in England. It's happening here too. Weather systems are shot to hell. The seasons aren't seasons anymore. Earthquakes and great floods in places that never had them before. They call it global warming. I call it a global warning. And you know what, it's all right there in John's book of Revelation. Disasters that level cities. The sun heating up so much, everyone is scorched."

"Don't forget the giant hailstones," Ben said. "*And there fell upon men a great hail out of heaven, every stone about the weight of a talent.*'"

"You know your Bible. That's about seventy-five pounds," Cleaver said. "Then there are the plagues. Well, Benedict, I hardly need to remind you about the superbugs that threaten us all, the rise of other diseases like the avian flu and untreatable new strains of tuberculosis." He waved his hands in the air expansively. "Then you open up *New Scientist* magazine and what do you see? Plagues of African locusts in the south of France. Just like the Bible says. And who knows what else is just around the corner?" Cleaver thumped on the table with a flourish. "I'll tell you who knows. John knows. And he tells me everything."

"Just to hear it the way Clayton tells it," Miss Vale breathed, "it sends a shiver down my back."

"I wish that was all of it," Cleaver replied. "But in the middle of all this chaos, John already predicted the rise of the one-world government. Satan's one-world government. '*And he causeth all, both small and great, rich and poor, free and bond, to receive a mark in their right hand, or in their foreheads: and that no man might buy or sell, save he that had the mark, or the name of the beast, or the number of his name.*'" Cleaver smiled. "Does that sound familiar, Benedict?"

"'*Here is wisdom,*'" Ben said. "'*Let him that hath understanding count the number of the beast: for it is the number of a man; and his number is six hundred threescore and six.*' Book of Revelation, chapter thirteen, verses sixteen to eighteen."

Cleaver nodded. "You're an educated man. But do you understand what this is telling us? It's already happening. The forces of evil are already getting a grip on us. A one-world currency. They've already started it. Look at your euro over there. Credit cards. You use a credit card, Benedict?"

"No, I don't."

"Smart move. But then there's the barcodes. The number six-six-six is already right there, all around us. And even more insidious technologies to get inside our heads are being developed right now, as we sit here talking." Cleaver helped himself to more food. "Then you have the instability in the Middle East," he went on. "More signs. The Bible already prophesied that God's chosen people of Israel would receive their Promised Land. Now, the reestablishment of the nation of Israel in 1948 is a true sign that we are living in the Last Days. We're witnessing the unfolding of God's plan. And now we're ready for the next phase."

"Which is what?"

"That's one your Bible scholars are missing. You have to dig a little deeper for it. It'll happen in Israel. Israel is the linchpin of Bible prophecy; it's the center where the whole thing will play out. So what's going to actually happen, and my guess is it will happen before too many more years go by, is that there'll be a major military strike against the sacred nation of Israel. I'm not talking potshots across the West Bank, suicide bombers, and petty diplomatic upsets. I'm talking full-blown nuclear conflagration."

"How do you figure that?"

"'And thou shalt come up against my people of Israel, as a cloud to cover the land; it shall be in the latter days.'" Cleaver smiled grimly. "The perpetrator of the attack is Gog. The ancient kingdom of Magog, right there in Persia. What nowadays we call Iran. Those are the guys who will launch their missiles at Israel. That's what's going to really set things in motion, big time."

"You really believe that's what the Bible is saying?" Ben asked. "That the Muslim nations will declare war on the Jews?"

"There's no doubt about it whatsoever," Cleaver said. "And the results will be profound. The Islamic attack on Israel is what will precipitate the world into the events prophesied by the book of Revelation."

"You would consider the destruction of Israel to be part of God's plan?"

"God won't let Israel be destroyed," Cleaver said. "They can fire all the missiles they like when the time comes, but they won't harm a blade of grass. *And it shall come to pass at the same time when Gog shall come against the land of Israel, saith the Lord God, that my fury shall come up in my face.'* See? God will step in and protect Israel, and its enemies will be destroyed."

Ben smiled and didn't reply.

"Now things really start rolling," Cleaver said, undeterred. "In the aftermath of this terrible war, the world will reach a peace agreement, probably brokered by a European leader. Someone of great charm and charisma, who claims to be a friend of the people."

"You're talking about the Antichrist."

Cleaver nodded. "The rider on the white horse. Revelation, chapter six. He who comes to conquer, to wreak destruction and fire upon the earth and enslave us all. The son of Satan himself. And, I'm sorry to say it, but I think he might be an Englishman. No offense."

"None taken," Ben said. "And I think I know who he is."

Cleaver gave a chuckle.

Miss Vale frowned. "These things aren't to be taken lightly, boys."

"You're right, Augusta," Cleaver said. "Because then it gets pretty dark. The powers of the Antichrist will take control of the world. No pretending anymore, right? They'll just step in and take over. Anyone who protests will be slain. That's the start of the great Tribulation. John tells us all about it in the book of Revelation. Hail and fire and the destruction of the earth's vegetation. The sea will turn to blood. Poisonous locusts. Mass torture. Billions of people killed most horribly. The faithful will be hideously persecuted as the Antichrist strives to gain complete dominion. Seven years of the most terrible, terrible suffering. It'll make the Nazi holocaust look like a walk in the park."

"'*Then there will be a time of anguish greater than any since nations first came into existence,*'" Ben said.

Cleaver nodded gravely and glanced at Miss Vale, who was gazing down at her plate with a look of distress glazed in her eyes. "But not

THE HOPE VENDETTA | 149

for everyone," he said gently. "We can console ourselves that the Bible tells us that at some point during this time of Tribulation, the faithful will be delivered from pain and torture."

"The Rapture," Ben said. "'For the Lord himself shall descend from heaven with a shout, with the voice of the archangel, and with the trump of God: and the dead in Christ shall rise first: Then we which are alive and remain shall be caught up together with them in the clouds, to meet the Lord in the air: and so shall we ever be with the Lord.'"

"Amen," Miss Vale whispered.

Cleaver smiled at Ben. "I'm glad you've taken our Lord Jesus Christ into your heart, Benedict. It would pain me to think of you being left behind. Nobody's getting out of the Tribulation alive."

"Then after the seven years are over, Christ returns to confront his enemy at the battle of Armageddon," Ben said.

"That's exactly right," Cleaver replied. "And then begins the golden period for all the Christians who held on to their faith through the dark times. They shall be richly rewarded."

After dinner, they retired back to the drawing room, where a decanter of brandy and crystal glasses were set out on a tray. Miss Vale excused herself for a moment and left the room.

"This has been a very interesting discussion, Clayton," Ben said, settling into an armchair with his glass of brandy. "But there's something else I wanted to talk to you about."

Cleaver spread his arms. "Fire away, son."

"In fact, there's *someone* I wanted to talk to you about."

"Is that a fact? And who might that be?"

"That might be one Zoë Bradbury." Ben watched Cleaver's face and let the words sink in.

Cleaver tried hard not to let his composure slip too far. "Uh-huh?" He gulped a little.

"You know who I'm talking about," Ben said.

"I know of her," Cleaver said coolly, glancing at his fingernails. "She's a friend of Augusta's, I believe."

"And no friend of yours, apparently."

Cleaver looked hard at Ben. "What exactly do you mean by that?"

"I mean the twenty-five grand she got from you, and the ten million she wanted."

Cleaver was quiet for a beat. "You know about that?"

"And about Skid McClusky. I thought you might like to fill me in on some details I'm missing."

"Just who exactly the hell are you, mister?"

"Someone looking for answers. Someone who's going to get them."

Cleaver toyed with his drink. His face had paled noticeably. "I think, uh, Benedict, this strikes me as the kind of topic that we ought to discuss elsewhere. In private."

"That's fine with me," Ben said. "I'm sure you wouldn't want Miss Vale hearing too much. That's a sizeable investment you have there."

Cleaver said nothing.

"But don't think you can get away from me," Ben continued. "You're going to talk to me."

The old lady came back in, followed by a maid carrying a silver tray with a coffee jug and three delicate white porcelain cups on little saucers. She smiled. "I've been thinking," she announced as she sat down. "I wondered whether our new friend would like to attend the tournament tomorrow."

Cleaver laughed nervously. "Augusta, I think that wouldn't be Benedict's cup of tea. Him being English and all."

Miss Vale blinked. "They don't shoot rifles in England?" She frowned at Cleaver. "Clayton, are you all right? You look as if you've seen a ghost."

"I'm just fine, thank you," Cleaver said. "Maybe I overate a little."

"What kind of tournament?" Ben asked.

Cleaver was fighting hard to stay natural in front of Miss Vale. "It's just a little event I hold out at my place once a year," he said in a strangled voice. "But—"

Miss Vale chuckled. "A little event? Clayton's being modest. All the best rifle shooters from across Georgia, Alabama, and Mississippi take part. Twenty bucks a ticket, and we're expecting over two thousand people."

"All strictly for charity, of course," Cleaver interjected, trying to smile.

"Of course," Ben said, staring at him.

"And this year all proceeds will be going to the Vale Trust Charity Hospital. That's one of the many projects that my charity supports," Miss Vale explained, seeing Ben's quizzical look. "We help the poor and underprivileged families in Georgia and Alabama who can't afford health insurance." She smiled sadly. "Last summer we opened a new wing to provide free treatment for child cancer patients. They do such good work there that I really want to expand it. So for this year's tournament I've organized a special sponsorship initiative that I'm hoping will raise a lot of dollars to allow us to help the needy."

"Sounds like wonderful work, Miss Vale," Ben said, not taking his eyes off Cleaver.

"You must come along," she replied. "It'll be a great day."

Cleaver reddened and cleared his throat. "But, like I said, Augusta, maybe it's not something Benedict would—"

"I'd love to," Ben said.

29.

The good Reverend Cleaver's place lay ten miles to the west of Savannah. As the morning wore on, away from the Georgia coast the atmosphere was even more humid and stifling. The land was flat and beautiful, with oak woodlands stretching off the highway as far as the eye could see in every direction.

The signs for the shooting tournament led Ben off the main road and two miles down a private drive. Other cars were heading the same way, and as he rounded a bend he came into a large field filled with hundreds of vehicles. He found a parking space and climbed out into the baking sun, slinging his bag over his shoulder.

Miss Vale had gone off early that morning in her chauffeur-driven limo, positively sparkling with excitement to get started with the organizing for her special charity event. She'd been so caught up with phone calls and last-minute details that Ben hadn't had the chance to ask her more about the sponsorship initiative she'd mentioned. He looked around the parking field and spotted her stately white Lincoln Continental in the far corner.

Cleaver's land must stretch for miles, he thought. This field alone was at least four acres. The crowds of spectators were wandering into an adjoining field several times larger, where scores of stalls and tents had been set up and at least a couple of thousand people were milling around, eating and drinking, talking and laughing in the sun. Clearly this was a fun family event, judging by the number of women and children present.

It was a big media event too, with TV trucks parked up near the entrance to the main field, cameras and journalists everywhere. The center of the field was dominated by a large tent that bore a sign for the Augusta Vale Trust. Nearby, hot-food vendors were dishing out paper plates stacked with fried chicken, buttery corn on the cob, burgers and fries. At a National Rifle Association stall, people were handing out leaflets on gun safety. Others were selling guns, ammunition, books and magazines, ear defenders, hunting gear, and a wider range of shooting accessories than Ben had ever seen in one place before.

He walked over to the fence and shielded his eyes as he scanned the shooting range itself. It was an impressive setup: a vast cleared space among the trees stretching far away into the distance, with targets set up at marked ranges of 100, 500, and 1,000 yards. In the distance, a massive ridge of earth had been bulldozed up to create a safe backstop, preventing stray shots from landing somewhere in the next state. A cordoned area had been set aside for spectators to watch the shooting, while the shooters' firing point was well equipped with mats and rifle rests. Clustered around the main range, smaller events were going on. There was even a kids' range, where NRA instructors were showing children the basics of shooting and safety with small-caliber junior weapons.

From the competition schedule nailed to a post near the adjudicator's hut, Ben saw that the small-bore competitions had already been shot that morning. Names of the winners were posted on a blackboard nearby. The main event of the day, though, and what most of the crowd had come to watch, was the open-class full-bore rifle shoot. Already, a lot of the big-bore rifle shooters were assembling on the firing point, opening up kit boxes, and preparing their equipment.

But the shooting competition held no interest for Ben. He was here to catch hold of Clayton Cleaver, take him somewhere private, and press some truth out of him.

He'd pretty much planned his strategy. He liked simple plans, and this one was very simple indeed. If Cleaver didn't confess right away, he was going to beat out of him what had happened to Zoë and where she was. If she was dead or alive, either way, Cleaver's fate was sealed. There was Charlie to pay for. Once Ben no longer needed him, he was going to take Cleaver to a quiet spot somewhere and blow his brains out. Leave him where he lay. Then home, and try to pick up where he'd left off.

He wondered where Cleaver was. He could see the house in the distance, a large neoclassical mansion with columns and porches, white and glimmering through the trees. His fists clenched with rage, and for an instant he felt the urge to walk straight over there and find him.

Then he spotted him. *Of course.* He should have expected that the man wouldn't be far from the crowd and the cameras. Cleaver was in the middle of the throng clustered around the Augusta Vale Trust tent, surrounded by press photographers, shaking as many hands as he could, the big, broad smile never leaving his face. Miss Vale was there too, looking elegant and gracious as she attended to all the people around her and delegated tasks to her assistants. As Ben approached, she caught sight of him and waved. He smiled and waved back.

As he came closer, he saw Cleaver's eyes shoot him a glance. Suddenly the Reverend seemed to have a pressing engagement elsewhere. He melted away into the crowd.

"Catch you later," Ben muttered under his breath.

Miss Vale took his arm as he joined her. "Isn't this just wonderful? Look at all the people." She beamed up at him. "There's someone I want you to meet." She turned to two of her assistants nearby, a thickset woman with ginger hair talking to a petite and very attractive Japanese girl in her early twenties.

"Harriet, where's young Carl?" Miss Vale asked anxiously. "It's quarter to twelve. It starts in fifteen minutes."

"I think he just arrived," the ginger-haired woman said.

"He's cutting it a little fine. I shall have to scold him."

The Japanese girl caught Ben's eye and smiled at him.

"Let's go meet him," Miss Vale said.

They started walking towards the parking field. Harriet and the old lady were deep in conversation. Ben followed behind, and the Japanese girl walked with him.

"I'm Maggie," she said. "Pleased to meet you."

"Ben," he said. "You work for the Vale Trust?"

She nodded. "Miss Vale has been telling us all about you," she said.

"Really? So who's this Carl we're going to meet?"

"One of Miss Vale's protégés," Maggie replied. "The Trust puts a lot of young kids from underprivileged backgrounds through college. The aim is to support and empower them. Carl Rivers is only nineteen, but he's already a champion rifle marksman. The Trust has been paying for his training, and we're hoping that one day he'll represent the U.S.A. in the Olympics."

"Impressive," Ben said.

"Miss Vale has organized a special sponsorship event for this year's match," Maggie said. "She's put a hundred thousand dollars of her own money in the pot, and she's persuaded a whole lot of wealthy folks to back Carl too. He's up against pro shooters from five states, but we're hopeful. If he wins the full-bore rifle class, we'll have raised about half a million for the hospital. It's really important."

"Miss Vale told me about the children's wing," he said.

Maggie nodded. "So sad."

They reached the parking field. Away from the rest of the cars was a section cordoned off closer to the ranges, for competitors only.

"That's him over there," Maggie said, pointing.

Ben looked. A young black kid was standing next to a badly beaten-up old Pontiac. He had a friend with him, a gangly, gawky-looking white teenager with jeans ripped at the knees and thick glasses that magnified his eyes so much they almost filled the lenses. The friend was unloading a long black rifle case from the back of the car.

"I don't suppose Carl Rivers is the one with the glasses," Ben said.

Maggie laughed. "No, that's Andy; I don't think he'd be much of a shot."

Carl was in the middle of an animated discussion with his gawky-looking friend and hadn't seen them approaching. He was leaning with his right hand against the side of the car as Andy laid the rifle case down on the grass. Whatever they were joking about, Carl suddenly threw his head back and burst out laughing. Andy was laughing too, his big eyes creased up with mirth behind the glasses. Then he reached up quickly and slammed the car trunk shut. Right on Carl's fingers.

Carl's laughter suddenly became a scream. He thrust his injured hand between his legs, hopping around in a circle.

Miss Vale went rushing over to him. "Dear child, let me take a look."

"Shit, what happened?" Maggie said in alarm.

Carl was obviously in a lot of pain. Ben examined the damage. The first three fingers of his right hand were mashed and bleeding.

"Can you flex them?" Ben asked.

Carl tried, and whimpered.

"Could be broken," Ben said.

"There's a first-aid tent not far away," Miss Vale said, shooting a look at Andy, who was standing to one side, biting his lip in distress. "They can take a look at it, but I think you need to get this seen to by a doctor."

"She's right," Ben said.

"Yeah, but I'm supposed to be shooting here today," Carl protested.

Just as he said it, there was an announcement over the loudspeakers that the full-bore rifle event would be starting shortly, and would the competitors please make their way to the firing line.

They walked him quickly to the first-aid tent, where a nurse examined the fingers as best she could, bandaged him up, and told him he needed to get to a hospital soon for an X-ray.

"I can't. I've got to shoot," he argued.

"Not with those fingers, you can't," the nurse said, tight-lipped. "Unless you can learn to shoot left-handed, son, you can forget it."

Carl left the first-aid tent almost in tears with pain and frustration, and they headed back towards the car. Andy trailed in their wake, all penitent and full of useless suggestions. Miss Vale was calm, though the disappointment was clear in her eyes. "The important thing is that you get to the hospital and get that seen to."

"But the money," Carl said. "The money for the charity."

"Nothing you can do, child," she said resignedly. "We'll see if we can reorganize it next year."

"Is there nobody else who could shoot in his place?" Harriet asked. "What about Carl's friend?"

"Andy couldn't hit the side of a house at twenty feet," Carl muttered. He kicked a stone in disgust.

The percussive detonations of rifle shots were coming from the direction of the range, as the shooters started warming up and making their last-minute zero adjustments.

"They're starting," Carl groaned.

"Maybe I could help," Ben said.

Carl turned and looked at him.

"You, Benedict?" Miss Vale said in astonishment. "Can you shoot?"

"I've done a little," he replied.

They were nearly back at the Pontiac. The rifle case was still lying on the ground behind the car, and Ben walked over to it.

"The range goes out to a thousand yards," Carl said, nursing his hand, frowning. "Any idea how small a target is at that distance?"

Ben nodded. "Some idea."

"If you want to give it a go, I have no problem with that," Carl said. "You're welcome to use my rifle. But you'd be up against guys like Raymond Higgins. And Billy Lee Johnson from Alabama. He's an ex–marine sniper school instructor. These are world-class shooters. They're gonna walk all over you."

Ben unslung his bag and dropped it on the grass. He squatted down next to the rifle case and flipped the catches. "Let's see what you've got in here," he said.

30.

Ben opened the case and peered down at the scoped rifle inside. "May I?"

"All yours," Carl said.

Ben lifted the weapon out of the foam lining and checked it over. It was a bolt-action Winchester Model 70, chambered in .300 H&H Magnum, an extremely potent caliber that launched its slim, tapered bullet at well over two thousand feet per second. The kind of rifle that, in the hands of a gifted shooter, could reach out to incredible distances. A top-flight instrument, with probably hundreds of hours invested in bringing it as close to perfection as was humanly and mechanically possible. It had a heavy competition-grade barrel. The action was slick, and the scope alone was worth as much as the Chrysler Ben was driving.

He took out a cigarette, clanged open his Zippo, and thumbed the wheel. It had run out of fuel. He swore softly and patted his pockets for the book of matches he remembered taking from the hotel. Finding it, he struck a match and lit up. "Anything I need to know?"

"Trigger's awful light," Carl said. "Watch out for accidental shots."

"What's it zeroed to?"

"Point of aim at three hundred yards," Carl said.

Ben nodded, turning the rifle over in his hands and peering through the scope. He laid it back in the case, opened Carl's ammunition box, and inspected one of the long, tapered cartridges. "You handload your own ammunition?"

Carl nodded. Ben could see in his eyes the love he had for his sport, shining through the pain. Target shooters like Carl devoted a huge amount of time and energy to handcrafting their own match-grade ammunition, selecting the best combination of case, bullet, and powder and putting it all together with extreme precision and attention to detail on the most expensive handloading presses they could afford, striving for the ultimate perfection in performance and accuracy. And it was all so that the shooter could drill a little round hole in a piece of paper. Their whole world was a little black circle on a white background. The closer together they could group those little round holes in the dead center of the circle, the more trophies they could take home.

That was where the huge gulf opened up between the pure target shooter like Carl and those men who were trained to use these rifles on a real target, a human target. Ben had been one of those men, once. He wondered if the young shooter had any idea of the nightmarish destruction a round like this could inflict on a man, when used for that more applied purpose. At a thousand yards, the descending arc of the bullet as it ran out of kinetic energy meant that it would strike its target from above. Aim at a man's forehead from that extended kind of range, and the shot would take him on the crown of his skull and drill downwards through his whole body.

Ben had been a young SAS trooper when he'd first seen the remains of a man shot that way. The Iraqi soldier had been hit in the head by a .50-caliber sniper round at twelve hundred yards. He had been peeled apart, exploded into pieces by the bullet and the hydrostatic shock that followed in its wake. One of his arms had been found nearly a hundred yards away.

The sight of the shattered corpse had haunted Ben a long time. What had haunted him more was that the sniper who had taken that extreme long shot, dug into the dirt on the top of a hill after hours of waiting in absolute stillness, had been him.

Today, the only casualties would be tattered pieces of paper. It made the fearsome weapon seem almost benign.

"You think you can do it, Benedict?" Miss Vale asked, standing over them with a worried expression.

"I can try," he said. "It's been a while since I did any rifle shooting."

"We'll be praying for you. Carl, you need to get to the hospital. Can Andy drive you, or shall I call someone?"

"I'm not leaving here till this is over," Carl said. "I want to watch him."

The match referee's voice announced over a loudspeaker that the full-bore rifle competition was about to start.

"We'd best hurry," Miss Vale said.

Ben tossed away his cigarette, picked up the rifle case and his bag, and headed towards the ranks of competitors. Carl followed, his eyes red with pain, clutching his hand. Miss Vale went to talk to the match referee and within half a minute had persuaded him to let the substitute shooter come in.

There were thirty competitors on the firing line. Ben stepped over the rope cordon and took his place on the line. He dumped his bag on one side of his shooting mat and the rifle case on the other. Opened up the case and lifted out the Winchester. It was too late for sighting-in shots, or to warm up the rifle's bore. A hundred yards away, range officers were taking down the practice targets and putting up fresh ones.

As he slipped on Carl's electronic ear defenders and settled himself into the prone position that his sniper training had instilled in him so long ago, Ben hoped he hadn't taken on more than he could deal with. His heart was beating fast. It had been a long time since he'd taken shots like this. Too long.

He glanced over at the shooter in the next lane. The man had his name stenciled, military-style, on the green metal ammunition box at his side. B. L. Johnson. The ex–marine sniper Carl had mentioned. For a second they made eye contact. Johnson had the look about him that Carl didn't have—the look of a man who hadn't shot only at paper targets. He smiled, not friendly, not aggressive. Just a little, knowing smile. Then he went back to his rifle.

Ben felt his heart begin to race as he peered through the scope at the targets. Only a hundred yards away, but the target face was no bigger than a dinner plate. It was divided up into a series of concentric rings, and at its center was a black circle the size of a saucer. The very middle of the black was a ring that shooters called the "X ring." It was the size of a large coin. The X-ring was worth ten points, the next ring outwards worth nine, the next worth eight, and so on.

The tournament rules were brutally simple. The shooters would engage targets at one hundred, five hundred, and a thousand yards. Ten shots per target, and anything below a ninety score was a disqualifier. It was a tough course of fire. Ben held his breath as he clicked in the magazine and worked the smooth bolt of the Winchester.

Here we go.

The crowd was silent.

Glancing back over his shoulder he saw Carl, Miss Vale, and her assistants huddled at the cordon twenty yards behind the firing line, watching. At the old lady's elbow was Cleaver, staring coldly at him.

The referee gave the command to commence firing.

Ben thumbed off the safety catch. He did a quick ballistic calculation and let the crosshairs hover on a point a few inches low of the center of the target to allow for the three-hundred-yard zero.

To his left, Billy Lee Johnson's rifle boomed, dust flying up off the ground near the muzzle.

Ben controlled his breathing. The sight crosshairs wavered against the target. Up, down, sideways. Sweat ran down his brow and prickled his eyes. He blinked it away.

In his mind, he saw Charlie again. He thought of the bombing victims on Corfu, the maimed and the dead. Thought of Nikos Karapiperis, and Zoë Bradbury, and the torment that her family was going through. Rhonda and the child who would never know its father. All because of the man standing behind him. He could feel Cleaver's presence there, almost touching him.

Different people reacted differently to anger. For some, it was a form of stress that affected their concentration, dulled their thinking, and slowed their reactions. He'd seen it happen many times.

But for him, it was different. He'd always been able to control his rage, to channel it, making the energy work for him instead of against him. It made him focus. He could feel every tiny detail of the texture of the rifle stock in his hands. He peered through the scope. Now the sight picture held rock steady. The target was sharp and clear. In his mind, he was aiming right at Cleaver's head.

He hardly felt the smooth trigger face against the first joint of his finger. The trigger broke and the rifle kicked back hard against his shoulder. He lost the sight picture for a moment, and when he brought the rifle back to aim he saw the little black hole he'd made in the target. The first shot had cut the edge of the X ring.

Looks like you haven't lost it, he thought.

And an hour later, he knew it for sure.

After the first round, seven of the thirty shooters had been eliminated from the competition. There was a twenty-minute break so that the range officers could take down the targets and set up the new ones, four hundred yards farther downrange. They were slightly larger than the first ones, but through the sights they were minute.

Round two began. Ben had imagined that the five-hundred-yard course of fire would have a devastating effect, and it did. When it was over, only nine shooters were left. He was one of them. So was Billy Lee Johnson. Now, when he looked at Ben, the smile was gone.

But Ben wasn't interested in Johnson. He was enjoying the fact that Clayton Cleaver was still there, watching. Ben was giving him a message, as surely as if he was telling him to his face. He wanted Cleaver to fear him, and he knew it was working.

Then the five-hundred-yard targets were taken down, and the survivors settled in for the real test. At a thousand yards, things looked very, very small, even through the magnifying lens of a powerful scope. But it wasn't simply a question of holding the gun steady and pulling the trigger. At such extreme range, there were many other factors involved. The wind could send a bullet's trajectory way off course. It had to be anticipated. So did the parabolic arc of the bullet as it gave way to the forces of the Earth—and from such a range Ben expected it to drop several feet. He had to compensate by aiming high, and that was where the true art of the sniper came into play.

The referee gave the call to fire. Ben worked the bolt and peered through the scope. He could barely see the target. It was such a tiny thing, almost outside the realm of his physical senses but so, so tangible in his mind's eye that it was the center of everything.

Fuck it.

He fired. Bolt back, case ejected, bolt forward, next round chambered.

Fired. The rifle bucked like a live thing in his arms. He worked the bolt again. He was lost in a world of his own, deep in the zone. Nothing existed except him, the target, and the forces trying to prevent him from hitting it. Even the rifle didn't exist—it was just an extension of his mind and body.

In that moment, not even Cleaver existed. He let go. Kept firing until his ten shots were spent. Only then did he look to see how he'd done.

He exhaled deeply. There was only one hole in the target. It was a ragged vent where all ten shots had gone in. A perfect score. His heart jumped. He'd won.

Except he hadn't. The range officers came bouncing back uprange in their golf buggies, and the results were announced to the crowd, amid a lot of cheering. Two shooters had come through the final round. Him and Billy Lee Johnson, neck and neck. It was a tie.

The marine sniper ambled up to congratulate Ben. "Pretty hot shooting, friend. Where'd you learn?"

"The Boys' Brigade," Ben said.

"Tiebreaker, guys," the ref said. "How do you want to settle it?"

Johnson grinned. "Your choice," he said to Ben.

"Whatever I want?"

Johnson nodded. "You call it."

"Let's bring it back a little," Ben said. "One hundred yards. One shot, best man wins."

"One hundred? Are you kidding?"

Ben didn't reply.

"Whatever you say," Johnson said. He rolled his eyes at the ref, who shrugged his shoulders.

They walked out and set up the targets at a hundred yards. "Hold on," Ben said. He kneeled down in the grass to tie his shoelace.

Johnson and the ref turned and headed back towards the firing line. Ben got to his feet and jogged after them to catch up. As he approached the cordon, he could see the eager faces of the spectators all watching him closely. Miss Vale was still there, and there was Cleaver still at her elbow and still staring coldly at him. Ben returned his gaze all the way to the firing point. Cleaver's face turned from white to red. Then he broke eye contact and glanced down at his feet.

They took positions. "You first," Johnson said.

Ben took his time aiming. The sun was hot on the back of his neck. The cicadas were chirping loudly all around, mixing in the warm air with the murmur of anticipation from the crowd.

The trigger broke under his gentle squeeze. The rifle recoiled harshly upwards and back, the image in the scope lost in a blur.

The crowd's murmur grew in volume as everyone searched the target for a bullet hole. At that short range, every mark on the paper could be seen clearly with spotting scopes and binoculars.

"You missed." Johnson was grinning. "Way, way wide."

"Not even on the paper," someone called out from the crowd. There was a general mutter of disappointment.

Ben looked back through the scope and smiled.

"Hold on," said another spotter. "Look down. He weren't aiming no paper target."

Carl had seen it. He slipped under the cordon and walked over to Ben's side. His eyes were wide. "Holy shit," he breathed.

Johnson had seen it too. His face went pale.

In the short grass at the foot of the target, two matches were stuck in the ground a few inches apart. One of them was lit, its pale flame flickering in the breeze.

"He struck the goddamn match," someone yelled.

Carl's mouth was hanging open, speechless.

The mutter of the crowd became an excited buzz. People were staring at him in amazement. "Best shooting I ever saw," the ref said, clapping him on the shoulder. "One in a million. Hell, ten million."

"Impossible," Johnson said. "He lit it when he was over there."

The ref shook his head. "No way. It'd be burned all the way down by now. That's why you waited so long to fire, right, mister?" He smiled at Ben.

"To hit a match at a hundred yards," Carl mumbled. "That's one thing. But to strike it and light it . . . ?" He blinked and broke into a grin.

"Your shot," Ben said to Johnson. "Still one match left."

"Where the hell did you learn to do that?" Johnson asked.

"Old army trick."

"They don't learn to do that in my army."

"In my army, my regiment, they did."

The marine sniper had laid down his rifle. "I can't equal that," he said. "I'm not even going to try." He put out his hand, and Ben shook it.

It was over. Ben quietly packed Carl's Winchester into its case and gave it back to him. The young guy took it in his good hand, still grinning through his pain.

Back at the cordon, Miss Vale embraced Ben warmly. "I thought I was going to faint with tension," she whispered in his ear.

"Someone had better drive Carl to the hospital now," Ben said. He felt a presence beside him and looked down to see the petite figure of Maggie, gazing at him admiringly. "I'll take him," she volunteered. "I think Andy already left. He felt bad about what happened."

Ben nodded. "Thanks. Good to have met you, Maggie." He turned to Carl. "You take care."

"Man, I still can't believe what I just saw," Carl said as Maggie took his elbow. As she led the young guy away towards the parking field, she smiled back over her shoulder at Ben.

Miss Vale was hanging on to his arm, gushing praise. Ben just smiled graciously. Then the ref stepped up. "You have to come collect your award," he said to Ben. "The press are waiting for you."

"Later," Ben replied. He was searching the crowd. The space where Cleaver had been standing before was empty. "Where's Clayton?" he asked Miss Vale.

"He had a phone call to make. Some pressing matter he just remembered. He's gone back to the house."

"I'll see you afterwards," Ben said.

"Where are you going?"

"Clayton and I have some business to discuss."

31.

Up close, the Cleaver house was impressively grand, with a neoclassical façade and tall white stone columns. Ben marched up the steps to the front entrance, walked straight in, and found himself in a hallway. It could have been as opulent as Augusta Vale's, but it had the look of a place that had seen better times.

A woman darted out of a doorway. She looked like staff, maybe a housekeeper or a personal assistant. She saw him and her eyes widened.

"Where's Cleaver?" he demanded.

"Who are you?"

"Where is he?"

"I don't know," she said. But the nervous glance up the winding staircase behind her told him what he wanted to know. He shouldered past her and went striding up the stairs, two at a time, ignoring her protests. Finding himself on a long galleried landing, he started throwing open every door he came to.

The fourth door he opened revealed Cleaver at the far end of a room, sitting at his desk. Ben slammed the door behind him and walked inside. He glanced around him and saw he was in a study. There wasn't much furniture in the place, and blank spaces on the walls marked where paintings had once hung. The room had a sad look about it. Obviously Cleaver had yet to collect his share of the Vale fortune.

Cleaver stood up, a little shaky. There was a bottle of bourbon and a glass in front of him.

"Time for our little talk," Ben said. "Had you forgotten?"

Cleaver sank back down into the leather desk chair. Ben sat on the edge of the desk, two feet away from him.

The door burst open, and two big guys in suits came rushing in. They saw Ben and tensed, ready for trouble. "Everything OK, sir?"

"Send them away," Ben said. "Or be responsible for what happens to them."

Cleaver waved his hand at them. "It's all right. Everything's under control."

The men shot lingering looks at Ben as they filed out and shut the door behind them.

"You're no theology student," Cleaver said.

"I am. But I wasn't always. We all have our secrets, Clayton. And you're going to tell me yours."

"Or?"

Ben reached into the canvas bag and drew out the .475 Linebaugh. He pointed it at Cleaver's chest. "You just watched me take out the center of the target at a thousand yards. I'm not going to miss you from here."

"All right," Cleaver said. "Let's talk."

"Where's Zoë Bradbury?"

"I really couldn't answer that."

"Think hard. You can still talk with no legs."

"I mean what I said. I don't know where she is."

"Don't test me," Ben said. "Not wise."

"What is it you think I've done?"

"She was blackmailing you. You decided you didn't want to pay."

"I did pay," Cleaver protested. "I paid the money without hesitation. And I'll pay the rest, when I get it. Just like I said I would. I'm a man of my word."

Ben raised the pistol to the level of Cleaver's head and cocked it. The metallic *clunk* filled the silence of the room.

Cleaver's brow beaded with sweat as he stared down the muzzle of the revolver. "She's in trouble, right? Something's happened to her?"

"You're asking me that?"

"I never laid a finger on her," Cleaver insisted. Panic was edging into his voice. "All I did was get some of my guys to follow her."

"All the way to Greece. I know the rest."

Cleaver frowned. "Pardon me?"

"I'm tired of games."

"You said Greece. What's Greece got to do with anything?"

"Greece is where you planted the bomb to kill Charlie Palmer," Ben said. "Where you had your agents murder Nikos Karapiperis and snatch Zoë. Let me tell you something. Kaplan and Hudson are dead."

There was a look of blank incomprehension on Cleaver's face.

"And I saw what your people did to Skid McClusky's legs," Ben added.

Cleaver held up his hands. "Hold on. You are making one big mistake here. I never heard of any Kaplan and Hudson, or Charlie Palmer or Nikos whatever. I don't know anything about Skid Mc-Clusky's legs. The only place I sent my guys was round to Augusta's to spy on that little brat screwing around."

Ben hesitated. When you pointed a gun at someone who wasn't used to it, and you showed you were serious about firing it, what generally came out was the truth. Cleaver had the look of a man who was genuinely frightened and sincerely spilling out his heart to save his life. Yet what he was saying seemed impossible. "What are you talking about, Cleaver?"

"Look, can you just take that gun away?" Cleaver said. "I can't talk with a goddamn gun in my face."

Ben uncocked the revolver and lowered it a little.

Cleaver cleared his throat and took a long sip of his bourbon. He paused to wipe the sweat off his brow.

"Tell me exactly what's been happening," Ben said.

Cleaver gave a deep sigh. "You know about the money I'm getting from Augusta. I don't know how you know, and I won't ask."

Ben nodded. "Go on."

"Augusta has an awful lot of money," Cleaver said. "She's a

billionaire. Now, she's a fine Christian lady and she offered me that hundred million out of the kindness of her heart. But she doesn't just give it away. She can't. Most of it's tied up in holdings and trusts and real estate. It isn't like there's some bottomless pit of dollar bills that she can dip into whenever she wants."

"And so, when Zoë Bradbury turned up again, you were scared she might change her mind."

"Damn right I was scared," Cleaver said angrily. "That girl is the most cunning and manipulative little bitch I've ever had the misfortune to know. One minute I'm about to get all this money, the next here's this spoiled brat from England dropping hints about funding she needs for this project and that dig and that research trip. And here's Augusta, with no kids of her own, talking about her like she was the daughter she never had, and how special and wonderful she was, and all that crap. You do the math. I really thought I was going to lose out in a big way." Cleaver knocked back another slug of bourbon. "Then when I finally met the brat, I could see that all she was after was Augusta's dough. That big talk was all lies. She just wanted it for booze and good times. She's nothing but a gold digger."

"Takes one to know one," Ben said.

Anger flashed in Cleaver's eyes. "What, you think I should have refused Augusta's generosity? It's been years since the book came out. All the money's gone, and a lot more besides. I'm deep in debt. You have no idea what it costs to run an operation like mine—and, well, maybe we did overstretch ourselves a little."

"It looks like you've been selling off the art and furniture," Ben said.

"I have. Things have been awful difficult. Augusta was offering me a lifeline. I had to take it. I'd have been crazy not to."

"Cut the crap and tell me what you did."

"OK. Whenever she was around Augusta, little Miss Bradbury'd be acting all virtuous. Long skirts, high-collar blouses. Just dripping with good ol' Christian piety, like butter wouldn't melt. But I knew she was screwing around all over town. I knew what she was getting up to behind Augusta's back, and right under her roof, with the likes of Skid McClusky. To name just one of her many conquests while she was in Savannah."

"Your men told you this?"

Cleaver nodded and mopped more sweat. "I had a few guys follow her around. I knew I'd get some dirt on her. And it wasn't hard to dig up. She was sneaking her fellas into the carriage house. More than one at a time, sometimes."

Ben guessed where this was leading. "So you got your guys to catch it on video. And you used it to turn Miss Vale against her."

"Augusta never knew who sent the tape," Cleaver said. "It was from a well-wisher. She never mentioned it to anyone. But I could tell it soured her. Next time I was there for dinner with her and Zoë, there was this atmosphere. That's when I knew my plan had worked. The money was mine again for sure."

"But then Zoë turned on you," Ben said.

"She guessed I had something to do with the change in Augusta. A while later, when she'd left the U.S. and I thought I'd never hear her name mentioned ever again, I got a call."

"I know. Twenty-five grand up front, and ten million later."

"Then you know everything," Cleaver said. "I paid, and I'll pay more. No problem."

"Just like that? Why?"

"Why do you want to know? I've told you the truth. I'm ready to pay her the money. If something's happened to her, it's got nothing to do with me. Now, sir, if you don't mind, I think this conversation is over. I have business to attend to." Cleaver started getting to his feet.

"Stop. You're not going anywhere." Ben raised the gun again.

"You don't believe me?"

"I want the rest. I want to know about the prophecy."

Cleaver slumped back down in his chair. "So that's why you were so keen to talk prophecies last night."

"What was in the box that Skid McClusky delivered to you?"

"Just a fragment of pottery. Nothing more."

Ben remembered what Tom Bradbury had told him that day in Summertown about Zoë's discovery of ancient pottery fragments. "I don't understand," he said. "Why pay ten million for a piece of pottery?"

"I can't tell you," Cleaver said.

"You're not leaving here unless you do." Ben cocked the gun. "And you'd better believe it. So talk."

"I had it carbon dated," Cleaver replied wearily. "It was the right age."

"The right age for what?"

Cleaver looked up at him abruptly. "The right age to have been around when the book of Revelation was written."

Ben stared and blinked. "I don't understand."

"She let me see one tiny piece," Cleaver said. "She still has the rest of it."

"The rest of what?"

"The rest of the evidence. She says that she found a collection of pottery tablets engraved in Ancient Greek, going back to biblical times. She says they prove beyond any doubt that Saint John wasn't the author of Revelation."

"And?"

"And that's it. That's all I know about them. She didn't give me a lot to go on. But I have to believe she means what she says, and that it's true. I can't afford not to."

"You don't sound very sure of your ground," Ben said.

"All right. All right. I'll level with you. You've seen my book. You know what it's about."

"That John the Apostle spoke to you."

Cleaver nodded and made a face.

Ben smiled. "You're trying to tell me that John didn't really speak to you."

"No, of course he didn't," Cleaver muttered. "How the hell could he? He's been dead for nearly two thousand years."

"I didn't really think he had, Cleaver."

"I only said it to give me an angle," Cleaver said desperately. "An edge over all of the other End Times preachers out there."

"You mean the honest ones," Ben said. "The ones who aren't just taking everyone for a ride."

"Whatever. But everything I've built is based on that book. All of this." Cleaver gestured at the view from the window. "Millions of Americans buying into the idea that I have a direct line to Saint John. That he personally vouched for the truth of all the prophecies that he wrote in the book of Revelation. And now that little bitch says she's dug up something that could screw it all up for me. The evidence that theology scholars have been looking for for centuries to end the debate about who the real author of Revelation was."

"But she'd bury the evidence for ten million dollars."

Cleaver made a helpless gesture. "That's what she said. And I had to take it seriously, didn't I? I mean, if she was just some two-bit student, I could call her bluff. But she isn't. She's a respected academic, believe it or not. She writes books. If she tells people about this, they'll take it seriously. Hell, she could get on TV with it. A hundred of your goddamned scholars waiting in the wings to pounce on it. It would finish me. No more book sales. It would mean the end of my political career."

"And bye-bye to the hundred million dollars."

Cleaver nodded sadly. "The little inchworm threatened to tell Augusta. Said she'd make me out to be a big con artist."

"But you are," Ben said. "You just admitted it."

Cleaver gazed out the window for a few moments, then turned and looked hard at Ben. "Sure. I'm a con artist. I'm a hustler. But that's all I am. I never hurt anyone. I never sent anyone to Greece. I don't know about bombings or leg-breaking. I met Skid McClusky once, when he brought me the box. That's it. I gave the man his money and he left." Cleaver's face was turning red. He stood up behind the desk. "I'm leaving now. You can shoot me if you want to. But you'd be shooting an innocent man."

"If I find out you've been lying to me," Ben said, "I'll come back. And I *will* kill you. Up close or from a thousand yards away, you won't see it coming. You know that."

But as he watched Cleaver walk out of the room, something was telling Ben that he'd got this whole thing very, very wrong.

32.

When Senator Bud Richmond had first started out in politics, he'd been just another hapless rich boy aiming vaguely for the top. The son of a Montana logger who'd worked his way up to become a multimillionaire industrialist, Bud had never done a proper day's work in his life and was more concerned with his golf swing, his lady friends, his fishing trips, and his beloved Porsche 959 than with serious business.

Two years ago, Irving Slater, his chief of staff and personal assistant, had been despairing of Richmond and on the point of handing in his resignation. As he saw it, he was still only thirty-seven and wasting a promising career on an indolent jackass who thought politics was just a game.

But then something had happened: a pair of unconnected incidents, six months apart, that had turned Bud Richmond's world around and ended up presenting Irving Slater with the chance of a lifetime.

One day shortly after his fiftieth birthday, Richmond had been about to board an airliner heading from his home state of Montana to Washington, DC, when he'd had a premonition. Like a faraway voice in his head, he'd said later, telling him that under no circumstances should he get on that plane. To the great irritation of Irving Slater, he'd refused to board it and waited for the next one. When his intended plane had crashed on takeoff with few survivors, he'd started talking miracles.

The second miracle had taken place when Richmond was driving his Porsche along the mountain roads near his home. Rounding a bend, he'd suddenly and inexplicably been seized by the urge to stop and look at the beautiful sunset, something he'd never done before. After ten minutes of gazing at the sky, he'd climbed back in the Porsche and raced on. A mile down the road he came across the wreck of a coach. A massive landslide had just tumbled down from the mountain and crushed it. Out of thirty-nine passengers, only two survived—and, according to their account, the rocks had hit the bus at the exact moment that Richmond calculated he'd have been in that spot if he hadn't stopped to admire the view.

In Richmond's mind there was only one explanation: God had spared his life for some higher purpose. The conversion was instant. Over the eighteen months since the second miracle had occurred, Bud Richmond's political angle had changed dramatically. And it was actually working for him. He grew up, took himself seriously. And his followers loved him. Born again, suddenly Richmond had an unstoppable zeal for life and work—and suddenly he was getting support from a whole new section of the community that had never shown him much interest before and that Slater had never counted on: the massive evangelist movement. More than fifty million of them. Slater quickly saw the angle. Over fifty million votes equaled a heady potential for the White House.

Irving Slater couldn't believe it. That the motherfucker had become a devout and driven man seemed far weirder than the miracles that he alleged had happened to him. But the wave was rising fast, and the chief of staff was ready to ride it.

Suddenly Slater was buried deep in the Bible. His boss's cast-iron belief in the End Times prophecies of the book of Revelation led him to study that text in extreme detail and read every scrap that had ever been written about Bible prophecy. He'd been stunned by the power of the belief that so many American Christians held: that at any time, the world could be plunged into the Tribulation and Rapture events foretold in the Good Book. It struck him two ways. First, privately, as utter hooey. Second, and much more important, as the deepest and richest political gold mine anyone had ever stumbled upon.

As he sat and watched the Richmond publicity machine gain

more and more fervent support, the first germ of a crazy, ingenious idea had begun to form in his mind. Everywhere the senator held his conventions and rallies across the United States, auditoriums were packed with the faithful who flocked to hear him. His TV talk-show ratings soared. He was hot property. Donations flooded in.

And that, as far as Slater was concerned, was just the beginning. Here were millions of people believing deeply in the literal truth of these prophesied events. Millions of people actually *wanting* it to happen—if it was God's will, if the fulfillment of prophecy was warfare, then so be it. *Wanting* the world to be plunged into darkness and chaos and war, so that God would come and rescue them from their drab, dull, stressed-out miserable lives and confirm to them, if there had ever been any tiny inkling of a doubt in their minds, that it was all true after all and their souls really were worth saving.

But before God could step in, Revelation told of an incredibly bleak period of suffering through which even the most faithful would have to endure. All those millions of people would need a leader to follow through that time. A mythical figure, like Moses, leading the chosen people to glory.

And Slater watched Richmond and wondered. Richmond and Moses. It made him smile. But then he looked at the faces of the crowd and he began to believe in the possibility. If Richmond made it to the White House, it would be him, Irving Slater, the man behind it all, who would wield all the real muscle.

But to make all that happen, something incredible, something unspeakable, would have to be done. There would have to be a way of making those events actually come about. For that, Slater needed help. A lot of help.

He found it soon afterwards, when he met a fanatical End Times believer at one of Richmond's social events. He met them all the time. But what made this man different was that he was a U.S. intelligence operative, and not a junior one. Slater had been stunned at what the man told him about the hidden vein of End Times belief deep in the infrastructure of America's intelligence agencies.

Suddenly Slater's crazy idea was taking quantum leaps towards reality. Through his new associate's contacts he gathered together a core group of agents. Most were committed End Timers; others, men like CIA Special Agent Jones, were more interested in the promise of power and the cash rewards that Slater was able to skim from Richmond's political fund to payroll the growing operation. Around the central core was an outer circle of agents who would do what they were told by their superiors but had no more idea what was really going on than did the unwitting Bud Richmond at the epicenter of it all.

Slater had been blown away by the speed and power with which he'd been able to build up his secret agency. The End Times Stratagem had been born.

They got planning.

The plan was grand in scale but simple in concept.

It was a plan of war. A war that, if the prophecy's power to influence global behavior was to be believed, shouldn't be entirely impossible to provoke.

According to the prophecy, the conflict would start in the Middle East. That didn't seem like a hard thing to manage. It was God's will, after all. All it required was a helping hand to roll things along, a spark to set the tinderbox alight. A *big* spark, something guaranteed to outrage the Islamic world like nothing that had ever happened before. Slater and his associates had long ago figured out what that spark would be. It was just a question of giving it the green light.

For the plan to work, the blame for the atrocity had to fall on the heads of the old enemies of Islam—the Jews. It was all right there in the Bible. The war that would escalate into the beginning of the End Times would begin with the massive retaliatory attack by the Muslims on Israel. The fire and brimstone prophesied in the Bible would take the form of nuclear warheads. As the world teetered on the brink of devastating war, millions of U.S. voters who recognized these as biblical events would be convinced that the end was finally nigh. End Timer votes would flood in. Richmond would be unstoppable.

It was insane, atrocious. Millions of people would die, for

sure—Jews and Muslims, maybe even Americans too. But Slater didn't care about that. The logic was perfect, beautiful and elegant, as the simplest ideas often were. He didn't believe for one moment that the war would kick-start the countdown to Armageddon—just the countdown to power, for him. And time was on his side. All he had to do was slowly groom Bud Richmond for his future role as the leader of the faithful.

But Richmond had competition. He wasn't the only influential figure banging the End Times drum. Slater had teams of agents watching every other potential Christian figurehead, one in particular: Clayton Cleaver in Georgia. Slater had been sitting with Richmond in the limo on their way to a press conference when he'd received the shattering report back from his sources that had turned everything around. It was the start of the Bradbury crisis.

As he thought back to all the events of the past months, Irving Slater paced up and down in his huge office in Bud Richmond's Montana home base, the sprawling house nestling in the mountainside. The vast windows of his office gave him a sweeping panoramic view of the thousand-acre Richmond range.

He stopped pacing and took a swig of milk from the bottle on his desk. Then he flopped in a soft leather armchair opposite a giant TV screen on the wall, grabbed the remote, and hit PLAY.

The DVD was of a current affairs panel-discussion program that Bud Richmond had participated in three months earlier. Slater couldn't stop watching it.

The program had been a great PR builder for Richmond. Slater had paid plants in the audience to fire tailor-made questions at the senator, and he'd written all of Richmond's responses himself. It was all going smoothly to begin with. Richmond had been in fine form, and Slater had been congratulating himself. The combination of the jackass's sincere belief and Slater's own smooth and witty script made for a great show.

But then, two minutes from the end and just when they were almost home and dry, some damn long-haired student in the back of the room had stuck up his hand and asked the fatal unscripted question out of the blue.

Watching the screen, Slater aimed the remote and skipped ahead to that terrible moment.

The student put up his hand. The camera panned across and zoomed in. "Senator, many scholars have doubts about the legitimacy of the book of Revelation as a Bible text. What do you think about that?"

Cut to camera two, and Richmond filled the screen. "I've read all they have to say," he replied calmly. "But my faith remains solid and sure."

The student had more to add. "But if someone could prove that Saint John hadn't been the author—that Revelation wasn't the true Word of God—would that not undermine your faith in it, sir?"

Watching the program on live TV, Slater had been gripping the edge of his chair.

Richmond had hesitated a second, then nodded solemnly. "OK." He'd inched forward across the table on his elbows, fixing the student with that fervent look of his. "Let's say some scholar came up with real, concrete evidence that Saint John did not really write that book," he'd said. "Let's say they could actually prove that the prophecies in Revelation were not truly based on the Word of God." He paused again for dramatic effect. "Then I would have to revise my belief in it. But I would also take that as a sign from God, telling me that I had to move in a new direction." Then Richmond had smiled broadly. "And I have to tell you," he added, "I'd be darn relieved, knowing we didn't all have to go through the Tribulation." The crowd had laughed.

At the time, the sense of unease that Richmond's ad-libbed answer had instilled in Slater had been only slight and temporary. He'd soon forgotten about it.

But then disaster had struck. When the surveillance team watching Clayton Cleaver in Georgia had informed him that Cleaver was under fire from a blackmailer, Slater had realized that in the light of Richmond's comments, all their careful plans were in serious trouble.

He'd never heard of any Zoë Bradbury before. When he googled the name he began to worry even more. This was a legit Bible scholar with a high-enough profile to blow everything apart. If what she was saying was true, and if she could give the critics the evidence they needed to prove that the book of Revelation hadn't been written by John the Apostle, that its very legitimacy as a New Testament text was in question—that the book was a *fraud*, for Christ's sake—the End Times Stratagem was dead in the water. Revelation was the central pillar holding up the End Times roof. To undermine its authority would shake the whole movement down to its roots. Not only that, but Richmond was now saying he'd be happy to walk away from it if he thought it had lost credibility. His standing with the evangelical voters would deflate like a punctured football—and with it Slater's visions of the White House.

Slater was a businessman, and his mind worked pragmatically. It hadn't taken him long to figure out the options.

One: buy her off. She wanted ten million from Cleaver, but why should she care where the cash came from as long as she got rich? He could double that figure to make her go away. But what if she kept coming back for more? What if she went ahead and spilled the beans anyway? How could she be trusted?

He'd preferred option two: grab her and make her lead them to the evidence. They'd destroy it for good, and then they'd bury her along with her claims.

So Slater had called on his contacts. His chief associate within the CIA had delegated the task to his man Jones, who in turn had sent a team to Corfu to snatch her. Now Bradbury was in their custody, somewhere nobody would ever find her. But there were too many problems and complications. He couldn't afford to wait. It was time for decisive action.

He turned off the DVD playback and sank back in the soft armchair, massaging his temples. On the low table in front of him was a hardwood bowl filled with chocolate bars. He grabbed three of them, tore off the wrappers, and swallowed them voraciously.

Gulping down the last of the chocolate, he snatched his phone from the arm of the chair and stabbed the keys.

His associate's voice answered on the second ring.

"We need to talk," Slater said. Pause. "No. You come here. I'm alone. I sent the jackass on vacation for a few days."

"Give me three hours," his associate replied.

"Be here in two."

33.

D r. Joshua Greenberg pulled the rental Honda off the highway and into the parking lot of the roadside diner. Grabbing his briefcase from the passenger seat, he climbed out and groaned. He'd been on the road a long while. He stretched and rubbed his eyes.

A Freightliner truck roared past with a blast of wind and a cloud of dust and diesel fumes. The doctor turned towards the diner and slowly, stiffly, climbed the two steps up to the entrance. The place was quiet—a few sullen truckers and a couple of families taking a late lunch. He took a booth in the corner, settled on the red vinyl seat, and ordered coffee. He didn't feel like eating. The brown liquid that the waitress shoved under his nose wasn't really coffee, but he sat and drank it anyway.

He sat there for thirty minutes, staring at his hands on the table. He should be moving on. They'd be expecting him back at the facility, to deliver the package to Jones. It was still two hours' drive away.

He gave a short, bitter laugh. *Facility.* That was a fine word for a semi-derelict hotel in the middle of nowhere that was being used as an illegal detention center for a kidnapped innocent young woman.

He glanced down at the briefcase next to him on the seat. Reached across, unsnapped the catch, dipped inside, and came out holding the little bottle. He set it down on the table in front of him. It was amber glass and held just under 100 milliliters of clear, slightly viscous fluid. There was no label. It looked innocuous enough. It could have been anything, some kind of innocent herbal remedy even. But he knew that if he were to empty the contents into the bubbling coffeepot behind the counter, every cup served out of it would make its drinker a candidate for the nuthouse within a day.

First they would become unusually chatty and uninhibited, happily revealing even the most intimate secrets about themselves. Then the drug would go to town on the unconscious mind, liberating every shred of darkness from inside—every repressed fear, every angry or bitter emotion, every disturbing or violent thought. It would all come flooding out, overwhelming the conscious mind in a wave of rage and paranoia and grief and terror, the whole spectrum of the most extreme emotions a human being could experience, all at once, relentlessly, for hours.

There was no stopping the feedback loop. Madness was the inevitable result, and there was no antidote.

He shuddered. And he was on his way to hand this over to Jones to give to an innocent young woman. To ruin her forever.

He sank his head into his hands.

How the hell did I get involved with this terrible business?

He knew perfectly well how. One small mistake, building on the errors of his past that he thought he'd left behind. One small mistake had ruined everything.

Joshua Greenberg had come from a poor background and spent his life trying to make up for it. His father was a Detroit factory worker, and his mother cleaned offices. The two of them had worked their asses off to put their only child through college. He'd done them proud, graduated in medicine and gone on to specialize in neurology and psychiatry. At the age of forty-eight, he was a successful man with his own New York private practice and a lectureship at Columbia, where he was head of his department. The big house in the Hamptons had two acres, a pool, and stables, and it was everything his wife, Emily, had ever wanted. His two teenage daughters had the Arab horses they'd always wanted, and he'd built a luxurious annex onto the house so that his elderly, proud parents could be close by.

The ghost from his past was something that he'd never thought would catch up with him again. It had been his freshman year at college, the first time away from home for a nervous eighteen-year-old. His roommate had been Dickie Engels.

He'd never forget Dickie. He was a lawyer's son, and the two years he had on Joshua had been spent traveling around France and Italy, places that seemed as far away as the moon. Compared with Joshua, Dickie was a true man of the world. He smoked Sobranie Black Russians, knew about wine, and had read Tolstoy and James Joyce. For six months Joshua worshipped him from a distance, fervently hoping his burning feelings wouldn't show. Once, tipsy after drinking the first champagne of his life, he'd been on the verge of kissing Dickie. It had never happened, but soon afterwards Dickie had asked to be transferred to another room. Then, a few months later, Joshua had met Emily and the shameful incident was forgotten. He moved on and got on with life.

Until James happened, fourteen months ago. He remembered clearly the first time he'd laid eyes on his dazzling new student. The thick black hair, the satin skin, the deep brown eyes. Suddenly the old feelings had started returning. It started taking over. It wasn't just a crush. And the beautiful young man seemed to feel the same way, taking more than a casual interest in his overweight, middle-aged lecturer. Joshua had initially tried to avoid him and evaded the repeated invitations for "coffee sometime."

Then one day Emily had announced, to Joshua's horror, that she planned to organize a party at their home for all the first-year students. There was no way out of it, and Emily could be very forceful. It would have looked odd to protest.

The night of the party had been stormy. Joshua had been mixing himself a drink in the kitchen when he felt something brush his arm. James had crept up behind him. They'd kissed in the flash of the lightning from outside.

Joshua was smitten. After that first night they'd started meeting up in his car in the college parking lot. It was crazy, looking back.

James had never gone all the way with him—always found a reason to get away when the petting got heavier. Joshua had taken to hanging around outside the student's window at night, hoping for a glimpse of him, telling Emily he was working late.

One day, James wasn't there anymore. Joshua was told he'd transferred to UCLA. He never heard from him again.

But he'd had bigger concerns than a broken heart. The day after James's disappearance, the devastating package had arrived in the mail. The photos were crisp and the faces unmistakable. The note was short and to the point. The doctor would be contacted and his cooperation appreciated.

At first Joshua had felt compelled to explain everything to Emily. She'd understand. But then he realized that, no, Emily would not understand. Emily would flip. She'd leave him, take away his beautiful daughters. He'd lose his home. His parents would be mortified beyond words. Then, no doubt, the pictures would find their way under the noses of his employers at the university. His teaching career would be over, and the scandal would be sure to wreck his private practice too.

It had been a few weeks before he'd been contacted again. The phone call had lasted twenty minutes and the instructions had been clear. He'd said to Emily he was going away to a seminar. Someone had dropped out at the last minute, and he was needed.

That was the start of quite a few unexpected seminars that took Joshua away from home for weeks at a time. He never really knew who his employers were. The money was generous, and he tried not to think too much about what they were making him do.

The sessions took place in anonymous gray buildings across the country. It was always more or less the same. A car would pick him up at the airport. The men in suits would drive him in silence and he'd be ushered to some quiet, empty room where the subjects were being held. Some of the experimental behavior modification program involved weird pharmaceuticals and brainwashing techniques. Joshua was required to evaluate the subject's state of mind, conduct tests, administer treatments that he'd never even heard of before. He never knew who the men were. He tried to persuade himself that all this must be in the interests of his country. But sometimes at night he'd wake up covered in sweat at the memory of the things he'd seen and helped carry out.

Once or twice he'd tried to break away. Then out came the photos again, and the threats.

But this time was different. This was worse. The approach had come through a different channel. The place he'd been called away to, out in the Montana wilds, was dark and run-down. The whole setup wasn't right. The subject wasn't some sullen prisoner that he could convince himself was a threat to homeland security. She was just a slip of a girl, and he was being coerced to destroy her. Jones terrified him. They all did—even Fiorante, the tall, attractive auburn-haired woman who was the youngest and sole female agent on the team. She might be beautiful, but he was damn sure she was deadly.

Joshua stared again at the bottle on the table and knew he couldn't go through with it. He was going to get her out of there. And then he was going back to New York to tell Emily everything. Let the chips fall. He didn't care anymore.

He left the diner and continued on his journey, planning what he was going to do. He stopped at a small town on the way and found a little general store, where he bought what he needed and hid it in the trunk of the car. Then he followed the long, winding road out into the wilds.

The hotel loomed up in front of him as he parked the Honda near the entrance. He stepped out, got his things from the car, and buttoned up the long overcoat he was wearing, then walked briskly up the steps to the glass doors. Punched the security code into the panel on the wall, waited for the click, and pushed through the door.

The familiar, detested smell of the place hit him as he strode through the dingy corridors. There didn't seem to be anyone around. He checked his watch, sweat breaking out on his brow. His heart was thumping rapidly.

He made his way quickly up to the top floor, to Zoë's door. The same big man in the dark suit was standing there as usual, eyeing him as he approached.

"What's with the heavy coat, doc?"

"Got a chill," Joshua said. He sniffed for effect.

"You're sweating."

"Maybe coming down with the flu. Can you let me in?"

"You're not scheduled to see her," the agent said.

"I just realized," Joshua stammered, "I left my BlackBerry in there."

"No signal up here anyway, doc."

"Sure. But I need it. It's got important stuff on it."

"Careless," the agent said.

"I know. I'm sorry."

"One minute," the agent said. "No longer."

"Thanks." Joshua smiled weakly and pushed through the door. It shut behind him and he heard the click of the lock.

Zoë had been sleeping. She sat upright in the bed, eyes wide at the sight of him standing there with his hair a mess, not in his normal white coat.

"I'm not supposed to be here," he whispered. "Do as I say and don't ask any questions. I'm getting you out of here."

The agent was thinking about his coffee break when he heard the commotion from inside the room. He cocked his head and listened for a moment, then unlocked the door and burst inside.

The girl was lying on the floor beside the bed. Her knees were drawn up to her chest and she was shaking violently. The guard stared down at her.

The doctor was kneeling on the floor next to her. He glanced up in alarm. "She's sick. Really sick."

"What the hell happened?" the agent asked, horrified.

"Some kind of episode," the doctor said. "She woke up when I walked in and the next thing I know, she's convulsing. Wait here—I've got some medication in the car." He jumped up and headed towards the door.

"What do I do?"

"Do nothing. Don't touch her. Just stay with her."

The agent stood and stared at her. Her whole body was shaking, rigid. Her hair was wet. She was foaming at the mouth. His mind was suddenly full of what they'd do to him for letting her get sick on his watch. Thank Christ for the doctor.

That was his final thought.

Joshua had stepped out of the room. He'd quickly unbuttoned the overcoat and drawn out the baseball bat that had been thrust through his belt, the handle trapped under his armpit. He strode back into the room, holding the bat in both hands. His mouth was dry. He'd been a reasonable ballplayer in college. The thought of smashing a bat into a man's head made him cringe, but he had no choice. He swung hard and felt the horrible thud vibrate down the shaft. The agent crumpled to the floor, facedown.

Zoë scrabbled to her feet, spitting foam and undissolved pieces of Alka-Seltzer. She stared down in horror at the spread-eagled body of the agent.

"Hurry," Joshua whispered. He dropped the bat. Took off the overcoat and wrapped it around her slender shoulders. Seizing her arm, he led her out of the room and locked the door behind them.

Zoë was glancing frantically this way and that as he guided her down the corridor and towards the back stairs that nobody ever seemed to use. She was weak from captivity and lack of exercise, and breathing hard as they ran down the stairs. He kept a tight grip on her arm. His own heart was hammering frantically.

The next landing down, he glanced furtively out of the fire doors and saw that the corridor ahead was deserted. He jerked her arm and they ran on. She stumbled, and he helped her to her feet.

"Slow down," she wheezed.

"I can't. We've got to get out. It's not far now."

A door opened to one side, and suddenly Joshua found himself face-to-face with the female agent, Fiorante. They both stopped dead, eyes locked.

But the woman didn't move. Didn't say anything.

Something told him to keep running. He pressed on quickly, dragging Zoë behind him.

"She saw us." Her voice was panicky.

He didn't reply. The entrance foyer was just up ahead. He was running hard now.

Ten yards to the entrance foyer. Five.

His hand was on the cold steel handle of the front door.

Then a voice cut through the empty building.

"Just where is it you think you're going, Doctor?"

Joshua whirled around. Jones was standing a few yards up the corridor. Beside him was the Fiorante woman. Two more agents were running up behind, pistols drawn.

Joshua yanked his car key from his coat and pressed it into Zoë's hand. "Blue Honda," he panted. "Just go. Get out of here. Now." He knew they wouldn't shoot her. He didn't care about himself, not anymore.

Jones stepped forward, his gun held loosely at his side.

Zoë hesitated.

"Go!" Joshua yelled at her.

"There's nowhere to run, Zoë," Jones said calmly as he walked up closer. He was smiling. "It's a wilderness out there. You're safer here with us."

Zoë stood frozen in the doorway. She stared helplessly at Joshua, and then at the agents. The female agent wouldn't meet her eye.

Then Jones took three more steps, and she screamed as his strong fingers gripped her wrist and yanked her hard away from the entrance. He flung her into the hands of the two other men. She fought and kicked, but she was weak. They held her by the arms as Jones turned towards Joshua Greenberg.

"Don't hurt him," she pleaded. "Don't—"

As the two agents dragged her back up the corridor, she heard the shot and threw her head back over her shoulder to see the blood splatter up the glass door and the doctor slump to the ground at Jones's feet.

She screamed all the way back up to her room.

34.

t was just after 1:30 p.m. when Ben left Cleaver's house and slipped away through the crowd. A few minor competitions were still in progress, but with the main event over the throng was thinning out. He spotted Miss Vale near the tent, talking to reporters.

She didn't notice Ben as he made his way quietly back towards the parking field. He felt bad about slipping away without good-byes or explanations, but he needed to be alone to think.

He got into the Chrysler and drove aimlessly, heading vaguely west and vaguely south. He crossed over the Altamaha River. Drove through farmland, past tumbledown shacks and corrugated barns, huge open fields where the earth was rich and red under the blazing sun. Past trailer camps where mean-looking white-trash inhabitants stood at the side of the road and gesticulated at his car as he drove by. After about an hour he was lost deep in the country with no idea where he was.

He drove feeling numb and defeated. He'd made mistakes in his life before, but this time he'd been completely wrong; as mistaken and off the mark as he could have been, and then a bit more. He'd been so sure that he was on the right track with Clayton Cleaver. All he knew now was that the man was a rogue, a con man, and an opportunist. But that didn't make him a kidnapper or a murderer.

He tried to salvage what he could from the mess inside his head and make sense out of what was left. But he had only questions, lots of questions, swirling around without a hint of an answer. Was Zoë still alive? Maybe even still on Corfu? Had he come to the States for nothing? He'd taken the truth of Kaplan's word for granted. Maybe that had been a mistake too.

He thought about the piece of pottery Zoë had discovered and used to blackmail Cleaver. She'd told Skid McClusky that the prophecy would make her rich. What had she discovered? If she really could prove her claim, its impact on Christian theology would be massive. Cleaver had been perfectly right: revisionist scholars had been waiting in the wings for years for the ammunition they needed to shoot the book of Revelation down as an illegitimate Bible text. But the implications went well beyond simply ruining the career of one obscure southern Bible-thumper. It could be the biggest event in years—as important as the Dead Sea Scrolls or the Turin Shroud. Maybe even bigger, if it could force a major revision of the Bible itself.

He kept coming up with the same questions. Who else would be threatened by Zoë's discovery, and so threatened that they would go to such lengths to suppress it? Or was suppression the aim? Perhaps her discovery of ancient pottery tablets had some other intrinsic value—a monetary value that someone was prepared to kill for?

Basically, he was guessing. He was adrift in a sea of possibilities. He needed to act, and act fast. But he didn't know what to do, or where to go. Back to Greece, hoping to pick up the pieces and not be caught by Stephanides again? Or simply back to Oxford, admitting defeat and facing telling the Bradburys that he'd lost their daughter? It was a disaster.

The sudden sharp blast of a siren jerked him back to the present. A police cruiser filled his rearview mirror, the light bar on its roof flashing red and blue through the dust on his back window. It gave another screeching burst, and he swore and flipped on the indicator to pull off the road. The car crunched to a halt in the dirt, and the police cruiser pulled in behind him. Dust floated in the air around the two vehicles. He watched in the mirror as the doors opened and two cops jumped out and walked towards him, one on either side of the Chrysler.

It wasn't a routine check or a speeding ticket. The cops had their weapons ready. The one on the left had pulled a revolver from his belt. The one on the right was clutching a short-barreled pump shotgun. This was serious. The cops were acting on specific information, and whatever they'd been told about him, it was making them jumpy as hell.

Ben sat quietly with his hands on the wheel, watching them, thinking fast. Why was he being picked up? What did they know?

The cop with the revolver stalked round to his window and twirled a finger. Ben rolled the window down and looked at him. He was young, mid-twenties. His eyes were round and nervy.

"Kill your engine," he yelled.

Ben reached out slowly and turned the key. Silence, apart from the chirping of the cicadas all around them.

"License," the cop said. "Nice and easy."

Ben moved his hand carefully to his pocket and slipped the license out. The cop snatched it from him, glanced down at it for a brief moment, and nodded to the one with the shotgun as if to say *It's him, all right*. Now he looked even more scared.

"Step out of the car," he yelled. "Hands where I can see them."

Ben opened the door and slowly stepped out. He kept his hands raised and held the cop's gaze, sizing him up. The young officer was jumping with adrenaline, his face tense and twitchy. The revolver muzzle was trembling slightly as he pointed it at Ben's chest.

The gun was two feet away. It was a Smith & Wesson Model 19. There were two ways to fire it. With the action cocked, it took only a light flick of the finger to drop the hammer. The alternative was the double-action mode, simply pulling the trigger to rotate the cylinder and bring the hammer back to fire. But that required a heavy tug, and Ben knew that unless the cop's pistol had been specially worked on by a gunsmith, the Model 19 had quite a tough action. More effort meant more time needed to shoot.

The gun wasn't cocked. What that told Ben was that he had about half a second longer to step in, disable the cop, and take his gun away. Then about another half a second to turn it on the one with the shotgun. He wouldn't hurt them badly, just take them out of circulation for a while.

But that would lead to all kinds of trouble that he didn't want. "What's wrong?" he said quietly instead.

The cop flicked his gun at the car. "Up against the vehicle. Hands on the hood."

Ben sighed in exasperation and spread his hands on the warm metal of the Chrysler. The one with the shotgun covered him from three yards away. The other walked back to the police car and started talking into his radio, looking nervous and fidgety.

Ben heard the sound of tires on the dirt and the low rumble of V8 engines. Keeping his hands planted on the car, he craned his neck to look. Two big black muscular Chevrolet SUVs were pulling up behind the police cruiser. Clouds of dust rose and settled. Sunlight reflected off the tinted windows of the vehicles.

The doors opened. Ben counted five people, two men and a woman from one car and two more men from the other. They were all smartly dressed in dark suits. The oldest was the guy stepping forward with the craggy face, slicked-back hair, and dark glasses. He was about fifty, lean and rangy. He was smiling, showing uneven teeth. The youngest was the woman. She might have been about thirty-five, with sharp features and a scowl on her face. Her auburn hair was tied back, gently ruffled by the warm breeze.

The lead guy flashed a badge at the two cops. "Special Agent Jones. We can take it from here, officers."

The cops stared at the badge like they'd never seen one before. They lowered their weapons.

Jones motioned to one of the agents, who walked round to Ben's passenger door, yanked it open, and grabbed the canvas bag from the seat. Jones took a pair of surgical rubber gloves from his jacket pocket and slipped them on before taking the bag from the other agent and reaching inside.

"Well, now, look what we found." Jones chuckled as he drew out the .475 Linebaugh. He dropped the bag on the ground at his feet and turned the big revolver over in his gloved hands, admiring it.

Flipped open the loading port, he spun the cylinder. Then he twirled it around his finger, cowboy-style, and one of the other agents laughed. Jones turned to Ben with a ragged smile. "Now that *is* a nice gun."

Ben didn't reply. He was thinking hard and fast.

The agents all stepped closer. The woman's eyes were fixed on Ben, and as he watched her he thought for a second he could sense some kind of doubtful hesitation on her face. The scowl was gone.

Jones took out his phone and dialed. "It's me. Good news. Got your Mr. Hope right here. OK."

Ben frowned. This was weird procedure.

Jones snapped the phone shut and turned to the two cops. "I don't think we'll be needing you anymore, officers," he said, dismissing them with a gesture.

The cops glanced at each other and started walking back to their cruiser. They had their hands on the door handles and were about to climb inside when Jones seemed to have an afterthought and called them. "Hold on a minute, officers. Just one thing."

The younger cop narrowed his eyes at him. "What?"

Jones smiled again, a knowing kind of smile that made his whole face crease up and his eyes become slits. He glanced at the .475 revolver in his hand.

Then he thumbed back the hammer, raised the revolver out to arm's length, and shot the younger guy right through the face from ten feet away.

35.

With a whir of pulleys and thick steel cables, the cable car glided smoothly out across the abyss. The cold mountain wind whistled around it, buffeting the metal capsule and making the floor vibrate under the feet of the two men inside.

Irving Slater loved it up here. Suspended high over the rocky valley, he could see for miles all around, and it gave him a feeling of invulnerability. He felt like an eagle perched on his mountain vantage point. That's what predators did—take the high ground, survey their territory from a position of complete control. Nobody could touch him up here, and nobody could listen in on sensitive conversations. The howling wind would kill the signal from even the most sophisticated listening device. Slater was fanatical about surveillance, and even though he'd had the Richmond House swept for bugs a hundred times and never found a thing, this was the one place he was truly comfortable when it came to talking serious business.

The cable was five hundred yards long and stretched from the boarding platform near the Richmond house to a landing bay on the other side of the valley. He'd had a remote device rigged up that allowed him to guide the car from inside, move it out as far as he wanted and then let it hang over the thousand-foot drop like the last apple on the tree.

Nobody else ever came here anymore. Dirk Richmond, Bud's father, had installed the cable car system at great cost many years ago, soon after he'd bought the thousand-acre range on the edge of the Rocky Mountains, to allow the family to access the ski slope on the mountain across the valley. But neither Bud's mother nor the indolent jackass himself had ever shown much interest in healthy outdoor pursuits, and old Dirk had gone to his grave a long time ago now, a vastly wealthy but embittered and disappointed man, largely thanks to his waster of a son.

Slater aimed his remote at the control booth and stabbed the red button in the middle. There was a muted clunk of linkages and pulleys from overhead, and the cable car juddered to a halt. Slater dropped the remote in his coat pocket and stared out through the Perspex window across the valley for a few moments, hands on the rail, letting his body move to the gentle swing of the cable car as the wind whipped all around it.

Then he turned to face his associate and smiled at the sweaty anxiety on the man's face. "You should be used to it by now."

"This place gives me the creeps."

Slater's smile melted abruptly. "Progress report," he demanded.

The associate gave a nervous shrug. "Bradbury isn't saying much yet. We're still working on it."

"That's what you said last time. Why are we even keeping her alive? And I don't suppose you've located the lawyer either."

"McClusky?"

"You guys let any other lawyers slip through your fingers who might know where Bradbury hid the evidence and be totally able to sink us?"

"We're still looking."

Slater's eyes bored into him. "You do that. How hard can it be? What about Kaplan and Hudson? Go on, surprise me. Tell me they turned up."

"Not yet. And I have a feeling they're not coming back."

Slater made a dismissive gesture and frowned out across the mountain valley. "So you have nothing whatsoever good to tell me?"

He pulled a chocolate bar out of his pocket and tore the wrapper off. "Want some?"

The associate shook his head and coughed nervously. "There's been a development." He reached into the briefcase propped between his feet. Handed Slater a slim manila folder.

Slater munched and flipped the file open. The first thing his eyes landed on was a blown-up passport photo of a blond-haired man in his thirties. "Who is he?"

"His name's Hope. Benedict Hope. Englishman. A few days ago our agents reported he was on Corfu, Greek island. He went out there to meet up with Palmer. As you know, Palmer was there—"

"I don't need a history lesson," Slater snapped. "Palmer was there looking for Bradbury, and he talked to some Greek asshole. I know. But I thought it was all taken care of."

"We thought so too. The Karapiperis hit and the bombing were dressed up to look like a drug gang reprisal. But this guy Hope got away. We already knew that from Kaplan and Hudson, but we only just found out who he is."

Slater brushed the photo aside and thumbed quickly through the printed sheets underneath. Military records for Palmer and Hope. He skipped through Palmer's first, brows tightening as he scanned down the text. Hope's record was much more extensive, and he took more time over it. By the time he'd finished reading, alarm was building up in his chest. He looked up. "Have you read this?"

The associate nodded.

"Remarkable. The youngest major 22 SAS ever had. Decorations coming out of his ass. He's either a goddamn hero or he's a dyed-in-the-wool stone killer. Either way, he's the kind of man who should have been on my team."

"We tried to dig up more about him, from after he left the army," the associate said. "There isn't much. He operates as a 'crisis response consultant,' moves around a lot, hard to pin down. He's real careful about covering his tracks. We don't even have a home address for him."

"Crisis response consultant," Slater echoed under his breath. "Kind of loose terminology. Covers a lot of ground."

"We think he took out Kaplan and Hudson."

"That would certainly figure." Slater shut the file. "What the hell's going on here? How does a damn archaeology academic come to have two ex-SAS guys on her trail? How is a man like Hope mixed up in this?"

"We don't know. Maybe he was working with Bradbury."

Slater looked up sharply. "Then he could know everything. He and Bradbury could be working together in this. Partners, for all we know."

"Possible."

Slater glared. "So what you're telling me is that this already fucked-up situation just got even more fucked-up. We have a former special-forces officer on the loose, who's taking out our agents and may know everything that Bradbury and McClusky know. In other words, we just went from dealing with a deadbeat ambulance chaser and a frightened little girl to dealing with a trained fucking killing machine who's at the very least the equal of any soldier ever produced by the U.S. Army. You do realize that, don't you?"

"I realize that," the associate replied dully.

"And have we any idea where this bastard might be?"

"I was coming to that. He's here."

"What do you mean, here?"

"He passed through U.S. immigration, Atlanta, two days ago."

Slater hung his head in frustration. "And you're going to tell me the CIA can't catch him?"

"Our people got to the airport late. He slipped out of there."

Slater stared hard at his associate. Shook his head in disgust.

"We have to be cautious," the associate said. "This isn't exactly official Agency business, Irving. And Hope isn't exactly an ordinary guy."

"I pay you people a lot of money," Slater said. "He's one man. One man. You have dozens of people on the payroll, and access to a hundred more at least. Is he really that smart, or are you really that inept?"

The associate's temper was rising. "We've done everything you told us to do. We acquired Bradbury. Took care of Karapiperis. Brought in

Herzog for the bombing. These things are not easy to do. It's not like organizing a press conference. One slip, we all go down."

Slater snorted derisively. "If I'd known what a bunch of lames you people were, I'd have paid Herzog to do the whole thing."

"He's a mercenary," the associate protested. "He believes in nothing."

"What does it matter what he believes in? The fucker could be a Satanist for all I care."

"That's not what this is about."

Slater looked at him levelly. "Oh, you think this is about doing God's work? Let me tell you, this is business, first and last. Herzog gets the job done, and he doesn't leave tracks that a blind man could follow."

The associate was about to reply when his phone rang. He turned away from Slater and answered, talking softly. His eyebrows rose. "You're sure?" he said. "OK. You know what to do." He shut the phone and turned back to Slater with a grin of triumph.

"Well?"

"That was Jones. He got Hope."

Slater smiled for the first time in the conversation. "That's more like it. Good. Now bring this bastard in, and let's get him talking."

"You know I can't be there," the associate said. "I can't be seen."

"No, but I sure as hell will. I want to meet this character."

"I'm not sure you do."

"Oh, I do," Slater insisted. "And then I want to finish him."

36.

The flat punch of the explosion ripped through the air. The cop's face disintegrated in a mess of red, and he was sent sprawling backwards with the impact of the heavy bullet. He flopped down into the dirt, legs kicking.

Then Jones cocked the .475 revolver a second time and shot the other cop before he had time to react. The bullet caught him in the chest, blowing his heart and lungs out through his spine. Blood spattered against the windshield of the police cruiser. The cop crumpled into the dust without a sound.

For a moment nobody moved.

The report of the gun rolled around the open countryside. The two cops lay motionless. Jones turned his back on them.

Ben stared at Jones, and then at the other agents. One of them was grinning. Two were impassive. Then he saw the expression of horror on the woman's face. She hadn't been expecting that.

"Hell of a kick these things have got," Jones mused, weighing the big revolver in his hand. He took off his dark glasses and fixed Ben with a wry look. "Looks like you're in deep shit now, Mr. Ben Hope."

Ben stood away from the Chrysler. He pointed at the two dead cops. "Why did you do that?"

"I didn't," Jones said. "You did. We all saw you do it. It's your gun, your prints all over it."

"What do you want from me?"

Jones smiled. "Answers. But not here."

He walked up to Ben. The smile was gone now. He cocked the pistol again and stuck it in his face. "You're under arrest, cop killer."

Ben looked around him at the agents. Five on the ground, at least two more behind the tinted glass of the cars. He evaluated distances, positions, body language. His eyes flicked from Jones to the muzzle of the gun and then back again. This was the second time in a few minutes that someone had pointed a pistol at him like this. He'd let the young cop do it to him, but there was no way he was going to tolerate it from this guy.

Besides, Jones had just made a big tactical error. Maybe he was too used to pointing a short, stubby Glock or SIG in people's faces. Or maybe he was just cocky and showing off in front of the others, like some kind of movie hero. But the long barrel on the hunting revolver meant that its muzzle was just four inches from Ben's head.

One of the first lessons he'd been taught, many years before, was never to hold a gun too close to the other guy. It was just asking for trouble. An expert military shooter would stand back and keep some distance between himself and his enemy, precluding any attempt at a disarming move. And disarming moves were something that had been instilled in Ben through endless training. They'd saved his life more times than he cared to remember.

He debated it for an instant. Could he do it?

These are U.S. government agents, and there are five of them. You won't make it.

He hesitated.

Fuck it. Go for it.

The move took less than a second. He grabbed the end of the barrel and jerked it sharply back towards Jones's face. The curved edge of the revolver's ebony butt caught the agent right in the teeth and smashed through them into his mouth.

Jones screamed, blood spraying from his lips. Ben yanked the gun back the other way, tearing it out of the man's fingers. Jones went down onto his back in the dirt, writhing and clutching his face, pieces of teeth spilling out from between his fingers.

Then, before anyone could react, Ben was hitting the deck, rolling fast in the dust, grabbing his bag, reaching for the latch on the Chrysler's door. He ripped it open and threw himself behind it, using it as a shield, just as the agents pulled their guns.

There was a ragged volley of gunfire. Bullets thudded into the door.

He cocked the gun and was about to shoot back, but then hesitated. Did he really want to do this? Getting into a gun battle with government agents was a lot more trouble than he'd reckoned on. He didn't want to hurt anyone unless he had to.

But something was telling him he had to. One of the agents was in his sights. No point in shooting to wound with a gun like this. Going for the shoulder would tear off an arm and kill the guy anyway from blood loss and shock. He fired, dead center of mass. The gun boomed and kicked savagely, and the target went down like a tree.

Five-shot gun. Three rounds gone.

More gunfire tore through the bodywork of the Chrysler. Ben half stood up behind the bullet-riddled door. The woman had her pistol leveled at him. She was looking right down the sights at him. Only had to pull the trigger.

But something told him she wouldn't shoot. So he shot the agent next to her instead. The bullet sent the guy spinning violently back against one of the big black SUVs.

Two more agents had spilled out of the black Chevrolets and were tearing guns from holsters.

Time to go.

Ben leaped into the Chrysler and dove down into the footwell. He twisted the key and threw it in drive, one hand on the wheel and the other punching down hard on the gas. The big car lurched violently forward, wheels spinning, door flapping open. He drove blind for twenty yards, staying down as bullets smashed through the bodywork and shattered windows sprayed him with broken glass, then hauled himself up into the seat as the Chrysler swerved wildly down the road.

The agents were running back to their cars. The woman was helping Jones to his feet. Then the black SUVs were spinning their wheels in the dust and coming after him.

The twisting country road was empty and Ben used all of it, clipping the apex left and right as the heavy car slewed on soft suspension. The windshield was an opaque web of cracks. He used the barrel of the revolver to knock away the shattered glass. Wind roared into the car. A straightaway opened up ahead of him. The needle climbed. Eighty. Ninety.

They were still right behind him. The revolver had one round left. It wasn't a gun he could reload on the move, like any modern automatic. It was a hunter's gun. A gun for a patient man. Every cartridge case had to be hand-ejected and reloaded one at a time. No good at all.

A shot boomed out and Ben ducked as the side mirror and most of the window frame were torn away in a storm of plastic and metal fragments. He threw a glance over his shoulder and saw an agent hanging out of the window of one of the SUVs, the wind tearing at his hair and clothes, bringing a stubby shotgun back to aim. Another shot, and a wad of lead pellets ripped through the Chrysler and took a bite out of the seat next to Ben.

Swerving all over the road, he reached out behind him with the revolver. Last shot. He fired without aiming. The recoiling pistol almost took his hand off as the huge bullet cannoned through what was left of the back window and smashed into the front of the SUV. In the mirror the big vehicle skidded, slewed sideways, and rolled. The shotgun shooter was spat out of the window as the car flipped over, wreckage spilling across the road. The second vehicle swerved around it and kept coming.

Ben was driving like he'd never driven in his life. More shots rang out. There was a bend up ahead in the narrow road, trees and bushes on both sides. He threw the Chrysler into it.

An old man was leading a mule across the road, right in front of him.

He instinctively twisted the wheel and the car sailed off the road. It smashed through the foliage. Branches speared through the broken windows. He was almost shaken out of the seat with the impact as the Chrysler hurtled down a bank.

For a second he thought he could see a way through and that he was going to make it.

But then, too late, he saw the fallen tree trunk. There was nothing he could do.

The Chrysler was still doing about fifty when it crunched into the trunk. Ben was thrown forward violently into the inflating airbag. The rear of the car rose up, wheels spinning, engine roaring. The Chrysler turned right over on its nose and then came smashing down on its roof.

The impact stunned him for an instant. There was ringing in his ears and the taste of blood on his lips. He was upside down, wedged against the steering wheel, with the buckled roof pressing hard on his shoulder.

Running footsteps, a cracking of twigs. Voices. A cry of "Down there!"

He kicked against the dashboard, forcing his body out through the buckled window. He somehow managed to get himself twisted round, and crawled out of the wrecked car. Then he reached back inside the window and grabbed his bag and the empty Linebaugh. An unloaded gun was still a better weapon than bare hands.

He was in dense thicket, tangled thorn bushes sprawling all around him like coils of barbed wire, tearing at his hands and face as he struggled to get away. He broke free of them, staggered to his feet, and glanced around him, breathing hard, heart pounding, forcing his brain to focus after the numbing impact of the crash. Trees and bushes blocked his view in all directions. He could hear voices through the screen of vegetation behind him. He slung the bag over his shoulder and broke into a sprint, ripping through the scrub and darting through the narrow gaps in the trees.

He beat back a low branch and suddenly there was an agent standing there, gun raised. Ben didn't slow down. He slid to the ground and skidded through the dirt with his right leg straight out in front of him. His foot caught the man's knee and brought him down. The 9mm pistol in the agent's hand went off, the shot going wide. Then Ben was on top of him, and clubbed him hard over the head with the butt of the empty revolver. The agent went limp in the dirt, still clutching his pistol. Ben tossed the hunting revolver into the bushes and ripped the 9mm from the guy's fingers. The magazine was full. The ugly black steel was comforting in his hand.

But now the echoing report of the gunshot over the treetops had drawn the others. He could hear the voices converging on him, and the crackle and rustle as they came chasing through the bush. They were close.

He ran on. The dry red earth underfoot turned to slippery mud as he stumbled into a stream. He leaped over rocks and scrambled up the opposite bank, fingers raking in the dirt.

The woodland was thickening now. He clambered over fallen trees and through sprawling thickets of thorns. Then the foliage parted and he could see a grassy rise up ahead. He made for it, away from the voices. There was still a chance of escape.

The thump of his heart was met by the deafening chop of rotor blades. A helicopter burst out from over the knoll, banking steeply, only twenty feet from the ground. It roared in towards him like a bird of prey, nose down and tail up, the wind from the blades tearing at his hair and clothes and flattening a wide circle of grass. A pair of shooters hung out of its open sides, wedged in tight with automatic rifles trained on him. Gunfire ripped a swath of earth at his feet. He turned and ran back the other way, threw himself behind the husk of a fallen tree, and rattled off three double-taps at the helicopter as it roared overhead, punching a line of holes in the black fuselage. The blasting wind of the rotors blew up dust, tore up vegetation debris, and made his eyes water. The chopper veered sharply up to avoid the tree line and began banking to come in for another pass.

A 9mm pistol was no kind of weapon against aircraft and military rifles. But it was all Ben had. He squared the sights on the advancing helicopter and loosed off five more rounds. Nothing happened. The chopper kept coming. The shooters were bringing their weapons back up to aim. He saw the red dot of a laser sight rake across his leg, and he jerked it away just in time. A storm of splinters flew up from the tree trunk before he even heard the shots. He hauled himself to his feet and ran for the cover of the bushes as bullets tore up the ground in his wake. The chopper passed overhead. He ran fast and blind through the thicket, leaping over rocks and ruts. Twice he stumbled and almost went down. Thorns tore at his hands as he swiped them out of his way, and then he was suddenly in a grassy clearing.

But he wasn't alone there. Two agents had headed him off. They were fifteen feet away, yelling at him to freeze, a pistol and a twelve-gauge pointed right at his head.

For a moment it was a standoff. He kept the gun trained on them, wavering it from side to side. His mind was racing. Shoot the one with the shotgun first. The guy with the pistol would probably get off a round, but a single bullet was more likely to miss than the devastating hail of pellets from a short-barreled scattergun at this range.

But a second later the odds were sinking fast as more of them stepped out of the bushes. The woman was to his right, at three o'clock. Jones was at ten o'clock. Then another guy appeared behind the first two. Five on one. With a circle of guns trained on him, there was nowhere to go and no other choices.

He tossed his weapon and put up his hands.

The woman was frowning at him down the barrel of her gun. The look in her eyes seemed to be telling him he'd made it worse for himself by running. That seemed to matter to her. He didn't know why, but he somehow knew she didn't want to be there, and she wished this wasn't happening.

Jones's eyes burned furiously in the mess of blood that was his face. He gave a garbled command, and two agents grabbed Ben's arms and flung him down on the leafy ground. He felt the bite of a plastic cable-tie around his wrists. A knee in his back and the hard steel of a gun against his head. Then a sharp prick as someone jabbed him with a needle.

"You're going sleepy-bye for a while, motherfucker," he heard Jones say through smashed lips.

After that, Ben was diving down into a black pool and the voices around him became echoes and died away to nothing.

37.

After what seemed like a thousand years drifting through a hazy universe of disconnected dreams and nightmares, Ben was jerked awake by the sound of voices. He sat bolt upright, and the first thing he realized was that he was sprawled on a bare mattress in the corner of a dingy room. The next thing he noticed was that his wrists were chained to the wall. He stared down at the steel cuffs biting into his flesh. Followed the line of the long chain from his left wrist, up the pitted wall and round a sturdy metal pipe, then back round to his right wrist. He tugged. The pipe was solid.

The time on his watch was 8:36 p.m. Five and a half hours since his capture. Where the hell was he?

He began to orientate himself as his mind cleared. His prison looked like some kind of old meat locker. It had no windows and a single door made of riveted sheet aluminum. But it had been a long time since it was last used for storage. The floor was thick with dust, and cobwebs hung from the walls. The place had the musty, mousy smell of a building that had been lying empty for years.

The voices outside grew louder. Footsteps. Shadows in the strip of light under the metal door. There was the rattle of a padlock, then the door clanged open and two big men strode into the room. One was thin and wiry, with veiny, clawed hands, his graying hair in a crew cut. The other man looked like a failed weight lifter who spent as much time on cheeseburgers as he did on the bench press, three hundred pounds of lardy muscle underneath a tiny bald head with a black goatee.

Both of them were wearing dark suits, white shirts, somber ties.

They weren't taking any chances. The wiry one stood back a few yards and aimed a pistol at Ben's head while the muscular guy approached him, bent down cautiously, and unlocked his left cuff.

"The room service in this place is terrible," Ben said.

The chunky guy gave a minute smirk. Without a word he yanked the bracelet harshly off Ben's wrist and dragged it out on the end of its chain through the gap between the wall and the pipe.

Ben eyed them both. Their movements were brisk, practiced, professional. With his hands free, for a moment he was tempted to make a move against them. The lardy one, close enough for Ben to smell the grease on his breath, would be no problem. But from the way the wiry one was pointing the pistol, focusing keenly down the sights at him, fingertips white on the black steel, he knew any move would be his last.

The big guy grabbed his free wrist and clapped the bracelet back on, painfully tight. Then he reached in, took a meaty fistful of Ben's shirt, and yanked him powerfully to his feet.

"Walk," he said in a deep voice. Ben met his eyes. They were empty. "Walk," he repeated, shoving Ben with a big hand.

The pistol was on him all the time as he stepped out of the meat locker and found himself looking around at industrial kitchen equipment.

Like the locker, the kitchen was neglected, abandoned-looking. Garbage bags piled up in corners had long ago been torn up by rats and mice, rubbish strewn across the dusty tiles. More debris was piled up on worktops and in sinks that hadn't seen water in years. Cookware and glassware sat on cobwebbed shelves. A knife was embedded in a moldy old chopping board.

He was in a restaurant, or a hotel. Wherever it was, the place had been closed down a long, long time ago. There was a chill in the air that was more than just damp walls. Where was he?

The two men prodded and shoved him across the kitchen and through a set of double doors into a murky corridor. In the gloom was the steel door of an old service elevator. The muscular guy jabbed the button on the wall and the door split in the middle and glided open. Ben felt the gun in his back and stepped inside.

The elevator had the same decaying smell as the kitchen. Ben walked the three steps to the far corner, turned, and leaned back against the wall. The pistol in the wiry guy's hands was still pointed straight at his face from across the elevator. The muscular guy followed, his weight making the floor shake. He pressed a button. The elevator whooshed and rattled under their feet. Nobody spoke. Then the door slid open on the ground floor, and Ben was shoved out into another corridor. The walls were flecked with black mold and the feral stench of mice and rats was even stronger.

"Keep moving," the muscular guy said, leading the way. Ben walked slowly, feeling the gun in his back, taking in his surroundings. They walked him to a second elevator and took him up to the first floor, along another dingy corridor. They passed several doorways. Old hotel rooms, brass-plated numbers blackened with tarnish. The muscular guy stopped outside room thirty-six and rapped on the door. A voice answered from inside; Ben heard footsteps, and then the door opened.

A rangy man with slicked hair stood in the doorway.

"I know you," Ben said. "How're the teeth?"

Jones scowled, showing the gaps in his mouth. "Get him in here," he commanded the other two. His voice was squashy and distorted by his swollen lips. Ben was shoved inside the room and thrown down in a chair. He sat quietly, the chain lying across his lap.

He was in a makeshift office. The room was bare apart from a few chairs, a cheap desk, and a table with a DVD player and monitor. He didn't suppose they'd brought him up here to watch a movie.

Jones shut the door and moved to the middle of the room, rubbing his lips and jaw, his eyes full of hate. Ben didn't recognize the other man. He was sitting on the desk, grinning with white teeth and almost jovial in his manner. Probably late thirties, slender, not tall, expensively dressed, flamboyant red hair. The watch on his wrist was chunky gold, its bezel studded with diamonds. He had the look of an intelligent man who didn't have to be brutal to be in charge but was very used to giving orders. Someone always a step ahead, who had every angle sussed out well in advance. Someone very dangerous.

"Nice place you've got here," Ben said.

The man grinned more widely. "Really, you think so?" His voice was nasal, and he moved his hands a lot while talking. "I guess, being British and all. I personally think it's a shithole. I can't believe what it's costing me. When I'm through here I'll have my guy fly me the eighty miles back to civilization."

"You talk a lot," Ben said.

"So will you," the man answered. His smile dropped a notch.

"I don't think we've met."

"My name's Slater. I think you already know Agent Jones here." Slater took a slim chocolate bar out of his pocket and started unwrapping it. "You like chocolate, Mr. Hope?"

Ben shook his head. "And I don't think you should let Jones have any. His dentist wouldn't approve."

Jones glared. Slater smiled. "All right, I appreciate humor but I'm not here for laughs. Don't make this difficult. Believe me, it's going to be a lot more pleasant if you don't fuck around with us."

"You're not going to get a lot out of me," Ben said.

"Oh, I think we will," Slater replied. "Major."

"I'm not a major. I'm a theology student."

"Right." Slater chuckled. "Must be some other Benedict Hope that comes up all over the CIA computer, with the same face as you."

"It's the truth," Ben said. "I'm just a theology student now."

"A regular man of God."

"I was trying to be," Ben said. "You guys got in the way."

"You were talking theology with Clayton Cleaver?"

"You could say that."

Slater suddenly got serious. "Why are you working with Zoë Bradbury?"

"You people are way off the mark. I'm not working with her. I'm looking for her, but I barely know her. Up till eight days ago, I wouldn't have known her in the street."

"So two SAS guys go all the way out to some Greek island looking for someone they barely know, just like that."

Ben shrugged. There was no reason to lie. "Like I said, I'm a student. Her father is one of my tutors. After she disappeared, he asked me to go to Corfu to find her. I said no and sent an old associate of mine who needed the work. He ran into difficulties, so I went along to help."

"That's it?"

"That's it." Ben looked hard at Slater. "Then someone blew him up. I thought it was Clayton Cleaver. That's why I went to talk to him. But I was wrong. Now I have a different theory. I think you killed Charlie, like you killed Nikos Karapiperis and all the other innocent people, because you need to know where Zoë put the rest of the ostraca she was blackmailing Cleaver with." Ben paused. "Now I've answered your questions, you answer mine. What do you need the ostraca for? Why are you doing all this? The Agency get religion all of a sudden?"

"That's not your concern," Slater said.

"If you needed what she had, maybe you should have thought about asking her before you killed her."

Slater pursed his lips. "What makes you think we killed her?"

"If she was alive, you wouldn't need me to tell you."

"She's alive," Slater replied. "Not only that, she's right here. You'll be meeting her sometime soon."

Ben was thinking furiously. *She was alive.* There was a chance. Possibilities filled his mind. But he didn't let Slater see what he was thinking. "You've had her two weeks, and you can't make her talk? I thought you were tough guys."

Jones pointed a finger. "You're going to tell us, asshole."

"You should keep your mouth shut, Jones," Ben said. "It wasn't the world's greatest sight before I smashed your teeth in, but it's a real eyesore now." He turned to Slater. "I think I get it. She doesn't know, does she?"

Slater just watched him impassively, munching on his chocolate.

"The scooter she hired on Corfu went missing the same time she did," Ben continued. "So I think she was on her way to meet Nikos Karapiperis when your guys tried to catch her. Experts like Jones here. I think they scared her, and she panicked and crashed, and that the reason she isn't talking to you is because she doesn't remember. She's got amnesia from a bang on the head, and you're scared she isn't going to remember. Basically, you're screwed."

Slater crossed his arms. "You're a very smart man, that's for sure. Shame we couldn't find a job for you on our team."

"Smarter than you," Ben said. "A cageload of monkeys could have done better. But that's what happens when you hire a brainless piece of shit like Jones to do your dirty work."

"A man in your position should be trying to make me happy," Slater said. "You're not making me happy."

"I haven't even started yet," Ben replied. "You're wasting your time on me. Even if I did know what you wanted to know, I wouldn't tell you."

"Even smart guys can get into the shit, and you're in a whole heap of it. We can bury you forever. You shot two cops, for a start."

"That was Jones," Ben said. "He's the real hard guy here."

"We have a whole bunch of witnesses who watched you murder two officers in cold blood," Slater said. "Then there's the question of the two missing agents in Greece. I figure you for that as well."

Ben didn't reply.

Slater grinned. "Don't remember? Did you get a knock on the head too? Let's see if this refreshes your memory." He gestured to Jones, who aimed a remote at the flatscreen monitor on the table. It flashed into life and Ben recognized the scene right away. It was crisp color footage of him and Charlie sitting at the café table on Corfu. The sound was muted.

Slater let it play for a few seconds, and Ben watched himself shifting around in his seat as Charlie unfolded the story to him. Then the kid with the ball came past, and moments later he saw himself jump up and run out into the road to save the child from the oncoming van. Charlie was up on his feet. It was the moment just before the explosion.

"OK, you made your point," Ben said. He didn't want to be reminded of that moment. He'd relived it enough times over the last few days.

Jones drew his scabbed lips back over his jagged teeth. He aimed the remote and his thumb stabbed the pause key just as the shock wave erupted across the café terrace and hit Charlie, ripping his body apart in a red blur. The image froze. Jones gazed at it and seemed satisfied.

Ben stared at the screen. He was seeing the blast in a whole new way. When the bomb had exploded, he'd been on the other side of the road behind the cover of the van, with his face down close to the ground. He'd hardly seen a thing.

This image was taken from a completely different angle. It showed the direction of the blast, and it told Ben exactly where the bomb had been. Memories flooded through his mind. He remembered the little boy with the ball. The man at the nearby table with the laptop. He remembered the way the man had shouted at the kid. Most of all, he remembered the fierce look in the man's eyes.

He'd never forget that face. Especially not now.

He barely remembered that the man had slipped away while he and Charlie had been deep in conversation. That's what people did in cafés, finish their drink and slip away—each table its own private, self-contained world. Nothing unusual about it. But he wished now that he'd taken more notice. Frozen up on the screen, caught in the exact moment it fragmented and belched fire and death across the café terrace, the laptop case was a dark blur under the empty table.

Ben turned away from the screen and stared hard at Slater, then at Jones. "So I was right. You planted that bomb."

Slater waved his hand in the air. "I'm a businessman. I don't plant bombs. I just pay other people to plant them."

"That recording was the last thing my agents sent to me before they went off the grid," Jones said. "What did you do to them?"

"They're both dead on a beach," Ben replied. "If you're quick you might find them before the crabs finish what's left of them."

Slater smiled. "So you've decided to be straight with us."

"I'll tell you something else too," Ben said. "I'm going to kill you soon."

"Is that a fact?"

"Yes. That's a fact. Jones too. I'd get those graves ready."

There was a silence. Slater paled, and covered it with a nervous laugh. "I was hoping you were going to be reasonable. This isn't making it any easier for you."

"You've let me see your faces," Ben said. "You wouldn't let me out of here alive anyway. So even if I knew where the ostraca were, which I don't, I wouldn't give you the pleasure."

Slater tossed his empty chocolate wrapper into a bin. "Fine. But there are quick and easy ways of dying, and there are slow and horrible ways to suffer."

"I'll have to decide which one you deserve," Ben said.

Slater sighed. "My God, you're so stubborn. OK, let me show you something else." He gestured again at Jones. The agent pressed another button, and from inside the DVD player came the clunking, whirring sound of the disc changer. The screen was blank for a few moments, then another image came up. A close-up shot of a gaunt, wasted man in grimy fatigues. He was in a filthy cell, or a cage, clutching at the bars. There was bright light shining in his face, showing the glistening fresh wounds and bruises on his jaw and cheek, the livid swelling of his right eye.

"What you're seeing here is from classified CIA archives," Slater said. "You don't need to know what this is about. Same old story. Let's just say the guy is privy to certain information, and these other guys want to get it out of him. He's a tough fucker, like you. He's resisted all kinds of torture. When the camera zooms out, you can just about make out the blood on his feet where they tore out his toenails. Any time now. There."

Ben watched the images on the screen as Slater stood up and walked around. "See, I'm a bureaucrat," Slater said. "I'll admit it. I like to hear the truth from people, but I'm not a guy who's comfortable around blood and violence—at least not at close range."

"It's different when you're just making a phone call, isn't it?"

Slater ignored that. "I could have you beaten into catmeat right now," he said. "I could have them cut off your fingers and ears, cut off your balls, fry you with electricity, dunk you in a tub, string you up by the thumbs, all that kind of shit. With your background, I'm sure you have a pretty good idea of what's involved. But that's more Jones's line. Personally, I'd rather get what I want without the mess. I like things clean and clinical. If I have to have someone fucked up . . ." Slater smiled. "Well, take a look at this guy."

Ben was watching. As Slater talked, the prisoner on-screen was being forced down in his chair by guards in unmarked uniform. A third came into shot and stabbed a syringe in the man's neck, pressed the plunger home, and jerked the needle out with a squirt of blood.

Slater reached into his jacket pocket, took out a small amber bottle, and laid it down with a clunk on the desk. Then he reached into the other pocket and brought out a small leather case. He unzipped it and laid it open on the desk beside the bottle. There was a syringe inside. "Know what this stuff is for?"

Ben gazed across at the bottle. "Yes, I do. But I thought Jones asked us not to discuss his personal condition."

"Oh, that's so funny. You know what this is."

"I've heard about it."

"I thought you would have. The very best of its kind. Vintage stuff. Hard to get. Unfortunately, the good doctor who supplied it won't be joining us." Slater gestured at the screen. "Now, this guy, he was like you. He absolutely insisted he didn't know what they needed to know. Boy, he was so sure of himself. But then he talked, all right. One shot was all it took. Within an hour he was telling them everything, and then some. Remarkable. And you know what, they didn't even have to put a bullet in his head afterwards, because look what happened."

Jones thumbed the remote again, three times. The image accelerated to eight times the speed, and suddenly the picture changed: new camera angle, different lighting. The same man, but he had changed too. Radically. He'd gone from being a terrified, beaten-up prisoner to being a babbling, screaming lunatic jerking on his cage bars, eyes wild, teeth bared, foaming at the mouth. He was on a different planet.

"Total insanity," Slater said. "The same guy, just six hours later. That's what this shit does to you. The effects are irreversible, permanent. Sometimes they kick in within an hour or so. Some of the tougher ones hold out for much longer. But they all go the same way sooner or later. Raving psychosis till the day you die. You understand what I'm saying?"

Jones smiled. He paused the image on the screen, laid down the remote, and folded his arms in satisfaction.

"I understand," Ben said.

"Good. Because I want you to think about that."

"Thinking of giving me a cocktail?"

"Straight, no chaser," Slater said. "But not just yet. Here's what we're going to do." He looked at his watch. "It's just after nine p.m. You have till ten to think about what you'd like to tell me. Then I'm going to reunite you with your friend Bradbury, and you can watch while I have this serum pumped into her. We'll see what she has to tell us. You can listen in. It'll be fun. And then, when I come back here in the morning, I'm going to let you see what it did to her before it's your turn." Slater smiled. "I'll be far away, sipping on a glass of Krug while you're sitting in your cell downstairs enjoying your last hours of sanity. Soon afterwards, when you're screaming in your cage like an animal, I'll sign a paper turning you over to a state nuthouse, where you'll live out the rest of your miserable life, battering your head off a padded wall."

"Why waste the taxpayers' money?" Jones said. "We should just dump his raving ass in a backstreet somewhere."

"I like it," Slater said thoughtfully. "Now, enough talk. Jones, get your guys in here."

Jones opened the door. The two men who had brought Ben up in the elevator were standing out in the corridor. "Take this prick back down there and lock him up," he said. He pointed at the muscular one. "Boyter, you're posted outside his door. McKenzie, you get back up here ASAP."

"You have one hour," Slater said to Ben.

Boyter gripped Ben's arm. "Let's go, shithead."

Ben stood up, shook off Boyter's chubby hands, and moved towards the door. He stopped, turned, and fixed Slater in the eye. "Remember what I said earlier," he said softly. Then he was gone.

Jones watched with a smirk as Boyter and McKenzie herded the prisoner down the corridor towards the elevator. He turned to Slater. The man looked a little less composed than he had a second ago.

"Don't worry about him," Jones said. "He's history already."

38.

Slater paced while Jones smoked. Five minutes passed, then ten.

"Relax," Jones said.

"I never relax." Slater looked at his watch. "Those cigarettes reek. What's keeping your guy McKenzie? I thought you told him to get back here ASAP."

"He'll be right back," Jones said. "Probably went to the bathroom."

Slater shook his head. His jaw was tight. He ran his fingers through his hair. "Something's wrong. I can feel it."

"You're nuts. Hope's locked up tighter than a fish's asshole."

"If that's so, I want to see for myself. I have a bad feeling."

"You and your feelings," Jones grunted. "OK, let's go."

"I'm not going down there with just you alone. How many people have you got in the building?"

"Including me, there are a dozen agents in the place. You're not telling me—"

"That's exactly what I'm telling you. Leave two watching Bradbury. I want the rest with me."

Jones protested loudly, but Slater insisted. Jones got on the radio. "Fiorante, join Jorgensen on the prisoner's door. Everyone else, my office, right now."

In two more minutes the seven agents were collected in the corridor outside. Slater cautiously stepped out of the office. Jones led the way, exasperation showing on his face.

"Not the elevator," Slater said. "We take the stairs."

"I think the guy got to you," Jones sneered. "You're spooked."

"Cautious is what I am," Slater said. "And smart."

They reached the bottom of the stairs, turned through the dingy lobby, and trotted down another flight towards the basement kitchen.

"Get your guns out," Slater whispered.

"You're nuts," Jones said again. "There's no—"

He batted through the double doors leading to the kitchen. Then he stopped dead and his mouth hung open. "Oh, shit."

"Told you," Slater muttered.

"What the fuck happened here?"

Slater shot him a sideways look. "I think that's pretty obvious, don't you?"

The kitchen was littered with debris. In the middle of it, Boyter and McKenzie were lying dead, the fluorescent striplights reflecting in the broad pool of blood inching slowly across the floor.

Slater peered down at Boyter and wondered for a moment what the strange circular object stuck to the side of his head was. Then it hit him. He had the snapped-off stem of a wineglass buried deep in his temple. McKenzie was lying at an angle to his colleague, his face blue, tongue hanging out, a livid weal around his throat where he'd been throttled to death with a steel chain. The handcuffs lay open on the floor, next to a small key. The men's jackets lay open, holsters empty.

Slater and Jones stared at each other. "Hope's loose in the building," Jones breathed.

"No shit. And you're going to find him."

"We'll find him," Jones said.

"You'd better. You lost him. He stays lost, you're dead. Understand?"

"We'll find him," Jones said again. "You get back up to the office."

"No way. I'm getting out of here. This place isn't safe for me."

"It's not safe for anyone."

"You're expendable. I'm not." Slater stabbed his finger at the agents. "You, you, and you. Escort me the fuck out of here." He started walking away, then stopped and turned. "And Jones?"

"What?"

"You take him *alive*. Clear?"

"We'll get him," Jones said.

Slater almost sprinted to the lobby, three agents close behind with drawn guns. He tore open the front door, left the building with jittery haste, and ran towards the sleek Bell chopper that was sitting in the middle of the parking lot. The pilot saw him coming, put away his flask of coffee, and fired up the motor. The prop slowly began to turn as Slater wrenched open the hatch and piled inside. Minutes later, he was a rapidly vanishing speck over the treetops.

With Slater out of the way, Jones gathered his agents around him. "OK, people, he's only one man. With McKenzie and Boyter gone, that still leaves ten of us in the building." He picked up his radio. "Jorgensen, you still there?"

"Right where you put me," said the voice in his ear.

"Fiorante with you?"

"Yes, sir."

Jones nodded. He jerked his pistol at the men. "Cash, Muntz, get up to the top floor and join them. That's where Hope'll be headed." He grinned. "He wants to get the girl." He glanced quickly around him, calculating tactics. No way Hope was going to get past four people on the door. Meanwhile, two teams of three men each could scour the place and head him off. "Bender, Simmons, you're with me. Kimble, Davis, Austin, take the left side of the building. Stay in contact. You see him, take him down. He's way too dangerous to keep alive."

"Slater said not to kill him," said Austin.

"I don't give a shit what Slater said." Jones touched his tongue against his teeth, felt the ragged edges that were such a constant reminder of the man. "I want this fucker bodybagged in the next ten minutes. Let's go."

39.

Ben almost pitied the two dead men. Whomever they were used to dealing with, they'd been too slow. They just hadn't seen it coming.

He'd left them where they dropped, found the key in the big one's pocket, and taken the silenced Berettas they were packing. Both fully loaded. He nodded to himself, tucked one pistol in his right hip pocket and the other in his back pocket. Glanced quickly around the kitchen. Yanked the knife out of the old chopping board. The stainless-steel blade was serrated and still sharp. He stuck it carefully in his belt.

He'd already figured out his escape route. He strode over to a square hatch on the kitchen wall and yanked up the sliding metal door to reveal the dumbwaiter. Next to the three-foot-square hole was a dusty old wall panel with three plastic buttons, two arrow-shaped, one pointing up and the other down, the middle one marked stop in faded writing.

He hit the up button with his palm, hoping the thing still worked after all these years. There was a dull clunk, and the dumbwaiter jerked up an inch before he hit the stop button.

Good enough, he thought. The space was just about large enough to cram himself in. It stank of old grease, damp, and mouse shit. He reached out from inside, felt for the up arrow, and hit it. Felt the dumbwaiter jolt under him and the sensation of rising upwards. He withdrew his arm quickly inside as the wall came down. A glimpse of brickwork and then blackness. The dumbwaiter rose up, grinding and vibrating. In the darkness he took one of the pistols and checked it again. There was no telling what he was going to meet up there.

From somewhere over his head there was a screech, as though the cables were about to snap. He braced himself but nothing happened. The dumbwaiter gave a shudder and then stopped. He reached out and pushed gently, opening a pair of double doors three feet square. His guess had been right. He was in the hotel bar, in a little serving area behind the bar itself. He lowered himself out of the hatch, thankful to be out of the claustrophobic space, and crouched down in the dust behind the old bar.

He figured he was on the ground floor. Where would they be keeping Zoë? Upstairs in one of the rooms? It was only a guess, and a vague one, but it was all he had. At least he was close now. Only about a dozen guns in his way. He could worry about that when he started meeting them.

He snapped off the safety on the pistol and crept silently out through the barroom door, sweeping the muzzle left and right, surveying the scene through the sights as he moved cautiously down the murky corridor. He kept in the shadows, tight against the wall, senses fully alert, the gun in front of him, drawing on the ability for complete silence and stealth that had made him legendary among his old regiment. He could hear running footsteps and voices from the lobby. They'd have broken up to hunt for him. Maybe two, three men per team, and probably at least two teams with whomever was leftover allocated to guard Zoë's room.

Up ahead, the corridor was L-shaped and opened up into a wider hallway with doors on either side. One was ajar, dusty light streaming out of what must once have been a TV room.

He froze. Someone was coming the other way. Three men, running. He shrank back into the shadow, the light from the open door creating enough contrast to mask him. He could have reached out and touched them as they ran by. He let them pass.

When the third man was two yards past him he stepped out into the corridor, raised the gun, and shot him in the back of the head. The man collapsed, hit the floor, and squeaked along the linoleum under his own momentum. Before the other two could register what had happened, Ben fired two more shots in such quick succession that the report of the silenced gun sounded more like one prolonged muted bark than two separate shots. The men's bodies jerked and they stumbled against each other and went down. A gun slithered across the dusty floor.

Ben gathered up their weapons. More Berettas, all the same model. He ejected the mags out of the three pistols and slipped them in his pockets. Then he stepped over to the three bodies and looked down at them.

He'd never enjoyed the cautionary head shot. It was something that had been schooled into him a long time ago. He'd never wanted to do this again. But every military tactician since ancient times said it was the right thing to do to make sure your enemy never got up once he was down. It was slaughterhouse-brutal, but it made immaculate sense.

Three head shots at point-blank range with a high-powered handgun are a lot messier in reality than in the movies. Shielding his face against the blood splatter, he did the job fast, stepping from one inert body to the next. The 147-grain semi-jacketed hollowpoint bullets had split the men's skulls apart and blasted brains up the wall. The corridor filled with the ripe stink of blood and death.

There'd be more of it to come. He moved on.

40.

Jones dashed along the corridor, stabbing the pistol out in front of him at every turn and doorway. Many of the lights were flickering or dead, casting long black pools of shadow everywhere. He stumbled, cursing, over a pile of old cardboard boxes and paint cans. Snatched up his radio. "Kimble. Talk to me."

Silence.

"Shit," Jones said. "Jorgensen. You still there?"

"Copy. We're still up here. No sign of him yet. You?"

"Nothing. The fucker's like a ghost. OK. Out."

Jones rounded a corner. The coppery tang of fresh blood hovered in the air, mingling with the smell of damp and rot. He saw three dark shapes lying in the shadows up ahead. He signaled to Bender and Simmons behind him to halt. They stared at the three dead agents on the floor.

"That makes five of us he's taken out, just like that," said Bender. "He's just playing with us."

"I don't think splitting up was such a great idea," Simmons muttered at his shoulder.

Jones gritted his teeth and nearly screamed at the pain. He wiped sweat out of his eyes. "We need more people. A lot more people."

"We don't have any more people," Bender said.

"I can get a hundred men in here and nail that motherfucker," Jones spat. "I just need to make one call." He thought for a moment. It would take a few hours to get reinforcements in place. He'd have a lot of favors to call in first, and the kind of manpower he was thinking of took time to organize.

A fresh idea occurred to him. "All right, listen, fuck this. We're going up to the top floor and join up with the others there. That makes seven. I don't care how good this guy is, no way can he get past seven of us." He grinned. "Then we're going to stick that little bitch Bradbury with the syringe. Right now. I'm tired of waiting games. Let's find out what she knows."

"Slater isn't going to like it."

"To hell with that cowardly bastard. He wants to play leader, he should stick around more."

They stepped over the dead men and ran on up the corridor. Jones reached the elevator first and hammered the button for the first floor. They said nothing, faces downcast, as the elevator whooshed upwards. Then the doors glided open and Jones was dashing towards his office door.

It was open, lying an inch or so ajar.

He fought to remember. No. He hadn't left it open. He'd locked it.

He drew his gun. Cold fear began to knot his intestines, and the gun shook in his hand. *Control yourself.* He held the weapon out in front of him and prodded the door tentatively open with his left hand. It creaked. He pushed it open a little farther. He stepped inside the room, heart thumping.

The office was empty.

So was the desk. And the canvas bag had gone.

"Hope," he breathed. "Hope was here."

Simmons was behind him, staring with big eyes.

"He took it," Jones gasped. *"He fucking took the bottle."*

41.

There was a cry from outside the office. Simmons and Jones locked eyes for half a second, then Jones grabbed the door handle and they burst out into the corridor. Night was falling outside, and the shadows in the building were deepening. Jones flipped a light switch. Nothing happened. Cursing, he peered into the darkness. "Bender?" he called out softly.

There was no reply.

The whites of Simmons's eyes glistened in the murk. "Where'd he—"

He never finished the sentence. Jones felt the wet spray of blood hit his face almost before he'd registered the muffled cough of the gunshot. Simmons fell against him, making a terrible gurgling sound from his throat, clawing at his arm, and then slumped to the floor. He kicked a few times, then the gurgle became a deathly rattle and he stopped moving.

"I'll kill you!" Jones screamed. He punched his gun out to arm's length and kept firing wildly until the magazine was empty. He ejected it, slammed in a fresh one, and let another fifteen shots loose down the corridor, as fast as he could work the trigger.

Then the hot gun was empty again. He stood there, gasping, panting. The corridor was darkening fast. Other than a shaft of dull gray light coming from one of the cobwebbed windows, he was in blackness. He turned, groping his way in the dark. He desperately reached for the light switch again. Nothing.

That was when he felt the cold blade of the knife against his throat. He froze, hand still on the switch.

"I knew you'd come back here," said a voice close behind him. "That's why I took out all the bulbs from this corridor."

Jones wanted to gulp but he could feel the edge of the steel pressing lightly against his trachea. "Hope?" he whispered.

"Tip for you," Ben said. "If you're going to keep a man locked in a kitchen, don't leave sharp knives lying around. Someone might get cut."

"What are you going to do?" Jones quavered.

"I'm going to slice your head off."

Jones rocked dizzily on his feet with terror.

"Unless you take me to Zoë," Ben said.

"She's guarded," Jones said in a strangled voice.

"Maybe I can convince you to have your people stand down," Ben said. "Then I'm going to take her out of here, and you're going to come with us so you can tell me what's going on."

"I just follow orders. Slater's the guy you want."

"I'll get to him in good time," Ben said. "But I think you know plenty. Maybe we'll get to try out that truth serum on you."

"You are so fucking dead, Hope."

"Not before you. Now move." Ben shoved him down the corridor.

In the elevator, Jones pressed the button for the second floor. Ben slipped the kitchen knife into his bag and kept one of the Berettas aimed steadily at the agent's head.

The doors whirred open. Ben grabbed Jones's wrist and bent it up sharply behind his back. He shoved him out of the gap, keeping the gun on him. They stepped out into the white corridor. The smell of fresh paint lingered in the air. The whole upper floor had been redecorated, but in a hurry.

"What's up here?"

"Just the girl," Jones said. "And twenty agents. You haven't a chance in hell."

"I've been taking chances in hell most of my life," Ben said. "Shut up and walk."

Jones walked slowly, breathing hard and sweating from the pain in his arm as Ben kept it within half an inch of breaking. Up ahead, the corridor bent round to the left. Ben quietly thumbed off the safety on his pistol, every muscle tight, watching everything. He felt Jones tense, and he knew they were close. He let go of Jones and drew the second Beretta.

They rounded the corner. Ten yards away the corridor came to a dead end at room thirty-six. Between them and the door stood three agents, two men, one woman. They saw him standing there with Jones and pulled their guns. Suddenly the corridor was filled with yelling.

Ben remembered them from before, especially the woman. Her auburn hair was tied back under a baseball cap. The 9mm she was holding looked oversized in her small hands, but she knew what she was doing with it. Her blue eyes were locked hard onto his. He tried to read the look on her face.

He moved towards them, using Jones's body as a shield, his left pistol hard up against the base of the man's skull and his right aimed down the corridor at the three guns pointing back at him.

"I just want Zoë," he yelled. "Then it's over."

He moved closer. Five yards. He felt the blood pulsing through his temples. The agents' faces were tense, nerves frazzling. Fingers on triggers, muzzles steady. One slip, one shot, and nobody would escape the frenetic exchange of bullets at such close range.

"Step away from him and lay down the weapon!" one of the men shouted.

Ben saw the flicker in his eyes at the same instant he sensed the sudden movement behind him. He reacted a fraction of a second too late. It all happened at once. A powerful hand grabbed his left arm and jerked his gun away from Jones's head. At the same time a fist slammed sideways into his ear, and his vision exploded in a flash of white light. Jones scrabbled out of his grasp. A volley of silenced gunfire, bullets tearing down the corridor all around him. A searing impact to his left shoulder as he felt a 9mm round punch deep into the deltoid muscle.

Something to worry about later. He fired point-blank at the agent who'd attacked from the rear. The guy crumpled. Ben caught him as he fell, spun him around, and felt the impact as bullets thwacked into the man's body. But he was caught off balance and the dead agent crashed to the floor on top of him, knocking the pistol out of his left hand. As he struggled to kick the corpse off him he glimpsed Jones running away back down the corridor, heading for the elevator.

The three agents were moving forward, guns extended, aiming right at him. The woman's face was steely.

Impossible odds. Three guns against one. There was no way he could bring them all down before they got him. Lying on his back, he punched out the Beretta one-handed and fired, taking down the man on the left. Swiveled his sights across in a blur.

Too late. He could see the other man's finger already taking up the slack on the trigger. Their bullets would cross in the air. He was dead.

Then everything changed.

The woman stepped back, twisted to one side, and put a bullet between the shoulder blades of the agent next to her. His mouth burst open. The gun dropped from his hands. He went down on his face.

Then silence. Just the two of them left alive in the corridor.

Ben got to his feet, eyeing her warily. His shoulder was on fire, his heart racing. He blinked the sweat out of his eyes and raised his weapon one-handed at the same instant she trained hers back on him.

They circled each other for a few moments in a silent standoff, pistol muzzles almost kissing. He was aware of the blood running freely down his left arm and dripping fast from his fingertips, the soft *plop* of the drops splashing onto the floor the only sound in the smoky corridor.

"Put it down," he said.

"You put yours down," she replied in a tight voice.

"Everyone's dead. It's just you and Jones."

"Who the hell are you, Ben Hope?"

"Just someone looking for Zoë Bradbury."

"You want to get her out of here? So do I."

"Show me."

She bent down, very slowly, and laid the gun on the floor. Then stepped back and watched him. "See? I'm on your side," she said. "Trust me."

He kept the gun on her, frowning and confused. "Who are you? Why are you doing this?"

"I'm Alex Fiorante, CIA. I'm not one of them."

"Could have fooled me, Alex."

"These people aren't regular Agency. They're some kind of rogue unit."

He was quiet for a moment, breathing hard, still aiming the gun at her. "Where's Zoë?"

She pointed. "Right behind that door. You want to get her out? Then let's do it. We don't have a lot of time."

"I want to know what's going on," he said.

"I'll tell you everything I know. After."

He squatted down and scooped up her fallen pistol. Every movement of his left arm was agonizing.

She watched him tuck her pistol in his belt. "You can trust me, I swear."

"Maybe I will," he said. "But I don't think we're there yet. Open the door."

Alex kneeled down next to one of the dead agents and rolled the heavy corpse over with a grunt. She reached into his inside pocket and came out with a key, her fingers stained with the man's blood. She wiped the blood on his clothes, walked the two steps to the door, and unlocked it.

"You first," he said. She stepped inside and he followed her, holding the gun to her back and looking around him at Zoë's prison.

It was empty.

42.

Then he heard the whimper from under the bed. He pushed Alex against the wall. "Don't move." He squatted down and peered under the bed.

For the first time in nearly twenty years he was finally face-to-face with Zoë Bradbury. Unlike the happy, smiling young woman in her photo, her face was pale and thin from nearly two weeks of incarceration. She shrank away from him with a look of terror.

"Zoë, I'm a friend." With the rising agony in his shoulder it was a struggle to keep his tone soft and reassuring. "My name's Ben Hope. I've come to rescue you. Your parents sent me."

She shrank farther away, back against the wall.

"Come on out," he said. "I'll take you home. It's over."

She wouldn't come out. He had no time to mess about like this. Jones was still in the building. Ben grabbed the steel bed frame and slid it away from the wall on its casters. He reached down and grasped her arm. She squealed with fright.

"Look, I know you've been through a lot," he said. "I know how you're feeling. But you need to cooperate with me." He jerked her to her feet, and she stared at him in bewilderment. Then she caught sight of Alex Fiorante across the room and started wriggling to get free of his grip. "She's one of them!"

"Zoë, it's all right," Alex said gently. "Ben and I are going to get you out."

"No! No! She's one of them!" Zoë struggled harder, her voice rising into a scream.

Ben hit her with a straight jab to the jaw.

She went down without a sound. He gathered her up and slung her over his right shoulder. The pain was excruciating.

"That's one way of doing it," Alex said.

"Let's go." Ben pushed open the door and surveyed the corridor. No sign of Jones. They paced cautiously down the hall, stepping over the dead bodies. Blood was dripping fast from Ben's left arm, leaving a trail as he walked. His shirt was soaked with it.

The elevator had gone. Ben pressed the wall button and heard it lurch into motion down below. "Stand back." He aimed his gun at the doors, bracing himself.

The elevator was empty. They rode it down to the ground floor and crept out into the deserted lobby. Zoë's limp body was becoming a dead weight. Ben wiped the sweat out of his eyes, fighting to stay alert.

Alex pointed. "The exit is this way." They hurried outside. He suddenly felt chilled to the bone as the cool night air hit the sweat on his body. He glanced all around him, taking in his surroundings for the first time since they'd caught him and brought him here.

The derelict hotel was perched high up on a rocky mound, with a narrow road snaking down through the trees and disappearing into the distance. The dying sunset was an explosive panorama of red and gold behind the rugged line of mountains. On the other side of the sky the moon was rising. Vast plains and forests stretched out for miles in every direction.

He turned to Alex. "Where are we?"

"About fifty miles south of Chinook, Montana. One road in, one road out. A million acres of nothing all around us."

"What the hell are we doing in Montana?"

"Getting out of it, if we have any sense."

There were a few vehicles parked outside the hotel. "We'll take that one," Ben said, pointing to a GMC four-wheel drive parked opposite. Alex trotted over to it and reached inside the driver's door to flip down the sun visor. A key dropped into her palm. "I'll drive."

Ben opened up the rear and laid Zoë gently down on the backseat. She stirred and groaned. He was sorry for what he'd had to do to her, but there was no time to worry about it now. He climbed in beside

Alex as she gunned the engine into life. "There's a first-aid kit under the seat," she told him. He opened the box and sifted through. Bandages. Surgical tape and scissors. A tube of codeine tablets. He swallowed two of them and leaned back in the seat, pressing hard against his wound to stem the bleeding.

Alex accelerated hard away from the hotel. The road was narrow and twisty, forest on either side.

"We can't stay on the road," he said faintly. "I don't want to come face-to-face with forty of your Agency friends, FBI, and whoever else. If you see any kind of path, take us down it."

"You're crazy. You'll lose us in the wilderness."

"That's the idea."

Alex was a good driver, and the big GMC felt solid and planted on the loose surface as she kept her foot hard on the floor. After a couple of miles there was a gap in the trees, and Ben saw a dirt road snaking away to the right. "There."

She threw the car into it, skidding into the turn. The car shuddered and hammered over the uneven ground. Branches and bushes skimmed past in the lights, raking the windshield. Ben pulled the bloody material of his shirt aside and felt the wound. The bullet hole was in the fleshy part of the shoulder. He didn't think it had hit bone. The whisky flask was still about half full, and he sluiced the wound with it, grimacing at the sting, as Alex drove. He peeled off his shirt, unraveled a length of bandage, and started binding himself up.

"How bad is it?" she said, glancing across, raising her voice over the engine roar.

"Fine," he muttered. The pain was dulling as the codeine hit his bloodstream.

"It's not fine. We're going to have to get that bullet out of you fast."

"Just keep moving," he said.

The road carved deep into wilderness. After about six miles it was so overgrown that they were driving blind, crashing through dense undergrowth. On the backseat, Zoë was groggily propping herself up, rubbing her face where Ben had hit her and holding on to the door for support as the GMC lurched wildly from side to side.

Alex's eyes were concentrated fiercely on the windshield, hands tight on the wheel. After a few more miles she was forced to slow to a crawl, and the road had petered out to nothing. The GMC battered its way through a giant thorn bush and broke free, and suddenly they were in open countryside with an ocean of dark prairie stretching out in front of them. The stars were out and twinkling, and the mountains were a jagged black silhouette against the sky.

"The Montana Hi-Line," Alex said. "Where the great plains meet the Rocky Mountains. Nothing but wilderness."

After a dozen more brutal miles, the terrain was becoming increasingly rough and the rocks and ruts were forcing them to take a wild path. Alex was getting exhausted, shaking her head to stay focused. Then the GMC lurched violently sideways and pitched to the left, almost going over. Ben felt himself sliding across the seat and braced himself with his legs. In the back, Zoë cried out. The car ground to a halt, something clanking from the front end. Alex swore and pumped the accelerator, but the wheels had lost traction and were spinning in the dirt. She swore again.

Ben opened his door and jumped down, clutching his shoulder. The bleeding had stopped, but his shirt and jeans were black with blood. He staggered in the dark, light-headed with pain, cold sweat on his brow. The GMC was tightly bedded into a rocky rut that had been hidden by bushes, impossible to spot in the dark. "We'd need a tractor to tow us out," he said. "We walk from here."

Zoë's jaw dropped open. "My God, this is your idea of a rescue? I'm not walking out there."

"Fine," he said. "You stay here to fend for yourself, among the rattlesnakes and grizzlies." He turned to Alex. "We'll need to conceal the car. It's easy to spot from the air."

"You think they'll come out in helicopters?"

He smiled weakly. "Wouldn't you?"

They salvaged what they could from the car—there were a couple of blankets in the back, bottled water, a Maglite, some matches, binoculars. Ben packed all the stuff into his bag, together with the first-aid kit. Then he and Alex explored the wooded valley around them, gathering branches and bits of shrub by flashlight and building them up in a mound around the car. There were a hundred questions he badly wanted to ask her, but right now they had more important priorities. He felt he could trust her, though he didn't know why.

After a few minutes the vehicle just looked like a big clump of vegetation under the moonlight. Ben nodded to himself and hefted the heavy bag onto his good shoulder. They set out across the rocky terrain, the moon lighting their path. Ben kept Zoë close by him, grabbing her arm to keep her moving when she fell back. She was sullen and unwilling, and complained loudly whenever she stumbled over a rock or a tree root.

He ignored her protests and trudged on. Every so often he glanced up at the stars to maintain their northerly course. Alex had said the hotel was fifty miles south of Chinook. It made sense that the closer they got to civilization, the more likely they would be to come across a road or a farm from where they could work out their next move. And Ben knew that sooner or later he'd need medical attention. Untreated, the wound would fester. He was thankful for the recent tetanus booster he'd had—but he'd seen gangrene set in quickly in lesser wounds than this.

As he walked he could feel his energy gradually dwindling and the grinding pain in his shoulder beginning to intensify again. He fought the urge to take another painkiller. He couldn't afford to waste them. There was a lot of distance ahead, and a lot of pain.

43.

The ground sloped steeply upwards ahead of them, rising out of the forested valley, the cold wind whistling about their ears. They walked wearily in silence, and after a while Zoë lost the energy even to complain anymore.

At the base of a towering limestone mountain, fifty yards above the valley, they found a cave entrance shielded from the wind by an overhanging lip of rock. Ben shone the Maglite inside, checking for signs of wild-animal habitation. The cave would have been an ideal lair for a grizzly or a mountain lion, but there were no traces of droppings or half-finished kill. Alex and a resentful Zoë gathered dry boughs and fern leaves for bedding while Ben built a fire at the back of the cave, arranged so that the smoke would rise up to the roof and escape through the entrance. He lit the tinder with a match, and after a few minutes he had a good blaze going. Exhausted from pain and drenched with cold sweat, he collapsed on the leafy floor. Alex joined him, frowning in worry as she settled next to him. She felt his brow and ran her fingers through his damp hair.

Zoë flopped down opposite, ignoring them. She grabbed a blanket for a pillow and lay down. She was asleep soon afterwards.

Ben prodded the fire with a stick. "It's time for you and me to talk."

"I'll tell you what I know," Alex said. "But it's not a hell of a lot."

"Tell me about Jones."

She sighed. "I was assigned to his unit eight months ago. I never liked the guy. He's a class-A creep. I was about to request a transfer to a different unit when things started getting strange. I was part of a team watching a guy called Cleaver. Phone taps, e-mail intercept, close surveillance, the works."

"But nobody told you why."

"The Agency works in mysterious ways a lot of the time. You accept that they don't always disclose everything to the field agents. But this was different. Only Jones ever saw the transcripts of calls. The rest of us were kept in the dark. I even started listening at doors, and that's how I knew some agents had been sent to Greece."

"Marisa Kaplan was one of them," he said. "Know her?"

"No, but I found her name on a file. One I could have got in a lot of trouble for looking at. She's ex-CIA. No longer active."

Even less active now, Ben thought. He didn't say anything.

"Then about eight days ago," Alex went on, "there was this sudden flurry of activity. Jones was all keyed up, on the phone a hundred times a day, real grouchy. Next thing, a team of us were scrambled together and posted up here in Montana."

"That was when Zoë was brought here from Greece."

She nodded. "They flew her by private jet as far as Helena, and then brought her out here by chopper. We were told she was a key witness to a terrorist bombing in Greece. But I never bought it. The Agency just doesn't operate that way. I've never seen a holding facility like this. I think they're using government resources for their own unofficial business. I was just about to report it to the top level. But I didn't do it."

"Why didn't you?"

"Because of what happened to Josh Greenberg. I didn't know him well, but he seemed like a good guy. Jones shot him in the face."

"Jones seems to like shooting people in the face," Ben said.

"When that happened, I was just too scared to think straight. I felt isolated. I wish I'd done something."

"I know the feeling."

"But I didn't know who I could trust. Then suddenly the call came through that we were all to fly back down to Georgia. They'd found out about you. You know the rest."

"I remember you from the day they caught me," he said. "The look on your face. I could see you were different."

She glanced at him. "I shouldn't have let them take you that day. I should have done something."

"There wasn't much you could have done. You'd just have ended up like the two cops. These people are killing anyone who stands in their way."

She gazed through the firelight at Zoë's sleeping form. "I don't know what the hell she's got that they want," she said. "But they want it pretty damn badly."

"Maybe more than you know," Ben said. He spent the next fifteen minutes telling Alex everything that had happened. Her eyes widened in stunned horror as he described the bombing. Then he went on. One baffling detail after another. Laying it all out. Skid McClusky. Clayton Cleaver. Augusta Vale's hundred million. Zoë's discovery. The blackmail.

She listened carefully to every word. By the time he'd finished, she was staring at him in bewilderment, struggling to grasp the enormity of it. "It's so weird," she breathed. "None of it makes sense. Why would they want some piece of pottery? Why is some obscure matter of theology important to them?"

"How long was your team watching Cleaver for?"

"Months."

"So that's how they found out about Zoë. When she tried to blackmail him, they picked up the phone call. Then when Skid McClusky went to Cleaver's office to deliver the box, they were already watching. They were the ones who went after McClusky. And if his ex-girlfriend hadn't turned up, they were going to torture him to death."

Alex's brow crinkled in concentration. "So what you're saying is that the whole thing with Zoë is just incidental."

"Cleaver is the key," Ben said. "It all revolves around him. But I don't think he even knows it. The question is, why were they watching him in the first place?"

There was silence as they both sat trying to puzzle it out.

"They're planning something," she said. "I just know it."

"Planning what?"

"I wish I knew."

"Who's Slater?"

She looked blank.

"He was with Jones in the hotel. Red hair. Small build. Sharp suit. Didn't look like a cop or an agent. He's in charge of it. Jones answers to him."

"I never heard of any Slater," she said.

Ben's shoulder was cramping, and he tried to make himself more comfortable against the hard wall of the cave. Agony lanced through him like a blade, and he shuddered. He was suddenly terribly weary from the mental effort of trying to work all this out.

She looked at him in concern. "You're in a lot of pain, aren't you? There's some codeine left."

"Save it for tomorrow," he muttered.

"Let me take a look at it."

"I'm OK," he protested.

"I'm not going to let you die on me, Ben. I need you as much as you need me." She reached across and started unbuttoning the bloody shirt. He resisted, then relented and leaned back as she drew the shirt off and carefully unwound the bandages. "You've done this before," he said faintly.

"Three years at medical school, before I dropped out to get a taste of adventure, travel the world. Dumbest thing I ever did." She shone the Maglite across his chest and shoulder. "And you've been shot before," she added, noticing pale scars on his torso.

"Twice before. That one's a shrapnel injury."

"Quite a collection," she said. She inspected the wound closely. "I don't think there's any internal bleeding, Ben. But we need to get that bullet out of there. You ought to be in the hospital."

"Out of the question," he murmured. But he was too weak to protest. Alex bundled a blanket under his head, and he lay back on it as she bandaged him back up, winding the gauze expertly into a tight and secure dressing. Then she helped him get his shirt back on and draped a blanket across him. "We should get some sleep," she whispered.

He watched in the flickering firelight as she made up a bed of fern leaves and settled herself into it. After a few minutes the steady rise and fall of her body under the blanket told him she was sleeping. He lay awake for a long time, listening to the yap of the coyotes in the distance.

Sometime in the night he woke to see Alex gazing at him in the dying glow of the fire. Her head was resting on her hands, her hair draped across her face. The last of the flames flickered in her eyes. "You were dreaming," she whispered sleepily. "About someone you love."

He didn't reply.

"Are you married?" she murmured. "Is there someone waiting for you at home?"

He hesitated before answering. "No. There's nobody. What about you?"

"There was someone," she said. "Back where I live, in Virginia. His name was Frank. I guess we never had much of a chance. It ended a couple of years ago. We never saw each other—he had his veterinary practice, I was always up at HQ or out in the field somewhere. It just kind of died on us." She smiled sadly. "I suppose I gave my heart to the Agency."

"I did that once," he said. "Gave everything I had to a badge. Then you realize one day how little it really means."

There was silence for a while.

"Something Jones said about you," she said softly.

"What did he say?"

"He said you were one of the most dangerous men alive."

He shook his head. "It's men like Jones who are the dangerous ones."

"I saw your file."

"That's my past, Alex. It's not me."

She raised her head up a little and brushed the hair away from her face. "So who are you, Ben Hope? Really?"

"I'm still working that one out," he whispered. Then he rolled over and closed his eyes.

44.

rving Slater's first reaction, after Jones had sheepishly called him from the hotel to say that Hope had got away with Bradbury and one of the agents, had been stunned silence. That had quickly modulated into pure rage, a blistering superfury that had reduced Jones almost to tears on the phone.

But now, a couple of hours later, he'd calmed down. Not enough to be able to flop down on the giant sofa opposite the fifty-inch screen. But enough to think clearly and gain a perspective on this whole thing.

And he'd come to a decision, one that he'd resisted for months but now realized he'd delayed for much too long.

He picked up the phone and dialed. Waited. A voice answered.

"It's me," he said.

"It's late."

"Never mind that. Listen. Change of plan. This is getting out of hand. I've decided to fast-track the Stratagem."

There was a sharp intake of breath on the other end of the line. "Why now?" the associate asked.

"Something's come up," Slater said. "Something very interesting that suits us perfectly." He described it.

"They'll all be there? Their president and the four members of the Supreme Council?"

Slater smiled. "All right under the same dome. And a lot of other very important people. Talk about giving them a slap in the face, huh?"

"If we can pull it off . . ."

"Call Herzog. It takes place in three days. Tell him I'll double his price if he can make the date."

"You're sure about this?" There was a tremor in the associate's voice. "It's a big step."

"It's a very big step," Slater agreed. "But this is the time. We do this now, or never. 'There will be no more delay.' Book of Revelation. See? I read the Bible too. We wait any longer, we're going to get fucked."

"This is an important moment," the associate muttered. "I wish you wouldn't curse like that."

"Don't be so fucking pious. It's boring."

"Is Richmond ready for this?"

"He will be. I'll make sure of that. You worry about your end. Do it now."

Slater ended the call. With jubilation in his step he trotted across to the drinks cabinet. Yanked the bottle of Krug out of the ice bucket and poured himself a large glass. He raised the champagne in a silent toast to himself and his moment of glory. Downed the glass in one.

His heart was beating. He'd done it. No more waiting. He topped off his glass and lay back on the sofa, barely able to contain his excitement. He aimed the remote at the giant TV and stabbed a couple of keys. His favorite satellite porn channel filled the screen, and he savored that for a while as he polished off the Krug.

Then the phone rang. Slater muted the groans and gasps from the surround-sound speakers and picked up.

It was the associate ringing back.

"It's settled. Three days."

"Tell Herzog he's a pro."

"I think he already knows that." The associate hung up.

Slater gulped down the last of the champagne, wiped his mouth with the sleeve of his silk shirt, and dialed a number.

Jones answered on the third ring.

"It's me," Slater said.

"No sign," Jones said, anticipating him. "But we're searching. We'll get them. It's under control."

"I've heard that before. And when you do find them, I want them dead."

"All of them? Bradbury too?"

"Bradbury too."

"But the ostraca—"

"We've gone beyond that now," Slater interrupted. "The plan's altered. Jerusalem is going ahead."

"Jesus Christ."

"Exactly. Hallelujah."

"How soon?" Jones breathed.

"Three days," Slater said. "So. You find them. And bury them."

"With pleasure."

45.

Ben opened his eyes to the morning light and smelled roasting meat. Alex was squatting down next to the fire, and he saw that she'd built it up and was cooking a rabbit over it using two pronged sticks and a spit.

"Something smells good," he said.

She glanced round at the sound of his voice, and there was genuine warmth in her smile. Her hair was tousled. "You're hungry. That's a good sign."

He lay back against the cave wall, watching the way she was running the fire hot to minimize smoke. The juices from the rabbit were dripping fast into the flames, sizzling and popping. He let his eye wander down the curve of her body, noticing for the first time how attractive she was. She was tall and slender, with an athletic grace to her movements.

His gaze rested on the butt of the Beretta sticking out of the back pocket of her jeans.

She seemed to read his thoughts. "You can have it back, if you want. I hope you don't mind that I took it from you while you were sleeping. But Zoë needs to eat. And so do you. You look pale."

He sat up slowly. It felt like someone was sawing off his arm at the shoulder with an angle grinder. He reached for the codeine and popped two tablets in his mouth. "I don't mind. You keep it."

She smiled. "So you trust me now."

"Do I have a choice?"

"Not really." She poked the serrated knife into the rabbit's flank and drew it off the spit, laid the roasted carcass on a flat stone, and started carving pieces off. She offered one to Zoë on the point of the knife.

Zoë wrinkled her face up in disgust. "I'm not eating that."

Alex frowned. "You'll need your strength. Looks like we have a lot of walking to do today."

"I'm vegetarian."

"Good," Ben said. "More for us. But if you think we're going to carry you, you're wrong."

Zoë pointed at Alex. "I'm not going anywhere with her. It's thanks to her that Dr. Greenberg was killed."

"I didn't want that to happen," Alex said. "There was nothing I could do to stop it."

Zoë grunted and huddled tighter into her corner. She sat and watched them darkly as they ate.

"Never mind her," Ben said. "If she wants to starve, that's fine. This is good."

"I never shot a rabbit with a nine-millimeter before," Alex replied. "I was scared there'd be nothing left." She wiped her mouth, got up, walked to the entrance of the cave, and took out her phone.

"Put that away," Ben said. "If there's any signal up here, they'll track us from it."

"OK. But as soon as I get to a landline I'm making a call."

"Yeah, right," Zoë burst out. "She's going to call *them*."

"No, little lady," Alex said sharply. "I'm going to have you taken into protective custody until we can get this whole thing sorted out."

Ben shook his head. "No chance. She's my responsibility. She's not going anywhere near the CIA. I promised her family that I'd get her home safely. That's what I aim to do."

"She has no papers. How the hell are you going to get her out of the U.S.?"

"By delivering her to the nearest British consulate. Her parents can come and collect her."

"And then what?"

"And then I'm going after the people who started all this."

"On your own? You think that's the solution—killing more people?"

"That's not what I wanted," he said. "I wanted a life of peace. I didn't ask to be brought back in."

"But now you're here."

"And I mean to finish it."

She shook her head. "It's not going to work, Ben. You're wanted for murdering two police officers. You'll get picked up before you get anywhere near these people. You have to do this thing my way. I'm your only alibi, remember."

"You're in just as much shit as I am," he said. "Try explaining to your superiors why you killed one of your fellow agents and aided a fugitive."

Alex said nothing.

Ben turned to Zoë. She was slumped against the wall with a sulky expression, staring into space. "You have a lot of explaining to do," he said.

"Me?"

"Yes, you. Where are the ostraca?"

She huffed. "I don't know what you're talking about."

"I thought Greenberg said you were making progress," Alex said. "You still don't remember anything?"

Zoë screwed up her face and sank her head in her hands. "I want to go home."

Ben stared at her. "How do you even know you have a home, if you don't remember anything?"

Zoë looked up and fired a filthy look at him. "Piss off. Leave me alone."

"You have no idea what I've had to go through to find you. People have died because of your stupid little scheme."

"Easy on her, Ben," Alex said. "It's been a tough time for her too."

Ben was quiet for a moment. "All right. I'm sorry. I didn't mean to be hard on you."

"You almost broke my jaw last night," Zoë said, rubbing it.

"I'm sorry about that too." He reached out and laid a hand on her arm. Pain stabbed through his shoulder with the movement. She pulled away from him.

"We'd better make moves," Alex said. "This could be a long day."

They killed the fire, wrapped the remnants of the rabbit in fresh leaves, and stowed them in Ben's bag. After packing up all their kit they took turns washing in the cold stream at the bottom of the wooded slope. Then they left the cave behind them and set out across the harsh terrain. To keep moving due north would mean going over the mountain, so they skirted its base through miles of fir and spruce trees.

"We could walk for weeks and find nothing," Alex panted. "This is one of the biggest states, with one of the smallest populations. We should have stayed on the road."

After a few more miles Ben was beginning to think she was right. Apart from the occasional buzzard, the only sign of life they saw for hours was the big elk that stepped out of the trees as they passed, stared at them for a moment, and then vanished like a ghost.

They stopped and rested awhile, then kept moving. Ben's head was spinning and his shoulder was throbbing badly. After just a few hundred yards he had to rest again.

"You're in a bad way," Alex said. "Listen. I can move faster on my own. I could scout ahead. Maybe I'll come across a road or a farm. I'll come back for you. With luck I won't be more than a few hours."

He knew he couldn't argue. "You be careful."

She smiled. "I can take care of myself. Back before you know it, OK?" She checked her pistol, took a long drink of water from the bottle, and headed off without another word.

It suddenly struck him that he hated to see her leave.

"She'll come back with Jones," Zoë said, watching Alex walk away. "You're pretty naïve, letting her go off on her own."

He ignored that. "She'll be gone awhile. We need to find a place to rest up."

After a few minutes of hunting around they came across a broken spruce, its trunk bowed sideways at a right angle. Ben grabbed a branch. "Help me pull this down," he said.

"What are you doing?"

"Making a shelter. We can't just sit out in the open, where we can be seen from the air."

She frowned. "They'll be looking for me, won't they?"

He nodded. She took hold of another branch of the bent tree, and together they strained and heaved downwards. With a crackling of timber, the trunk gave. The heavy canopy sagged right down to the ground, forming a space they could crawl into without being seen. He settled himself into the leafy den, resting against his bag.

Zoë crawled in after him and arranged a blanket on the ground. She lay down and sighed loudly. "I'm so fucking exhausted," she complained. "My feet are killing me, and this place crawls with insects. Jesus, I'd give anything for a soak in a hot bath right now."

Ben ignored her. After a few minutes, when she realized he wasn't going to react to her huffing and puffing, she shut up and they sat in silence for a while. The pain in his shoulder was dulled by the codeine, but it still hurt badly. He drifted in and out, and time passed. He checked his watch. Alex had been gone more than half an hour.

"I'm so hungry," Zoë groaned.

He pulled the bag out from behind him, undid the straps, and reached inside for the package of leaves. He opened it and tossed it across in front of her. "Eat. Alex went out of her way to prepare this for you."

"I can't eat dead things."

"Then you're not hungry, are you?"

"I'm starving."

"You look it," he said.

She glanced down at the rabbit in distaste, glanced back up at him, hesitated, then picked up a piece with her fingers and took a small bite. Then a bigger one. After two more bites she was chewing away happily, except when she thought he was watching and she would pretend to be revolted. He smiled to himself at the display. When she'd finished and was covertly licking her fingers, he reached for the drinking flask and tossed it over to her. "I know how unpleasant that was for you," he said. "Wash it down with this."

She twisted the cap off and sniffed. Her eyes lit up. She took a long gulp, then passed the flask back to him. He took a small sip and returned it to her. As she drank some more, he took out his cigarettes. He offered her one, and she refused. "Smoking kills you slowly," she said.

"Good. I'm not in any hurry."

She chuckled. "I haven't had a drink for weeks," she said. "This stuff's going to my head a little."

"Finish it," he said, lighting up a cigarette.

She drank down the last of the Scotch, screwed the cap back on, and leaned back, stretching. She gazed up at the blue sky through the leafy canopy. "So good to be outside," she breathed. "Feels like I was cooped up forever."

"I'll get you home soon," he promised.

"You saved me. I haven't thanked you."

"You can thank me when it's over." He closed his eyes again. Waves of hot and cold were washing over him. He needed to get this bullet out.

She nodded. "I don't understand. How do you know my parents?"

"I'm one of your dad's students."

"You? A theology student?"

"I get that a lot," he said. "I was a soldier before. But now I'm look-ing for a new direction."

"The Church?"

"Maybe."

She smiled. "What a waste. You're far too dishy to become a vicar."

"Thanks. I'll bear that in mind."

"Have you got a girlfriend?"

He shook his head.

She smiled again. "You're not gay, are you?"

"Not that I know of."

"Good." She moved a little closer to him. Brushed a lock of hair away from her face. "I wonder how much longer she's going to be away for."

"Alex? Probably quite a while."

"I'm glad we can talk like this," she said.

"Me too."

"You're nothing like any of Dad's other students I've ever met. They're all wimps."

The sun was overhead now, rays filtering through the branches. Zoë squinted up at the dappled sunlight. "Getting warmer," she said. She peeled off her heavy sweater and laid it down on the ground. She was wearing a flimsy top underneath. She leaned forward and smiled again.

"Your bangle just slipped off," Ben said, pointing down at the gold bracelet that was lying in the leaves.

"Shit. That's always happening."

"You should be careful," he said. "It looks expensive."

"It was my great-grandmother's."

He nodded thoughtfully and was quiet for a few moments. "Shame about Whisky," he said suddenly.

"Yeah, it's loosened me up a lot," she answered. "Wish we had more of it." She giggled.

He shook his head. "I wasn't talking about the drink. I was talking about Whisky. He got hit by a car. He's dead."

Her eyes widened in horror. She drew away from him, her body snapping rigid. "What? When did this happen?"

"While you were partying on Corfu."

"Those bastards never told me," she said.

Then she clapped a hand over her mouth, realizing what she'd done.

"No, they didn't tell you," he said. "Because it's not true. I just made it up. Your dog's alive and well. And I think you've just given yourself away, Zoë Bradbury. You walked right into it."

She went red. "I don't know why I remembered that. I don't remember anything else."

He grabbed her wrist and held it tight, ignoring the pain in his shoulder. "No, of course not. Apart from the fact that your father is a theologian and all his students are wimps. That you don't eat meat.

That you're wearing your great-grandmother's bracelet. That a couple of weeks ago you were living it up on a Greek island. You know what I think? I think you know a hell of a lot more than you're pretending."

She struggled against his grip. "Let me go!"

He shook her. "No chance, Zoë. For once in your life, you're going to tell the truth."

46.

Zoë broke away from him and crawled out of the shelter. Ben followed her, grabbing for her ankle. She kicked back at him and caught his injured shoulder. He cried out and collapsed in the dirt as she scrabbled out and made a run for it. "Where do you think you're going?" he yelled after her.

Zoë ran through the trees, swiping branches out of her way.

Then she stopped and screamed. A figure stepped out from the bushes.

It was Alex, hot and red-faced from her long hike. Her hair was messed up and full of leaves, and her jeans were soaked to the thigh from where she'd been wading through water. "Zoë? Where are you off to?"

Ben caught up with them, panting and clutching his shoulder. His eyes blazed as he saw Zoë. "Right, you little fucker. You're going to talk."

Alex stood there looking bewildered. "What's going on here? I just came back to tell you good news. There's a farm up over the ridge, about two miles away."

"What's going on is that this one's got her memory back," Ben said. "She's been holding out on us."

Zoë burst into tears and fell to her knees in the dust.

Alex stared in disbelief. "Is this true?"

"Come on, let's have it," Ben said. "Where's the ostraca? What's this all about? What do Jones and Slater want with it?"

"I don't know," Zoë sobbed.

"You won't leave here until you tell us the truth," Ben said.

"I mean it!" she screamed up at him. "I don't know what they want it for. I was only using it to blackmail Cleaver!"

"Tell me where it is," Ben said, trying hard to curb the fury in his voice. "Then maybe we can get out of this. We can use it against them."

Zoë was shaking her head violently, her face streaked with tears and dust. "I can't tell you where it is," she sobbed.

"Why not?" he demanded.

"Because . . . because . . . I can't say it." She burst into tears again and raked her face with trembling fingers.

Alex stepped over to her and took her arm. "Don't be afraid. We're trying to help. Tell us. Then we can all cross over to the farm. It'll be over soon."

Zoë wiped her eyes and glanced up at Ben with a look of fear. She sniffed and hung her head.

"Well?" Ben asked.

"I can't tell you because . . . it doesn't exist." Her shoulders sagged. "There. I've said it. Happy now?"

Ben was stunned into silence for a few seconds. "What?" he said quietly.

Zoë sat up, her feet planted apart in the dirt. "It was all a bluff," she whispered. "It was all lies, all right? There *is* no evidence. I made the whole thing up."

Ben was struggling to make sense of what she was saying. "But the fragment you sent Cleaver, that you got Skid McClusky to take him in the box. It was for real. Cleaver had it verified."

Zoë shook her head tearfully. "He had it radiocarbon dated, that's all. The fragment was the right age. Why do you think I chose it? But the inscription on it was meaningless. Nobody could have verified that. I only found a few shards. For all I know it was some ancient Hebrew recipe book or an accounts sheet. There wasn't enough left to make sense of."

Ben stared at her, his rage mounting. The pain in his shoulder was gone. "A recipe book," he echoed.

"I wasn't even sure Cleaver would fall for it," she blurted. "It was just a crazy idea I had one day on the Turkish dig. I didn't have to work out the details because I knew I could bluff it. I thought it would be a way to get back at the bastard, shake him up a bit. That stupid book. Who's he trying to kid?" She reddened. "And why should he get all Augusta's money? She was my friend first. I should be the one to have it."

"And this is the truth?" Ben said. "There never was any evidence about Saint John and Revelation?"

"If there is," Zoë sniffed, "it's still buried in the sand somewhere."

Ben started shaking as it sank in. He thought of Charlie. In his mind he was replaying the moment when his friend had been blown to pieces. "I don't suppose it would make any difference if I told you about the people whose lives have been destroyed thanks to your little scheme," he said. "Never mind your family are going crazy with worry. Nikos is dead. Did you know that? Do you even care?" The pain was returning now, like a piece of molten steel in his flesh.

Zoë glanced up at him in alarm, then screwed her eyes shut and said nothing.

"Not to mention the victims of a bombing in Corfu that you don't even know about," he said. "But which you caused. And the doctor who risked his life to help you, and died trying. And your friend Skid McClusky, hiding in a dingy motel with his legs smashed. All of it thanks to you, you stupid little twit." He was getting breathless with pain. He fought the urge to grab a fistful of her hair and smash her face in. "I've always treated women just the same way as men. But if you were a man, Zoë, I swear this would be your last day. You have no idea what you've done."

There was a long silence, the only sound Zoë's quiet sobbing, the rustling of the leaves in the breeze, and the call of a buzzard somewhere high overhead.

Alex was the one to break the silence. "So where does this leave us?"

Nobody replied.

Nausea came over Ben like fever. He felt something tap his foot and looked down. His left hand was slick with blood, fingertips dripping fat dollops onto the forest floor. Alex saw it too, and her eyes flashed worry.

Then came the steady thump of rotor blades in the distance. Ben looked up. The chopper was just a dot on the sky, but it was getting rapidly bigger.

"Company," Alex muttered.

"Under cover," he said. "Now." He grabbed Zoë's arm and hauled her roughly off her feet, sending her tumbling into the bushes. Alex ducked in after her, and Ben squatted close by. He could smell Alex's hair, her hot skin. Even in his pain, there was a strange tingle from the feeling of closeness.

The chopper approached, its thudding roar filling the air. Then it swooped over the wooded valley, shaking the trees, and was gone.

Alex let out a long breath. "You think they found the car?"

Ben shook his head. "They're combing the whole area. That's what I'd do. Jones must have called on every resource he could muster up." He got to his feet, listening to the fading thud of the chopper. "Time to move on."

47.

The long, weary two miles felt like they were Ben's last. He could feel his strength ebbing away with every step. Alex led the way, carrying his bag, stopping frequently to help him across the difficult terrain. Zoë followed silently, thirty yards behind, her face pale, avoiding Ben's eye as they threaded their way through the pine trees and down a long, rocky slope to a river.

"We have to cross," Alex said. "The water's fast-flowing but it's not deep." She took his hand and they waded out. He stumbled and fell, and the impact of the icy water made his body spasm with chills. Alex helped him stagger to his feet. "Just a little farther," she said, and tried to smile reassuringly.

He gritted his teeth and fought back the dizziness. One step at a time, he made his way across the river and then collapsed on the rocky bank. Zoë caught up after a few minutes, and then he willed himself to keep moving. The ground sloped sharply back up from the river. Then, at the top of the next rise, Alex took the binoculars from the bag and rested on a rock to scan the valley below. "There it is," she said happily.

Despite the pain and exhaustion, Ben noticed the spectacular view from up here. Open prairie stretched for miles in front of them, and the early-afternoon sun was sparkling off the snow on the distant mountain peaks. Alex handed him the binocs, and he focused on the rambling range of farm buildings a mile away across the waving grassland. The place looked like a typical small hill farm, with assorted barns and horses grazing behind white-painted fences.

"I don't see anyone about," he said. "But there's smoke coming from the chimney."

"Let's get down there and take a look," Alex replied.

It took another forty-five minutes of painfully slow progress to reach the farm. They walked inside the gate and followed a dusty path between run-down timber outbuildings towards the house. Ben rested against a fencepost while Zoë hovered uncertainly in the background and Alex approached the farmhouse. One window was boarded over, and the porch steps were worm-eaten and supported on bricks.

She thumped on the door. "Hello? Anybody around?" There was no answer. She stepped back from the house, gazing up at the windows, then shrugged at Ben.

The sun was hot and high above them now, and he shielded his eyes from it as he scanned around the farmstead.

Then he saw the body.

The old man was lying in the long grass a hundred yards from one of the horse paddocks. Ben and Alex hurried over to him. She kneeled down next to the limp figure in the worn-out jeans and red check shirt and felt for a pulse. "He's alive," she said. Ben fetched a pitcher of water from the nearby paddock and splashed some of it on the old man's face. He groaned, blinked, and tried to sit up. His hair and beard were long and white, and his face was tanned to leather. He winced in pain and grabbed his ankle. Ben saw that it was badly swollen.

"Damned colt there pulled me off my feet," the old man said, pointing. In the paddock, a young chestnut looked up from his grazing and gazed across at them, trailing his lunging rope from his halter.

"Don't try to talk," Alex said to the old man. "We'll get you in out of the sun."

They helped the old man up the broken-down porch steps and into the farmhouse. The house was cool inside and smelled faintly damp. Through a shady hallway was a sitting room with wallpaper hanging off the walls and a low couch that looked as if it had been there since the fifties. They laid him down. Ben wiped the sweat out of his eyes and gently peeled back the old man's trouser leg. "Looks to be just a bad sprain," Alex said, peering down at it.

"Mighty glad you folks turned up," the old man said. "Don't get a lot of visitors out here." His wrinkled eyes focused on Ben's bloody shirt, but he said nothing. He extended his hand. "Riley Tarson's the name."

"Ben Hope. This is Alex."

Zoë had wandered into the house, standing idly, watching from a distance.

"What about this little lady?" Riley asked. "She got a name?"

"Yeah," Ben said. "Trouble." He eased off the old man's boot, then turned to Alex. "I think I saw some comfrey growing outside in the yard. You know how to make a decoction? That'll help ease the swelling."

"No need," Riley said. "Ira keeps a jar of some damned Indian potion on the kitchen shelf."

"Ira?"

"He helps out on the farm. Ain't here, though. Rode out two days ago to chase up a missing steer. Not been back since."

"I'll see if I can find the jar," Alex said. Zoë trailed after her.

Riley eyed Ben carefully. "You're a little out of your way, mister. It's my guess you're no ordinary travelers."

"You guessed right," Ben said.

"And I guess that chopper earlier was out looking for you. Right about that too?"

Ben said nothing.

Riley's old face creased into a grin. "I know what them helicopters are. I got no love for no G-men."

"They're CIA," Ben said quietly. "They're looking for us."

"I have no problem with that, son. If you was fixing to harm me or rob me, you'd have done it by now. I don't know your business, and the less I know the less I have to tell. A man's actions is all I care about." Riley grunted. "Now, the sonofabitch in the helicopter, he came down low while I was lying there in the dirt. Saw me and just smiled and flew off. If you hadn't showed up, I wouldn't have made it through till morning. So you ask me to pick sides, I won't be picking his and that's for sure."

Alex came back into the room, holding a big jar full of greenish lotion. Ben examined it. "That's comfrey, all right," he said. "It'll help." He smeared it over the swollen ankle, then immobilized the foot with the cushion, rolling it carefully around and strapping it up with tape. "You need to rest up awhile," he told Riley.

"You don't look too good yourself," the old man said. "I seen gun-shot wounds before."

Ben suddenly felt faint again. The old man's lips were moving, but all he could hear was a rumbling echo in his ears. The room began to spin, and then he was dimly aware of Alex's cry as he crashed to the floor.

48.

Consciousness came and went. Like a slow-motion strobe effect, there were periods of blackness where he drifted and floated for what seemed like eternity. In between were bursts of sound and light and activity. He was dimly aware of climbing the stairs, an arm around Alex's neck as she supported him. Then a room. A bed. The feel of crisp sheets against his skin. Blood on white cotton. Alex bending over him, her face looming large, concern showing in her eyes. He blacked out again.

When he opened his eyes, the red light of dawn was creeping across the wooden floor of the unfamiliar room. He blinked and tried to lift his head off the pillow. His shoulder was freshly bandaged. There was pain, but it felt different.

He felt for the ring around his neck. It was gone.

He looked around him. He was in a large bedroom, simple and traditional. In stark contrast to the downstairs, the room was clean and tidy, as though it was never used. He was in a brass-framed double bed, covered with a patchwork quilt. There was a washbasin in the corner, and on the wooden rocking chair next to his bed were fresh clothes: a blue denim shirt and clean jeans, neatly folded. Carefully placed on top of the clothes was the gold wedding ring with its leather thong.

Alex was next to him. She was slumped on the bed, her tousled hair across the quilt, one arm draped over his legs. He wondered how long she'd been watching over him before she gave in to sleep.

She stirred and opened her eyes, looking directly at him. She seemed to have that ability, which he'd seen only in wild animals and trained soldiers, to go from a dead sleep to a state of perfect alertness, with none of the yawning puffy-eyed waking-up stages in between. She smiled and sat up on the bed. She'd changed out of her woolly sweater and was wearing a farmer's checkered shirt a size too big and knotted at the waist.

"Welcome back to the land of the living," she said.

"You did it?"

She nodded. "I had to go in deep, but it came out clean. It didn't hit any bone. It flattened a little but didn't mushroom. No fragmentation." She reached for a tin cup on the bedside table and rattled it. He looked inside at the crumpled bullet rolling around in the bottom. It looked small and innocuous now.

"You saved my life," he said. "That's twice now. I have some catching up to do."

She took the cup from his hand and pressed cool fingers gently to his brow "You're still burning hot. Get some rest."

He lay back against the pillow. "We have to get moving."

"Not for a few days. Riley says we can stay here as long as we need."

"How is he?"

"Sleeping. He'll be fine." She smiled. "He seems to think you and I are an item."

"Where's Zoë?"

"She has a room down the hall. She's tired, Ben. You need to go a little easier on her."

"I could kill her."

"She feels bad."

"She ought to."

She stroked his forehead, brushed a strand of hair out of his eyes. Outside, the dawn light was brightening. He could hear horses neighing in the distance, and a dog barking. "I should go and see to the horses," she said. "Riley won't be up for a while yet."

"Stay a minute."

She smiled again. "OK."

They sat in silence for a few minutes.

"You were dreaming a lot," she said. "Last night. You were feverish for a while."

"Was I?"

She nodded. "You were talking in your sleep again."

He didn't reply.

"You were talking to God."

"I don't have a lot to say to him."

"You asked for his forgiveness, Ben. Like it really mattered to you. What happened? What did you do that you want to be forgiven for?"

He rolled over away from her.

"I want to help you," she said.

He glanced back at her. "Why?"

"I don't know. I just do." She smiled. "I kind of feel I know you now. I undressed you and put you into bed. I've been up to my elbows inside your shoulder pulling that bullet out of you. Your blood all over me. I've packed your wound and patched you up. Bathed you and sat here half the night mopping sweat off you. So why won't you let me help you with this? It's good to talk, right?"

"Bad things have happened," he said. "Things I don't want to talk about."

"Bad things happen to everyone."

"I know that."

"It's not your fault Charlie died," she said. "I know you blame yourself, but it's not fair. You didn't know what was coming. You were only trying to help your friend."

He was about to reply, then shut his mouth.

"What?"

"Nothing," he muttered. "Maybe you should see to the horses now. Just don't stay out in the open too long. The helicopter might come back."

She smiled. "You can't get rid of me that easily."

"Maybe you're right," he said. "About Charlie. Maybe it wasn't my fault."

"There's something else, isn't there?"

He closed his eyes.

"Tell me."

After a long pause, Ben said quietly, "I can't."

49.

As the morning rolled by, Ben could feel his strength slowly returning and his impatience mounting. He lay on the rumpled sheets reading his Bible, working through all the facts in his head.

He couldn't stop thinking about Slater. Who was he? Not an agent. Not a cop. He wasn't a warrior like Jones. He was a leader, an organizer, a brain. Obviously a man with considerable power at his fingertips. One of the movers and shakers. A politician, maybe, but not a prominent figure—Alex had never heard of him. Perhaps one who preferred to stay in the shadows, working behind the scenes. And one who, for some reason that was still a complete mystery, was politically interested in Clayton Cleaver and, by extension, politically threatened by Zoë's ostraca discovery.

Religion and politics. Cleaver was aiming at governorship, but he was still only small potatoes in the larger game. What if someone else, someone far higher up the ladder, someone with much more to gain or lose, had a stake in this too? Votes and power were a big motivator, worth killing for.

But some inner voice told Ben there was something else to it. Did political ambition alone explain how Slater, or the forces he represented, was apparently able to hijack CIA resources to enable his plans? Something bigger was going on.

And as Ben leafed through the Bible on the pillow next to him, that thought kept returning and chilling his blood.

After a while he couldn't bear the inactivity any longer. Just after midday he got to his feet, feeling a little woozy but much stronger. He was wearing only a pair of shorts. Alex's dressing was tight around his chest and shoulder.

He picked up the ring and hung it back around his neck. Walked over to the window and looked out at the farm buildings and paddocks, the sweeping prairie and the mountains in the background.

Something caught his eye. In one of the barns, among old farm implements and junk, was the rusting hulk of an ancient Ford pickup truck. He gazed at it for a moment, then nodded to himself.

He went to the washbasin and splashed cold water over his face, then walked back over to the bed and pulled on the jeans that had been left out for him. They fitted well, and he wondered whose they were. Not Riley's, not with a thirty-two-inch waistband. He remembered the old man had mentioned a helper, Ira. He pulled on the shirt that had been left out too.

The aroma of coffee was floating up from downstairs, and someone was moving about down below. Ben ruffled up his hair in the mirror and made his way down the wide wooden staircase.

He found Alex down in the big farm kitchen, standing at an old cylinder-fed gas stove, frying strips of bacon in a battered pan. She turned in surprise as he walked in. "I was just about to bring you something to eat."

"What other U.S. political figure uses the Bible as a campaign platform?" he asked.

Alex stared at him for a moment. "You mean, apart from a president who said God told him to go to war with Iraq?"

"Lower down the scale," he said. "Someone working hard to make it to the top."

"There are a thousand evangelical political wannabes out there," she answered. "Some are bigger than others. But I can't just pluck one name out of the hat. Why are you asking about this all of a sudden?"

"It's nothing. Just thinking. Probably way off the mark."

"You shouldn't be up so soon."

"I feel a lot stronger."

"You look it. But you can't just spring up like a jack-in-the-box. You should rest awhile longer."

"I'm not going back to bed. There's a truck out there. Looks old, but maybe it'll get us out of here. I'll give Riley double what it's worth, so he can replace it with a better one."

"Nice thought," she said. "But we're not going anywhere in that, at least not yet. I already tried it. Battery's all right, but the starter motor seems to be gone."

"A doctor *and* a mechanic," Ben said.

"Make good coffee too. Want some?"

"Love some." He gratefully accepted a mug from her and took a sip.

"I made French toast, too. And some bacon and beans." She laughed at his expression. "You don't have French toast where you come from?"

"I only know Irish toast," he said. "That's regular toast, soaked in Guinness."

"Try some. It's fried bread with sugar."

He sat down at the table and ate. "Where's her ladyship this morning?"

Alex jerked her thumb upwards. "She won't come out of her room."

"Riley?"

"He's stubborn, like you," she said. "He's limping around out there tending to the animals. Tough old bird. Told me he was a marine once."

"Vietnam?"

"Korea," rasped a voice. They turned. The front door creaked open and Riley hobbled into the kitchen, his gnarled hand clutching a stick. "Something smells good." He lowered himself stiffly into his chair at the head of the table. Alex passed him a piled plate and he muttered a few words of Grace before he dug into it. The three of them ate in silence for a while, then Ben mentioned the old truck in the barn.

"If you can get it going, it's yours," the old man said. "Tell you what, you dig real deep in the back of that old shed, you'll find another truck there under a tarp. Engine gave out years back, but I reckon the starter on that one's still in good shape. Might be worth a try."

"We'll check it out."

Riley reached across and took a bottle from a nearby cupboard. It was filled with clear liquid. "I always have a drink after a meal. Care to join me?" He popped out the cork and sloshed some into three mugs. He took one for himself and slid the other two across the table. "Mighty good stuff," he said. "Distilled it myself."

Ben sipped it. It tasted about twice the strength of Scotch. "Reminds me of poteen. Irish moonshine."

"Knowed a guy who ran a sixty-nine Dodge Charger on it," Riley muttered.

Ben watched him appreciatively. He was a tough old man, but with a good heart. "I wanted to thank you for letting us stay here. There was no need to give up your bedroom for me. I'd have been happy with the barn."

Riley scratched his beard and smiled sadly. "That's Maddie's old room. I don't go there much. She'd have wanted you and your lady here to use it."

Ben and Alex exchanged glances and didn't reply. Then the door creaked open and they all turned to see Zoë standing there uncertainly.

"Pull up a chair, miss," Riley said.

Alex stood and went over to fetch the pan from the stove and a fresh plate. "Come and eat something, Zoë."

Zoë looked subdued as she sat at the table and picked at the food that Alex pushed in front of her. Ben ignored her. Riley finished his food, licked the plate with relish, and drained the last of his moonshine. "That was darn good." He leaned back in his chair and took out a battered pack of Lucky Strikes. Ben accepted one, and they lit up.

Zoë glanced over at the cheap plastic phone that hung on the wall in the corner of the kitchen. "Ben," she said sheepishly, "would it be OK for me to call my parents?"

Ben was about to say no, but before he could speak Riley cut in. "Phone don't work, miss," he said. "Been gathering dust there for the last two years. Never paid the bill. Maddie, she used to call up her sis once in a while. But I never much liked talking on that thing anyway. I like to look a person in the eye when I talk to them." He jerked his thumb back over his shoulder. "Nearest phone's at the Herman place, 'bout nine miles west across the ridge there."

Zoë turned to Alex. "What about your cell phone?"

"You won't get reception up here," Riley said. "Hermans don't get it neither."

"Fine. Then I'll go to the Herman place," Zoë said. "Is there a horse I can borrow?"

"You're not going anywhere," Ben warned her.

Just then, the sound of hooves in the yard made him turn to look out the window. Through the dusty pane, a bronzed young guy with glossy black hair and a denim jacket was dismounting a tall gray horse and tying it up to a rail.

"That's Ira," Riley said. "Must have found that steer." He rose from the table and hobbled outside to join the young guy.

Zoë was watching keenly out the window. Ben followed her gaze and knew what she was thinking. Ira looked as though he had a lot of Native American blood. He was handsome and fit-looking, about twenty-three.

"Remember what I told you," Ben said. "You stay indoors. People are out there looking for us."

She didn't reply.

"Good," Ben said. "Now let's see if we can get this truck started."

50.

"ou're going to round off that nut," Alex was saying. "Then you'll never get it loose."

Streaks of sunlight shone through the gaps in the old wooden slats of the big barn, casting bright stripes across the dirt floor and the farm junk that lay around inside, piles of fencing posts and stacked-up tools and drums of oil, sacks of fertilizer. Some hens were scratching and clucking in the hayloft up above.

Ben peered out from under the chassis of the even-more-ancient pickup they'd uncovered at the back of the barn. His face was sprinkled with red flecks of rust from where he'd been trying to loosen the bolts holding on the starter motor.

"Use the chain wrench instead." She passed it down to him.

He laid down the one he'd been using and took the wrench from her. As he looked up at her, her attractiveness struck him for a fleeting moment. It wasn't the first time he'd noticed it. Her auburn hair was tied back, wisps falling out, tousled and sexy. It was hot in the barn, and she'd rolled up her shirtsleeves to the shoulder. There was a smear of oil on the shiny, toned muscle of her upper arm. The check shirt was unbuttoned a long way down. She brushed a lock of hair away from her eyes.

"You learned this mechanic stuff in the CIA?"

She grinned back at him. "Try growing up with four older brothers who were all car crazy."

Ben got the chain wrench around the stubborn bolt head, and it loosened with a crack. He soon had the starter motor free and pulled himself out from under the truck. He stood up, wincing.

She reached out and placed a hand on his shoulder. Her touch felt soft and warm through the denim shirt. "You should take it easy," she said. "I can do this."

"You've done a lot already."

She looked at the starter motor in his hands. It was just a heavy lump of rust, trailing wires. "Think it'll work?"

"Who knows?"

She took it from his hands. The touch of her fingers on his lingered a little longer than it needed, almost a caress. She looked up at him. "I'm glad, though."

"Glad about what?"

"Despite all that's happened, everything that's going to happen, I'm glad I met you. Glad you're OK. Glad to be here with you like this. I'm just scared I might not know you for long."

He made no reply. They stood there for a few moments. Her blue eyes gazed into his, holding them, letting him look deep into them. Her lips were slightly parted. "You're lonely, aren't you?" she murmured. She touched his hand again, firmer and longer, her fingers intertwining with his. "I know. I can see it. Because that's how I feel. Lonely. Alone. Needing someone."

Feeling his heart pick up a step, he stroked her bare arm. Her skin was warm and smooth. He moved his hand up to her shoulder. Caressed her hair and cheek. His thumb ran close to the corner of her mouth, and she bent her head down to kiss it tenderly. They moved closer. Her hand gripped his more tightly, almost urgently.

When the kiss came, it was hungry and passionate. He pulled her close to him, exploring, feeling her arms around his back, the heat of her body, her hair on his face.

Then he pulled away, with an effort. "I can't."

"Why are you afraid to kiss me?" Her eyes searched his. "We both want to. Don't we?"

"Yes," he said. "I do want to. But this can't happen."

"But why? Why fight it? We don't have a lot of time together."

He couldn't find the words. He'd never been able to find them, even just thinking about it alone, even in his darkest moments.

"I lost someone," he whispered. "Someone close. Closer than I even knew. Not long ago."

She bit her lip and sighed. Stroked his hair. "I saw the ring."

He closed his eyes. Nodded slowly.

"You want to talk about it?"

"She died," he said.

"What was her name?"

"Her name was Leigh."

"How did it happen?"

He looked up. "She was murdered."

Hearing it like that, the finality of it, the horror of it struck him all over again. Suddenly he was seeing the whole thing in his imagination, like a nightmare film reel that wouldn't stop turning.

He saw the black blade of the knife. Going in.

Piercing deep inside her, taking away her life.

The last look in her eyes. Things she'd said as she lay dying that would stay with him the rest of his days.

He took a long, deep, slow breath. "It was my fault. The man who killed her was someone I was supposed to have protected her from. I failed. He came back, and he took her away from me."

He was quiet for a long time. Then he whispered, "I miss her. I miss her so much."

Alex laid a hand on his arm. Her touch felt warm and reassuring. "You didn't kill her, Ben. That isn't a burden you should be carrying."

He shook his head, feeling the pain rise up. He swallowed it back down. "I might as well have," he said. "Every day I ask God to forgive me for letting it happen. But I don't think God's listening to me. In fact I don't think he ever has, not once in my whole life. He deserted me a long time ago."

"You don't mean that."

He took her hand and squeezed it gently. "Find a better man than me, Alex. I'm not what you need."

"You are a better man," she said. "I hardly know you, but already I can see it."

He said nothing.

That was when they heard the chopping beat of rotors, and the gunfire churning up the farmyard outside, and Zoë's scream.

51.

Zoë had been wandering idly about the house, bored, listless. After being cooped up for such a long time, she felt full of pent-up energy and hated lying around doing nothing.

Out of the window she could see Ira in the paddock a hundred yards or so from the house. He was training a young horse, the colt that had pulled Riley off his feet and twisted his ankle. The sky was cloudless and blue, and the meadow grass was swaying gently in the breeze. Suddenly she was desperate to be outside, to be out talking to Ira. He was so attractive. She loved the loose, easy way he moved, athletic and supple and toned. She smiled to herself, imagining the feel of his skin.

Ben had told her to stay indoors, she remembered. *Stuff him.* Did he think she was stupid? She'd hear a helicopter long before she saw it or it could see her. She was tired of being treated like a child.

She walked out to the paddock, feeling the sun on her face and the breeze in her hair. Ira saw her from a distance, and she approached him with a warm smile. "Hi. I'm Zoë. You must be Ira."

Ira jumped down off the colt's back, wiped his hands, and met her at the paddock fence. "Good to meet you, Zoë," he said.

Zoë had always liked to flirt, and she was good at it. Ira responded to her quickly—she knew that not many pretty young blond women turned up on his doorstep like this. Within a few minutes they were laughing and joking comfortably together, lots of eye contact, lots of touches, most of it coming from her. Ira was a little overwhelmed by her attentions, but she could see from the look in his eye that maybe being stuck out here in the wilderness would have its compensations.

"You like to ride?" he said.

"Yeah, I ride. Never used an American saddle before, though."

"It's easy," he said. "Like a big armchair. Want to give it a go?"

"Will you give me a leg up?" She clambered through the fence, and she enjoyed the feel of his strong fingers on her leg as he helped her into the saddle. Ira'd done a good job of breaking in the colt, and she found him responsive as she walked him up and down the paddock, getting the measure of him. Then she put him into a trot.

"Don't rise to it," he called. "Keep your butt down in the saddle. Go with his rhythm."

She mastered it quickly, then flipped the loose end of the rein left and right to urge the colt into a long-striding canter. Ira stood in the middle of the paddock and she rode round and round him with her hair streaming out behind her, dust flying up from the colt's hooves.

"This is great," she was about to say. But the look on Ira's face shut her up and made her turn and look. She gaped in terror at what she saw. The colt wheeled, unsettling her in the saddle.

The shadow passed over her.

The helicopter roared in out of the sun, nose low, tail up.

The colt reared, and Zoë felt herself flying. She tumbled into the dust. Ira was running to her, eyes wide with alarm. The black chopper moved in closer, like an attacking shark, its noise filling the air, hurling up dust and dirt with the wind blast. Zoë scrambled to her feet. The red dot of a laser sight raked across her body. She screamed. The colt was rearing and bucking in a crazed panic.

Then suddenly the ground was whipped up by automatic gunfire.

Ira had Zoë's arm and was dragging her out of the paddock and back towards the house. The man with the rifle, hanging out of the side of the chopper with one foot on its skid, let off another prolonged burst that kicked up stones in her wake as she sprinted and stumbled. She threw a terrified glance over her shoulder, and her eyes met those of the man she'd hoped she would never see again.

Jones grinned at her over the top of the M16. He fired again, savoring the moment, the rifle hammering in his arms. His heart gave a little jolt as the bitch tumbled and fell. But then the Indian was yanking her back to her feet, and he realized that she'd just tripped.

He yelled at the pilot to hold the chopper steady, and brought the gun back up to aim. But the targets had made it to the house, staggering inside, slamming the door shut. He cursed and let off a long blast that strafed the front porch. Windows burst apart and splinters flew as bullets tore through the fabric of the house.

Inside, Ira was dragging Zoë across the floor, covering her body with his own. Glass shards flew around them. The curtains fluttered, ripped to rags by the gunfire that punched through the walls and churned up the floor. Zoë was screaming.

Ben and Alex ran from the barn to see the chopper hovering over the yard, just twenty feet from the ground. Ben drew the Beretta from the back pocket of his jeans and raised it up as the chopper veered round to face them, coming lower, skids almost on the ground.

Ben had recognized the figure with the rifle instantly. He didn't hesitate to fire. Jones quickly withdrew and scrambled out of sight as Ben loosed off a string of double-taps that punched holes into the fuselage. Then the chopper veered off suddenly, climbed steeply, and roared overhead. Ben put a couple more shots into its underbelly, but 9mm ammunition just wasn't enough to make an impression. He swore.

They ran to the house as the chopper made its escape. Ben pounded up the porch steps and threw open the door. He saw Ira inside, lying protectively across Zoë's body. "Anyone hurt?" he shouted. Ira shook his head, dazed, getting up and helping Zoë to her feet.

Riley came stumbling into the room, eyes bulging in horror. He was clutching a scarred Ithaca shotgun in his fists.

The dust was settling in the house, silence descending in the aftermath of the attack. Ira helped a weeping Zoë upstairs as Riley paced the wrecked kitchen, still clutching his shotgun and cursing loudly.

Alex followed Ben back outside. He stood on the porch steps and scanned the horizon thoughtfully, his eyes narrowed against the sun. "That was Jones. And he'll be back."

"He's going to bring an army with him," Alex said. "A few hours, tops. We should get out of here."

"See if you can get that starter motor transplanted."

"Where are you going?"

But Ben was already heading back inside. "Riley, I need to know if you have some kind of rifle in the place."

The old man stared at him for a second. There was a gleam in his eye, a fire that looked like it was returning after lying dormant a long time. He grunted and beckoned for Ben to follow. He hobbled down a passage and pushed open a door leading down some wooden steps to a crumbling basement. On a homemade rack on the wall was a rifle. It was slender and compact, walnut and blued steel. The old man lifted it down and handed it to Ben without a word.

Ben examined it. It was a .22-caliber underlever Marlin. Welcome, but more of a rabbit or squirrel gun than anything else.

Riley saw Ben's face and smiled. "I know what you're thinking, son. It's heavy iron you want."

Ben said nothing.

"Let me show you something." The old man hobbled across the basement, into the shadows, where packing cases and broken furniture were piled up and thick with dust and spiders' webs. He started clearing things out of the way, panting with the effort. He stooped down low and dragged something heavy across the floor. Ben looked down. It was an old trunk.

"I haven't opened this since I came home from Korea," Riley said. "Guess part of me never wanted to see it again. But if there's any truth in fate, maybe now I know why I hauled the damn thing back halfway round the world." He blew dust off the lid and opened it.

Inside the trunk was a load of old packing material. Riley scooped it out and dumped it on the floor. Underneath was a layer of sacking cloth. It was smeared with grease and smelled strongly of old gun oil. Riley gripped the edge and peeled it back. "Here it is," he said. "I couldn't hardly lift it no more. But I was pretty useful with it, back in the day." He stepped away to let Ben see.

Ben blinked. "I don't believe it. You've got a BAR."

Browning Automatic Rifle. It was a model he'd seen only once before, a hefty American light machine gun that had been used from the First World War and been decommissioned during the sixties. The kind of weapon that belonged in a military museum—but this one looked brand-new. Gray gunmetal and oiled wood and iron battle sights, the way things used to be before the era of rubber and polymer, red dot optics and lasers.

Ben reached inside the crate and lifted it out. It was heavy and oily. He checked it over. The rifle was in perfect condition, the bore clean and the action slick. Even the canvas sling was as new. The magazine was long and curved, and there were five more like it in the bottom of the trunk.

Riley smiled. "Special high-capacity antiaircraft version. We used to shoot down planes with these babies." He waded deeper into the basement and knocked some more junk out of the way. Reached down with a grunt and dragged a heavy metal ammo case into the middle of the floor. It was olive green, rusty around the edges with faded yellow lettering on the side.

Riley flipped the steel catches and the lid creaked open. Old brass gleamed dully from inside. Neatly stacked bottleneck cartridges, more than a thousand of them. They were .308 military issue, well preserved, lightly greased. Over half a century old, primers still gleaming. "All you need to start a goddamn war, son."

"This is where it's going to happen," Ben said. He unclipped the magazine and started pressing rounds into it.

The old man watched him and nodded to himself. "You got the look of a soldier. Tell me I'm right."

Ben nodded. "Was, once."

"Unit?"

"British Army. Special Air Service."

"I heard about you people. Black ops. Iranian Embassy siege in London, right?"

"Ten years before my time," Ben said. "I served in the Gulf. Afghanistan. Africa. Mostly covert ops. Things you don't want to know about, and neither do I."

Riley snorted. "Classified shit."

"Doing the dirty for the men in suits to feather their nests. Never again."

"Same men in suits that have business with us today."

"Pretty much the same species," Ben said. "But it's me they have business with. This isn't your war, Riley. I'd appreciate it if you stayed out of the way."

Riley spat. "We'll see about that, boy. I've been at war with the damn government for fifty years. And you saved my ass. Least I can do is return the favor."

"These are bad people."

"I ain't exactly an angel myself, sonny. I'm old, but I can still kick ass when I have to."

Ben nodded his gratitude. "There are some other things I'm going to need," he said.

52.

Ben walked back to the farm buildings. Alex was just stepping back from the newer of the two old trucks, wiping rusty grease off her hands with a rag. There was a smudge of oil on her cheek. She looked anxious, but smiled through it when she saw him approaching.

"You did it?"

She walked round to the driver's door, opened it with a creak, and climbed up inside the cab. "Moment of truth."

The truck fired up with a roar and a cloud of blue smoke. Her face broke into a wide, triumphant grin as she gunned the engine. She hopped out of the cab and ran over to him, beaming, and hugged him. "Now let's get out of here," she said.

He said nothing.

"What?"

"It's not that simple, Alex."

"What are you saying?"

"You go. Head nine miles west across the ridge and get to the Herman place. It's time to call in your people. They'll take care of Zoë."

There was alarm in her eyes. She shook her head adamantly. "We all go. There's still time."

He put his hand on her shoulder and rubbed the warm skin of her neck with his thumb. "We'd never make it, out in the open. They'd soon overtake us. And if we leave Riley and Ira here alone, they'll be killed. I can't have that on my conscience. Someone has to stop these people. You go. Let me stay here and meet them."

"You stay, I stay."

He shook his head again. "I want you somewhere safe," he said. "I couldn't bear . . ." His voice trailed off.

"I couldn't bear if anything happened to you either," she whispered.

"Trust me. Nothing will happen."

"You don't know what you'll be up against."

"I have a pretty good idea," he said.

She sighed. There was a catch in her breath. She stroked his hand. A tear hung on her eyelash, and he smiled and wiped it away. She laughed through the tears. "This is crazy," she sniffed. "I never thought anything like this could happen to me." She gazed into his eyes for a second, then held him tight. He could feel the urgency, the yearning, in the way her arms were wrapped around him.

For a brief instant he lost himself, feeling her against him, the scent of her hair. He closed his eyes. Part of him wished so desperately that he could freeze that moment. That this could be simple, and that his options were open.

But they weren't, and it was anything but simple. It never could be.

He gripped her arms and gently pushed her away from him. "Now you have to go," he said.

She nodded regretfully. "All right. I'll go."

They drove the truck round to the front of the house, checked the oil and the tires and the fan belt. Everything seemed fine. Ben went to fetch Zoë from her room, and explained to her that she was leaving. She nodded quietly and followed him back downstairs, climbed in the truck, and sat quietly.

It was hard to watch Alex leave, but Ben was glad that she and Zoë were escaping to safety. He tried not to let his feelings show on his face as she started up the engine and pulled away with a last wave. He shielded his eyes from the sun and watched the truck lurch away down the uneven lane towards the gate.

Then it ground to a halt. The driver's door flew open, and Alex jumped out. She ran back to him, wrapped her arms around his neck, and kissed him. "You take care, Ben Hope. That's an order."

"This isn't good-bye," he said. "Now go. Get out of here."

She ran back to the truck, tears in her eyes. She threw herself back in the driver's seat and put her foot down, wheels spinning on the gravel.

This time, she kept driving. Ben stood and watched the truck bounce over the open ground until it reached the winding country road that snaked away towards the ridge in the distance.

Then Alex and Zoë were gone.

Now he had work to do.

The next hour was a time of sweat and dust as he made his preparations. He studied the layout of the farm, thought about the line of attack, considered how he would do it.

It would be one man against many. They would come heavily armed, and they were professionals who'd hit hard and fast. But it was possible. Just about possible. He had an edge. The biggest edge of all.

He found the things he needed and stacked everything up against the side of the barn. Some of it was heavy, and he dusted off an old hand truck to shift things around with. Riley was too fragile to join in, but Ira was a quick and willing helper.

As he and Ben were loading up the hand truck, the young guy stopped and looked up. "There's going to be a bunch of them, right?" He seemed to relish the idea.

"They won't take any chances this time," Ben said. "They want to finish it here. But I want you and Riley out of the way, understand?"

"I'm Blackfoot Indian." Ira's voice was soft but full of pride. "The way I see it, these people are the descendants of the men who took my people off our land and dumped us on the reservation. They took away our sacred birthright." He nodded solemnly. "If now's the time to take something back from them, man, you couldn't drag me away with ten wild mustangs." Then he grinned. "Anyway, I want to see this."

Ben looked at him. "Don't romanticize war. What you're going to see today will be the worst thing you've ever witnessed in your life."

When things were in place, Ben helped Ira herd the horses away to the safety of the far paddocks, a quarter of a mile away across the rolling grassland. The sun was beating down savagely and his shoulder throbbed. When the last horse trotted in through the paddock gate and went off to join the others among the lush grazing, Ben checked his watch. It was just after four in the afternoon.

Just about time.

And as he looked up to the blue sky above the mountain peaks, he could see his instinct was right.

They were coming.

53.

There were three of them, black dots against the sky, flying in V-formation, the thump of their rotors building in volume as they rapidly approached.

Ben told Ira to head fast for the farmhouse basement and to make sure Riley stayed there with him until the fight was over. Ira hesitated for only a second or two before he ran for the house, and Ben made for the block-built storeroom where he had the BAR set up on its bipod at one of the upper-floor windows. He bolted the door behind him, climbed the rickety stairs, and settled in behind the weapon. Beside him on the floor was his bag, bulging with spare magazines for the rifle and a Beretta pistol.

The choppers closed in fast and hovered over the farm, their thudding beat deafening, flattening the grass with the wind blast and frightening the horses in the distant paddocks.

From his hidden vantage point in the storeroom, Ben peered through the sights of the rifle and watched as the helicopters descended, maintaining their formation, one in front and two behind. Men in black burst from the open sides of the lead chopper and slithered rapidly down rappelling ropes, like spiders on silk threads, dropping towards the ground. Six of them, three on each side, clad in tactical body armor, goggles, helmets, armed with automatic rifles. A slick display of intimidating power that was guaranteed to strike fear into most hearts.

Now it was time for Ben to make use of his edge. It wasn't so much the BAR, now loaded and cocked and ready to lay down a wide field of fire across the farmyard. It wasn't so much his years of extensive battle training. It was an innate thing, something that had helped him become the soldier he'd once been.

He didn't like killing. But he knew he had a gift for it. His instinct, right from the start of his military career, had been to go right at them. Hit them with everything. Speed. Aggression. Surprise. Maximum impact. If these people had come looking for war, he was going to give them a war like they'd never seen before. If he didn't get out of this, he'd at least make a hell of a mark.

So before the six troopers had even touched the ground he was already flipping off the safety on the BAR and opening up on the chopper above them. He went for the fuel tanks. Where a flimsy pistol round had no chance of penetrating, nine hundred rounds a minute of high-velocity .308 full metal jackets sliced like a hot razor through a pat of butter. The tanks ruptured with a screech of ripping metal and fiberglass and a deafening explosion as the chopper erupted into flame and crashed to the ground, a spreading fireball engulfing the troopers. They had no chance.

No quarter, no pity. You don't give it, because you don't get it from the enemy. Ben fired into the flames, the BAR bucking like a jackhammer in his arms, spent cases rolling across the floor at his feet, and the smell of cordite filling the air. He saw burning men struggling to get to their feet, arms waving, staggering back, collapsing into the inferno.

A second explosion ripped the chopper apart. A massive unfolding mushroom of flame blossomed upwards. Black smoke rose in a huge column. Flaming debris showered across the farmyard.

One down.

The two remaining aircraft pulled back, their pilots hauling them up into a steep escape climb. They roared over the farm and banked in a swooping parallel arc. Then they streaked back towards the buildings. Men in black tactical gear were hanging out of their sides, bringing their weapons to bear.

Ben tracked the leading one through the sky. Spent cartridges streamed from the hot breech of the BAR as he launched round after round into the fuselage. A ragged string of holes punched through its body. A fleeting glimpse of the spray of pink mist as someone inside was hit. Perspex shattering and crumpling under the heavy fire.

The chopper veered at a crazy angle, lost altitude, and nosedived. The beat of its rotors became a lopsided *whumph-whumph-whumph*, throwing up billows of dust as it gyrated out of control. For an instant it looked as though it was going to plow straight into the ground right in front of the house—but then the blades caught the edge of the cowshed roof and the aircraft tore through the wooden structure, planks and splinters and pieces of corrugated iron spinning in all directions.

Two down, one to go.

The third chopper thudded overhead, climbing to avoid the flying, bouncing wreckage.

Seconds later, what remained of the black-clad troopers from the crashed second chopper were spilling out of the cowshed door, weapons poised. Ben caught them in his sights and hammered them down in a bloody swath from left to right.

This was too easy.

Then suddenly it wasn't.

Modern military longarms were fitted with muzzle flash suppressors to conceal the telltale blast of flame from enemy spotters. The BAR belonged to a generation before those kinds of refinements. So when the torrent of gunfire tore through the storeroom roof and sliced down through the building all around him, Ben knew the bright yellow-white flash that pulsed from the barrel of the heavy rifle had given away his position to the pilot of the third chopper.

Fragments of tiles and torn roof beams rained down on him. Windows exploded and chunks of masonry flew as the third chopper hovered over the building and poured down the combined fire of at least two or three assault rifles.

Ben rolled, grabbing the big Browning, dragging his bag with the spare magazines across the floor after him. He hefted the weapon up vertically and fired back up through the roof at the belly of the chopper. Dust showered down into his face.

The craft veered away, spinning towards the house. Ben leaped to his feet, looped the bag over his shoulder, scrambled down the creaking steps to the ground, and burst outside into the blinding sunlight.

He was in the junk-strewn alleyway between the storeroom and the ruins of the cowshed. Thirty yards to his left was the gutted-out shell of a dead tractor. Fifteen yards closer, sitting up against the walls of the buildings on either side, were two shapeless heaps covered with tarpaulins. Various farm debris was piled up around them.

To his right, beyond the gap between the buildings, the third chopper was hovering steady above the farmyard. As Ben watched, six men streamed down from its sides and hit the ground. He flattened himself against the wall. The men didn't see him as they dispersed among the buildings, signaling to one another.

But the pilot had spotted him. The machine's nose dipped and it came on, tracking up between the buildings, gaining speed, the front tips of its skids almost raking the ground.

Ben sprinted away from it, heading towards the cover of the wrecked tractor. Gunfire crackled behind him as he sprinted between the two tarp-covered heaps on either side of the alley. He ran faster. Threw himself behind the tractor as bullets whipped up a snake of dirt and dust in his wake.

He raised the rifle. The helicopter was bearing down on him, just a few yards away, sending up a violent dust storm.

Now it was right between the tarp-covered heaps.

Right where he wanted it.

He fired. Not at the chopper but into the heap on the left. Then the one on the right. He emptied the magazine into them, in a scything arc of fire. Then he dropped the empty rifle and hurled himself flat on the ground behind the old tractor.

The blinding flash of light obliterated everything.

He'd found the tall propane gas cylinders in the barn earlier, spares for the old kitchen stove. Next to them he'd found the sacks of four-inch nails that he'd bound to them with rolls of duct tape, wrapping up each one tightly in turn as Ira held the cylinder steady. Hidden under the dirty tarps, they were a crude, giant version of a nail bomb.

Just one problem: he hadn't intended to be this close when they went off.

In the closed space between the buildings the effect was devastating. The massive explosion took the chopper straight in the face.

It was as though it had hit a wall. It was flung down to the ground like a child's toy, buckling and crumpling. The windows burst inwards. The rotor blades flew into shards. Then the fireball from the propane cylinders touched off the gasoline bombs and jerricans he'd set up along the sides of the walls, hidden behind farm junk. A sheet of flame closed in on the chopper, rolling in through its open sides like liquid, rinsing it out, incinerating everything that lived in there. Burning men tumbled out, screaming, flailing, falling, dying.

Ben kept his face to the dirt as the spreading fireball rolled over him. Its heat seared his back, and for one terrifying instant he thought he was going to burn. But then the hot breath of the flames drew away from him, and he staggered to his feet.

Everything around him was destroyed. The shattered buildings were on fire. Bodies lay strewn across the ground, and the stench of charred flesh filled the air. The chopper was a blazing skeleton.

Ben stepped out from behind the tractor. The rifle was lying in the dirt a few yards away. He went to snatch it up, then saw that a piece of flying shrapnel had crushed the receiver. He swore, grabbed the pistol from his bag, and emptied out the useless BAR magazines.

Then, suddenly, the troopers who had landed from the third chopper were back. All six of them, darting between the shell of the burning aircraft and the wrecked buildings. Weapons raised, fire reflected on their goggles.

And now Ben realized with an icy shock that he was in trouble. More men were coming down the other way. Their leader's face split into a wide grin.

Jones. He must have landed a fourth chopper somewhere behind the trees, using the first three as a distraction. There were five troopers with him, all clad in tactical battle gear, all aiming the same M16 assault rifles.

A dozen men in all. Maybe 350 rounds of high-velocity rifle ammunition, all for him. And he was trapped right in the middle, with no time to get back behind cover.

"Got you now," Jones yelled. "You're all alone."

54.

When Ben heard the next gunshot his body involuntarily tensed up solid like a boxer tightening up to take a punch. In that suspended-animation breath of time that is all a man has to ready himself for sudden death, he waited for the impact of the bullet that would kill him.

What happened instead was that one of the troopers was suddenly jerked off his feet, as though someone had hooked him up with a cable to a speeding train. He landed spread-eagled in the dust, his rifle clattering to his side. The boom of the gunshot echoed across the farm.

"Not quite alone," a voice shouted.

Suddenly there was chaos. Shots seemed to be coming from all directions. The snap of a small-caliber rifle and another trooper went down, clutching his head. The rest scattered, flinging themselves down behind whatever bits of discarded farm machinery, rusted-out drums, or stacked tractor tires offered them shelter.

Whoever was shooting was moving from cover to cover. It had to be someone who knew the layout of the farm blindfolded. Another rolling boom, and a trooper screamed as his thigh burst open with a spatter of blood. Another snappy report and the man next to Jones fell forward without a sound.

Two shooters. The .22 Marlin and the Ithaca shotgun. Riley and Ira had joined the party.

Ben dived back behind the tractor. To his left, four troopers were pinned down under cover near the burning chopper. To his right were Jones and his team, crouched behind a pile of firewood logs.

They were firing sporadically at nothing, panic showing in their movements. Ben punched the pistol up and shot one. Return fire ricocheted off the tractor's fender. He fired again. Hit another.

But then he saw something that made his heart stop. At the end of the alleyway between the wrecked and now blazing cowshed and the storeroom building, ten yards from Jones and his remaining men, Ira was stepping out into the open with the .22 Marlin in his hands. His chin was high and there was a glint of pride in his eyes. Old Riley Tarson hobbled out behind him, the shotgun clamped in his fists, thunder in his face. "You people have no right to be here," he yelled.

Jones whipped his rifle round towards the two men. Ben let off four rapid rounds from across the alley and Jones flung himself back down in the dirt behind the log pile.

Then it was mayhem, shots rattling back and forth across a wild V of fire. Ira went down, grimacing in pain. Riley stood his ground, working the pump on his old Ithaca, loosing off blast after blast. The Beretta kicked and boomed in Ben's hands until it was empty.

The gun battle was over as quickly as it had begun. A strange silence hung over the farm. The alleyway was littered with dead men.

Jones was the only intruder left alive. He burst from cover, threw down his empty rifle, and ran for all he was worth, shielding his face with his arm as he stumbled through the flames of the burning chopper and disappeared among the buildings.

Riley dropped the shotgun and crouched down beside the fallen Ira. The young Indian was clutching his leg, groaning in agony, blood seeping between his fingers.

Riley looked up as Ben approached. "Figured you might want a little help," the old farmer said.

Ben nodded. "I owe you one."

Ira grinned weakly up at him. "Whipped 'em good, didn't we?"

Ben crouched and examined the wound. "It's just a graze," he said. "Riley, you'd better get him out of here. There might be more of them coming."

"Where are you going?" Riley said.

"To get Jones." Ben turned and started walking fast. Ejected the empty magazine from the pistol and let it drop down into the dust as he slammed in another.

Fire was crackling up the side of the cowshed, blocking his way. He ducked inside the wrecked storeroom, battled through the flames, and ran out through the front entrance into the yard just in time to see Jones stumbling over to the big barn. He was moving clumsily in his tactical gear. Ben crossed the yard after him and walked inside the barn. It was one of the few buildings that hadn't caught fire.

It was dark and cool inside. Ben looked about him.

Then Jones was bursting out of the shadows and the prongs of a pitchfork were flying at Ben's chest.

Ben sidestepped the thrust, and the fork embedded itself in the timber wall.

Jones staggered away, hatred in his eyes. He reached down and ripped away the Velcro strap holding his tactical combat knife in its leg sheath. He whipped the blade out and crouched low, like an animal about to pounce.

"You shouldn't have come here," Ben said quietly. "Big mistake."

Jones let out a wild scream and charged at him. He swung the knife at Ben's throat. Ben stepped into the arc of the swing, caught the wrist, and twisted it hard. The knife spun out of Jones's grip.

The CIA man cried out in pain. He writhed away and backed farther into the shadows of the barn, moving towards the ladder that led up to the hayloft, glancing wildly around him for anything he could use as a weapon. He stumbled over an empty drum and knocked over a stack of fencing poles. Grabbed one of the poles. It was five feet long, thick pine, sharpened to a crude point. He tried to throw it like a spear, but it was too heavy and crashed against the rusted housing of a large circular saw with its point sticking upwards at an angle.

Ben kept coming. Jones had nowhere to run to now.

"You're in my world now," Ben said. "You're weak and you're unarmed, and you're finished. You should never have got in my way."

Jones let out a strangled noise and scrambled up the rickety ladder. Ben followed him up to the raised platform thirty feet above, where

cobwebbed bales were stacked up in the dusty shaft of light streaming from a gable window. He raised the pistol and aimed it at Jones's
head.

Jones dropped down on his knees in the hay, his face contorted.
"Don't kill me. Please."

Ben lowered the gun and thrust it in his belt.

"No," he said. "I'm not going to kill you." He reached into his bag.

Jones screamed in horror as Ben took out the bottle and syringe.
He unslung the bag, let it fall, and stepped towards the CIA man.
Jabbed the needle into the bottle and pulled back the plunger. Jones
tried to scrabble away. He was blubbering with terror now. Ben
grabbed him, threw him down in the hay, and jabbed the needle deep
into his neck. He pushed the plunger home.

Jones screamed again, broken teeth bared in gibbering fear. "What
have you done to me?"

Ben stood back. He tossed the empty syringe into the shadows.

Then Jones went to pieces in front of his eyes. He battered his
head against the floor. Tore out his hair. Stuffed his fingers down
his throat in a desperate attempt to vomit the drug from his system.
Tears poured down his face.

"Tell me how it feels, Jones," Ben said. "Knowing that in a few
hours you'll be as insane as the poor bastard on the video."

"Kill me," Jones sobbed, bits of hay stuck to his wet face. "Please
just kill me."

"No chance," Ben said. "You're going to tell me everything." He
leaned back against the hay bales and watched as the drug circulated
through the man's veins. After a minute or so, Jones's frenzy dimin-
ished and he seemed to relax. He slumped down in the hay.

The transformation was weird to watch. It took a few more minutes for the man to start loosening up. His face hung expressionless,
as though the muscles had been anesthetized. His eyes rolled back in
his head. Then he began to talk, in a mumbling voice.

Ben knew what he had to do. He was at the end of a thousand-
mile trail of dead government agents and police. That added up to
some of the worst trouble he'd ever been in, and it was going to take

a lot of very persuasive evidence to get him out. He only hoped Jones was about to provide just that.

He reached back into his bag and found the oblong shape of his phone. He took it out, turned it on, and activated the video camera function. Pointed the phone at Jones.

He spoke loudly and clearly. "Tell the camera who you are."

The agent's eyelids fluttered. "My name is Alban Hainsworth Jones," he muttered without hesitation. "I work for the CIA."

Ben nodded. Looked like the stuff was working. Now to press on. "Tell the camera the name of the person who was kidnapped on Corfu by former government agents Kaplan and Hudson, with the collusion of active members of the CIA."

Jones's eyes darted back and forth. His fingers were twitching and clawing, as though there was some desperate internal struggle going on to hold in the truth despite the chemical signals flooding his brain. "Zoë Bradbury," he mumbled. "Zoë Bradbury was kidnapped by U.S. agents and brought to an unauthorized secure facility in rural Montana for questioning."

"What was your part in this, Agent Jones?"

"To extract the information from her using brutality and torture if needed," Jones said. "And to eliminate any opposition, which is why I murdered Dr. Joshua Greenberg and two Georgia police officers." Sweat was pouring off his brow. His face was contorting, veins standing out in a livid Y-shape on his forehead. The conflict inside him seemed to be tearing him apart.

Ben held the camera closer. "Why was Zoë Bradbury's information so important?"

"Because of Jerusalem."

"Explain that."

Jones's eyes rolled back in his head, so that just the whites showed. His lips peeled back to show his jagged teeth. He looked like a zombie. It sent a shiver down Ben's spine.

"Too late to stop it now," Jones muttered. "It's in motion. It's inevitable. It's going to happen in less than twenty-four hours."

"Too late to stop what?"

"It was never about the girl. It was about war."

"What war?"

Jones's eyes rolled back down and focused on him. He smiled weirdly. "The war in the Bible," he said.

Ben processed the words. They were like a slap in the face. They wouldn't sink in. "Keep talking."

Sweat dripped down the man's nose. It was pouring off him faster than anything Ben had ever seen. Pooling in the hollow at the base of his throat, soaking rapidly through his clothes. He seemed to be on fire. His eyes were rolling and darting alarmingly. "The end of the world," he croaked. "The End Times. Armageddon. They're starting it. They're going to make it happen. Starting in Jerusalem."

"What are they going to do?"

"Something massive," Jones said. "And there's nothing you or anyone can do to stop it."

Ben was stunned, hardly able to think straight as his mind raced to make sense of this. "Slater's in charge of all this? Who is he?"

Jones's grin was frozen and wild. He was beginning to shake violently. He mumbled something incomprehensible.

"Speak clearly," Ben said.

Jones looked up at him. His eyes were rimmed with blood. "I'm going to go mad," he whispered.

"Yes. You are. Now answer the question."

It might have been the effect of the drug, or it might have been just the horror in the man's mind, knowing that he was going to spend the rest of his life as a babbling lunatic. But something snapped in Jones's head. Ben read it in his eyes—but reacted too slowly.

Jones was suddenly rearing up to his feet. Ben reached out to press him back down, but there was some kind of mad power in him that allowed him to force past.

Before Ben could stop him, Jones had covered the ten steps to the edge of the hayloft platform. There was no rail or barrier to stop him. He didn't slow down. He hurled himself off the edge and sailed out into space, twisting in midair. Ben caught a glimpse of the wild light in Jones's eyes as he dropped towards the floor below.

He didn't hit the floor.

His fall was arrested by the upward-pointing fence post that he'd tried to spear Ben with earlier. It caught him between the shoulder blades, and his falling weight drove it right through him, through organs and rib cage and right out of his chest. The wooden point protruded grotesquely, slick with gore.

Jones stared upwards at Ben. His head was thrown back at an unnatural angle. The blade of the old circular saw was embedded in his skull. Blood and cranial fluids oozed down the rusty steel disc, down the housing of the machine to the dirt floor.

Ben shut off the phone and dropped it in his pocket. He grabbed up his bag and climbed back down the ladder. His mind was still reeling from what Jones had said.

They kidnapped Zoë to start Armageddon.

It seemed insane, and for a moment he wondered whether what he'd heard was genuine or the brain-frazzling effects of a drug that turned men insane.

But no. There had been something in Jones's eyes, even as his sanity was slipping away. He was telling the truth.

Ben stood staring at the CIA man's corpse, trying to understand what he had meant.

Then he tensed, alerted by the sound outside. He ran to the barn door and out into the sunlight. The wreckage in the yard and the alleyway was still blazing, hot on his face. Through the shimmering heat haze and the slowly rising pall of smoke he saw the helicopters landing beyond the farm gate. Four of them, so dark-green as to be almost black, the letters FBI in white across their sides.

The first one to touch down was the big twin-prop Boeing. Ben hadn't seen one since his army days. Hatches slid open. A man stepped out. He wasn't wearing tactical clothing, but a gray suit. His sandy hair fluttered in the whipping blast of the rotors as he hurried across the grass, keeping his head low.

Behind him was Alex. Her eyes were wide as she took in the devastation of the farm, the burning buildings, the wrecked choppers. Then she caught sight of Ben and her face lit up.

Ben walked towards them out of the carnage. He reached for the Beretta in his belt and tossed it away into the dirt.

More personnel were spilling out of the helicopters as they landed. The gray-suited man strode purposefully up to Ben. His hand went to his jacket and came up holding a badge. Armed agents swarmed round his flanks, pistols trained on Ben.

Ben wearily raised his hands.

"I'm Special Agent Callaghan," said the gray-suited man. "And you're under arrest."

55.

Ben was frisked and ushered briskly into one of the choppers by big, silent men in dark suits and dark glasses. He watched through a window as Callaghan put Alex and Zoë on the second chopper and boarded with them.

The flight took a long time, and it was evening when the helicopters touched down at a private airstrip where black SUVs stood on the runway together with men with guns. Ben was escorted across the tarmac to a sleek jet. The guards kept him away from Alex and Zoë.

Some time later, the jet landed at what looked like a military airfield. More black cars were waiting for them. Ben was marched across to one of them, a door held open for him, an agent sitting on either side of him. Callaghan climbed into the front passenger seat and the car took off at high speed, leading the way for a procession of vehicles. Nobody spoke.

But Ben could guess where he was being taken.

Langley, Virginia, CIA headquarters. As the cavalcade of cars approached the vast sprawl of buildings, he saw that his guess was right. Armed security personnel guarded the tall steel gates that bore the eagle-and-star seal of the Central Intelligence Agency. Callaghan flashed a card as they went through, and a series of gates glided open for them. They drove through building complexes with thousands of windows, illuminated like starships in the dusk, past floodlit lawns where rows of U.S. flags fluttered in the breeze. Everything was immaculate, a monument to unflinching national pride and self-possessed superiority.

Then the car stopped and Ben was led inside a building. The place was milling with activity, more layers of security to pass through and hundreds of workers swarming through the wide corridors. Callaghan walked briskly, and Ben followed, aware of the men in black suits right behind him. Glancing over his shoulder, he spotted Alex fifteen yards behind. She was being escorted along by more of the same dark, taciturn men. She smiled at him, but it was a nervous smile. Zoë was nowhere to be seen.

Ben followed Callaghan through an open-plan labyrinth of operations rooms that were heavily cluttered with desks and computer terminals, staff and security personnel swarming everywhere. The place looked like the London Stock Exchange. Rows of clocks displaying the times in different countries. Hundreds of monitors flashing and blinking, giant screens on the walls showing news broadcasts from all over the world. Brightly lit electronic political maps of the globe, animated to show movements and developments that Ben could only guess at as he walked by. Everywhere he looked, scores of people were glued to the screens as though American national security would collapse into rubble and anarchy if they glanced away for just an instant.

At the far end of the last operations room they walked through was a set of glass sliding doors. The room beyond was hidden behind vertical blinds. A security guard rose from a desk as they approached. Callaghan handed him a card. The doors glided open with a slick *whoosh*, and Ben followed Callaghan into a long conference room.

In the middle was a glistening table, surrounded by leather chairs. Three walls were paneled with wood; the fourth was a large mirrored window flanked by a pair of flags, the U.S. Stars and Stripes on the left and the emblem of the CIA on the right, embroidered in white-and-gold thread. The ceiling was low and studded with spotlights.

The silent agents ushered Alex into the room and left. The doors glided shut and clicked. She glanced at Ben, clearly full of things to say but feeling compelled to stay quiet. He held her gaze for a second, putting reassurance in his eyes.

Seated at the head of the conference table was a large, broad-shouldered black man in his early sixties, wearing a somber suit and a navy tie. There was an air of gravity about him, like that of a judge. Callaghan walked around the table and took a seat to his right, straightened his tie, and looked to him for the first word. It was obvious who was in charge here.

"My name is Murdoch," said the big man. His voice was deep and mellifluous. Ben could clearly see the intelligence in his eyes. Murdoch gestured at the chairs on his left, calm and slow in his movements. "Please. Take a seat."

Ben sat, and Alex sat three feet away. She coughed nervously.

Ben was determined to seize the initiative here. The place was designed to intimidate. That wasn't going to happen. "Where's Zoë?" he demanded.

"Miss Bradbury is in very good hands," Murdoch replied calmly. "Agent Callaghan here is in charge of her protection."

"She's in CIA custody?"

"She's safe," Murdoch said. "That's all you need to know." He pursed his lips, formulating his thoughts. He leaned heavily on the table and gazed at Ben with penetrating eyes. "This is a very ugly situation. For all of us," he added meaningfully. Then his eyes darted across and the steady gaze landed on Alex. "Agent Fiorante, you realize you're in a lot of trouble here. Before we get started, have you anything to say?"

Ben could feel the tension in her, like a crackle of electricity next to him. She clearly knew what he'd already guessed, that on the other side of the mirrored window there were people watching and listening, filming and transcribing every word that was being said in the room.

"Nothing that isn't already in the statement I made on the way here," she said coolly.

"Let's run through it again, for the record," Murdoch said.

Callaghan smiled coldly.

Alex spoke carefully, measuring every word. "I was part of Jones's team, under the impression that we were taking part in authorized operations. However, during that time I witnessed a number of incidents that I found highly suspect, to say the least. I can testify that Jones personally executed the two Georgia police officers as well as

Dr. Greenberg at the facility near Chinook, Montana. It all happened right in front of me. I will further testify that Jones and his associates were using the Montana facility to imprison and, if we hadn't intervened, to torture and murder Zoë Bradbury."

"And you didn't think to report any of this to your superiors at the time," Callaghan cut in from across the table, staring aggressively at her.

"Sir, Agent Jones was my immediate superior. And I was concerned for my safety. That said, I regret my actions."

Murdoch's face was impassive. He nodded gravely. "This is an issue we can address later on." He turned to Ben. "Let's talk about you. I've seen your military record. We know exactly who you are. So there's no point whatsoever in pretense."

Ben returned his steady gaze. "I had no intention of concealing anything from you."

"You were hired by Miss Bradbury's family to locate her."

Ben shook his head. "I was helping a friend. I had no professional involvement."

"Whatever you say. But the body count is beginning to look like one of your old military operations. First Greece. Then Georgia. Then Montana. Our investigation team is still pulling dead men out of the Mountain View Hotel. All either active or former government agents. The farm where we found you resembles a war zone. From what I can see, Major Hope, you leave a trail of devastation and mayhem in your wake everywhere you go."

"Only when people stand in the way," Ben said. "And you can call me Mr. Hope."

"Right. I see you're retired."

"I'm a theology student."

Murdoch's lips curled into the faintest of smiles. "So would you mind telling me what exactly has been going on with this Bradbury kidnapping?"

"It was never really about Zoë Bradbury," Ben said. "She's only an incidental part of it. It's about something bigger. Much bigger."

"Like what?"

"Like war," Ben said. "The war to end all wars."

"This is making no sense to me," Murdoch rumbled. "Let's take it from the top. You're claiming that Special Agent Jones was part of some kind of ghost organization, working from within the Agency."

"Right under your noses. He and his associates have been making use of your resources for their own aims."

"Which are?"

"It took me a while to work it out," Ben said. "But like I told you, I study the Bible. It's all in there. It's been there for thousands of years, written into prophetic scripture."

Callaghan shook his head in confusion.

"The book of Revelation," Ben said.

"Give us a break," Callaghan sneered. "The Omen. Number of the Beast."

"Can't you shut this cretin up?" Ben asked Murdoch.

"Shut up, Callaghan," Murdoch said, keeping his eyes on Ben. "Mr. Hope, I would like you to explain this to me clearly."

"The organization is a militant evangelical Christian cell. Their goal is a terrorist strike in Jerusalem."

Callaghan burst out laughing. Murdoch glanced at him, his serious expression holding.

"If you don't believe me," Ben said, "maybe you'll believe one of your own people. You took my phone away from me at the farm. Let me have it back."

"Who do you want to call?" Callaghan chuckled. "Your lawyer? Or your priest?"

"Give him the phone," Murdoch said.

Callaghan made an exaggerated gesture of surrender, reached down into his case, and brought out a clear plastic bag. He tipped the phone out of it. Ben picked it up, turned it on, and scrolled through the menu. Then he placed the phone on the table with the screen facing the two men and played back the video recording of Jones for them.

The man sat framed on the tiny screen. He talked. They watched and listened. Callaghan loosened his tie and shifted in his seat.

Murdoch's somber expression grew darker. The playback ended with Jones disappearing out of the frame, and the sound of the wooden stake punching through his body as he fell to his death. Ben reached across and turned it off.

"You realize this confession was obtained illegally," Murdoch warned. "It doesn't constitute evidence."

"Nothing very legal about any of it," Ben said. "I administered the truth serum that Special Agent Jones was going to give to Zoë Bradbury. They didn't exactly have a doctor's prescription."

Murdoch glared heavily at him. "Keep talking."

Ben filled in what he knew. He started at the beginning and worked his way through to the end, leaving out nothing. By the end of it, he knew he had Murdoch's attention. Deep furrows had appeared on the man's brow.

But Callaghan was staring skeptically. "This Slater, the guy you claim Jones was taking orders from. Shame he never mentioned that name during his statement."

"It's true," Alex cut in, glancing nervously at Ben.

"Did you personally meet this man?" Callaghan asked her harshly.

She paused a beat, then shook her head. "No, sir, not as such."

Callaghan smiled and pointed at Ben. "So we only have his word for it."

"You got a first name for him?" Murdoch said.

"I never got around to asking," Ben replied. "We weren't really on first-name terms."

"So basically you have no idea who he is," Callaghan said.

"I could describe him," Ben said. "He's about my age, North American Caucasian, red hair, slight build, about five-eight, professional, moneyed, expensive watch."

"Not exactly hard data," Callaghan spat.

"But still, I'd like to know more about him," Murdoch cut in. "If this guy exists, he's on our database." He laid his hands flat on the table, lips puckering in concentration. "Let's leave that aside. I just don't get what you're telling me here. Why does a Christian group want to start a war?"

"Let me make it simple," Ben said. "Someone is staging a deliberate attempt to force biblical prophecy to come true. Perhaps because they truly believe it's going to happen. Maybe they're tired of waiting for God to make the first move. Or maybe it's a trick, to make it look as if it's about to come true, in order to dupe millions of believers into thinking the End Times are about to start. Either way, I believe the motive is largely political."

"Involving whom?" Murdoch asked calmly. "And at what level?"

"I don't know. But it's at a high level. Whoever this is, they have a lot to gain by steering the world towards war and generating mass panic, or mass euphoria, among a core of more than fifty million American voters."

"This is totally absurd," Callaghan said. "Crazy. Purely speculative."

Murdoch ignored him, watching Ben with a look that said he was taking this very seriously now. "How do you get to this conclusion?"

"Think of Jerusalem from a strategic point of view," Ben said. "You've got the holiest sites of Judaism and Islam side-by-side in the same city. A place of anger and frustration. A religious powder keg, just waiting for a spark to set it off. And it's ground zero for the End Times movement. Fifty million pairs of eyes glued to it, interpreting every incident that takes place there, and every development in world politics, strictly and exclusively in terms of apocalyptic Bible prophecy."

Murdoch nodded. "OK, I'm with you. Go on."

"The prophecy states that the war will begin with an attack on God's chosen people of Israel," Ben said. "Now, what would you do if you wanted to set something like that in motion?"

Murdoch thought for a moment. "I'd take advantage of the religious tension in Jerusalem. I'd look for a way to provoke Muslim leaders into wanting to strike at the Jews, big-time."

"So the first blow struck would have to target the Muslims," Ben said, "in the certain knowledge that the Islamic world would want to launch a strong reprisal against their enemies."

"Therefore we're looking at an initial attack on Islam."

Ben nodded. "Correct. Something that would significantly upset the Islamic world. Something designed to shock and provoke them like nothing ever before, that would be guaranteed to gain that kind of dramatic response from them."

Murdoch raised his eyebrows. "Specifically?"

"I'd be speculating," Ben said. "An act of terrorism. A high-level assassination. Very daring, and extremely insulting to them."

Murdoch clicked his tongue. "That's a pretty broad field. We have no idea what's planned, or who the perpetrator would be. We don't know where to start."

"We do know two things," Ben said. "One, it's going to happen within something like the next twenty hours. And two, it's going to get blamed on a Jewish operative."

Callaghan grimaced and slapped his palm on the table. "This is ridiculous."

Murdoch paid him no attention. "Let me tell you why I'm worried about this," he said. He turned to the mirrored window, and Ben saw that he'd been right. Murdoch gestured. "Stop filming, stop transcription."

Then he turned back to Ben and Alex. He frowned. "What I'm about to tell you does not leave this room. Three months ago an Israeli Mossad agent, a professional assassin known to the CIA as Salomon, vanished suddenly off the radar screen. Presumed dead. No body was found, and nobody has stepped forward to claim responsibility for his killing, if that's what it is. This *is* highly speculative, but I don't find it hard to put Salomon's disappearance together with what you've told me here today."

"I wouldn't be surprised if you find his prints on the assassination weapon," Ben said. "And his wallet full of credit cards lying nearby." He smiled. "Like the ones they just happened to find in the burned-out wreckage of nine-eleven, with the terrorists' IDs on."

Murdoch's eyes narrowed. "I'm going to ignore that comment."

"I know all about dirty war," Ben said. "You don't get used as a pawn without learning how the game works."

Callaghan slumped back in his seat, staring hard at his colleague. "You're not going to take this man seriously, are you, sir? He's a loose cannon. An anarchist."

Murdoch slowly turned and glared at him. "I take this very seriously indeed," he rumbled. "And, Callaghan, if you have nothing more constructive to say, I suggest you say nothing at all."

Callaghan went quiet.

Murdoch leaned across the table. He pinched the bridge of his nose, then exhaled noisily. "OK," he said. "I'm going to have to clear this with my superiors. But when they hear what I have to say, it's extremely likely that you, Mr. Hope, will be on a flight to Israel."

"To do what?"

"To try to stop this catastrophe from happening, if indeed that's what's being planned. You'll be supplied with everything you need once you touch down in Jerusalem. Callaghan will put you together with our people there."

Ben shook his head. "I don't work for you."

"Consider yourself enlisted. Unofficially, of course."

"I gave you the information," Ben said. "I've done my part. Now I want to go home. This is your problem."

Murdoch's frown lines deepened. "I think that, if you're right about this, World War Three is going to be everybody's problem. And apparently we don't have a lot of time to figure out a solution." He clicked his tongue thoughtfully. "I can't send company agents in on this. It's the kind of situation where an outsider would be more useful to me. Someone who can't be traced to us."

"You mean, if something were to happen to me," Ben said. "Collateral damage. Easy to bury."

"Consider it a favor to us," Murdoch said. "And of course we'd show our appreciation by forgetting the incident in Georgia. Maybe there's some delinquent with other murders to his name that we can find to pin the cop killing on. You get my drift?"

"Sir, can I remind you I'm a witness to the fact that Agent Jones murdered those two officers?" Alex protested.

"I think you should keep your mouth shut, Agent Fiorante. There's also the issue of your involvement in this situation. You admit to having shot a fellow agent. That's not something we can just skip over lightly." Murdoch settled back in his chair and folded his hands across his belly. "So, Mr. Hope. Either you cooperate with us in this matter, or you'll be charged with the murder of two police officers and several government agents. And Agent Fiorante will spend the next decade in a federal prison for her own actions. Your choice."

"What makes you think I'm the right man for the job?"

"Let's not mess around, Major. The clock is ticking. If it comes down to a sniper-counter-sniper situation, I have evidence that proves to me that you're just about the best guy in the world for this job." Murdoch reached into his pocket and took out a matchbox. Slid the tiny drawer open with his finger. Took out a spent match and tossed it on the table. "Ring any bells?"

Ben stared at it. "Let's say I go along with this. I have some conditions."

Murdoch nodded. "I'm a reasonable man. I'm listening."

"I want Zoë Bradbury flown home to her family."

"Not an option," Callaghan cut in. "She's a witness."

"She's also a victim," Ben said. "A victim of the fact that your agency is corrupted and people within it are abusing its power. So, unless you want that information getting out there, you arrange for her to be flown home under close guard and given top-priority police protection in the UK until these people are caught."

Murdoch thought about it for a moment. "OK, agreed. But she will have to come back here to testify, if required."

"And I want your personal guarantee that in return for my cooperation, there'll be no question of any charges leveled at Agent Fiorante."

Murdoch nodded slowly. "Anything else?"

"I left behind a complicated situation in Greece. There's a Corfu police captain called Stephanides who'd probably like to talk to me again."

Murdoch waved his hand. "We can take care of that. He never heard of you. Anything else?"

"That's it."

"Then we have a deal," Murdoch said. "And you're on your way to Jerusalem."

56.

I t was after 10 p.m. when Ben and Alex emerged from the conference room. The operations office was still as bustling and hectic as before. Murdoch led them down a hallway and through a set of doors to a computer lab that was so crammed with equipment there was barely room for the half-dozen or so staff manning it.

Callaghan was hunched over a terminal with one of the technicians. He looked up as Murdoch walked up to him. "There are over twenty-two thousand males named Slater between the ages of thirty-five and forty-five in the United States," he said.

Murdoch leaned on the desk. "Can you narrow it down? Hair color, height, build, profession."

"It's going to take a while to factor in those kinds of parameters," Callaghan said testily.

"Don't take too long. Time is short."

Then Ben and Alex were left alone in a quiet lobby for a few minutes while Murdoch went off to make some phone calls.

"Thanks for what you did in there," she said. "It's not fair, what they're doing to you."

"Promise me two things," Ben said.

She nodded. "Name them."

"First, you'll make sure Zoë gets back to her family safely."

"Of course I will. And the other promise?"

"That you'll look after yourself. Have a good life, all right?"

She smiled uncertainly. "This is your way of saying good-bye?"

"Maybe. I don't know what's going to happen."

"Can I give you a call sometime?"

"I'd like that," he said. He told her the number of his cell phone. She repeated it.

A door swung open and Murdoch reappeared. "It's done," he told Ben. "Your plane leaves for Israel at midnight."

"What happens when I get there?"

Murdoch frowned. "You'll appreciate that we're improvising this to a large degree. I'm hoping I'll know more by the time you touch down in Jerusalem. Our agents there will be figuring out the likely targets. You'll be contacted." He looked at his watch and winced. He turned to Alex. "You're working under Agent Callaghan now. We're releasing Miss Bradbury into your care. She knows you, she'll feel safe with you. She's a little uptight, and maybe you can help calm her."

"No problem," Alex said. "She can come home with me tonight."

For the first time that evening Murdoch looked pleased, real warmth in his eyes. "Thank you, Alex. There'll be three agents outside your door, although I have a feeling Miss Bradbury's no longer under threat." He gestured towards the door, looking expectantly at Alex.

She hesitated, glanced at Ben.

"So this is it," he said to her.

"I guess so," she replied. "I'll see you around, then."

"Sometime," he said.

She touched his hand. Their fingers interlocked for a brief moment, then parted. Murdoch noticed it and looked away.

"Take care," Alex murmured, and then she turned and Ben watched her walk away and disappear through the door.

"Now let's see if you and Callaghan can find your man Slater," Murdoch said.

Ben spent the next seventy minutes alone with Callaghan in a dark room filled with screens, sifting through the hundreds of ID photographs that the agent and the computer lab tech had narrowed down from the original thousands of files. When they'd gone through the whole lot, Ben sat back in his chair and shook his head.

Callaghan narrowed his eyes. "You're sure about that?"

"Absolutely sure," Ben said. "I never forget a face."

"Then he gave you a false name. Which I knew all along. I can't figure out why Murdoch can't see it. It's obvious. And it leaves us with a big fat zero. Waste of time."

Ben said nothing.

Callaghan peeled back his sleeve to check his watch. "Let's move. I need to get you on that flight."

57.

The CIA staff vehicle pulled up outside Alex's little white wood house in the sleepy town a few miles from the headquarters at Langley. Alex and Zoë climbed out of the back doors, and two agents walked them up the pathway through the tiny garden to the front door. The street was empty and quiet. Alex opened the door, and the guards checked all over the house. Everything was fine. They returned to the car. In a few hours another would come to take its place.

Alex showed Zoë inside the open-plan living room. "Make yourself at home," she said, flipping on lights. The house felt a little cold and unlived in, she thought, and went over to the fireplace and turned on the imitation gas fire for instant flames. She checked her answering machine. No messages. *Life with the Company.*

Zoë flopped on a white leather sofa, rubbing her eyes.

"You look exhausted," Alex said. "I think we both could do with a drink. What do you say?" She walked through to the neat kitchen and took a bottle of red wine from the rack, opened it, and poured them each a large glass. Zoë accepted hers gratefully.

"Well, here we are," Alex said.

Zoë smiled. "Here we are."

"It's been a hell of a time, hasn't it?"

Zoë nodded. "I don't even want to think about it. It feels so strange to be here. I can't wait to get home."

"Your parents will be glad to see you again."

"I called them from Langley."

"How did it go?"

"They cried."

"There'll be more of that when you get there," Alex said.

"Probably."

"I'm going to heat up some dinner. You like pizza?"

"Anything."

"I just remembered you're vegetarian. It has pepperoni and anchovies. Want me to scrape them off yours?"

"Leave them on," Zoë said. "I could eat a pickled donkey."

Just then the phone rang, and Alex answered on the speakerphone.

"It's all arranged," Murdoch's deep voice said on the line. "Miss Bradbury is booked on a commercial flight to London from Arlington in the morning. Callaghan will be at your place just after ten to pick her up and escort her to the airport."

"Copy that," Alex said.

"Then I want you to take some leave for a while," Murdoch said. "You've been through a lot."

Alex thanked him, and the call ended.

Zoë was starting to look warm and relaxed on the leather sofa in front of the fire. She peeled off her cardigan and tossed it down on the floor. "So it looks like you're on vacation."

"I could use it, I tell you." Alex went back into the kitchen and fished the pizza out of the freezer. She stuck it in the microwave, and a few minutes later the two of them were sitting at the maple wood breakfast bar, washing down the pizza with more wine.

"This is such a cosy little place," Zoë said through a mouthful.

"It does the job. It's practical and functional. I'm barely ever here, so it suits me fine."

"You live alone, then?"

"Just little me."

"No boyfriend?"

"No time."

Zoë emptied her glass and set it down, a smile playing on her lips. "You like Ben, though."

Alex was just raising the bottle to top off their glasses. She froze. "That obvious?"

"Pretty obvious."

Alex sighed. Raised her eyebrows. "Not much of a secret agent, then." She poured the wine.

"He likes you too."

Alex didn't answer.

"But I don't think he likes me very much," Zoë said, frowning as she took another sip.

"I don't know that's true," Alex lied.

"I don't blame him. I've been a shit to him. In fact, I've been a shit to a lot of people."

"You were under a lot of stress."

Zoë shook her head. "No excuses. I want you to know that I'm really sorry for what I did, and all the trouble it caused."

Alex smiled and patted her arm. "It's over now," she said. *Just the small matter of World War Three about to start*, she was thinking. "Your part is, anyway."

"Will you be seeing Ben again?"

"I don't know. I hope so. Maybe."

"If you do, will you tell him something from me?"

"Sure."

"Tell him I never meant for his friend to be . . . for what happened to his friend. I never wanted anyone to be hurt. It was just a stupid hoax. I didn't think it through."

"I'll tell him, don't worry." Alex smiled warmly.

Zoë gazed into the middle distance for a while. "I'm so sorry about Nikos," she whispered. "He's dead. And it's my doing." She sniffed. "And Skid. His poor legs. He didn't deserve that."

"No, I don't suppose he did."

"I'm going to change," Zoë said. "Things are going to be different from now on. It's time I grew up."

"Why don't we open another bottle of that wine?" said Alex.

58.

The searing white heat of the sun hit Ben as he stepped off the plane. He grabbed a taxi outside the airport and leaned back against the hot plastic seat, wishing he had his whisky flask, trying not to think about why the hell he was here as the battered Mercedes hurtled him towards his destination.

Jerusalem. The city that the Talmud described as having been given by God nine parts of all the beauty of all the world—as well as nine parts of all its pain.

The skyline was white under the cloudless blue sky and the scorching sun. It was in many ways like any other Middle Eastern or North African city, smoky and noisy and buzzing like an ant's nest—a sweltering, heaving throng of thousands of cars and buses and locals and tourists all crammed into a few square miles where the modern jostled with the ancient, the high-rise buildings on the outskirts contrasting sharply with the architecture of two thousand years of religious history. Names like Ammunition Hill and Paratroopers Road were a stark reminder of the bloodiness of the city's past.

Jerusalem had passed through more hands than most historic cities in its time, and all had left their mark, with Christian, Jewish, and Muslim architecture vying for domination. Which, Ben thought to himself, perfectly mirrored the tense political role that this place had played for so very long. A role that might now be about to reach a chilling climax, if what Jones had said was true.

By 4:30 p.m. he'd checked in at his hotel, a drab, sleepy joint on the edge of the city, within earshot of the ululating prayers blaring from a nearby mosque. His room was basic and functional, but he wouldn't have given a damn if it had been crawling with cockroaches.

What the hell was he going to do? He was itching with frustration. It seemed crazy sending him here with so little to go on. The clock was ticking and there was nothing he could do about it.

He showered and changed, spent a few minutes studying the map of the city, then paced his room, impatiently clutching his phone, waiting for the call Murdoch had promised would come. But there was nothing.

Fuck it. He stormed out of the room and made his way down to the hotel bar. The place was empty apart from the wizened old barman. Ben pulled up a stool and lit up the first of the cigarettes he'd bought at the airport. A tall, cool beer made more sense to him in the choking heat than a double Scotch. He leaned on the bar, sipping his drink and watching the smoke curl and drift. His shoulder still ached. Montana seemed a million miles away. So did Alex.

It was two minutes past five when his phone finally went.

"Hope. Callaghan here. Write this down."

Ben took a small notebook and pencil out of his pocket. "I'm listening."

Callaghan spelled out an address in Jerusalem. "It's within the Old City, at the southwest end of the Jewish Quarter," he said. "You have a rendezvous at eighteen-thirty your time."

"Who with?"

"Someone with information. They'll provide you with everything you need."

"One of your people?"

"Let's just say it's an operational house."

"Sleeper agent?"

"Call him an asset."

"What does your asset have for me?"

"It seems you were right," Callaghan said. "There's some vital and sensitive intel to pass on. Something big is about to take place. We think it's the target. Best you hear it from our guy."

"That was quick."

"Yeah, well, things are moving quickly now. Thanks to your input," he added grudgingly.

"What's his name?"

"It's not important. He's expecting you." Callaghan sounded impatient. "I know this is irregular. But you don't need me to tell you, time is of the essence. So get over there. We're depending on you."

"What about Slater?"

"Still working on it. Leave it with us. Out of your hands now, OK?"

"And Zoë?"

"Deal's a deal. I'm on my way right now to Fiorante's place to pick her up and put her on a flight to England."

"I'll be checking to make sure she got there."

"You do that, buddy. And, Hope?"

"What?"

"Good luck." Callaghan ended the call.

Ben put the phone away and sat for another minute, sipping his drink. His zigzag chase across the world looked as though it was entering its final phase. He only hoped that what Callaghan's contact had to say would be worth it.

He left the hotel, stepped out into the scorching sun, and took a taxicab that sped him towards old Jerusalem. Time was ticking rapidly by, but there was nothing he could do other than kill time before his rendezvous with the CIA asset.

He entered the Old City through the Damascus Gate, a frenetic melee of shoppers, tourists, street traders, money changers, beggars, and hawkers. He walked by clustered street stalls selling everything from food, newspapers, and cans of Israeli cola chilled on blocks of ice to counterfeit Levis and electrical goods. A squad of Israeli soldiers swaggered through the crowds. Open-neck khaki uniforms.

Dark glasses. Galil assault rifles with grenade launchers, cocked and locked. Welcome to Jerusalem.

He was deep in thought as he spent a while walking through the ancient heart of the city. The place was a maze of shady winding streets and sun-bleached squares, every inch of them echoing some chapter of its long and tumultuous history.

Ben wandered on and found himself following in the footsteps of a million Christian pilgrims as he walked the Via Dolorosa, the Path of Pain, along which Christ had dragged the cross on the way to his crucifixion. The sacred route led him into the heart of the Christian quarter of the Old City. He stopped and stepped back to gaze up at a towering building, shielding his eyes from the sun's glare. He recognized this place from his theology studies.

The Church of the Holy Sepulchre. It was one of the most revered sites in Christendom, marking the site of Christ's burial and resurrection. Its pitted stonework bore the marks of centuries of religious graffiti carved there by pilgrims through the ages who had crossed the world to pray here.

The old church was still attracting visitors today. Crowds of Western tourists were drifting in and out of the arched entrance, an endless procession of brightly colored T-shirts and shorts and cameras and guidebooks, staring around them in awe at the two-thousand-year-old architecture. The scent of sunblock wafted on the air, and the gabble of voices, many of them American, echoed off the high stone walls.

Ben watched them and wondered. Why were they here? Were they just ordinary people who had traveled thousands of miles to visit and photograph some old building? Or might there be, for some of them, a deeper religious motivation? How many of these people might have come here to reflect on and marvel at the apocalyptic events that they believed were going to befall the world in their own lifetime, to pay homage to the spot where it had all started and was all going to end?

Even if they had, that didn't make them mindless warmongers. Those millions of evangelical believers whose collective support could feather the nests of men like Clayton Cleaver, or provide the incentive for darker political forces to manufacture wars, could have no idea that their religious devotion might be so misused and perverted. They could have no concept of the ways that Bible prophecy could be manipulated as a means to power or to destroy lives.

Or could they? Ben ran over the span of human history in his mind. Was it really such a surprise that a few powerful, cynical men would take advantage of the innocent faith of the many? Wasn't that what powerful men had been doing since the dawn of civilization— playing God, the most dangerous game of them all?

He glanced at his watch. It was approaching six-fifteen. Time to move. He took the slip of paper out of his pocket with the address he'd copied down. In a nearby street he found another battered white Mercedes taxi that was vacant. He showed the address to the heavily bearded driver. The guy nodded, Ben climbed in, and the car took off.

In a few minutes he would know what was going to happen.

And all he had to do then was figure out a way to stop it.

59.

A lex answered the door to find Callaghan standing there in the breezy sunshine with two agents. They stepped inside the house. "She ready?" Callaghan said.

Zoë was coming downstairs. "Here I am."

"You got everything?" Alex asked her.

"I didn't bring a lot with me." Zoë smiled at Alex. "So it's good-bye, then. I suppose I won't see you again, will I?"

"I suppose not. Safe journey home, Zoë. Take care."

"Thanks for what you did for me." Zoë grasped Alex's hand and gave it a squeeze. "I won't forget."

Alex watched her walk across to the black GMC and climb into the back. The agents climbed in with her. Callaghan got into the front passenger seat.

Alex gave Zoë a wave, shut the door, and walked back inside the house. "That's that," she muttered to herself.

Then something caught her eye. A glimpse of gold on the wooden floor under the coffee table. She walked over to it and picked it up. It was Zoë's valuable old bracelet. It must have slipped off when she took off her sweater.

"Shit," she breathed. Zoë had been through a lot with that bracelet, must be attached to it. Alex bit her lip for an instant, deciding what to do. She glanced out the window. The GMC was just moving away out of sight up the long street. Its brake lights flared red, and it took a left turn and disappeared.

On the spur of the moment, Alex decided to follow. The airport was just a few miles away—she could catch up with them there and give Zoë the bracelet.

Her VW Beetle was parked a few yards down from the house. She grabbed the key from the hook near the door and raced outside.

She'd started the engine and pulled away down the street by the time she thought about phoning Callaghan on his cell phone. *Shit.* Her phone was still in the house. Too late to go back for it now. Never mind.

Alex gunned the Beetle down the street between rows of quiet suburban homes, took the left turn, and accelerated out of town towards the highway. Traffic thickened. She caught sight of the big black GMC ahead, eight or nine vehicles between them. Keeping an eye on it, she followed the familiar route. She put on a CD of Creedence Clearwater Revival as she held the VW at a steady sixty.

In a few minutes they were approaching the turnoff for the airport. Alex glanced in her mirror, prepared to flick on her indicator and switch lanes.

But the GMC wasn't changing lanes.

It kept on going down the highway.

Alex frowned as it sped on ahead. The airport signs flashed by and were left behind. Strange. Hadn't Murdoch said they were taking Zoë straight to the airport? Then where *were* they taking her?

She drove on. Time passed. The CCR album came to its last track and ended. She barely noticed. The sky had clouded over now, and rain began to spatter on her windshield.

Now the GMC was heading off the highway and into open country. Woodland flashed by, and the traffic started thinning out. They were travelling farther and farther away from Langley and Washington, DC, heading God knew where. Something told Alex to hang back, and she touched the brakes to widen the distance between her and Callaghan.

Deeper and deeper into the country. Rain hammered against the glass, the wipers beating time. The road became snaky and narrow, and she hung right back so that she could just about keep the GMC in sight but without being spotted.

Now she was seriously perplexed. What was going on here? She wished she could call Murdoch at Langley. Stupid, *stupid*, to have left her phone behind.

The Beetle's dashboard clock was approaching 11 a.m. and the fuel gauge needle was beginning to dip worryingly into the red when the GMC finally pulled off the road. Trailing sixty yards behind, Alex saw the brake lights come on as it lurched onto an overgrown forest road, splashing through puddles. She followed cautiously.

The GMC bumped and bounced down the road until it came to a pair of tall iron gates half-hidden behind ferns. The rain was lashing down now.

Alex killed the Beetle's engine and coasted the final few yards, gently halting the car behind the cover of some bushes. She climbed out into the downpour and hid in the side of the lane, watching as one of the agents got out, walked up to the gates, and undid a padlock. Chains rattled loose. The agent creaked the gate open and the car drove through.

Seconds later she heard screams.

Zoë's voice.

No phone, no weapon. Alex had never felt so naked. She crept through the bushes a few feet, careful not to snap any twigs. Her hair and clothes were quickly soaked from the rain, sticking to her skin. She peered through the foliage. Beyond the gate was a large, sprawling house. It looked like some kind of hunting lodge, expensive, secluded. The gardens were overgrown, as though the place was used only occasionally.

Callaghan's men were dragging Zoë out of the GMC and towards the house. Callaghan led the way. He opened the door, and the men hauled Zoë inside, kicking and screaming. Then the door closed.

Alex's heart was thudding hard and fast. She checked her watch. It was 11:09 a.m. She tried to figure out where they were.

Alex crept through the open gate and moved quickly across the overgrown garden, moving carefully through the trees and shrubs to avoid being seen from the house's many leaded windows.

She crept right up to the house. Her heart was in her throat. She listened. There was nothing.

And then there was the click of a pistol hammer being cocked, and the hard metal of it to the back of her head.

"Careless," said a man's voice she'd never heard before. "You were following them. But I was following you."

She risked a glance behind her. The man with the gun was slightly built, expensively dressed, with a long black raincoat over his suit. His hair was gingery red. There was a twinkle of humor in his eyes. Rain pounded off the canopy of his umbrella.

"You're Slater," she said.

"And you must be Agent Fiorante. I've heard all about you."

The realization was dizzying. *Callaghan and Slater.* The whole time, they'd been in it together.

He twitched the gun barrel. "Move. Keep your hands raised. Lower them and you're dead."

Alex walked. He prodded her inside the house. It was somber inside. Dark wood paneling glistened dully in the darkness. A stone fireplace was filled with old ashes and blackened logs. The heads of animal trophies stared down from the walls, eyes glazed, spiky antlers and curled horns casting weird shadows. She shivered, dripping water across the flagstones.

Footsteps echoed up the hallway and a door crashed open. Callaghan strode in. His face was twisted in fury. Three more men filled the doorway behind him, pistols drawn.

"Surprise visitor," Slater said.

Callaghan stared at her. "That was smart of you, Fiorante. But there's a fine line between smart and dumb, and you just crossed it." He motioned to the other men. "Frisk her."

They searched her roughly, but carefully. "She's clean."

Alex brushed wet hair from her face and glared defiantly at Callaghan. "What have you done with Zoë?"

Callaghan smiled. "You want to go meet her? Be my guest."

Alex was dragged down a twisty, shady corridor by the agents as Callaghan and Slater led the way. There was a heavy iron-studded door in an alcove at the bottom of the passage, down some steps. Callaghan took a long iron key out of his pocket and unlocked it. He jerked the door open, and the agents shoved Alex inside. She tumbled down a flight of stone steps and landed hard on a concrete cellar floor. She tasted blood on her lips as she staggered to her feet.

Slater casually descended the steps towards her, that twinkle in his eye. He stopped halfway down and leaned on the iron stair rail. "What a shame," he said, eyeing her up and down. "She's so nice."

Alex heard sobbing behind her. She turned. Zoë was slumped against the wall in the shadows. Her face was wet with tears and there was a cut over her eye. Alex went over to her and held her. "You bastards," she hissed at them.

Callaghan walked down the steps and stood next to Slater. "I guess this is where we part ways, ladies." He reached into his coat and drew out a Glock 9mm. He pointed it at Zoë, then swiveled it to aim at Alex. Alex refused to flinch. No way would she show him fear.

Zoë whimpered, clutching her hand.

"Fuck you," Alex said.

"I really like this woman," Slater said. "She's feisty. Shame I can't get to know her better."

"She's a pest. And pests get eradicated." Callaghan squinted down the sights, getting ready to fire.

"Wait," Slater said.

Callaghan lowered the gun impatiently. "What?"

"Don't shoot them."

"What?"

"Don't shoot them. I have a better idea." Slater grinned. "How often do you come out here?"

"Not as often as I'd like," Callaghan said. "You know how it is."

"Say, once every four, five months?"

"In a quiet year."

"This a quiet year?"

"This is a crazy year."

"Well, how about we just shut these two up down here and come back in six months or so to see how they're getting on?"

Callaghan made a face. "There's going to be a hell of a stink down here."

Slater shook his head. "I never told you about my dog, did I? I had this retriever, when I was a kid. It was OK for a while, but then I got tired of the damn thing, so I shut it up in a basement to see what would happen. Took a pretty long time to die, actually. But I can tell you that the stink dies off after a while, once the rats have eaten most of the meat away. Maggots take their share, then the body fluids all dry up. You're left with kind of a dried-out husk."

"You're a sick bastard," Alex said.

"I like it," Callaghan said. "What do you think, ladies? Give you some time to get to know each other better. You might even try digging your way out. Only the foundations go down awfully deep and we're built on solid bedrock here."

"It'll give you something to do while you're dying," Slater said with a grin. He checked his watch. "We'd better move. The senator's plane is waiting for me."

Alex scowled at him. "Senator?"

Slater's grin widened. "Who did you think was bankrolling this thing, the Salvation Army?"

Alex blinked in disbelief. "A U.S. senator is behind this?"

"Oh, it's not like he even knows about it," Slater said. "Bud Richmond's just a rich boy evangelist jackass who barely knows what day of the week it is. I sign the checks, not him. He might be the one being set up to lead the faithful, but this is my operation."

"What the fuck are you people doing?" Alex yelled up at them.

Slater shrugged. "I hate the idea of a beautiful woman like you dying in ignorance. We're just about to open the curtain on the biggest show on earth, though unfortunately you won't be around to witness it. We aim big, and we're starting big. Something that'll make the Corfu bombing look like a firecracker."

Then he told her what it was, clearly enjoying the look on her face as she listened in horror.

"You're mad," she breathed. "You're completely insane."

"Just moving things along, Agent Fiorante," Callaghan said. "Don't think of it as our agenda. This is God's plan. If it leads to war, then that's the way God wants it to be."

"Though personally, you can keep the God bit," Slater added. "Callaghan is the religious nut here."

The CIA agent threw him a hard look.

"You can't get away with it," Alex protested. "They're expecting Zoë to turn up in England. When she doesn't, alarm bells will be ringing."

Callaghan smiled and shook his head. "Wrong again. They're not expecting her anymore."

"They made me call my parents from the car," Zoë sniffed. "Made me tell them I'd met someone and wouldn't be back for a while."

"And they're pretty used to that, aren't they?" Callaghan added.

"Then Murdoch will notice I'm missing," Alex said. "Either way, this will come back on you."

"Listen, honey," Slater cut in. "By the time anybody cottons on to anything, the world will be a very different place. They'll have more to worry about than you two."

"You can kill us," Alex said evenly. "But Ben Hope will be coming for you."

Slater and Callaghan exchanged amused glances. "Nice sense of timing, Agent Fiorante," said Callaghan. "Because right now it's coming up to 11:25 a.m. That's 6:25 p.m. Israeli time. Your boyfriend is walking into a trap, right as we speak. In five minutes, he'll be dead."

Slater chuckled. "Have a nice time, girls."

The two men turned and headed back up the cellar steps. Then the heavy door slammed shut and Alex and Zoë were left in darkness.

60.

Ben found the crumbling old apartment building at the end of a narrow cobbled alleyway. The street was quiet. A woman in traditional headgear saw him coming and retreated hurriedly through a doorway. He looked at his watch. Dead on time.

He checked the notebook again as he stepped into the cool shade of the apartment building. His footsteps echoed off the stone floor and the craggy walls as he climbed the stairs, glancing at the numbers on the doors.

It was a very ordinary abode. A sleeper working for an agency like the CIA needed to blend in totally with their environment, indistinguishable in their lifestyle from any normal member of the community. Sometimes their spouses were completely in the dark about their double life. They were usually people from an unassuming background, who would never attract the attentions of the police or other authorities. Their role was to gather low-grade intelligence, sometimes to act as messengers or assist more senior agents on missions in their area.

Ben came to the apartment number he'd been given and knocked on the door. He listened. There was no sound from inside. He checked his watch. He was right on time for the rendezvous. He knocked again.

The door opened. The man in the doorway was lean and hawk-like, with cropped black hair and a thick beard, casually dressed in jeans and a white shirt. His eyes were dark and intense. "Mr. Hope?"

Ben nodded.

"Come this way," the man said, motioning him inside.

Ben followed him into a living room. The place was small and sparsely furnished, the walls bare and white. They'd clearly been expecting him. On a table was a slim manila file, the bottom edge of some papers visible. Next to the file was a Heckler & Koch 9mm pistol, action locked open, and a loaded magazine. On a nearby couch was a disassembled sniper rifle with silencer and scope. *If this comes to a sniper-counter-sniper situation*, Murdoch had said.

"Callaghan told me you had something for me," Ben said.

"That is correct," the man answered with a mysterious smile. "Something important. But first, you will take coffee?"

"I don't have time for coffee."

The man smiled again. "You are right. You do not."

The movement was sudden and violent. Ben felt the wind of the attacker rushing up behind him before he could react. Something flashed in front of his face. He instinctively raised his hands to defend himself. The garrote bit harshly into his fingers. Ben desperately tried to wrench it away, but the attacker was powerful, dragging him backwards off his feet. The wire sliced through his flesh. He kicked and struggled.

The bearded man was smiling. He slowly reached for the gun on the table.

Ben was fighting for his life. The man with the garrote twisted and sawed. Out of the corner of his eye he saw a door open. Another man walked in, holding a long, curved knife.

The trap was sprung. Callaghan had lured him to his death.

Then he'd die fighting. He threw himself down to the floor. The strangler went down with him, tightening the wire even more. Ben could feel himself choking. He lashed out with his foot, kicking out in a wide arc over his body. It connected with the guy's face. Suddenly the garrote was loosening.

The knife guy was moving in closer.

Ben rolled across the floor and threw a sideways kick at the knife-man's knee. Hit the joint sideways with brutal force and felt the crunch. The guy screamed and dropped the blade to the floor.

Then Ben was on his feet. He grabbed the strangler's hair and drove a knee hard into his face. Whirling round, he delivered a web-hand strike to the knifeman's throat that crushed his windpipe. Then he spun back round to the strangler, putting all his weight into a backwards elbow blow to the face that impacted hard and smashed his teeth down his throat. The guy crashed to the floor, rolling on his back. Ben stamped down on his neck. Blood spurted out of his mouth.

The bearded man was fumbling with the gun, slamming in the magazine, and chambering the first round. He raised the pistol and fired. The report was deafening in the small room. Ben felt the shock wave of the bullet. Plaster stung his cheek as the shot plowed into the wall six inches from his head. Ben tore a picture frame from the wall and hurled it. It spun sideways across the room and caught the man's wrist. Glass splintered. The man cried out and dropped the gun. Ben threw himself at him, punching and gouging. The man was quick. A grab of the wrist, a twist of the body, and Ben was flying through the air. He landed on a glass-topped coffee table and crashed right through it. Then the man was on top of him, a knee hard in his chest and raining blows down on him. Ben lashed out with his foot and caught him in the solar plexus, sending him flying back. But the man recovered his feet in a backward roll and was closing in again.

The fight was fast and furious. Strike, block, strike, block, a blur of fists. Ben drove a hard punch into his throat. The man staggered back a pace, but he had an iron grip on Ben's arm and used it to send him spinning into a corner bookcase. Ben crashed hard into it and it collapsed on top of him. Books and broken glass and bits of shattered shelving everywhere. Ben grabbed a hardback volume and sprang to his feet.

The man was running at him again, unstoppable. Ben rammed the book edge-on into his face. Blood sprayed from burst lips. He followed up the blow with an elbow strike, felt the solid impact. The man screamed, his face covered in blood now. He went down. Ben was straight on him. He grabbed a fistful of hair and dashed his head against the floor. And again. And again.

Suddenly Ben could feel his phone buzzing in his pocket. The distraction made him hesitate for a quarter of a second too long. The man twisted up and fought back like an animal, scratching and pummeling wildly. They rolled across the floor, locked together. Then the man's scrabbling hand was on the fallen gun. The muzzle swayed up, its small black eye staring right into Ben's. He desperately grappled for it, fingers clawing at the cool steel. The muzzle twisted away. It was a contest of pure strength now, whoever could gain control of the weapon.

Then the gunshot blasted through the wrecked room.

61.

Alex was scouring the cellar for a way out, anything. The door was solid. The torch she found on a cobwebbed shelf cast a yellow, fading pool of light into the recesses of the dark space. She was hoping for a trapdoor, a coal chute.

Nothing. They were trapped. She sat on the hard stone steps, her head in her hands. She could think of only one thing.

Ben. It was a trap. She wanted to reach out to him, warn him, do something. But it was probably too late. They wouldn't have taken any chances with him. They'd have killed him. She felt her eyes well up.

"Alex?" Zoë whispered from the shadows. "They must have gone by now. Let's get out of here."

"Don't be funny."

"I'm not. Let's get out of here."

"Zoë, we're trapped. We can't get out of here."

But as Alex was staring at the shadows, she saw the little screen light up and her heart jumped. She shone the torch. "Where in hell did you get a phone from?"

"I took it from the Neanderthal sitting next to me in the car. He never noticed."

Alex laughed in amazement. "Smart move."

"I was a useful little pickpocket when I was fifteen," Zoë said. "Some things you never forget. And guess what—I've just recorded everything those bastards said. Thought it might come in handy."

"Let's make a call," Alex said.

Zoë jumped up to her feet, moving about the cellar. "Reception is really weak. Wait. I'm getting one bar. What's the number for police here, nine-one-one?"

"Don't call the cops. Give it to me." Alex ran over and grabbed the phone from her. The reception was dicey. The single bar flickered off, then on again. She tried desperately to remember the number Ben had given her. It came back to her in a rush. She prodded the keys as fast as she could.

Dial tone. She listened tensely. It kept ringing and ringing.

"Oh God. I think they got him."

Halfway across the world, Ben staggered to his feet and looked down at the corpse of his attacker. Half the man's face was blown away, blood and flesh and bits of skull and jawbone strewn across the floor from the point-blank gunshot.

Ben was breathing hard, shaking with adrenaline. The blood on his face was a mixture of his own and that of the three men lying dead in the smashed-up apartment.

The phone was still buzzing in his pocket. Should he answer it?

He fished it out with bloody fingers and stared at it for a moment. Then he pressed the reply key and held it to his ear.

"Ben? Is that you?"

"Alex?" He was startled by the sound of her voice. From her tone he knew instantly that something was wrong.

"You're all right. Thank God."

"He didn't help much."

"Callaghan is one of them," she said.

"I just found that out myself, the hard way. Where are you?"

"I'm with Zoë. We're shut in Callaghan's basement." She quickly told him everything—how she'd followed Callaghan's car, how Slater had caught her. What he'd told her about the Christian U.S. senator. "But Richmond doesn't know what's going on," she said, her words spilling out in a rush. "They're just using him as some kind of figure-head."

"All right, listen," Ben said, thinking fast. "Here's what we're going to do. Don't call the police. Can your vet friend Frank be trusted?"

"Absolutely."

"Then call him. Retrace your steps with him, so he can find you."

"I think I know more or less where we are."

"Good. There's got to be some way he can get you out of there. Make up whatever story you want, but he has to keep his mouth shut about this. Then you and Zoë need to lie low and stay safe. I'll contact you."

"There's more," she said. "I know what they're going to do. There's an important Islamic prayer sermon taking place at a mosque in Jerusalem. The president and four members of the Supreme Muslim Council will be there. They're going to blow it up."

Ben's heart leaped into his mouth. "Which mosque?"

"It's at the Temple Mount," Alex said.

"When is this happening?"

"Seven o'clock, Israeli time."

He looked at his watch. "But that's only twenty minutes from now."

"Go, Ben. You have to stop it." Then Alex ended the call, and he was staring at a dead phone.

It was as though the air had been sucked out of the room. A thousand thoughts rushed through his mind at once.

The enormity of it almost knocked the breath out of him. How stupid he'd been, how completely blind, not to have seen this coming. In its own terrible, horrible way it was a strategic decision of the most perfect kind.

The Temple Mount in the heart of the Old City was one of the most bitterly disputed sites in religious and political history. For Christians it was the spot where God had created the Earth, and the seat of his Final Judgment; Islamic lore named it the Noble Sanctuary, where the Prophet Mohammed had ascended to Heaven. It had once been the home of the greatest and holiest Jewish temple of all times, until the Romans had destroyed it in AD 70.

Built on the ruins of the great temple was the most sacred site of the Islamic world, after Mecca and Medina. The Qubbat al-Sakhra. The Dome of the Rock, a huge and magnificent octagonal mosque crowned with a golden dome that could be seen far and wide across the city. It was the epicenter of two millennia of Jerusalem's bloody religious past, fought over by dozens of nations in its time, and now, since the Israeli government had reluctantly handed over stewardship of the temple to the Muslims in 1967, the ultimate symbol of the struggle between Judaism and Islam.

And to destroy the Dome of the Rock, to desecrate such a holy shrine as this, and place blame on the Jews for the atrocity, would be to light a quick-burning fuse that would see the apocalyptic prophecy of the Bible fulfilled. Israel and the Muslim world would be at war. The United States would inevitably get involved, standing with Israel. The call to arms would sound across the entire Islamic world. The great jihad that fundamentalist Muslims had been waiting for would finally have dawned. Global conflict.

In a world tearing itself apart in blood and chaos, tens of millions of evangelical Christians would flock to the only leaders they felt they could trust. Meanwhile, events like 9/11 would become a daily occurrence. And worse, much worse. Ben remembered Clayton Cleaver's prediction of nuclear war, and an icy tingle ran down his back.

It was a doomsday scenario, and the clock was ticking faster than he could think.

Now it had to be stopped—and it was completely down to him.

62.

en thundered down the stairs, burst out into the hot sun, and sprinted up the street. Passersby saw him coming, a wild man covered in blood, running like the wind, and threw themselves out of his way. His footsteps pounded in the narrow streets.

As he ran he snatched a glimpse at his watch. Six forty-two.

Eighteen minutes.

On he sprinted, his breath rasping as he traced a winding path north through cobbled streets and alleys, scattering people aside as he went. He rounded a corner, glancing about him to get his bearings. Up ahead, the street was filled with market stalls and shops and crowds of locals and visitors. Taxis and other cars were honking their horns as they crawled through the bustle. A motorcyclist on a tall BMW trail bike revved his engine impatiently as he waited for a bunch of tourists to get out of his way.

Ben ran up behind the bike. The rider was wearing a backpack with shoulder straps. Ben grabbed a strap and hauled the motorcyclist off his machine, sending him tumbling to the ground. Before the BMW could fall on its side he grasped the handlebars, threw a leg over the saddle, stamped into gear, and opened the throttle. The BMW surged forward with an aggressive roar, and the crowd quickly dispersed to let him through. He raced up the winding market street, throwing the machine left and right, skidding between stalls and scattering startled pedestrians.

In his head he was counting seconds and measuring distances. The Old City was a small area of Jerusalem, its four quarters crammed into a space only two kilometers across at its widest point. The Dome of the Rock was situated only a short walk from the Church of the Holy Sepulchre, where he'd been standing earlier.

Ben raced on, riding wildly through markets and traffic, rattling over cobbles. Suddenly there was the howl of a police siren behind him. Flashing lights in his mirrors. There was a low wall edging the street to his right. A gap in the wall. A steep flight of stone steps leading upwards between craggy ancient houses. He threw the machine into a skid, twisting the bars. The front tire hit the steps with a shuddering bang that almost spilled him off. The tortured engine screamed as he hammered the bike up the steps.

The police car had disappeared in his mirror, but already he could hear the sirens in the distance, at least two or three, converging on his position.

A sign flashed by for Batei Mahase Street. He was heading the right way. But then he looked back in the mirror and saw more flashing lights. Two police cars, gaining fast.

Suddenly a bunch of children burst out of a doorway and ran out in front of him. He swerved to avoid them, lost control, and the BMW smashed into a shop front. He sprawled to the ground. The police cars skidded to a halt. Cops burst out, running towards him. He staggered to his feet, punched the nearest one and knocked him down. A second grabbed at his arm. Ben kicked him in the groin. Before the guy even started screaming, Ben was running.

Six forty-nine.

Eleven minutes.

But he was getting close now. Up ahead he could see the entrance to the huge esplanade leading to the Wailing Wall on the edge of the Jewish Quarter. The spectacular Dome of the Rock rose up beyond, the sun glittering off its gold roof.

Voices were yelling behind him, sirens wailing. He threw a glance behind him as he ran. More police were giving chase. He reached the Wailing Wall and sprinted along its side, scattering a crowd of robed clergymen.

Up ahead was the Moors Gate, the only way for non-Muslims to get into the Temple Mount complex. Ben ran through, past the ticket kiosk, barging through crowds of tourists. People yelled at him, then shrank away when they saw the blood on his clothes. Now he was sprinting across the vast paved esplanade of the Temple Mount, towards the Dome of the Rock itself. His lungs were burning and he felt as though his legs were about to give out any second. He willed himself to keep moving.

The huge building loomed up above him, its octagonal walls faced with blue marble and magnificent Koranic inscriptions and artwork. Crowds of Muslim worshippers were congregating outside the vast mosque, a buzz of excited veneration in the air.

Behind him, Ben could hear the shouts of the police as they battled through the crowd. He stole away, moving deeper in amongst the jostling throng. His mind was racing, heart thudding fast. The crowd of worshippers was filtering inside the building. Things were about to begin. The Muslim dignitaries were inside.

Four minutes.

He whirled round, glancing wildly in all directions. The bomb could be anywhere. It could be strapped to the body of any one of a thousand people all around him. It could have been planted weeks ago, waiting for a remote signal to set it off.

He imagined the magnificent building suddenly split apart by high explosive. Its noble golden dome spewing flame and debris as everything inside was torn to pieces. The fireball rolling into the blue sky above Jerusalem. The tower of black smoke signaling for miles around that something cataclysmic had just occurred.

Three minutes.

There was no chance of stopping it now.

That was the moment when he spotted the face in the crowd. It belonged to a Westerner, a small man in a light jacket and casual trousers. A leather bag hung from a strap over his shoulder. He could have been any one of a million tourists.

But Ben never forgot a face, and this one had been branded on his memory since Corfu.

His mind flashed back in a blur. The man with the laptop at the café terrace. The same sharp features. The same empty, impassive eyes. It was him. The bomber. Charlie's killer.

Ben shoved his way through the crowd towards him. The police were just twenty yards behind. He broke into a run. A woman screamed.

The bomber saw him. His eyes narrowed for an instant, and then he was gone, dashing away through the heaving throngs of people.

Two minutes.

Ben was running like he'd never run in his life, past smaller domes and ancient buildings. Down a flight of smooth, uneven stone steps that led to a labyrinth of massive pillars and arches. Ahead of him, the bomber was a flitting figure, darting through arches and cloistered alleyways, turning left and then right, people diving out of his path as he ran.

But Ben was slowly gaining on him. The clap of their racing footsteps echoed off the ancient stonework.

One minute.

Then he saw the man was reaching into the leather bag. Something in his hand. A small black rectangular shape. Remote detonator. He was punching the keys as he ran.

Entering a numerical code.

Ben's blood froze in his veins. He reached behind the hip of his jeans, and from under the bloodied shirt he drew out the bearded assassin's pistol. He fired. The bomber ducked low. The shot sang off a pitted stone wall. People screamed and yelled in alarm.

Then the bomber was darting down another alley, archways leading off in all directions. Ben was keeping him in sight, but only just. He couldn't lose him, not for an instant, or he could finish entering the code. Then he had only to hit a SEND key and it was over.

Hundreds would die, maybe thousands. Then more, a lot more.

It was exactly 7 p.m.

Far away, Irving Slater sat in the backseat of a speeding limo and watched the hand on the gold watch count down the last few seconds to glory. He leaned back against the leather and smiled.

"Showtime," he said aloud.

63.

The bomber dived through a crumbling stone arch, running flat out, the device in his hand.

Then suddenly he was cartwheeling through the air with a loud grunt of pain and surprise as the moped coming the other way knocked him off his feet.

Ben came skidding out of the archway just in time to see the bomber go sprawling across the narrow street in a tangle of arms and legs. The scooter crashed down on its side and slithered in a shower of sparks. The rider tumbled and rolled. The black detonation device went bouncing across the paving stones.

There was blood on the bomber's face. His teeth were bared in pain and concentration as he went crawling after the fallen device. Ben watched in horror from ten yards away as his trembling hand reached out for the tiny keypad. Then his fingers were closing around the device, dragging it towards him.

Ben dived at him and punched him hard in the head. He punched him again. The man's head lolled, spitting blood. Ben grabbed for his fingers, trying to wrestle the thing out of his grasp.

There was a sharp yell from behind. Ben turned. A young cop was standing three yards away, panting hard, pistol wavering, sweat on his face. He motioned with the gun. Ben could see in his eyes that he was scared. Scared, but serious. He screamed a command in Hebrew.

Ben raised his hands, slowly rising to his feet.

The young cop flicked the gun towards the bomber.

But the bomber just smiled. He sat up in the dust and cocked his thumb over the SEND key.

The sequence was complete. One keystroke and the world was going to change irrevocably.

Ben moved faster than he'd ever moved before. His elbow hit the young cop's face at the same time that he was already grabbing for the pistol. The shot was completely instinctive. He didn't aim.

The bullet hit the bomber's hand in a mist of red, blowing off half his fingers. The shattered detonator dropped to the ground.

The bomber kneeled there, nursing his damaged hand, staring up at Ben open-mouthed. "Who *are* you?" he croaked.

"Nobody," Ben said. Then he shot him in the head.

64.

Then it's over," said Murdoch. "You honored your end of the deal."

Ben was sitting on the edge of his bed in the Jerusalem hotel, feeling for a part of his body that didn't hurt. "And now you'll honor yours," he said. He didn't want to mention Callaghan and Slater to Murdoch. He had his own plans for them.

"I always keep my word," Murdoch said. "We'll take care of everything. As for you, you're a free man. You were never here. I never even heard your name."

The next call to make was to Alex. Ben used the number she'd called him from at Callaghan's house. He prayed she'd answer. That she was all right.

After a dozen rings, he started at the sound of her voice.

When she heard his, she burst out crying.

"I'm coming back," he told her. "Meet me at the Lincoln Memorial in Washington, DC, tomorrow afternoon, one o'clock."

He stood for a long time under a hot shower, washing away the blood and the dirt and the memories of the day. Then he grabbed his things and checked out. He made the airport in forty minutes, and within a couple of hours he was boarding a flight for Washington.

It wasn't over yet.

WASHINGTON, DC
THE NINETEENTH DAY

He was back on U.S. soil at midday. He made his way to the heart of DC and sat on the warm stone steps at the foot of the Lincoln

Memorial. Sunlight danced on the clear surface of the ornamental lake that stretched out in front of him. Beyond that stood the obelisk of the Washington Monument, and beyond that, the Capitol dome and seat of the U.S. Senate.

There was no sign of Alex yet. He took out his phone, thinking about the two calls he had to make. The first was to Augusta Vale.

She sounded happy to hear from him.

"Sorry I had to disappear like that," he said. "Something came up."

"I still have reporters calling me, wanting to know about the mystery shooter who stole the prize and vanished."

"I just wanted to thank you for your hospitality."

"Think nothing of it, Benedict. Anytime you're passing through Savannah, you must give me a call. You will always be a most welcome guest in my home. And if there's anything I can do for you . . ."

"There is one thing. Do you have Reverend Cleaver's number? I'd like to order a few copies of his book."

"Why, I'm sure he would be overjoyed to hear from you again," she said.

Ben dialed the number she'd given him. Cleaver sounded nervous when his secretary passed him the phone.

"How are you, Clayton?"

"Fine," Cleaver replied warily.

"And a hundred million dollars richer?"

"The money came through two days ago," Cleaver said, sounding puzzled. "How did you know that?"

"Intuition," Ben said. "And I'm calling you to make a deal."

Cleaver gulped audibly. "A deal? What kind of deal?"

"Don't panic, Clayton. I'm not going to take your money. Not all of it, anyway."

"That's very generous of you."

"Yes, it is. So here are my terms. They aren't negotiable. Ready?"

"I'm listening."

"First, you're going to donate a quarter of that money straight back to the Vale Trust, for the new children's wing."

"Of course, I'd already thought—" Cleaver blustered. "But twenty-five percent?"

"That's the deal," Ben said. "Here's the next part. I imagine once you've paid off the loan sharks you're going to want to refurnish your place. Your walls still bare?"

"Y-y-yes," Cleaver stammered. "But what—"

"There's a talented young modern artist in Oxford, England. Her name's Lucy Wilde. I want you to check out her website."

"What the hell has that to do with me?"

"You're about to become a patron of the arts, Clayton. You're going to buy up every piece of art she has for sale, and you're going to offer her a handsome commission for more. And I'll be checking, in case your definition of handsome is too different from mine."

"This is nuts," Cleaver protested. "I don't even like modern art."

"Get a taste for it," Ben said. "Now here's part three. A farmer in Montana needs some spare cash to renovate his property. Someone shot the place up a little bit. He also needs a new truck or two. I'll be sending you his address and a bank account number to wire the money to."

"How much spare cash?" Cleaver asked suspiciously.

"Nice round figure," Ben said. "Call it a million dollars."

There was a wheezing gasp on the other end. "You're killing me, Ben."

"I thought about that option. But I prefer this way. Are you ready to hear the next part of the terms?"

"Go on," Cleaver said wearily.

"Good. There's a certain Georgia lawyer who needs an operation to fix his legs."

Cleaver exploded. "McClusky? You want me to pay off McClusky?"

"That's right," Ben said. "Some setting-up money wouldn't be a bad idea either, to help him open up a new practice and get started again. How about three hundred grand? Wait, let's make it five hundred."

Silence on the other end.

"One more thing I want from you," Ben said. He paused. This was the part that mattered most to him. "I want a trust fund set up. One million pounds sterling."

"For who?" Cleaver snorted. "You?"

"For a child," Ben said. "One that isn't born yet, but who means a lot to me. The money's to be held in trust until the kid reaches eighteen, and then paid over in full. You'll be hearing from a solicitor in London, who'll set it up. You just need to sign on the line."

He'd given it a lot of thought. He knew there was no way Rhonda would ever forgive him for what had happened, no way he could ever explain things to her. What could he do? Go making excuses, write her a note? But at least he could do this for Charlie's kid.

"I hope I'm making myself very clear," he said.

"Oh, I understand," Cleaver muttered. "But what if I don't feel like going along with this generous business deal of yours?"

"I'll be watching you, Clayton. You'll find I'm not as forgiving as the loan sharks. I really don't want to have to shatter Miss Vale's illusions about you—but if I see you're not doing what I want, rest assured I'll be letting her know what a big huckster you are. Not only that, I'll be on the first flight over there and by the time I'm finished you'll be hard to tell from roadkill. And I always keep my promises."

"Now I suppose you're going to tell me I have to fork out another ten million to that goddamn Zoë Bradbury," Cleaver groaned.

"No, you can keep that money. I don't think Zoë Bradbury deserves another cent from you or anyone else."

There was a long silence on the line as Cleaver mulled over the terms. "I don't have much leeway here, do I?"

"Not a hair's breadth."

Cleaver let out a deep groan of defeat. "All right. You win. It's a deal."

As Ben was putting the phone away, Alex appeared. She was wearing black trousers and a burgundy leather jacket that brought out the color of her hair. She couldn't stop smiling when she saw him. She ran across the steps and hugged him tightly. "I never thought I'd see you again."

They embraced for a moment, then parted.

"Frank got you out?" Ben said.

She nodded. "Zoë and I have been staying at his place. Lying low like you said. She's still there."

"Good. She shouldn't leave there until this is finally over. Until Slater and Callaghan are dealt with, it isn't safe for her. Or for you, when Callaghan realizes you're still alive and a witness to everything."

"So what now?"

"Now I'm going to pay a visit to Senator Bud Richmond."

"Not without me," Alex said.

65.

The sleek Porsche 959 raced along the mountain road, wide tires gripping the asphalt as it came speeding around the bend.

It screeched to a halt as the driver caught sight of the broken-down Ford that blocked the road ahead, sitting at an angle with the hood up.

Bud Richmond climbed out of the car, smiling at the attractive auburn-haired woman he could see bent down under the hood, fiddling with the oil dipstick, looking distressed. "Can I help, ma'am?"

"Yes you can, Senator." Ben stepped out from behind the car. He aimed a gun at Richmond's face. Alex grimly slammed the hood shut.

"What's this about?" Richmond demanded.

"It's about Irving Slater," Ben said. "Let's go for a drive."

Forty minutes later, the senator was sitting ashen-faced in the back of the Ford after listening to Ben's account of Slater's plan. Alex had played him back Zoë's phone recording from the cellar.

"I can't believe what I just heard," Richmond said in a defeated voice.

"You were the biggest part of Slater's plan," Ben told him. "He's been using you all along."

"Sometimes he acted strangely," Richmond said. "All those furtive little meetings, out in that cable car. I always wondered."

"Now you know."

Richmond's fists clenched. "I knew he had his ways. I knew he didn't have a great opinion of me, called me a jackass behind my back. But I never once thought he would stoop to this . . . this abomination." His voice was trembling with anger. "Dear Lord, to think I have been allowing murderers into my midst. Agents of Satan." He looked up at Ben. "I'm just shocked. What can I say? Slater has to be brought to justice." Then he turned to Alex. "Have you informed your superiors of this yet?"

"Nobody knows anything about this except us," she said.

Richmond bit his lip. "Callaghan and Slater must be arrested. Let me make a call."

Ben shook his head. "That isn't the plan."

Richmond frowned in confusion. "Then what is?"

"Tell me about the cable car," Ben said.

66.

rving Slater had taken a sudden vacation when he'd heard that the Dome of the Rock was still intact. He'd been skulking incognito in his suite at the Bellagio, slugging bourbon and chewing chocolate, spending hours on the phone to his broker to talk about his options.

Worst case, he could be out of the country within a couple of hours. He'd been scouring maps of South America on the Internet. He liked the idea of Brazil. Those beaches in Rio, overflowing with foxy chicks. He could be happy there, and he could liquidate enough assets to be rich for a long time. It was a tempting escape route, if the shit hit the fan.

But as time had passed, his initial panic had subsided a little. Nothing terrible had happened. Nothing on the news. He'd been able to put his thoughts in order. OK, Hope was still alive—the trap had failed. But so what? Hope had nothing solid on him. There was nobody left alive who'd seen him at the Montana facility. There was no evidence linking him to Callaghan, and Callaghan had covered his own tracks well. Hope might come back from Jerusalem and go to Murdoch with accusations that he'd been set up, but he couldn't prove shit. The only real witnesses were the two bitches in Callaghan's basement. And they wouldn't be doing much talking to anybody. He was pretty much home free.

Late the next morning, he'd got a call. It was Richmond. The senator sounded agitated but happy. He said he'd had a communiqué from the White House. He'd been invited to a dinner to discuss religious policy in the Middle East. It was wonderful news. He needed Slater to come home from vacation right now to help him with his speech.

"Meet me at the ski chalet," Richmond said. "This evening, eight o'clock."

Slater glanced at the time, frowning. "I can just about make it if I leave now. But why the ski chalet?"

"We had a tip-off," Richmond said. "The house is bugged. My office, the whole place. We're dealing with it, but in the meantime we need to talk somewhere private."

Slater was stunned by the development. Maybe this was a break. Maybe he could somehow use this to claw his way back to making his plan work after all. As he paced and drank, he fumed about the bugs. Who the fuck could have planted them? But it didn't matter now.

After a rushed flight and a flustered limo ride, Slater finally made it back to Richmond's mountain residence. He was hot and needed a shower. His ass ached from hours of travel.

The old ski chalet was across the mountain valley from the house, accessible only by cable car. Slater trotted up the steps leading up to the wooden control room that adjoined the house. He stepped inside the docked cable car and aimed the remote from inside at the control panel. He was just about to activate it when he heard a voice.

"Wait."

It was Callaghan, stepping gingerly towards the cable car.

Slater stared at him. "What the fuck are *you* doing here?"

"Richmond called a meeting with me. Something about the White House."

"Why would Richmond want you?"

"I don't know. He said it was important. Where is he?"

"Across there," Slater said, pointing over the valley. "In the ski chalet."

Callaghan paled slightly. "Can't we meet him in the house?"

"The house is bugged."

"Seems strange to me," Callaghan said. "OK, if that's how he wants it, let's get it over with."

Slater pointed his remote and pressed the button. Nothing. He shook it and pressed again. This time there was a loud *clunk* from above their heads, and the car began to glide smoothly away from the house, out into space.

Halfway across the abyss, it suddenly stopped without warning.

"What the . . ." Slater tried the remote again.

No response. "Battery must be dead," he muttered. But the green LED was working fine. His heart picked up a step.

"If that gizmo isn't working," Callaghan said with a note of panic in his voice, "then how are we going to get back?"

That was when the phone rang in Slater's pocket.

From where Ben was wedged in the crook of a rock three hundred yards away, the cable car was a tiny cube dangling against the sky. He put away the remote that Richmond had given him after switching it with the dummy one that Slater was trying to use.

Slater answered the phone. "Senator, is that you?" His voice was edgy and tense, tinged with worry.

"Wrong again, Slater," Ben said into the Bluetooth headset he was wearing.

Silence on the line. "Who is this?"

"Look to your left," Ben said. "If your eyes are very keen, you'll see me. I'm the speck on the mountain."

"Hope?"

"You're probably wondering how this happened," Ben said. "Tell the truth, I can't be bothered explaining it to you. It's a need-to-know thing. And dead men don't need to know."

"Don't do this," Slater stammered. "I have a lot of money. I'll make you rich."

"It wasn't a bad plan," Ben said. "You're a clever guy. Callaghan too. And that was a smart move of his, erasing you from the CIA database." As he talked, he was undoing the straps on the padded rifle case next to him. He slid the weapon out. It was the Remington rifle that Bud Richmond's father had given him for his twenty-first birthday. It had never been fired. Ben unzipped the ammunition compartment and took out five of the long, conical .308 cartridges. He pressed them one at a time into the magazine, then worked the bolt. He settled in behind the rifle. Through the scope he could clearly make out the system of pulleys and wires on the cable car roof.

Slater must have heard the metallic noises over the phone. "I work for a U.S. senator," he protested in a panic. "You can't kill me."

"I've got a message for you from the jackass," Ben said.

"What? What the—"

"You're fired."

He snapped off the safety and took aim, ignoring the cries of panic from his headset.

He never even felt the trigger give. The butt of the weapon kicked against his shoulder.

Three hundred yards away, the cable parted. The ends thrashed wildly. Pulleys spun. The cable car lurched and fell ten feet, then was jerked to a stop by what was left of the wire.

Inside, Slater and Callaghan were screaming, hammering like lunatics at the windows, scrabbling desperately on the tilted floor.

Ben calmly worked the bolt, found his mark, and fired again. The echo of the gunshot rolled and whooshed around the mountain valley.

The cable car seemed to hang in midair for an instant as the cable gave. Then it dropped like a stone. It fell nearly a thousand feet before it hit the first crag. It burst apart. Wreckage tumbled down the mountainside. Somewhere among the hurtling, bouncing debris were the tiny matchstick figures of Slater and Callaghan as they fell screaming to the rocks a few hundred feet farther down.

By the time their bodies had hit the bottom, Ben was already packing up the rifle. He slung the case over his shoulder and started making his way down the mountainside.

67.

Alex was waiting down below in the car. Ben climbed into the passenger seat. She started up the car and headed along the dusty, empty road. They sat in silence for a while.

"I would have liked to know you," she said quietly.

"It could have been different," he replied.

"But it isn't, is it?"

"No," he said. "It's not."

"Won't you change your mind? Stay with me for a while. See how things go."

He said nothing.

"I know how you feel," she said. "But doesn't life have to go on?"

"I'm not ready, Alex. I'm sorry. That's just how it is."

Time passed. Miles under their wheels before they spoke again.

"What will you do now?" she said.

"Go home."

"Back to theology?"

He said nothing for a moment. Then he whirred the window down. The wind blew their hair. He reached into his bag and took out the Bible. Stared at it for a few seconds. The book couldn't mean the things it once had to him. Not now.

He tossed it out of the open window.

It hit the seventy-mile-an-hour blast and burst open, pages fluttering. Then it tumbled down the grassy embankment at the side of the road and was far behind them.

"I guess not, then," she said.

"What about you?"

She glanced over at him. "Do next? Same as you, Ben. Take stock of things. Look for a new direction. Maybe the Agency isn't for me after all. I signed up because I wanted to help people. I figure there are better ways for me to do that. So, I've been thinking I should go back to medical school."

He nodded. "That's a good decision. You'll make a brilliant doctor."

She reached across and squeezed his hand. "I'm going to miss you, Ben Hope," she said.

"I'll miss you too."

"Will you be OK?"

"I'll be fine," he said.

"Really?"

He smiled. "Really."

"Keep in touch."

He didn't reply.

"I know you won't," she sighed.

After a few more miles, a sign flashed up for a small town. He showed her a place where she could drop him off, and she pulled up on the grassy verge.

She said nothing as he climbed out of the car. He slung his jacket over his shoulder and watched as she drove away.

The car grew smaller and smaller until it was just a dust cloud in the distance.

The sun was setting. He turned and started walking towards the town.

Author's Note

Although *The Hope Vendetta* is a work of fiction, it is a fact that many millions of people across the world, the majority of them evangelical American Christians, fervently believe that we may at any moment be plunged into the apocalyptic End Times events that they claim to be forecast in the Bible. None of the biblical references in this book have been invented; it's all there in the Good Book for those who wish to study it. As far as these millions of people are concerned, the prophesied horror scenario is for real, it's coming, it's unstoppable and those of us who aren't ready for it are doomed to a hideous fate.

Bible study being such an enormous and complex subject, in the writing of *The Hope Vendetta* some liberties have inevitably been taken in the interests of drama, and to some extent it was necessary to simplify. Real-life End Times prophecy believers tend to borrow here and there from various parts of the Bible, piecing it all together across the board, rather than simply lifting ready-made ideas from one single source, as the characters appear to do in the novel. This is the reason why, in real life, End Times prophecies can differ slightly in their interpretation: some believe that the Rapture will take place before the Tribulation (known as pre-Tribulation belief), and others believe it will take place some time after the Tribulation has already started, meaning that all of us, faithful and unbelievers alike, would have to endure quite a long period of unspeakable nastiness together before the more fortunate are whisked away to Salvation. It is this "mid-Tribulationist" stance that I have attributed to Clayton Cleaver and the End Times conspirators in this story.

The book of Revelation, which in the story forms the basis of the End Timers' belief, is in real life only one of many prophetic texts of the Bible—others include the Old Testament's book of Ezekiel—but is by far the most intriguing, with elements such as the classic "666" reference now embedded in popular culture. Bible buffs will spot that I lifted certain quotations from Ezekiel, Daniel, and elsewhere. In this respect I am guilty of some scriptural sleight of hand. Apologies to the purists: *The Hope Vendetta* is fiction, after all . . .

. . . Then again, is it completely fiction? While researching this book I was struck by the number of strange events and apparent "signs" becoming visible to me as I delved deeper into the subject. Halfway through writing the book, I was woken up in the middle of the night by what turned out to be an earthquake, an extremely rare and bizarre event in my part of the world. Further research showed up all kinds of weird global events that, in a certain light, could be interpreted as signs that the End Times dice are about to roll: weather anomalies, plagues of African locusts in France, outbreaks of rare illnesses, growing social chaos, increasing tensions in the Middle East. On a larger scale, astronomers are now finding evidence of collisions between entire galaxies—unsettling echoes of the forecasts in the book of Revelation that "heavenly bodies will collide." The more I read, the more I began to find Clayton Cleaver's dire warnings eerily persuasive.

Is it really going to happen? We'll just have to wait and see.

Finally, I would like to stress that the negative portrayal of certain fictitious End Times believers in this book is in no way a reflection on real-life Christians, whatever their interpretation of Bible prophecy may be. Ben Hope is a fiction hero, and heroes cannot exist without villains!

Readers are invited to spot the hidden "Doomsday clue" within this Author's Note. A free signed copy of the book to the first five readers who contact me via my website with the correct answer.

I hope you enjoyed reading *The Hope Vendetta* as much as I enjoyed writing it. Ben Hope will be back.

Acknowledgments

The author wishes to express special gratitude to Stacy Creamer and Lauren Spiegel at Touchstone, without whom this book would not have been possible. Many thanks also to the rest of the editorial, design, and publicity team at Simon & Schuster for their invaluable contribution: Cherlynne Li, Renata DiBiase, George Turianski, Martha Schwartz, David Falk, Meredith Kernan, and Marcia Burch.

Last but not least, special thanks to my literary agent, the inimitable Noah Lukeman.